PROLOGUE

SHE WOKE TO the sound of voices and sat up in her narrow bed, rubbing her eyes. The toys on her shelves were only shapes in the darkness. But moonlight peeked in around the edges of the window curtains.

Out in the front room, Momma and Daddy were talking. He wasn't usually here at night, but he came when he could to the little cabin at the edge of the swamp.

He would hug her and tell her she was his special little girl. He would run his fingers through her hair and say it was spun gold.

Maybe he'd have a treat for her. A toy. Or some candy like the last time. Momma didn't approve of candy, but Daddy liked to give her a few pieces—and tell her to enjoy them when Momma wasn't looking.

She started to swing her skinny legs over the side of the bed. Then stopped. Momma and Daddy weren't speaking very loud, and she couldn't make out the actual words. But as she caught the tone of the conversation, the happy sense of anticipation dried up, like the drops of water on the ground in the morning.

Momma and Daddy were worried, the way they'd been that other time when Daddy had said the town was on the warpath. Only nothing bad had happened then. And everything had gone on just the way it always did.

She picked up Mr. Rabbit, her favorite stuffed animal, from the pillow and hugged his limp body to her, as Daddy's footsteps came rapidly across the wooden floor. Flinging the door open, he strode into her room and bent over her bed, scooping her into his arms.

"We have to leave. We don't have much time."

Momma came hurrying after him. "This is my home. I won't let them drive me out."

"You've been taking too many chances."

"No. I've tried to help people."

"And look where it's gotten you. Darlin', you have to listen to me this time."

"If I'd listened to you . . ." Momma's voice trailed off.

Daddy gathered her up and hugged her to him. "Come on little bit, you're going with me."

"No!" Momma protested, almost drowning out the voices in the background. There were people outside, she realized with a sudden spurt of fear. Angry people.

One of Daddy's arms tightened around her; the other reached for Momma. "Jenna, let me get you away from here, before it's too late."

"I can't."

She could feel Daddy's heart pounding, hear his voice rising.

"Oh Lord, don't do this to me, please."

"Come out and show yourself—you damn witch," an unseen voice screamed, making her cower against Daddy. Other voices joined the chorus. "Come out before we burn you out."

Daddy tried to keep hold of Momma's arm, but she

THE NOVELS OF RUTH GLICK
(WRITING AS REBECCA YORK)

KILLING MOON

A P.I. with a preternatural talent for tracking finds his prey: a beautiful genetic researcher who may be his only hope for a future . . .

EDGE OF THE MOON

A police detective and a woman who files a missing-persons report become the pawns of an unholy serial killer in a game of deadly attraction . . .

"Rebecca York delivers page-turning suspense."
—Nora Roberts

"Glick's prose is smooth, literate and fast-moving; her love scenes are tender yet erotic; and there's always a happy ending." —*The Washington Post Book World*

"A true master of intrigue." —*Rave Reviews*

"No one sends more chills down your spine than the very creative and imaginative Ms. York!" —*Romantic Times*

"She writes a fast-paced, satisfying thriller." —UPI

WITCHING
MOON

REBECCA YORK

BERKLEY SENSATION, NEW YORK

WITCHING MOON

A Berkley Sensation Book / published by arrangement with
the author

PRINTING HISTORY
Berkley Sensation edition / October 2003

ISBN: 0-425-19278-4

A BERKLEY SENSATION™ BOOK
Berkley Sensation Books are published by
The Berkley Publishing Group,
a division of Penguin Group (USA) Inc.,
375 Hudson Street, New York, New York 10014.
BERKLEY SENSATION and the "B" design
are trademarks belonging to Penguin Group (USA) Inc.

PRINTED IN THE UNITED STATES OF AMERICA

10 9 8 7 6

wrenched herself away from him and hurried into the front room. "I only tried to help. I've done nothing wrong," Momma called into the darkness beyond the walls of the house. Turning back to Daddy, she said, "I won't let them drive me from my home."

"It's too late." Daddy's warning was swallowed up by a rising babble of voices, like the wind tearing at the tree branches in a storm.

She was afraid of storms because one time a tree had fallen right across the path to the front door. But this was much worse.

She buried her face against her father's shoulder, her free hand clutching Mr. Rabbit. "Don't let them hurt Momma," she whimpered.

"I won't," he answered, starting toward the front of the house.

Before he could reach the living room, the window beside the door shattered, sending glass dancing over the wood floor.

Momma screamed, rooted to the spot where she stood.

Then a smell that was strong and dangerous filled the air—and a strange roaring noise howled through the house.

"Save her. Get her out of here," Momma screamed.

Her father cursed, started forward. But the heat from the front of the house beat him back. Still clasping her to his body, he sprinted across the bedroom, then bent to push up the window sash.

"Daddy! I'm scared, Daddy," she whimpered into the soft fabric of his shirt, trying to breathe through the cloud of smoke choking her nose and throat.

Daddy coughed and staggered, and she thought he was going to fall down, but he kept going.

"It's okay. Everything will be okay," he said. He said it over and over between coughs as he lowered her out the window. When she was standing on the ground, he quickly followed and scooped her up. His body curved over hers, he ran from the cabin. Behind her she heard a sound like thunder. Raising her head, she saw the whole house explode into flames.

"Momma! Where's Momma?"

Daddy put his hand on the back of her head, pressing her face into his shoulder and hunching protectively over her as he ran into the darkness of the swamp.

CHAPTER
ONE

THE LAST GUY who had walked in his shoes was a dead man, Adam Marshall thought as his booted feet sank into the soggy ground of the southern Georgia swamp. But he didn't intend to suffer the same fate. He had advantages that the previous head ranger at Nature's Refuge hadn't possessed.

Still, something was making his skin prickle tonight, Adam silently admitted as he slipped one hand into the pocket of his jeans. Standing very still on the porch of his cabin, he listened to the night sounds around him. The clicking noise of a bullfrog. The buzz of insects. The splash of a predator slipping into the murky waters of the mysterious marshes that the Indians had called Olakompa.

The Indians were long gone, but an aura of otherworldliness remained in this pocket of wetlands, which had managed to withstand the encroachment of civilization. It was a place steeped in superstition, and Adam had heard some pretty wild tales—of people who had been swallowed up by the "trembling earth" and of strange creatures that roamed the backcountry.

In the darkness, he laughed. He'd taken all that with a grain of salt. But maybe he could contribute to the myths while he was here.

This was a very different setting from his previous post in the dry desert country of Big Bend National Park.

He liked the change. Liked the swamp. For now. He never stayed any place too long. It didn't matter where he lived, actually. Just so he had the space he needed to roam free.

He looked up and saw the moon filtering through the branches of the willow oaks and cypress trees. It was huge and yellow and full, and he knew there were people who would think that the large orb in the sky had something to do with his unsettled mood. But it wasn't that.

He dragged in a long breath, detecting a scent that was out of place in the sultry air. Nothing he had ever smelled before, he thought, as he walked into the shadows under the oak trees.

Whatever it was had a strange tang, a pull, an edge of danger that he found disturbing. Of course, he was affected by odors as few people were. And by other things most folks took in stride. Coffee, for example, made him sick. And forget liquor.

Later tonight, he'd probably have a cup of herbal tea. By himself, since he was the only staffer who lived in the park—in the cozy cabin thoughtfully provided by Austen Barnette, who owned this three-hundred-acre corner of the swampland, along with a sizable portion of Wayland, Georgia.

Barnette was the big cheese in the area. And he'd gone to the expense and bother of hiring Adam Marshall away from the U.S. Park Service to show he was serious about running Nature's Refuge as a private enterprise. But there was another reason as well. Adam had a reputation for solving problems.

Most recently, at Big Bend, he had shut down a bunch of drug smugglers who had been bringing their cargoes across the drought-shrunken Rio Grande. He had tracked them to their mountain hideout and scared the shit out of them before turning them over to the border patrol.

He had done a good job, because he always demanded the best from himself as far as his work was concerned. It compensated for the other area of his life where he wasn't quite so effective—personal relationships. But he was damn well going to find out who had killed Ken White, the previous head ranger.

He walked to a spot about a hundred yards from his cabin, a place where he often stopped and contemplated the swamp before going out to prowl the park. It was a good distance from the house, where he was sure nobody would find his clothing.

Standing in the shade of a pine, he sniffed the wind again as his hands went to the front of his shirt. He unbuttoned the garment and dropped it on the ground, then pulled off his shoes and pants, stripping to the buff.

The sultry air felt good on his bare skin, and he stood for a moment, digging his toes into the springy layer of decomposing leaves covering the ground, caught by a push-pull within himself. The man warring with the animal clamoring to run free.

The animal won, as it must. Closing his dark eyes, he called on ancient knowledge, ancient ritual, ancient deities as he gathered his inner strength, steeling himself for familiar pain, even as he said the words that he had learned on his sixteenth birthday—the way his brothers had before him. As far as he knew, the only Marshall boys still alive were himself and Ross. But he didn't know for sure because he hadn't seen his brother in years.

It was when he prepared to change that his thoughts

sometimes turned to Ross, but he didn't let those thoughts break his concentration.

"Taranis, Epona, Cerridwen," he intoned, then repeated the same phrase and went on to another.

"Ga. Feart. Cleas. Duais. Aithriocht. Go gcumhdai is dtreorai na deithe thu."

On that night so long ago, the ceremonial words had helped him through the agony of transformation, opened his mind, freed him from the bonds of the human shape. Maybe they were nonsense syllables. He didn't know. Ross had studied the ancient Gaelic language and said he understood what they meant. Adam didn't care about the meaning.

All that mattered was that they blocked some of the blinding pain that always came with transformation.

While the human part of his mind screamed in protest, he felt his jaw elongate, his teeth sharpen, his body contort as muscles and limbs transformed themselves into a different shape that was as familiar to him as his human form.

The first few times he'd done it had been a nightmare of torture and terror. But gradually, he'd learned what to expect, learned to rise above the physical sensations of muscles spasming, bones changing shape, the very structure of his cells mutating from one kind of DNA to another. At least that was how he thought about it, because he didn't understand the science involved. In fact, he was sure modern science would have no explanations for his family heritage.

But the change came upon him nevertheless.

Gray hair formed along his flanks, covering his body in a thick, silver-tipped pelt. The color—the very structure—of his eyes changed as he dropped to all fours. He was no longer a man but an animal far more suited to the natural environment around him.

A wolf. Where no wolves had made their home for

decades. But now one had command of Nature's Refuge. It was his. And the night was his.

Once the transformation was complete, a raw, primal joy rippled through him, and he pawed the ground, reveling in the feel of the damp soil under his feet. Raising his head, he sucked in a draft of air, his lungs expanding as his nose drank in the rich scents that were suddenly part of the landscape. To his right an alligator had gone very still. And a bear had stopped and sniffed the wind sensing the presence of a rival.

The large black beast stayed where it was for a moment, then ambled off in the other direction, unwilling to challenge the creature with whom he suddenly shared the swamp.

Adam's lips shaped themselves into a wolfish grin. He wanted to throw back his head and howl at the small victory. But he checked the impulse, because the mind inside his skull still held his human intelligence. And the man understood the need for stealth.

Dragging in a breath, he examined the unfamiliar scent he had picked up. It was nothing that belonged in this natural world. Men had brought something here that was out of place.

The smell was acrid, yet at the same time strangely sweet to his wolf's senses. And it drew him forward.

Still, he moved with caution, setting off in the direction of the odor, feeling the air thicken around him in a strange, unfamiliar way as he padded forward.

Each breath seemed to change his sense of awareness. His mind was usually sharp, but the edges of his thoughts were beginning to blur as though someone had soaked his brain with a bottle of sweet, sticky syrup.

The air stung his eyes now, and he blinked back moisture, then blinked again as he caught his first glimpse of fire.

The flames jolted him out of his lethargy.

Fire! Where no fire should be. Out here in the open—in the middle of the park. The swamp might be wet, but that wouldn't stop a blaze from sweeping through the area, if the flames were hot enough. He'd read as much as he could about the Olakompa in the past few months, and he knew that in the winter of nineteen fifty-five, wildfires had burned eighty percent of the swamp area.

Fires were usually due to lightning igniting the layer of peat buried under some areas of the swamp.

He'd seen no lightning tonight, but it wasn't difficult to imagine a conflagration roaring unchecked through the park. Imagine birds taking flight, animals scattering for safety, the water evaporating in the heat.

His mind fuzzy from the smoke, he kept moving forward, toward the center of the danger. But when he took a second look, he saw that the flames were contained. A bonfire. Deep in the wilderness.

Tall, upright shadows moved around the flames, and in his bleary state, he could make no sense of what he was seeing. Then the wavery images resolved themselves into naked human figures—dancing and gyrating in the glow of the fire.

He shook his head, trying to clear away the fog that seemed to swirl up from the sweet, enticing smoke. For a moment he questioned his own sanity.

He'd heard people describe hallucinations that came from drug trips, heard some pretty strange stuff. Had his mind conjured up these images? Against his will, the circle of fire and the gyrating figures drew him, and he padded forward once more, although caution made his steps slow. He had come upon many strange things in his thirty years of living, but never a scene like this.

He blinked, but nothing changed. The naked men and women were still there, chanting words he didn't understand, dancing around the fire, sometimes alone, sometimes touching and swaying erotically together, sometimes falling to the ground in two- and threesomes—grappling in a sexual frenzy.

The thick, drugging smoke held him in its power, compelling his eyes to fix on the images before him, making the wolf hairs along his back bristle.

Getting high was deliberately outside his experience. He had never tried so much as a joint, although he had been at parties where people had been smoking them. But just the passive smoke had made him sick, and he'd always bailed out, which meant that he was ill-equipped to deal with mind-altering substances. Street drugs were poison to the wolf part of him. He was pretty sure that even some legal drugs could bend his mind so far out of shape that he would never be able to cram it back into his skull.

But the poison smoke had a stranglehold on his senses and on his mind. He was powerless to back away, powerless to stop breathing the choking stuff.

He took a step forward and then another, his eyes focused on the figures dancing in the moonlight. The smoke obscured their features. The smoke and the slashes of red, blue, and yellow paint both the men and women had used to decorate their faces and their bodies. He licked his long pink tongue over his lips and teeth, his eyes focused on sweaty bodies and pumping limbs, his own actions no longer under the control of his brain. Recklessly, he dragged in a deep breath of the tainted air. The fumes obscured the raw scent of the dancers' arousal. But he didn't need scent to understand their frenzy.

He watched a naked man, his cock jutting straight out from his body, reach for a woman's breasts, watched her thrust herself boldly into his hands, watched another woman join them in their sexual play, the three of them dancing and cavorting in unholy delight, the firelight flickering on their sweat-slick bodies.

His gaze cutting through the group of gamboling figures, he kept his heated focus on the threesome. He saw

them swaying together, saw them fall to the ground,
writhing with an urgency that took his breath away.

His own sexual experience was pretty extensive. But
he'd never participated in anything beyond one man/one
woman coupling. And some part of his mind was scan-
dalized by the uninhibited orgy. Yet the urge to join the
gang-shag was stronger than the shock. He felt as though
his skin were cutting off his breath, restraining him like
a straitjacket.

He had to escape the wolf. And in his mind, in a kind
of desperate rush, the ancient chant came to him, and he
reversed the process that had turned him from man to
wolf.

"*Taranis, Epona, Cerridwen,*" he silently chanted, the
words slurring in his brain.

"*Ga. Feart. Cleas. Duais. Aithriocht. Go gcumhdai is
dtreorai na deithe thu.*"

His consciousness was so full of the sweet, sticky
smoke that he could barely focus on the syllables that
were so much a part of him that he could utter them in
his sleep.

But they did their work, and his muscles spasmed as
he changed back to human form, the pain greater than any
he remembered since his teens.

He stood in the shadows, his breath coming in jagged
gulps, his eyes blinking in the flickering light, his hand
clawing at the bark of a tree to keep himself upright when
his knees threatened to give way. The sudden urgent
sounds from the campfire twenty yards away snapped his
mind into some kind of hazy focus.

"There! Over there," a man's voice shouted.

"Someone's watching."

"Get him."

"Kill him!"

"Before he rats us out."

The orgy-goers might have stripped off their clothing

in the swamp, but they hadn't abandoned the protections of the modern world.

A shot rang out. A bullet whizzed past Adam's head.

Without conscious thought, he turned and ran for his life, heading for the depths of the swamp where either safety or death awaited him.

CHAPTER

TWO

ADAM RAN FOR his life as another shot flashed by, too close for comfort. In some part of his mind, he knew a bullet in the brain would be a kindness, because these people were capable of tearing him limb from limb with their bare hands.

So he ran headlong through the untamed landscape, heedless of anything besides the sounds of the mob behind him.

Nothing mattered except escape. The pungent smell of peat, the sound of insects buzzing in the night, the muck under his feet were a jumbled mixture of sensations.

He might have been running on all fours or on two feet. He didn't know which. He only understood on a deep, instinctive level that staying alive depended on flight. Perhaps he was hallucinating now, but he felt the mob's hot breath on the back of his neck, heard the air hissing in and out of their lungs. He felt hands clawing at him and slipping off his sweat-slick body. Or perhaps that was only the indifferent branches of bramble bushes tearing at his naked flesh.

He splashed through ankle-deep mud, then broke through into water up to his waist as a layer of peat gave way beneath his weight.

Somehow he scrambled to higher ground, where sticky earth sucked at his bare feet.

In the darkness the sounds of pursuit diminished behind him, but still he kept up his frantic flight, his path lighted only by the silvery rays of the full moon.

He ran until he was exhausted, ran until he could run no more. Sinking to his knees, he swayed uncertainly, his hand coming to rest against the trunk of a tree.

As he tried to steady himself, the sickness at the back of his throat welled up in a great wave of nausea.

He leaned forward, retching up the food that remained in his stomach from dinner. The sickness exhausted him, and he rolled to his side, curling into a ball.

Perhaps God had mercy on him that night, because no predators found him as he sank into unconsciousness.

ADAM woke in the gray light of early dawn, to the sound of birds chirping in the trees.

For terrifying heartbeats, he didn't know where he was or even *who* he was. His head felt like a thousand coal miners were working away inside his skull with pickaxes, destroying brain cells as they went. When he tried to move any muscle in his body, the agony increased, so he lay very still, struggling to ride above the pain the way he did when he changed from wolf to man and back again.

Wolf to man.

The fundamental reality of his existence was his secret life as a wolf. Yet somehow he had forgotten all about that as he lay on the damp ground.

Jesus! He was in bad shape.

He closed his eyes, trying to will himself back to normal, although he couldn't exactly say what normal was. He felt as though he were hanging on to sanity by his fingernails.

Wild, disturbing images swirled into his mind. Some came back to him with his wolf's vision. Some were the perceptions of a man.

He saw flickering fire. Smelled a strange acrid smoke that was as sweet as it was pungent.

He squeezed his eyes more tightly shut, feeling the pounding of his heart as his fingers clenched and unclenched in the soft soil where he lay.

Had it all been a dream? A very vivid dream? Brought on by the hallucinogenic smoke?

He took a cautious sniff of the cool morning air. He didn't smell anything strange now. But that proved nothing.

To ground himself, he focused on the sensations of his body. It wasn't just his head that hurt. He ached in a wide variety of places. One spot in particular stung like hell. Opening his eyes, he looked down at the long red scratches that marred the flesh over his ribs. He'd been torn by brambles on his headlong dash through the swamp.

He didn't remember much of that. But he'd heard bullets whiz past his head. And he'd felt the primal anger of the men and women chasing him.

He was thinking about Ken White when he managed to climb to his feet. Ken White, the guy who'd held this job before him, had been found dead out here with a bullet in his brain.

Adam had smugly told himself that he wasn't going to end up that way. Now he contemplated his narrow escape.

He looked back toward the deep swamp, thinking he needed to find the campfire where he'd seen the drug and sex party. But not now. Not when he was naked and vulnerable and covered with grunge. First he was going home to shower, tend his wounds, and dress.

He raised his head, squinting in the early morning sunlight as he got his bearings. He had a good sense of direction, but he was swaying on his feet when he set out for his little cabin. His jaw rigid, he kept moving—hurrying now, wondering what he'd say if the staff found him wandering around naked.

Or if they found the place where he'd left his clothes, he thought, as he picked up his pace and angled toward the spot where he'd undressed.

Although he still wasn't back to normal, his brain was starting to work a little better. In his mind he contemplated the men and women he'd come upon the night before. He didn't know who the hell they were. And finding out was going to be a problem. His wolf's nose wouldn't be able to identify them when he encountered them again.

The smoke had drugged him, fogged his sense of smell and clouded his vision. The body paint had finished the job of hiding the party-goers' features.

A couple of the women had been blondes. At least one of them had been a real blonde he remembered. And the same woman had had big breasts that had bobbed up and down as she'd danced in the flickering light.

He gave a short bark of a laugh. Apparently he'd focused on breasts and female pubic hair. He couldn't recall the details of any cocks he'd seen. But that wasn't really surprising, given his sexual orientation.

He grimaced, thinking that what he knew about the orgy-goers was pitifully small. All his adult life he'd relied on his wolf senses. But now he was as deaf and blind as if he'd been thrown into a witches' cauldron.

*   *   *

TURNING from the water-stained sink, Sara Weston peered at her image in the full-length mirror on the back of the bathroom door, thinking that her rumpled old green pants and faded brown shirt made a kind of fashion statement. They were the perfect outfit for a tramp through the swamp.

She swiped a hand through her blond hair, backed away from the mirror, and walked toward the kitchen of her little rented house, hoping that she might be able to choke down some apricot yogurt for breakfast.

She'd spent most of the night huddled in her bed, sleep an impossibility as she listened to the unfamiliar sounds of the Olakompa. Animals splashing through standing water. Buzzing insects. The occasional passing of a car down the narrow road where her rented house was located.

Along with the sounds came something else. Something she couldn't identify that had drifted toward her on the night air like tainted mist. A mixture of old nightmares and new ones. When she'd finally fallen asleep, she'd dreamed of this house. Not as it was now. The paint on the walls was a darker shade. The furnishings were shabbier. And she'd seen a woman drifting through the rooms, a woman who had turned and held out her hand in invitation. To what? Sara didn't know. She didn't want to know.

She shook her head, denying her dreams. Her two nights in the motel where she'd stayed when she'd first arrived in Wayland had been bad enough. This house on the edge of the Olakompa was worse.

The air was different here. Thicker. Enfolding her in an unwelcome embrace that made her feel as though someone had pressed a malicious hand over her nose and mouth.

She tried to banish the unwanted image. But it wouldn't go away. She had always had uncanny judgments. She'd sense that a place or a person was good or bad. And usually those perceptions would turn out to be valid.

It was just one of the things that made her feel different from other people. Different in a way she had never wanted to explore too deeply.

So she kept a lid on the fanciful side of her nature. In her personal life. And her professional life, too.

When she'd been a teenager, she'd had a hard time deciding what she'd wanted to do with her life. She'd been attracted to art. And her high school teachers had encouraged her in that area. She'd been good. Too good, maybe. Because when she'd looked at her drawings and paintings, she'd thought they'd revealed too much about her inner self. And that had made her feel exposed.

So she'd backed away from creative expression. In college she'd taken a lot of science courses. Science was steady and down-to-earth. You dealt with facts and information and numbers. And the numbers didn't give away anything about the person writing them down.

Science had taught her to be measured and methodical. To study each new environment carefully. Before she'd come to Wayland, she'd read about the town. The early residents had raised cotton and tobacco. Then peanuts had become the major cash crop in the area. In the nineteenth and early twentieth century, a weaving factory had provided a lot of employment—until the jobs had gone to countries like Mexico and China where labor costs were lower.

Now tourism was an important part of the economy thanks to Nature's Refuge and the nearby national park that drew visitors to southern Georgia's unique and beautiful Olakompa Swamp.

Many of the same tourists who came to the parks also visited the cute little stores and restaurants along the four block commercial stretch that was now called Historic Downtown Wayland. In fact, the town was getting a reputation for the number and quality of its antique and secondhand shops. As well as the discount mall out near the interstate.

On the surface, Wayland had a good deal of charm— if you didn't poke too closely into the pockets of poverty that she'd seen in some of the outlying areas.

She'd done her homework. And now she would do the job that she'd contracted to do—a research project for Granville Pharmaceuticals. They wanted to find out if any of the plants native to the area had commercial medicinal value. And they'd hired her to conduct a six-month study of the local flora.

This morning, she supposed she should be opening the boxes of lab equipment that had arrived from UPS yesterday afternoon. But she needed to get out of the little house.

So she climbed into the secondhand Toyota, Miss Hester, that Mom had given her when she'd gone off to college in Chapel Hill. Almost eight years later, she was still driving the old rattletrap.

Mom had wanted her to get something better before she headed for Georgia. She'd protested that Miss Hester was just fine.

As she drove, she scanned the highway for the Nature's Refuge access road she'd been instructed to look for, then slowed when she saw the turnoff. Not the paved public drive that led to the front entrance, but the gravel track that skirted the edge of the vast swampland property.

The directions were very precise, and here it was.

Behind her on Route 177 a pickup truck honked, and she jumped, then watched the driver wave his fist in anger as he pulled around her and barreled down the blacktop. He probably was thinking, "stupid woman driver."

Goody for him. Turning off the highway, she came to a stop, peering uncertainly up the road, wishing that this job offer hadn't been so tempting.

Too bad none of the dozens of applications for tenure

track teaching had panned out. Apparently, the market for newly minted Ph.D. botanists was depressed.

"Don't worry dear; something will turn up," Mom had said, with that eternal optimism of hers. "You've always loved plants. I know you can do something with your special skills."

Sara smiled to herself. Right, she loved plants. Loved growing them. Loved knowing their names and their uses. But more than that, she'd worked long and hard to earn an advanced degree in botany, which now hadn't seemed worth the effort considering the costs involved.

When she realized her hands were clamped around the steering wheel, she unclenched them. With a sigh, she took her foot off the brake. The car drifted slowly forward as though it had a mind of its own and had somehow acquired information she didn't possess.

Something just out of her grasp.

With a shake of her head, she pressed down on the accelerator, fighting a sense of disquiet as she felt the shadows of giant trees close in on either side of the car.

Really, if you looked at this place objectively, it was beautiful, more beautiful than she'd imagined.

A low area full of water, cattails, duckweed, and water hyacinths ran along the side of the road. In the shallows a blue heron moved slowly away from her, poking its head below the surface, then lifting it gracefully again, and she stopped for a moment to watch its progress. She smiled as she saw a small brown lizard hop onto a floating leaf. There were eleven kinds of lizards in the swamp, and she guessed she was going to see a lot of them while she was here.

Starting up again, she drove a few more yards to a wooden barrier. On a nearby long-leaf pine was a large No Trespassing sign.

She'd been told to expect the gate. Carefully, she

looked around, probing the shadows under the trees before grabbing her knapsack and climbing out. .

It was early, but she could feel heat rising from the marshy land on either side of the desolate road as she walked toward the barrier.

Still, when a cloud drifted across the sun, she felt a sudden chill. Shaking it off, she walked to the padlocked chain that secured the gate and opened the lock.

With the bar out of the way, she returned to her car and drove through, then swung the wooden pole back into place and snapped the lock closed, thinking that escape was now impossible.

ADAM regarded his haggard face in the bathroom mirror. He looked like he'd been shot out of a cannon and missed the net.

With a grimace, he turned on the shower and stepped under water as hot as he could stand. After washing off the muck, he dabbed antiseptic on his scratches, shaved, and dressed in a clean pair of dark slacks and the green shirt that Nature's Refuge called a uniform.

At least he looked presentable. But his head still felt twice its normal size. Opening the refrigerator, he considered what to eat for breakfast. Nothing appealed to him, but he knew from experience that going without food was bad for his system. So he grabbed some chunks of stew beef and carried them to the table in his small dining room.

He liked the house that came with the job. All he had to do was step out the front door and walk a few hundred yards along a path to the main part of the park complex.

The built-up area of Nature's Refuge consisted of six structures. The largest was the administrative center with offices, a gift shop, and an auditorium where he and the other staffers gave nature talks. They also conducted tours of the swamp, both on foot along well-marked trails and boardwalks and in the trim skiffs moored in the dock area.

Chris Higman and Dwayne Parker had already arrived at the main office by the time he'd washed the meat down with a cup of blackberry tea and two ibuprofen.

Adam stopped inside the office door, automatically dragging in a deep breath, catching his staffers' familiar scent. Under normal circumstances he'd know whether either of these people had been part of last night's orgy. Today, he didn't have a clue. And the lack of knowledge made his chest feel tight.

"You two are always right on time," he commented, trying to sound like his usual chipper self.

"Maybe I'm anglin' for your job," Dwayne joked.

"I'll watch my back," Adam answered, striving for a light tone.

The door banged, and Leroy Hamilton came in. He was slightly older than Chris and Dwayne, and he'd been here a couple of years longer.

In the National Park Service, all the rangers had a college degree in a prescribed set of fields. That certainly wasn't true at Nature's Refuge. When Adam had come to the park, he'd found some of the staffers poorly trained and some of the procedures pretty lax, to put it mildly. But he was getting things into shape.

As he usually did in the morning, he went over the assignments for the day. But it was impossible to turn off his earlier thoughts. He'd established a pretty good relationship with the young men and women who worked for him. Now he couldn't help wondering if any of them had chased him through the swamp last night—intent on murder.

As far as he could see, nobody seemed the worse for wear this morning. But all of them certainly knew what area of the park would be good for an after-hours party.

He stifled a sigh. They looked like clean-cut kids. In fact, he knew they were all fine upstanding members of the local Baptist church, since each of them on separate occasions tried to get him to attend services.

Most of the people around here were churchgoers. So was there some kind of underground cult in town that went completely against the cultural norms?

He snorted inwardly at the sociological jargon. Obviously, he was in a strange mood this morning. Yet the question did bear asking. Had he seen local people out for a night of revelry in the swamp? Or were the trespassers from out of the area? Would they come again? And most of all, were they the same people who had murdered Ken White?

Maybe he'd find some clues when he located the place where they'd made their fire.

Leaning his hips against his desk, he gave the three staffers a serious look. "I thought I smelled smoke out in the park last night."

All eyes riveted to him.

"You hear anything about individuals illegally in the park?"

"No, sir," Leroy said immediately. The others echoed his answer.

"Well, I want to go out there and have a look."

"You want me to go with you?" Dwayne asked immediately.

"No. I'll handle it myself. Send Tim down to the ticket booth at the boat dock when he comes in."

"You got it, boss," Dwayne answered.

Picking up a walkie-talkie from the shelf near the door to the equipment room, Adam headed for the dock where he climbed into one of the motorboats tied up near the main channel. If you knew where you were going, sometimes a boat was the quickest way into the park's interior.

He was thinking about the party-goers again as he started the outboard motor, then settled down in the back of the skiff, his hand on the tiller.

The dark water was smooth as glass, an almost perfect mirror reflecting the trees that hung above the channel. An egret flapped away as the boat rounded a bend, and Adam thought he heard a gator splash into the dark water. Usually he enjoyed the wildlife in the park. This morning he was too preoccupied.

He wasn't sure exactly where he'd encountered the fire the night before, but he had a good idea of the general area, since he'd made it his business to get to know his domain. Fifteen minutes later, he cut the engine and tied the boat to the roots of a dead tree. Climbing out, he scrambled through muck that came several inches up his low boots, then made it onto more solid ground. Pausing again to get his bearings, he headed through the underbrush toward the open area he remembered from the night before, looking for signs of trampled vegetation and seeing none.

Cautiously, he stopped and sniffed the air. When he caught the barest whiff of the smoke, he froze. No way was he going to let that stuff take over his mind again.

For a long moment, he stood absolutely still, breathing shallowly in and out, his perception turned inward. When he'd smelled the stuff last night, he'd started feeling muzzy almost at once. As far as he could tell, nothing like that was happening now. Maybe the residue was at so low a level that it wouldn't hurt him.

Or just the opposite could be happening. Perhaps once you'd been bitten by this particular snake, it only took a little of the venom to wig you out again. And you wouldn't even realize it was happening.

He'd just decided to save his recon mission for later when movement on the other side of the clearing caught his eye, and he went very still. Something was there.

A large animal?

No—a person, dressed in green and brown that blended with the foliage. A guy who knew his way around in the backcountry.

Then the figure stepped out of the shadow of the trees, and he realized it wasn't a guy. Instead, he found himself staring at feminine curves covered by a long-sleeved shirt, cotton pants, and boots similar to his own.

She wasn't aware of him, giving him time to focus on her blond hair, caught at the nape of her neck by a simple band.

He zeroed in on that hair, thinking it was like what he remembered from some of the women last night.

Without moving a muscle, he watched her wander into the clearing. When he saw her kneel, saw her bring something shiny and metal out of the pack she was carrying, he leaped forward.

CHAPTER
THREE

"HOLD IT RIGHT there!"

The blond woman jerked around to face him, her hand clenched around a clump of sweet flag she was about to dig up with a small trowel.

"You're trespassing on private property," he heard himself say, surprised that his voice sounded normal, because he felt suddenly light-headed as he gazed into wide blue eyes that regarded him warily.

It was the remnants of the smoke affecting him, he thought. It had gotten to him again. He could smell its lingering presence more strongly than he had a few moments earlier, and now he wished he had backed away instead of letting himself be drawn forward into a trap.

But it was already too late, he knew on some deep, buried level. He might have tried to puzzle out what that meant. It was only one of the confused thoughts that swirled in his brain, thoughts that danced away before he could catch onto any one of them long enough to bring it into focus.

Last night the smoke had taken away the sharpness of his senses. Now his reaction was totally different. In the morning sunlight, he was suddenly and totally absorbed by every detail of the woman kneeling before him. His gaze lingered for a moment on a blond strand of hair that had escaped the band at the back of her neck and now curved seductively around her ear. Then he took in the triangle of ivory skin exposed at the throat of her shirt.

But more than the physical impressions, he saw that she was struggling not to show panic as she stared at him with those wide blue eyes.

That panic made his chest tighten. "It's okay," he said, then wasn't sure if the words had reached his lips or only echoed in his mind as he took her in.

What the hell was she doing out here, anyway? Had she returned to the scene of last night's clandestine party? Or was she engaged in some other crime? Like stealing plants from a private park.

He had to admit she didn't look much like a criminal. Her hair was the color of ripe wheat. Her face was heart-shaped and delicately made with beautifully curved lips, high cheekbones, and those blue, blue eyes, framed by dark-tipped lashes.

She was slender. About five five, he guessed. Her breasts were high and very nicely rounded. Probably she thought her hips were too generous, but he liked them the way they were.

He blinked, stood his ground, trying to explain in his mind why he was fixated on this woman. "The smoke," he said, and this time was sure he had spoken aloud, because she dragged in a breath, her nose wrinkling before she answered him.

"What smoke?"

"Don't you smell it? The leftovers from the party."

She tipped her head to the side, looking at him as though he'd lost his mind. Maybe he had. He'd lost it last night and thought he'd found it again in the morning. Now he struggled to remember what they had been talking about.

"You're trespassing," he managed.

She was still kneeling on the ground. Now she reached for a knapsack lying a few feet away, pulled it toward her, and thrust a hand inside. When it emerged, she was holding a small revolver. "Don't come any closer," she said, as she carefully stood up. "Raise your hands."

He'd been feeling spacey, as though his brain and his body belonged to two separate people, and there was no way to bring the two of them back together. The gun did the trick. Suddenly the muzzy feeling was gone. He stood where he was, raised his hands, palms toward her. "Be careful with that thing," he said.

"Who are you? What are you doing here?" she asked.

Had she been the one shooting at him last night? And now was he giving her a free second chance? Too bad he was pretty sure those old legends about werewolves weren't true. You didn't need to load your gun with silver bullets to bring down a member of the species. All you needed was nice hot, conventional lead.

"Who are you?" she asked again, her voice going an octave higher. He heard raw nerves in that voice, which made the situation all the more dangerous. His mind was doing swift calculations now. She didn't look like the kind of woman who was used to handling a gun, but that proved nothing, except that she could shoot him by accident.

"Take it easy," he advised. "You don't want to get arrested for killing the head ranger at Nature's Refuge."

"The head ranger! Don't give me that. The head ranger should be expecting me."

Expecting her? Who the hell was she? Some inspector the park's owner, Austen Barnette, had sent and forgotten to mention to his minions? That wasn't like the old coot.

Or was there some information about this woman buried in a pile of junk mail?

"I'm Adam Marshall," he said, his voice calm and steady. "Whom should I be expecting?"

Ignoring his question, she demanded, "Show me some identification."

He watched her eyes, gauging her level of jumpiness. Would she really pull the trigger, or would she hesitate a fraction of a second, giving him time to knock the weapon out of her hand?

Some part of his brain was viewing the confrontation from a distance like a kind of strange out-of-body experience. "Okay, my wallet's in my pocket. Don't drill me when I pull it out," he said, speaking calmly as he reached into his back pocket and extracted the wallet, then carefully opened it to his driver's license, which he held up for her to see.

She peered at the plastic-covered rectangle, then snapped, "That's from Texas."

"Yeah, right. I just took the job here four months ago."

"And you haven't changed your license?"

"I've been busy. If you've been in touch with Austen Barnette, you may recall that the previous head ranger was found shot dead in the park. So pardon me for being a little careful when I meet up with strangers out here."

She winced. After several second's hesitation, she lowered the weapon, and he managed to fill his lungs with air for the first time since the gun had appeared out of her knapsack.

"Thanks," he said, then asked, "So who are you?"

"Sara Weston."

The name was familiar, and he struggled to figure out the context. "The botanist," he finally said. "Working on the drug project for Granville Pharmaceuticals."

"That's right."

"I was expecting a fifty-year-old woman with gray hair

pulled back in a bun," he said, feeling foolish as the words came out of his mouth.

She made a face. "You don't have to be an old bat to be interested in the medicinal uses of plants."

"I realize that." He sighed. "But I'd be remiss if I didn't ask *you* for some identification."

She nodded and hunkered down to reach in her pack. As he had done, she pulled out a wallet with her driver's license—and also a letter from Barnette, giving her permission to take plant specimens from the park.

"You looking for a cure for cancer?" he asked.

"I'm looking for plants that native Americans and herbal healers have used successfully. Like this *Acorus calamus*," she said, gesturing toward the plant she'd been about to dig up.

"Sweet flag," he said.

"Yes. *Acorus calamus*. Or sweet flag. Or calamus or sweet root. It's been used to cure various ailments since biblical times. It looks like an iris, but it's actually related to jack-in-the-pulpit and skunk cabbage. The part used medicinally is the root. It shouldn't be peeled, because the active ingredient is right below the surface." She stopped abruptly, maybe because she'd become aware that she was lecturing him.

"Okay," he answered, "you've convinced me of your botanical expertise."

Color spread across her cheeks, and he couldn't stop himself from admiring the effect.

He told himself it wasn't likely that Dr. Sara Weston had been involved with the orgy-goers of the night before. But her turning up in this particular location the next morning was certainly a screaming coincidence.

"So are you just looking for cures for diseases, or are you interested in psychotropic drugs?" he asked.

"That's kind of a strange question. Why do you ask?"

"Because I caught some people having a drug party

last night," he said, watching her carefully.

Her eyes widened. "In the park?"

"Yes. Actually right around here. Maybe you can give me your professional opinion on what they were using."

"*Acorus calamus* has no psychotropic qualities as far as I know," she answered.

"But some of the plants here do," he said, "like pearly everlasting or ladies' tobacco, or whatever you want to call it." He tossed the observation over his shoulder. He was already marching past her and toward the clearing where he thought he'd seen the fire.

He waited with his nerves on edge, then relaxed when he heard her following him.

He stopped short when he saw the fire pit. Until that moment he hadn't been absolutely sure he hadn't dreamed it.

Looking around, he half expected to find some discarded article of clothing, but on first glance, there was nothing besides ash and charred wood and a bunch of footprints in the dirt to witness that anyone had been here recently. Apparently the party-goers hadn't been too wasted to take away their personal effects.

The smoke was stronger here. When he drew in a cautious breath, he caught the remnants of the stuff mixed with the unmistakable aroma of stale sex, at least to his werewolf-enhanced senses.

Could she smell that, too? he wondered, giving her a sidewise look. Her posture had turned rigid, and he couldn't shake the feeling that they were sharing a kind of secondhand intimacy.

She walked slowly toward the place where the fire had been, staring down at the cold embers. "Isn't it dangerous—lighting a fire out here?"

"Yeah, but they cleared a fairly large area."

He looked from her to the stone-ringed pit. He had sworn he was going to stay as far away from the smoke as he possibly could. Yet some impulse he couldn't analyze had seized hold of him. He found himself walking forward, picking up a stick, and stirring the cold ashes.

Gray flakes swirled. Caught by a little puff of wind, they rose into the air. The particles gave off the scent of the smoke that had captured him the night before.

Instantly, Adam's mind flashed back to the darkness of the moon-drenched swamp, to the wild movement of naked bodies dancing and coming together in the flickering firelight.

But this time was different. This time, in his imagination, he wasn't an outsider, silent witness to the orgiastic dancing. This time he was one of the participants, writhing and chanting among the press of bodies.

And he wasn't the only one. The pretty blond botanist was back there, too.

The nighttime scene was an overlay on the daytime reality. His gaze riveted to Sara Weston's face—to her body. Her eyes had gone unfocused. Her breath was a shaky gasp. And another flood of color suffused her face.

The remnants of the drug pulsed through his senses, and in that moment of illusion, he saw her as he had seen the dancers the night before. Naked and aroused, her nipples tight, her skin glistening with sweat.

But the smoke-induced hallucination was over before it had time to form into anything solid and real.

She was staring at him, as if she knew what had leaped into his mind.

"What just happened?" he asked.

"Nothing."

"Are you sure?"

"Perfectly."

He shifted his weight from one foot to the other. "What kind of psychotropic drug would use fire and smoke as a delivery system?"

"That's not my field. I don't know." She raised her

head, looking at him with assessing eyes. "Why did you stir up the fire?"

"I was making sure it was really out," he answered, wondering if she would call him on the lie. "As you pointed out, a fire here could be dangerous."

She only nodded, then said, "I'm sorry if we got off on the wrong foot. I was planning to stop by your office later today."

On some other morning, he might have accepted her words with a nod. Instead he said, "But you came out here first."

"I was anxious to get started," she answered.

"How did you get onto park property?"

"I have a key to the gate that locks the access road. My car's over that way," she said, waving her hand in the direction of the road that ran along the edge of the refuge and then branched off toward the interior. Probably she was glad for the change of subject. And probably he should bring the conversation back to the drug. Instead, he let it go because he wasn't feeling any more sure of himself than she looked.

"I wouldn't come in here in a car," he said.

"Oh?"

"The ground in the swamp can be wet and slippery. A truck with four-wheel drive is more suitable to the road conditions."

"Too bad I can't afford one," she snapped.

"I could ban you from the park."

"Austen Barnette might have something to say about that."

"You've been in touch with him?"

"It was my understanding that he was in favor of my research. I believe Granville is paying him a fee to allow me to collect specimens here."

"Yeah," Adam conceded. Barnette had told him that he'd worked a deal with Granville Pharmaceuticals. At the time he'd been annoyed, because as far as he was concerned, digging up plants for medicinal purposes in the park was incompatible with the concept of Nature's Refuge. What if Granville found some useful plant that only grew in the swamp? There would be all kinds of people tramping through the place, disturbing the natural environment. He'd wanted to explain that to Barnette, but he'd also been new on the job and unsure of how the owner would take advice from employees. So he'd kept his mouth shut.

Perhaps he was taking out his frustration on Sara when he said, "Do you mind telling me where you were last night?"

"In bed."

"Alone?"

Her face contorted. "Of course I was alone. What are you implying—that I was here at a drug party last night?"

"I have to check out every lead."

Her voice took on a sharp edge. "Well, I don't appreciate you implicating me."

He wasn't going to back down. "The park is pretty big. You have to admit, it's strange that I find a problem in this particular area—then find you here the next morning."

She shrugged. "I'm sorry if it seems odd to you. Perhaps the proximity of the road is a factor."

The urge to keep her talking burned inside him. But he didn't know what else to say. He'd set them up in a confrontational situation, and now he didn't know how to get out of it.

She took care of that problem for him. "I'm sorry. You'll have to excuse me; I must get back to work." She turned and retraced her steps.

He stood watching her. She was acting like she was the only person out here in the swamp, but he knew she had to be aware of his gaze.

She carefully ignored him as she bent to the plant she'd been digging up, looking totally absorbed in the task, except for the rigid set of her shoulders.

He watched her for several more moments, then he went back to the fire circle to look for clues.

This time he was careful not to stir the ashes. He should probably call in the sheriff, Paul Delacorte. As he recalled, there were rules about disturbing a crime scene. But he wanted a crack at the site first. Then he'd see if Delacorte had registered any similar trouble on his radar screen.

He kept his focus pretty much on the area where the orgy had taken place, starting near the fire pit and walking in an ever-widening circle, looking for evidence.

He saw several places where coolers or boxes had been set on the spongy ground. He saw places where he thought the participants might have been writhing together, but that was about all.

Sighing, he continued the visual search and doggedly kept from looking over to where Sara Weston was working.

He saw a stampede of feet where the party-goers had probably taken after the intruder the night before. He followed that trail into the underbrush, but came up with nothing.

Finally, on his way back, he allowed himself to raise his eyes to the spot where he'd last seen the botanist.

She was gone. Somehow, he'd known she would be.

CHAPTER
FOUR

STARFLOWER WOKE AND stretched languidly in her bed, the covers drifting down to expose her naked breasts. They were slashed by a line of scratches where one of her lovers had raked his nails across her tender flesh last night.

She fingered the marks now, gently, possessively, bringing back memories of the wild coupling.

She had loved the fire and the smoke and the frantic dancing. When the dancing had turned to touching and kissing and fucking, she had liked that even better.

She had felt her power build while she was with the others. She had felt as though she could do anything. Even though it wasn't quite true.

It was always that way when the clan gathered for a ceremony in the swamp. They were the chosen ones. And they had finally come out of hiding to claim their birth-right. Their strength was in their melding together. Falcon had said that would be true. And it looked like their leader was right.

Falcon had told them to pick names from nature. When she'd joined the clan, she had chosen Starflower because she loved the combination of sounds and because the name seemed unusual and elegant.

That wasn't the name she was known by when she went out among the sorry folk who populated Wayland and the area around the town. They thought she was like them. But she had powers they could only dream of.

She sent her thoughts across the room, toward the heavy vase that sat on the shelf below the window. With her mind, she tried to move it. She felt the glass vibrate, but the vase remained where it was.

"Shit!" She had thought that, after the energy flowed into her last night, she could move the damn thing, but it was too frigging heavy. Her gaze darted over the room. A pile of papers sat on the corner of the desk. From where she lay in bed, she was able to riffle them. One flew into the air and drifted downward toward the floor.

She felt a small zing of triumph. She had moved the paper. But it wasn't enough. She had to practice her talent. Falcon had told her to practice. But practicing alone was no fun. And it was hard work.

It was better when she was in the magic circle of the group, feeling their collective power and their sexual energy.

She smiled as she sat up, then pushed back her flowing golden hair. Her fingers caught on a piece of debris, and she plucked it out, holding it up. It was a twig, and she remembered now that her hair had caught on the low hanging branches of a tree as she'd followed the others headlong into the wilds of the park.

Razorback had seen the intruder and sounded the alarm. And she'd had no choice but to join the wild chase.

An outsider had seen them dancing around the fire under the witching moon, and he must be eliminated.

Secretly, she didn't go along with that logic. She had

sensed the watcher's presence in the darkness—even as Falcon had played with her breasts and run his hand down her butt crack.

But her mind had reached toward the man beyond the firelight. She had felt his potency. And she had wanted that potency between her legs.

She leaned back against the pillows again, touching her breasts, bringing the nipples to hard, sensitive points as she thought about the guy who had been watching them—watching *her*. Last night she had been sated. But this morning, thinking about the stranger in the darkness brought back her sexual desire.

Eyes closed, she let her hand drift down her body as she thought about the intruder. Falcon said he was dangerous. To the clan. To their plans. He had spied on them for his own purposes. But she had sensed his sexual arousal and his desire to join with them.

Then when the group had attacked him, he had run for his life, because he had no choice.

But he was no coward. She knew that.

The rest of the group might not understand. But she knew he was like them. Well, not exactly like them. But he was no one ordinary. She understood that much. And she would find out who he was and bring him into the clan.

She kept her thoughts on him as she stroked her breasts, pinched the nipples, then slid one hand down her body to her slick, wet sex.

Her finger slipped into the hot, swollen folds. She was sore from the night before, and it hurt to stroke herself. All of the men had had her in the frantic riot of sexual need created by the smoke.

But the pain this morning only added to her pleasure. And when her orgasm rocked her, she heard the vase sway on the shelf and tumble to the floor, where it broke in a shower of glass shards.

*   *   *

SHERIFF Paul Delacorte climbed out of his black-and-white cruiser and stood under the branches of a longleaf pine, looking at the open area near the ranger station at Nature's Refuge. The grounds were well kept, he noted, with plantings of flowers setting off the natural vegetation.

He hadn't been out here in a couple of months. Now he gave his surroundings his usual thorough inspection. As far as he could see, Adam Marshall was doing a right fine job of keeping up the park ambiance. Marshall had come here with a high level of enthusiasm. He had the place shaped up, but it still remained to be seen how far out on a limb he was willing to go to influence policy.

Paul had done some checking and knew that the man had joined the National Park Service right out of college eight years ago. He'd worked for them until accepting the head ranger position in Wayland. Paul wondered how the new head ranger liked the job, now that he'd been here a few months.

The rules at Nature's Refuge weren't quite like the rules that the federal government insisted upon.

Take for example, the large gator that lay sunning himself beside a cabbage palm. The gator's name was Big Jim, and he'd been a fixture at the park for over fifteen years. Paul knew the creatures looked like big scaly slugs, incapable of fast movement. But in reality, when a gator was hungry, it could strike with lightning speed. Big Jim had once snapped up a miniature poodle belonging to a tourist and dragged if off, squealing pitifully, into the swamp. That was back when Paul had first been elected sheriff, and as a black man, he'd been a little reticent about rocking the boat in Wayland. Basically, he'd figured he'd gotten the job because the population expected him to follow his daddy's tradition and not make waves.

He wasn't his daddy, of course. And he'd vowed he

wasn't going to be the black lackey of Wayland, Georgia. But he'd also known he couldn't come striding in with his degree from the state university and his top honors at the police academy and euthanize a beloved local icon. So he'd allowed Austen Barnette to persuade him that paying a fine—including a substantial sum to the owner of the poodle—would make up for the loss of the animal. And he'd gotten the assurance of the then head ranger, Ray Thompson, that the gator would be fed large portions of raw meat on a regular basis, to keep him away from the tourist's dogs and children.

Back then Paul was still feeling his way. Now he'd learned that if you were gonna run with the big dogs, you'd better know how to lift your leg in the tall grass.

Straightening his shoulders, he switched his thoughts from himself back to the park. There had been four head rangers since Ray Thompson had retired and migrated south to the Daytona Beach area. Most of them had been good men, except Hank Bradford, who had liked his liquor a little too much.

The face of Ken White flashed into his mind, and he clenched his fists at his sides. Five and a half months ago, Ken had been murdered out in the swamp, and there still weren't any clues about who had done it. Although Paul had his theories.

Which was why he was keeping a close eye on Nature's Refuge. From his position under the pine tree, he caught sight of Adam Marshall coming up the path from the boat dock.

Paul moved to intercept him—noting the man's flash of surprise as he spotted the navy blue uniform. Marshall stopped where he was, waiting for the law to catch up with him.

"What's new?" Paul said.

The ranger gave him an apprising look. "I have the feeling you might already have an idea," he answered.

"Nothing concrete," Paul allowed. It was hard to explain the feeling he'd picked up in town this morning. It wasn't something he could exactly articulate. It was simply a kind of vibration of dark excitement in the air. The kind of murky vibration he'd felt the morning after Ken White's death. Some people might have called it cop's instincts. Maybe that was part of it, but it also made Paul wonder about his own genetic heritage. Over the years, there had been a fair amount of informal interbreeding between the white folks and the blacks in Wayland. He knew he probably had as much white blood flowing through his veins as black. And he suspected some of his ancestors were involved with the strange doings that had erupted in the area over the years.

"Let me tell the staff I'm back," Marshall was saying. "Then we can go over to my cabin and talk."

"Appreciate it," Paul answered, leaning against a railing at the edge of the parking lot where he could keep an eye on Big Jim.

He was watching a flock of sparrows chattering in the bushes when Marshall returned several minutes later. Had it taken him that long to deal with the staff or was he collecting his thoughts?

Paul eyed the manila folder in Marshall's hand.

"The attendance figures by day of the week and month. I want to see if I need to switch staff schedules around."

"I guess there's a lot of behind-the-scenes management involved with running a place like this," Paul observed, straightening. Together he and Marshall crossed the parking area and stepped into a small grove about a hundred yards from the main complex.

Nestled among the trees were a pair of snug log cabins. They had been used for storage for a number of years. But Ray Thompson had had them cleaned up and turned into living quarters. He and one of his staffers had moved in when the park had had some problems with vandalism.

Marshall was living in one of the cabins now. The other was sometimes used for overnight guests.

"You like living out here by yourself?" Paul asked as the ranger opened the door.

"I like my privacy, yeah."

Was that a warning? Paul wondered, as the head ranger led him into a combination living/dining area with a small kitchen off to the side.

Paul looked around unobtrusively, making judgments about the man by the way he kept his personal space. The rooms were military neat, and Marshall hadn't bothered to set out any mementos that would give any clues to his past life. If he were going only by what he observed now, he'd think Marshall was trying to hide his background. But Paul had seen his performance appraisals. They were all good.

"Can I get you something to drink?" Marshall asked, walking toward the kitchen area.

"I remember you don't drink coffee. Or soft drinks."

Marshall laughed. "Yeah, I've got some nice spring water—or some herbal teas."

"Water is fine," Paul said.

The ranger brought a bottle out of the refrigerator and poured two large glasses. "We can sit out back," he said, leading the way to another door that opened onto a small patio shaded by black gum trees.

"Seems like a good place to set a spell," Paul commented as he settled into one of the two Adirondack chairs that looked out toward the natural area beyond.

Marshall took several swallows of water. "You didn't come here to talk about the bucolic scenery, did you?" he asked. "I'd like to know what did bring you out to the park."

"One of my periodic drop-bys to ask if you'd picked up anything on the Ken White case," Paul replied.

*   *   *

ADAM thought about his response as he set down his
glass on the low wooden table between the chairs and
glanced up into Paul's face, which was the color of English toffee.

"As a matter of fact, something did happen here last
night," he finally said. Growing up, he'd developed a
healthy disrespect for the law. The attitude came from
dear old Dad, who had supplemented his income as an
auto mechanic with breaking and entering.

The way kids did, Adam had absorbed some of his old
man's attitudes and prejudices. He'd had to learn the hard
way that the law wasn't the enemy. And he'd also had to
discard some of the racist attitudes his dad had brought
into the house. To put it mildly, his father had looked
down on anyone whose dark skin color wasn't the result
of a nice suntan. It wasn't until Adam had left home that
he'd bothered looking at black people any differently. His
first boss in the park service, Henry Darter, had been an
African American, and with the background of prejudice
Adam had absorbed from his father, he'd resented working for Darter—until he'd seen how the man had handled
a flash flood in the Big Thompson River valley. Darter
had saved a lot of lives that evening, and Adam had come
out of the experience with a totally different view of the
man.

Adam didn't like to think in stereotypes. But he
couldn't help noting that Paul Delacorte was a lot like
Henry. He might seem relaxed—even a bit slow, until you
saw the intelligence flash in his large brown eyes.

Delacorte got comfortable in his chair. "You plannin'
to share the information with me?"

Speaking slowly and deliberately, Adam started with
the background of the evening before. "I like to nose
around the park at night," he said, liking the double mean-

ing of the verb. "Kind of looking out that everything's the way it should be in my immediate environment, if you know what I mean."

"Like the way I drive around town in my cruiser, just making sure everything's peaceful."

Adam nodded, feeling a sudden current of kinship with the man. Probably that was what Delacorte had intended. "Last night I was out in the swamp, and I smelled something funny."

"Funny—like what?"

"Like smoke. When I got closer, I realized the smoke was hallucinogenic, and the people who had kindled the fire were high."

The sheriff sat forward in his seat. "Oh yeah?"

"As near as I can figure, they came out to the park to have a private sex and drug party."

"With marijuana? Coke?" the lawman asked.

Instead of answering, Adam asked, "You have trouble with any of those in town?"

"Of course we do. Wayland may look like a sleepy little southern burg, but it's not the Garden of Eden before the fall."

Adam laughed. "Yeah. Well, I don't indulge in anything stronger than herbal tea myself."

"Why not?"

"That's a pretty direct question. But I'll answer it— because I don't have anything to hide," he said, vividly conscious of the lie. "I guess you can think of it as an allergy. Or that my system's delicate. Anyway, drugs play havoc with my senses."

Delacorte nodded, and Adam had the feeling the sheriff was taking the disclaimer under advisement.

Adam went back to the original question. "They weren't smoking joints or snorting anything. They were inhaling some kind of stuff that they dumped into the fire. I was trying to get close, and they discovered I was watching them." He gave Delacorte a direct look. "And somebody started shooting at me."

The sheriff's exclamation interrupted his narrative. "Holy Moses." It was a mild curse, but about the strongest he'd heard the man use.

"I was unarmed. My only choice was to get the hell out of there—before I ended up as buzzard feed."

Adam watched the lawman, judging his reaction. He knew that on the face of it, the tale sounded like the head ranger might have been indulging in some of the shit he claimed he never used, yet he could see Delacorte working his way through the story.

"They chased you into the swamp?"

"Yeah."

"And then what?"

"Then I woke up the next morning wondering if I'd dreamed the whole damn thing. Only when I went back to the area, I found their fire pit."

Adam realized his hands were clamped around the water glass. He also realized the sheriff was watching him intently.

"That drugged smoke," he said. "It knocked you out?"

Adam shifted in his seat. "Like I told you, I've never been into mind-altering substances. So, yeah, I couldn't handle the smoke. That's why I can't give you any details about who the party-goers were."

He saw the sheriff nod.

"You've had trouble in the park before?" he asked. "Before Ken White?"

"Yeah."

"So would you mind cluing me in to what Austen Barnette neglected to tell me when he signed me up for this job?"

Now it looked like it was the sheriff's turn to decide what to say. Adam knew he was an outsider. And in a small town like Wayland, it took a while for a newcomer to be accepted.

On the other hand, he'd been willing to take a job in Nature's Refuge, after the last head ranger had died in the line of duty. He figured that should entitle him to the real scoop.

"We've had trouble in the Olakompa over the years," the lawman said.

"Other murders?"

Again, Delacorte hesitated, then said, "About twenty-five years ago. A woman was killed."

"Found in the swamp, like White?"

"She had a cabin about a mile north of here as the crow flies. It's a little longer by road. It happened there."

"Who killed her?"

"The case is still listed on the books as unsolved."

"You weren't the sheriff back then."

"No. It was my daddy."

Adam absorbed that choice bit of information—something everybody in town knew. "The sheriff's job in Wayland is hereditary?" he asked.

"No. I ran for the office and won it."

Adam nodded, considering what Delacorte had chosen to tell him. "Do you think that old murder is connected to Ken White?"

Delacorte hesitated for a moment before saying, "I don't have any evidence to link them."

"What's your gut feeling?" Adam asked.

The sheriff gave him a long look. "I'm reserving my judgment." He stood up. "I think you'd better show me the location where you found the campfire—and the people last night."

Adam set down his glass with a *thunk* and stood as well, certain that the sheriff had decided to end this phase of the interview.

He was pretty sure there was more to tell about Wayland's past problems. He was also pretty sure he wasn't going to hear about them this morning.

"You know the road at the east edge of the park?" he asked, and Delacorte nodded.

"There's a barrier across the lane. The fire pit was about a half mile farther up the road."

"You got the time to carry me up there now?"

"I've got the time. I want to know what the hell's going on in my park."

"I could station a deputy out here at night."

"No!" Adam's answer was instantaneous, and he immediately regretted that he'd spoken so quickly—like a man with something to hide.

Delacorte held up a hand. "Just a suggestion," he said, and Adam knew the sheriff was wondering if he was up to something unsavory at night out here. Like growing marijuana.

Probably he wouldn't like knowing that the head ranger was prowling the park in wolf form at night.

He'd thought that with his wolf senses, he'd be able to figure out what had happened to his predecessor. So far it hadn't turned out that way. But he did know that both Paul Delacorte and Austen Barnette had been expecting trouble. Unfortunately, the park's owner had chosen to withhold that information from his new employee.

"So, you have any choice suggestions for me?" he asked.

The sheriff hesitated for a moment. "Yeah. Don't sit with your back to the window."

CHAPTER
FIVE

SARA WALKED INTO the kitchen of the small cottage, turned on the tap in the sink, and let it run, waiting for the stream to cool before she drew a glass of water.

She downed it in several gulps, then stood staring out the window at the grove of trees that surrounded her rented house. There were black gum, sweet bay, and an old water oak hung with Spanish moss that must have been hit by lightning at one time. It was split up the middle. But somehow it had survived and grown in a lopsided fashion.

The trees would have been lovely if there had only been a few. But too many had grown up around the little house.

"Darkness at noon," she muttered.

Even in the middle of the day, it was dismal under the canopy of branches, as though the sun had gone into a permanent eclipse. She'd never liked the dark. And here she was in a house where mold and moss grew on the roof and the siding, like insidious unwanted visitors.

A light breeze fluttered through the leaves and the moss

hanging on the tree branches. It wasn't enough to do much for the damp, heavy air. But the rustling sound skittered over her skin like insect legs.

As if to ward off a chill, she folded her arms over her chest and rubbed her shoulders. This place gave her the creeps, and she had learned not to ignore her intuition. She wanted to throw her possessions into the car and flee. But that was not an option. Not when she'd effectively trapped herself here.

Granville Pharmaceuticals had written her out of the blue and offered her an enormous research grant. She'd been flattered and relieved to get a job. She'd taken a lot of the first payment and sent it directly to the outfit that held the note on her college loan, because the idea of being in debt for the next fifteen years made her throat close.

Of course, she felt that way now—closed in and smothered. And the sensation had nothing to do with her education loans.

The disquiet came from her immediate surroundings, this cabin and the wilderness around it. If she could, she would find another place to live and work. But she suspected that by the time she went through proper channels to move somewhere else, her stay would be almost up. So she switched on the kitchen light, then walked around the little house turning on the lights in every room.

They drove away the darkness but did nothing for the hot, sticky air.

The small dwelling had two bedrooms. She was sleeping in the larger one. The other was going to be her laboratory.

Granville had already shipped several long worktables, but some assembly was required, so she'd put that off until later. For the time being, the plants she'd dug up were resting in boxes on a plastic sheet, which she'd spread over the narrow bed in her makeshift lab.

She had pretentiously given Adam Marshall the Latin name of sweet flag. But she was just as conversant with the common names of the specimens she'd collected.

In addition to the irislike plant, she had lily of the valley, jimsonweed, and male shield fern. All of the latter were poisonous. And the jimsonweed was reputed to have psychotropic qualities, a fact she hadn't shared with Marshall.

She sighed, thinking she might as well go into the work room and start documenting the collection. Maybe she could even make some extracts from the leaves or the roots or the seeds and start testing them for antibacterial properties.

But instead of focusing on work, her mind strayed back to the morning in the swamp—to the moment when she'd met Adam Marshall.

She'd been so intent on the clump of sweet flag that she hadn't even been aware of him until he was almost on top of her. Or maybe it was the way he moved through the swamp, like an animal supremely adapted to the natural environment.

Those first moments had shaken her to her toes. She simply hadn't expected to meet up with anyone else out there in the middle of nowhere.

She'd taken in every detail of the man in those first charged instants. Somehow, when she thought of him, her mind filled with animal images. He was over six feet tall and as dark and dangerous-looking as a hungry bear. His eyes were black and deep set, glittering like the eyes of a bird of prey. He had a blade of a nose, nicely shaped lips, and dark stubble covering his cheeks and chin.

He'd looked like he'd had a hard night. Probably she did, too, she thought, her fingers unconsciously going to her hair.

She was in the act of smoothing back the unruly strands when she stayed her hand. What was she doing? The man wasn't even here, and she was fussing with her hair. Besides, it didn't matter anyway what he thought of her.

Even as the denial surfaced in her mind, she knew it was a lie. Some tender, feminine part of her did care what he thought about the way she looked.

She closed her eyes for a moment, thinking that a twenty-eight-year-old woman should have more experience with men. She'd dated, of course. But it was difficult for her to make connections with people. She'd always felt like there was a barrier between herself and them. A time or two she'd managed to overcome it. But often she hadn't felt like it was worth the effort. So her focus had always been on her studies or the things that interested her, like gardening or her art. And she'd had a good reason to study hard: she was determined to do well and she wanted to make Mom and Dad proud.

Now she was paying the price for her sexual inexperience—getting excited about a guy she met in the woods, a guy so different from the academics who had inhabited her world for the past ten years that she had no point of reference for him, besides the wild animal images she'd conjured up.

Above and beyond those images, she didn't like his manner. He'd practically accused her of being part of some drug cult, cavorting in the park at night. And when he'd stirred the blackened ashes of the campfire, a scene had flashed into her mind.

The darkness, the moon-drenched swamp, the wild gyrating of naked bodies dancing and coming together in the flickering firelight. It had caught and held her for only a moment, but it had shaken her to the core.

Against her will, the image came back to her now, and she squeezed her eyes shut, struggling to make the all-too-vivid picture vanish. She didn't want to see it. Didn't want to know about it. But it held her in its grip. And the most disturbing part was that she had put herself smack in the middle of the scene. She was one of the dancers.

"No!"

She spoke the word aloud trying to drive the nighttime scene from her mind. But the denial did her no good. The world around her disappeared. She was transported to the nighttime swamp. To the campfire with its smoke that clogged her lungs and made her head go muzzy. She heard low, chanted words. Words that stirred her senses.

Unconsciously, she swayed from one foot to the other, no longer feeling the smooth surface of the kitchen floor below her shoes.

Instead, she felt spongy dirt and tree roots under her naked feet.

Dancers moved around her. The smoke obscured their faces. But she saw the sweat gleaming on their bare bodies. And saw that they were aroused. The women's nipples were contracted to tight points. The men were fully erect.

One of them reached for her. With a little moan, she slipped out of his grasp.

Then a man leaped into the firelight. It was Adam Marshall. He was nude and magnificent and aroused.

"Sara." He called her name, called her to his side, and she swayed toward him, craving the feel of his body against hers. He pulled her into his arms, and the contact of naked flesh against naked flesh was glorious.

He drew her away, into the inky blackness beyond the reach of the fire. She knew that they were going to make love—in some dark, leafy place away from the rest of the group where they could have their privacy. And she knew that if she let it happen, her life would change forever.

"No."

"Come with me, Sara. I need you."

"No." Somehow, with strength she didn't even know she possessed, she wrenched herself away. From him.

From the vivid daydream that had hooked its claws into her flesh.

The kitchen blinked back into focus, and she stood there, gasping for breath, trying to clear the smoke from her lungs.

No, there was no smoke here. She was in the house Granville had rented for her. She closed her hand over the edge of the counter, feeling the hard surface digging into her palm, fighting a wave of unwanted sexual arousal that held her as she tried to figure out what had happened to her.

She'd had episodes like this before. Well, not quite like *this*. Nothing remotely sexual. But episodes where she seemed to leave the here and now and go someplace else.

The daydreams had been vivid. But they had never turned her on.

Lord, what had happened to her?

Adam Marshall had poked at the campfire. Maybe he'd stirred up some of the hallucinogenic smoke. Maybe the thick, evil stuff was still affecting her.

She'd felt it last night, too, she silently admitted. Felt some ugly presence reaching for her from the dark shadows of the swamp.

Now she understood what she'd sensed in the damp humid air beyond her grove of trees when she'd been awake in the dark hours.

Or was she making all that up? Not the feelings. But the images. Had they come from the overactive imagination she tried so hard to rein in all her life?

She gripped the kitchen counter more tightly, yet the frightening perception persisted.

"Stop it," she ordered herself. "You *will not* let your imagination run away with you."

The order did little to dispel the drowning sensations that threatened to overwhelm her.

Something was waiting for her in Wayland, Georgia—

something she didn't want to meet. Adam Marshall was part of it. But only part. There was more, and she'd didn't want to find out what it was.

She had been staring out the window unseeing when a flicker of movement brought her back to the here and now. A figure darting between the trees. A man.

She went very still as her gaze focused on him. Her heart gave a little lurch when she thought it might be Adam Marshall. Lord, had she sensed him out there? Was that the reason for the flash of fantasy that had taken hold of her?

It took only seconds to determine that it wasn't his tall, muscular figure she saw. And she breathed out a sigh of relief—and disappointment.

This man was older and more slender.

He must have caught sight of her in the window, because he stopped in his tracks. Across fifty feet of swampland, they stared at each other.

What was he doing here on private property?

She saw then that a wicker basket dangled from one of his hands. And she realized that he must be gathering some kind of food or plants from the area. Which might make him a valuable resource.

He didn't look threatening, yet she had decided not to take any chances. So she turned away from the window and picked up her carry bag where she'd stashed her gun.

Then she headed for the front door. By the time she reached it, the man had taken several steps into what passed for the front yard of the little house.

As she walked onto the porch, he stared at her with wide, surprised eyes.

"Can I help you?" she asked.

The basket in his hand bobbled as he came farther into the yard. "I didn't expect . . ." His voice trailed off. He was staring at her as though she'd dropped from the moon.

"Yes. Well, I'm renting the house for the next few months while I'm here for a research project," she answered. Really, she didn't have to make any explanations. But this was a small town. And people were going to be interested in what she was doing here.

From her position above him, she could see now that his basket was filled with small, dark fruit.

"Blackberries?" she asked.

"Black raspberries. Blackberries don't come into season for a month."

"Oh."

She studied the man. His skin was weathered, but up close he looked more fit than her first impression. Probably he was in his sixties. Probably he made his living in the outdoors.

"Hello," she said, making an effort to sound friendly. "I'm Sara Weston. I'm going to be here for a few months, investigating the medicinal properties of plants found in this area."

"Hal Montgomery," he answered, before backing away. "I'll see you around, Sara Weston."

Moments later he had disappeared into the underbrush, moving as silently as a ghost.

ADAM wiped his feet on the doormat that graced the wide front porch of the red brick mansion, feeling like he had when he'd been out in the woods and about to walk into his mother's kitchen. Well, not exactly the same. The tile floor in front of his mom's sink had been worn through. And the appliances were old and dented—from his dad's kicking them a time or two.

He looked at the gleaming white wood door frame and the leaded glass fan transom above the double doors.

Austen Barnette's southern mansion was a far cry from the modest East Baltimore home where he'd grown up.

And a far cry from the two-room cabin that went with the head ranger job.

He'd been here twice before, for his job interview. And then when he'd started work.

The first time the old man had flown him to Jacksonville from southwest Texas and put him up overnight at the Holiday Inn.

The next morning at nine o'clock sharp, a stoop-shouldered old man wearing a dark suit and white shirt had ushered him into Barnette's paneled den with its comfortably worn leather furniture. The lord of the manor had offered him coffee, which he'd declined. He'd settled for a glass of water as Barnette had asked him pointed questions about how he saw the present and future of Nature's Refuge. Apparently he'd passed the test, because a special delivery letter had arrived at his home in Big Bend National Park the next week.

He'd been elated to get the job. Now he was having second—and third—thoughts.

The door was opened by the same servant who had ushered him into the house the first time.

Stepping across the threshold, Adam took a moment to adjust to the dim light as he breathed in the aroma of lemon-scented furniture polish. On the surface, it seemed like nothing had changed since his first visit here five months ago.

"This way, sir." The old man gestured toward the hall.

"I didn't ask your name last time I was here," Adam said.

The butler or whatever he was called looked surprised. "I'm James."

"So what have you heard in town about the goings-on at Nature's Refuge?" Adam asked.

The man's eyes went wide—for just a second, then turned guarded. "Nothing, sir," he answered.

Adam smiled at him and waited a beat before saying,
"Well, if you change your mind about talking to me, you
know where to find me."

James didn't reply, and Adam didn't push it. He wasn't
going to interrogate Austen Barnette's house staff. Not
yet, anyway. But maybe after the man thought about it,
he might have something to say later.

Adam proceeded down the hall past a parlor where a
maid was dusting the furniture. The room was as he remembered it—quietly opulent, with a permanent aura of
cigar smoke that grated on his nerve endings. It wasn't
the only shock to his system. As always, it was difficult
to picture himself, the son of an auto mechanic and bur-
glar, in such a setting.

The mansion's owner was sitting in the same old-
fashioned swivel desk chair where he'd been on Adam's
last visit. But the man looked like he'd aged a couple of
years in the past few months. There was more white in
his salt-and-pepper hair and more sag to his wrinkled skin.

"Thank you for seeing me," Adam said.

"Nature's Refuge is important to me. I'm always available to speak to my head ranger."

"I appreciate it."

"Sit down." The old man gestured toward the chair
across the room.

Adam sat. Beside it on the table was a silver tray with
a cut glass tumbler and a pitcher of water.

Barnette picked up his own beverage of choice, coffee
served in a delicate china cup, and took a sip.

"What can I do for you?" he asked, setting down his
cup and clasping his hands in his lap.

Adam studied his employer carefully. He seemed com-
posed, yet there was an undercurrent below the surface of
that calm. Was he worried about something and unwilling
to make the first move? Or was he truly waiting for information about the park?

"The sheriff came to see me this morning," Adam began.

Barnette's raised his eyebrows. "Oh? Did he find out something about Ken White?"

"No. He was just checking in. But it was interesting that he picked this morning to show up." He waited a beat, waiting to see if Barnette would rise to the bait. When the old man remained silent, he continued. "We had an incident last night that I think you ought to know about."

"What?"

"I like to walk through the park at night—just to check on things. Last night, I came across some trespassers." Quickly he gave an account of the strange group who had invaded the park the night before, keeping his description to the drugged smoke and the dancing participants. "When they discovered I was watching them, somebody shot at me," he concluded.

"But you escaped unharmed."

"Yes."

Neither of them spoke for several moments, forcing Adam to direct the conversation once more.

"I got the feeling from Delacorte that you've had problems like this in the park before," he said.

"Not in the park!" Barnette answered.

"Not that anyone told you," Adam answered, giving the old man an out.

His employer nodded.

"Now we might assume that Ken White stumbled onto the same kind of thing I did, but he didn't happen to get away."

"I hired you because you're an excellent park ranger, and you have a reputation for solving crimes. Like that smuggling operation you shut down in Big Bend. And that cattle rustling gang in Montana."

"Yeah, well, it's easier to solve crimes when you have

the background to work with. What do you and Delacorte know that I don't?"

Barnette stared at him. "What did the sheriff say to you?"

"Nothing helpful."

"He knows his place in town."

"What's that supposed to mean?"

"It means that his family has lived in Wayland for a long time. They get along here."

Adam looked at his employer, understanding another facet of his personality. He saw Delacorte as a servant— just the way he saw James. Adam's own skin was a different color, but he suspected he fell into the same category. Hired help.

So how to proceed now? He could be a good little servant and go back to the park and watch his back. But watch for what—exactly?

He decided on the direct approach. "Why don't you tell me what I should know about problems in Wayland over the past few decades."

Barnette blinked. "That's a pretty open-ended subject."

"Yes, sir, it is. I'm trying to understand the sociology of the town," he said blandly.

Barnette shifted in his seat. "This is a good Christian community. I don't want outsiders coming in and judging us."

"You wanted an outsider—me—to come in and solve your problems. That's difficult to do when you tie my hands."

The old man thought about that. "I suppose your request is reasonable, but I don't want this discussion going any further than this room."

Adam nodded, thinking that he could agree for now.

"All right. We've had problems with goings-on in the swamp. The trouble . . . uh . . . dates back at least a hundred years."

Adam blinked. "That's a considerable amount of time." He waited for more information. When it wasn't forthcoming, he asked, "What are you talking about exactly?"

"You want to put a label on it? I don't have a label." Barnette stopped and fixed Adam with his stony gaze. "There's magic in the swamp. I'd like to think it's good magic. But sometimes it takes another form."

The revelation was so unexpected that he waited several seconds before asking, "Can you be more explicit?"

"Like what you saw last night."

"That wasn't magic. It was drugs."

"Call it what you want. Did you feel like something strange was going on? Something you didn't understand?"

"Yes."

"Well then."

"I'm not equipped to investigate magic," he said.

"You saw people. Find out who they are."

"How?"

"The same way you identified those drug smugglers in fifty-plus square miles of desolate Texas park."

Adam had no answer for the remark. He wasn't about to explain that he'd been operating last night with a hood over his senses. He needed more clues, and somebody was going to have to give them to him. Apparently, it wasn't going to be his employer.

Barnette gave him a dismissive look.

Adam knew that was his cue to leave. But he stayed where he was. "We should talk about Sara Weston," he said.

"What about her?" Barnette asked, his voice sharpening so that Adam wondered what he'd conveyed in his own tone.

He wasn't sure how he was going to answer until he heard himself saying, "Is she in danger—going into the swamp?"

Barnette's gaze turned inward. "I hope not," he said.

"It would look bad for us if something happened to Granville Pharmaceutical's researcher."

"Then why did you allow her to come here—now?"

"What do you mean—why now? Why not now?"

"You had a murder here less than half a year ago."

"I thought it would be all right. I thought with you here, we wouldn't have any more incidents . . ." He let his voice trail off, then asked, "Are you questioning my decision?"

"No," Adam lied.

"If she finds something important in the park, some plant that can cure diseases, then we'll get some great publicity. That will bring more visitors here."

"And if she gets shot by the . . . people I saw last night, that's going to drive the crowds away."

"I'm counting on you to make sure that doesn't happen," Barnette snapped. "You need extra help patrolling the refuge?"

"No."

"I didn't think so. I know you work alone. I know you find clues that other people miss."

If I don't get killed first, Adam thought. Aloud, he said, "I'll do my best."

"Keep me informed on what you find out."

"Yes, sir," he answered, silently reminding himself that if Austen Barnette could pick and choose what he wanted to reveal, Adam Marshall could damn well do the same.

The meeting had been far from satisfying. It was a relief to leave the old man's private sanctuary and step into the sun again. He stood on the wide front porch, breathing in the fresh air, thinking about why he'd taken this job in the first place. He'd wanted to get out of Texas. He'd wanted a challenge. He'd liked the idea of being in charge of his own park. Now he felt like he'd made his decision with only part of the facts he'd needed.

Across the lawn, he saw a man dressed in a plain white T-shirt and jeans working with a power saw, apparently replacing some of the wood siding on the wall of the detached garage. The guy raised his dark head and looked at him curiously. And he stared back, wondering if they had met.

Something about the workman was familiar, but he didn't know what. Maybe he'd seen him around town. He thought about walking closer. Maybe the guy was curious about the new head ranger out at the park. Maybe if they talked, he could get another perspective on working for Austen Barnette.

But something about the workman's posture kept him standing where he was.

After a long moment, the man lowered his head and went back to the siding, and Adam walked down the steps and back to his SUV, thinking he needed a better source of information about the hidden history of Wayland, Georgia. And he needed something else as well—a gas mask, which he was going to order from the Internet as soon as he got the chance.

CHAPTER
SIX

AMY RALSTON LOOKED up from her position behind the boat rental counter and watched her boss's long-legged stride as he came down the mulched path to the dock.

She was pretty sure that the sun shade over the window of the ticket booth hid her face, so she felt free to drink in the view of Adam Marshall. When he drew closer, she lowered her gaze and pretended to be sorting through receipts from recent customers.

It was impossible not to react to the man. He was nothing like the last head ranger. Ken White had been old—in his fifties at least. He'd had thinning hair and a pot belly. She had thought of him like a slightly gruff old uncle. She'd been sad when he'd gotten killed; she hadn't wanted it to happen.

Actually, she'd been more than sad. She'd been frightened by the implications.

After Ken's death, for a while, there hadn't really been anyone in charge at the park. Mr. Barnette had stopped by a time or two, getting driven over in that big black Cadillac of his. But he hadn't known anything about the day-to-day operation of the park. So he'd asked them to carry on with their jobs until he could get a replacement. It had worked fairly well, at least in the short run.

Then their new boss had arrived, and Amy had flipped over him. Not just her. All the female staff had a thing for him.

He knew it, too. But he kept things on a professional level. Unfortunately, because if he made a move toward her, she would be more than willing to do the dirty with him.

He was good-looking, with tanned skin, thick black hair, remarkable dark eyes, and a great body. But it wasn't just his looks that turned her on. There was something about him, something she couldn't define. You could maybe call it charisma.

The guy was a chick magnet.

"How's it going?" he asked, the question casual.

"Fine."

He glanced over at the boats moored in the narrow channel that led to the park's main waterway. "How many tours are out?"

"Dwayne just took a family of four on the hour excursion. Rosie left a half hour ago with another party. And we have a married couple interested."

She consulted her notes. "Mr. and Mrs. Carlton. I explained that we don't want too many boats out there at once. So they're coming back at three for the deluxe tour."

"I'll take them out," he said.

She looked up in surprise. Ken had been very conscious of his position as head ranger. And he'd made it clear that routine stuff was beneath his notice. He'd always given jobs like boat tours to the lesser members of the staff.

"Someone else can do it," Amy offered.

"No. I like to keep in touch with every aspect of the

operation." He laughed. "Even feeding Big Jim."

"Yuck." That was definitely one chore Amy tried to avoid. Feeding their "pet" alligator meant handling big chunks of raw meat from the refrigerator.

"PART of the job," Adam said, before moving down the dock and pulling up the engine of a nearby boat to check the propeller for weeds, which were a perennial problem in these nutrient-rich waters.

In addition to feeding Big Jim, he'd already taken care of putting out grain for the waterfowl that the park fed regularly so the birds would be on hand for visitors to look at.

Feeding wildlife went counter to what he'd learned in the U.S. Park Service, of course. The philosophy was that if you gave handouts to animals, you turned them into beggars. He'd abided by the policy when he'd worked for the U.S. government, even when it had meant watching snowbound moose starve. But he also saw no harm in providing food for birds the tourists liked to see around Nature's Refuge.

The simple act of scattering duck feed had given him time to decompress after his conversation with Barnette. And he was hoping that a tour of the waterways would continue the process.

As soon as he'd left the old man's mansion, he'd thought about driving into town and demanding that Paul Delacorte put him in the loop. But he was almost sure he wasn't going to get any more answers from the sheriff than he had from Barnette.

And that wasn't the only reason for heading back to the park. He knew himself pretty well. He knew that going off half-cocked was a bad idea. He needed to calm down. And taking a boat out into the still, dark waters of the swamp was an excellent way to do it.

The tourists arrived at five of three. Barbara and John Carlton were a couple in their late forties, he guessed, from Denver. They had never been to this part of the country before, and they were excited by the prospect of a swamp tour. Adam collected fifty dollars from them, got out life jackets, then helped the couple into the front of the boat, while he sat in back at the tiller and started the engine. Most local residents who took watercraft into the swamp paddled. But that wasn't practical for tourist expeditions because it would add too much time to each trip. So all of the boats at Nature's Refuge were motorized.

They putted slowly away from the dock, then turned into one of the narrow channels that lead into the interior of the preserve. In front of them, the water was still as glass. Rotting peat made it cola dark, creating a natural mirror that reflected the vegetation crowding in on either side of the boat. The effect was like being in a magic tunnel of greenery where you couldn't tell up from down.

Magic. Barnette had used that word. Probably he hadn't been referring to the scenery. But what had he meant?

Adam had thought of the Olakompa as a place that civilization hadn't been able to destroy, a refuge for the birds and animals that lived here. Now he wondered what secrets lurked beneath the dark waters. And really, the dimly lit, mysterious swamp was an easy place to become a believer in the supernatural.

And why not? A werewolf was a kind of supernatural creature. Perhaps his ancestors had sprung from a place very similar to this.

"It's like taking a trip into wonderland," Barbara murmured, her voice hushed. "Is the park all like this?" she asked.

Her husband had gotten out his fancy camera and was busily snapping pictures.

Adam brought his mind back to the tour.

"No," he answered. "We have these narrow channels. But they open up into what are called prairies, kind of water meadows. The higher elevations in the park are dry land. Well, higher is a relative term. We're about a hundred feet above sea level, in a natural depression. Some of the land is also boggy. And we have over seventy islands—I mean in the whole swamp, not just Nature's Refuge. The terrain makes for a variety of plants and animals."

The mention of plants sent his mind zinging back to Sara Weston. He'd met her where the footing was dry. But if she'd come to the swamp, she must be here to collect some of the aquatic specimens like floating heart, arrow arum, pickerelweed, or golden club.

The channels could be confusing, if you didn't know your way around. She'd need a guide. And he was the perfect choice.

He went into a little fantasy, imagining them alone in a boat out in this vast wilderness, pictured himself helping her with her work, the two of them silent but very aware of each other. Sexually aware, like they'd been this morning. But now she wouldn't be wary of him.

She'd want him as much as he wanted her. She'd put her hand on his arm, letting him know. He pictured his gaze locking with hers, before he steered the craft into a shallow waterway where they could reach for each other without worrying about the boat tipping dangerously.

He held the tantalizing image for several heartbeats, then ruthlessly wiped it from his mind. He'd thought that giving a tour would relax him. Instead, he was wound up tighter than a kudzu vine choking the life out of a tree trunk.

Embarrassed, he shifted in his seat, glad that he was sitting behind his passengers and they were looking toward the front of the boat.

His eyes scanning the shoreline. It didn't take too long

to spot what he wanted. He cut the engine, drifting toward the bank. "Look at that floating log," he said, pointing.

As the boat eased closer, a small alligator lifted its head out of the water and stared at them.

Barbara started in alarm. John began snapping more shots.

"One of the twelve thousand gators we have in the swamp," he remarked. "Decades ago, a lot of them were turned into shoes and handbags. Now they're protected." He wondered if the couple would also like to know that there were thirty-seven species of snakes in the area, including five poisonous ones.

Probably not, he thought, hiding a grin as he guided the boat around a bend and into one of the more open areas, past clumps of water lilies and tall grass.

He saw a wood stork feeding near the shore and dutifully pointed it out, so John could label his pictures later.

Usually he enjoyed giving these tours. He'd always been interested in wildlife. And he'd done a lot of reading on his own. Maybe he'd been trying to figure out where the werewolf fit into the natural order of things.

He realized he'd been silent for several moments and came up with another piece of nature lore as he guided the boat into another narrow channel. "White-tailed deer come down to the water for a drink."

"Don't the gators get them?" John asked.

"Rarely. They have almost no natural enemies."

"Are there wolves around here?" Barbara asked.

"They were last seen here in the nineteen twenties," Adam said easily. He didn't add that a wolf had been prowling the park for the past four months.

Barbara scanned the shoreline. "I'd like to see the deer."

"Maybe on the way back. They rest during the day, then become more active late in the afternoon."

"It's so amazing that this place survived into the twenty-first century," John mused.

"It almost didn't. The swamp's ecosystem came close to being destroyed in the early nineteen hundreds by a company dedicated to turning cypress trees into telegraph poles and floorboards. They took out four hundred and thirty million board feet of cypress before the easily accessible timber ran out. President Franklin Roosevelt stepped in and converted a large part of the swamp into a wildlife refuge in nineteen thirty-seven."

"He established Nature's Refuge?"

"No. Austen Barnette bought this area much later."

The waterway opened up again, and he steered the skiff through a grove of cypress trees, following a muskrat who swam away from them as quickly as possible.

When he came around a curve, something odd caught his eye. Something that looked as though it didn't belong in the natural environment.

From time to time he found junk floating in the water. Paper cups. Plastic jugs. He always scooped them up and brought them back to throw into the trash.

But this wasn't in the water. It looked like a piece of yellow paper tied to the trunk of a young cypress tree, standing out against the dark bark. It wasn't a bright yellow. It was faded, so that he might have mistaken it for something else. It could have been here for months, he supposed, getting drenched in the rain and baking in the sun. He didn't know for sure because he hadn't been in this particular corner of the swamp recently.

He could feel his heart rate picking up. He wanted to think that he simply didn't like finding something man-made tied to a tree where no human artifacts should be. But he knew it was more than that. Last night he'd encountered drugged smoke and naked people out here. Today there was something strange tied to a tree. Had the party-goers marked their territory?

The Carltons hadn't spotted the thing. He could steer the boat on by, then come back later, when he was alone. Probably that was what he should do, but he wanted to know what the damn thing was—now.

Barbara and John looked in the direction where he was headed and spotted the anomaly.

"What's that?" the husband asked.

"I don't know. It looks like someone left it for a marker," he added, plucking a phrase out of the air.

"Who would do that?"

"Maybe a poacher," he improvised even as his mind clawed for answers. The official entrance to the park was through the front gate, but it was always possible for someone to come in the back way. One of many back ways, actually.

The Olakompa Swamp was over six hundred square miles. Austen Barnette owned only a small corner of the watery real estate, about three hundred acres. That wasn't much in the grand scheme of things. But it was plenty of room for the birds and animals who lived here plus various assorted trespassers.

Like the group last night, he was thinking as he leaned out to examine the object. It wasn't paper, but cloth. In fact, it was a crudely made bag of old fabric, tied together at the top with a piece of rough twine. It looked like there was something inside.

Nothing heavy. But enough material to puff out the yellow fabric.

He pulled the boat as close as he could get, but it wasn't close enough to snag the thing without endangering his passengers, and that would be unforgivable. So he tied up to a cypress knee, then started to climb out.

A scream from Barbara had him leaping back, rocking the boat dangerously.

Both passengers gripped the sides of the craft, and he found himself sitting back down heavily.

When the rocking had stopped, he turned toward Barbara, struggling to keep his expression bland. Really, he wanted to chew her out for startling him, but he knew it was prudent to resist the impulse.

"What's wrong?" he asked.

"Over there. A snake."

He followed her outstretched hand, but if the creature had been real, it had already slithered away.

"Thanks," he said, then took his time inspecting the area before climbing onto the slippery surface of the tree root and finding a handhold on the rough bark. Carefully, he worked his way toward the object.

When he was close enough, he hauled out the penknife he always carried and cut the piece of rough cord that held the bag to the tree.

Moments later, he was back on the aluminum bench, where he stowed the thing at his feet.

John reached for it. Adam kicked it under his seat. "Leave it," he growled.

The other man must have heard the wolf tone in his voice, because he reared back.

"The tour's over," Adam said. "Sorry we have to return early, but I'll refund your money when we get back to the dock."

CHAPTER
SEVEN

FALCON LEANED BACK in his chair, stretching out his long legs under the table, and crossed his scuffed boots at the ankle as he sipped his Bud Lite. His head had been a little muzzy, but he'd put in most of a day's work.

He was still feeling a nice warm glow from the up close and personal contact with the clan last night.

Of course, he had to steer his mind away from the ending of the night's revelries. But that wasn't difficult. He was the kind of guy who could ignore inconvenient details when he wanted to.

He'd packed up his tools, and now he was relaxing at his favorite little café on Main Street.

Some part of him would have liked to see the core of Wayland shrivel and die like so many of the little southern towns with their boarded-up storefronts, trash blowing down the main drag, and all the action, such as it was, out on the highway in the Wal-Mart parking lot.

But there were some advantages to what the chamber of commerce liked to call Historic Wayland.

The town's core had survived the new development that had come to the cheap land on the outskirts of town. The old business district had transformed itself into a kind of yuppy tourist haven, with a few bright spots for the locals to enjoy.

Like the Good Times Café, with its down-home southern cooking at reasonable prices.

He saw the waitress step out of the kitchen. Her name was Betty Sue, and she was about his age, mid-twenties. She'd lived here all her life. Not like him. His family had left town, suddenly, in the middle of the night. They'd run for their lives and found a place to rent in Jacksonville, where his dad had gotten a job driving a delivery truck.

Daddy had scraped along. It had been better than getting burned up or ripped apart by the nice Christian folks of Wayland.

That had been twenty-five years ago. And now the son was back. And as far as he knew, the good people of the town didn't know who he was. But they were going to find out, and they were going to be sorry for what they had done.

Betty Sue came swishing over to the table and delivered his food. A hamburger and fries, nestled in a napkin-lined plastic basket to save on dishes.

She and the rest of Wayland were in for a surprise when the clan had consolidated their power. Just a few more weeks, and they would be ready to get even for the sins of the past.

He picked up the catsup bottle and shook it over the thick home-cut fries, being careful not to get the napkin soggy.

"Can I get you anything else?" Betty Sue asked.

He considered a suggestive answer, then thought better of it and shook his head as he bit into a fry.

Um, um good.

He had taken a seat by the window, and as he ate his fries and burger, he watched the car and pedestrian traffic. There were a lot of tourists. Which was good for business. But there were a fair number of townspeople out as well.

He watched a woman pushing a baby carriage. A family of four, the parents and kids all licking ice cream cones. An old guy leaning on a cane. An old lady with an ugly dalmatian on a leash.

Wayland looked like such a peaceful little town. Yet the things that had happened here would curl your hair.

Regular witch-hunts. Like in the middle ages. Only now the witches were getting ready to turn the tables.

He chomped off a bite of burger and bun, chewed, and swallowed, his thoughts turning back to the night before. To the smoke, the women, the feeling of strength that he knew came partly from the black waters of the swamp. And the unity of the group. It wasn't just having mind-blowing sex. It was the way they fed each other's power when they joined together. It had been his idea to gather up the descendants of the witches. He'd thought of it after he'd met Willow and found out her parents had run away from Wayland, just like his momma and daddy.

He and Willow had hit it off in bed real well. But he'd recognized the experience as something more profound— as a pooling of energy. And he'd wondered if he could multiply the effect. So he'd set about gathering the clan around himself.

Eyes closed, he relived the scene last night. Relived the orgiastic frenzy and the pleasure like a thousand suns bursting in his brain.

But this time he couldn't ignore the ending. The way everything had all come to a screeching halt in the moment when they sensed that guy watching.

After Ken White, Falcon had been sure nobody else was going to bother them. Then this guy had shown up.

Who the hell was he?

His hand clenched around the glass of beer, and he made a concerted effort to relax.

The guy had been naked. Ready for action.

Falcon gave a soft laugh. He'd also sensed the man's longing for a connection with them.

Maybe and maybe not. He'd decide, after they figured out who he was. Falcon already had a couple of candidates in mind. Actually, by chance, he'd gotten a look at one of them today. With his clothes on, he'd just looked like an ordinary guy.

Of course, Falcon knew that was true of himself, too. But he wasn't ordinary. He had power and the strength of his convictions. And he was going to make damn sure that nobody wrecked his plans. He and the members of the clan had waited too long to get revenge on this town that had killed their parents and their grandparents down through the generations. This time, the hunting and the terror were going the other way.

ADAM was feeling more in control by the time he reached the boat dock. Probably he shouldn't have over-reacted to the bag. Or to Sara earlier. But he'd been on edge since the moment he'd opened his eyes.

"Sorry for hurrying you back here," he apologized when he'd tied up and helped the Carltons back onto the planking. "I want to find out what's in this thing."

"No problem," John answered.

It was obvious from the tone of the other man's voice that he'd also like to know what was in the yellow bag. Adam didn't offer to share the information. Really, he would have preferred to have been on his own when he'd found the damn thing. He counted himself lucky that he'd been the one and not someone else on the staff.

Would they have brought it to him? Would they have pitched it in the dark water? Or would they have known what the thing was and hidden it? Ordinarily he wouldn't make that assumption. But he was learning that the town kept the secrets of the swamp to itself.

"I can give you a refund," he said. "Or if you're going to be in the area tomorrow, I can give you another trip into the swamp for free."

The couple exchanged glances.

"A free trip," Barbara said.

"Okay. Good." Free trips weren't something he handed out on a regular basis, because he knew that Barnette could be tight with his money. He wanted an accounting of how much was being spent and how much was being taken in, although he didn't insist that the park make a profit. Sometimes receipts were ahead of expenses and sometimes they weren't. If the operation needed extra cash, the owner had reluctantly supplied it.

But Adam didn't plan to push his luck in that department. He led the way to the service counter, where Amy was staring at them.

Her gaze flicked to the bag, then quickly away.

"You seen anything like this?" he asked.

"No."

He was almost positive she was lying, but he didn't press the point. Instead he asked her to write up a ticket for a courtesy trip for the Carltons. When that was taken care of, he headed back to his cabin. He didn't know exactly why he wanted to be alone when he opened the damn bag. It was just a feeling he had.

Probably it came from his wolf instincts. Subliminal awareness was always stronger when he was a gray shape running free in the darkness of the night.

But he wasn't a wolf at the moment. And he wasn't going to change now, not when someone could come marching up to his cabin and find a dangerous animal inside.

So he set the bag on the kitchen table, then started

working at the knotted twine that held the top closed. Of course, he could have slit it with his penknife, but he wanted to keep as much of the artifact intact as possible. And besides, the knot told him something about whoever had left the bag.

It wasn't any kind of expert knot. It was a crude series of ties, probably done in haste.

As he worked, he became aware that the makeshift bag was giving off a pungent odor. Stopping, he took a cautious sniff. The last thing he wanted was to find himself overcome by more drugged fumes like last night.

But this was a clean odor, not like the smoke of the night before. When he'd worked the knot loose, he carefully spread open the cloth. Inside was a collection of leaves and twigs and a few other things, like chicken feathers.

He lifted a sprig of something and sniffed. The unmistakable scent of feverfew filled his nostrils. It was hard to describe. Something like mothballs. But not as unpleasant as moth repellent. The sprig wasn't dried. It had been picked fresh and put into the bag, where it had wilted.

Its condition told him something about the length of time the bag had been there. Only a few days, because the herbs inside hadn't had time to go brittle.

Herbs. Yes. That was a good guess. In addition to the feverfew, he recognized the smell and the small leaves of a thyme sprig. There were others, too. But he wasn't an expert on the subject, so he couldn't be sure what they all were.

He looked at the chicken feathers mixed in with the greenery. They had some thick black stuff on the quill end, stuff he didn't want to examine too closely.

So what the hell was this collection of greenery and feathers and black gunk? A voodoo hex? An Indian medicine bag? A joke? A warning—left for whom and by whom?

That last question sent a shiver traveling over his skin. Not much scared him, but he didn't understand this stuff, and he didn't like it.

He had the feeling Sara Weston could tell him exactly what plants had been included. Maybe she even knew enough old-time lore to tell him what it meant.

Sara. His mind kept zinging back to her every chance it got. The two of them would make a great team, he thought. He loved the natural environment. So did she. She had all the qualifications to be a forest ranger's wife.

That thought stopped him cold. He'd met her exactly once. He didn't know how she'd like living in a cabin in the wilderness. And more to the point, he didn't want a wife. He had never wanted a wife. And the realization that the notion had popped into his head was startling. Even somewhat horrifying.

He fought a sudden impulse to get up and claw off his clothing so he could change into a wolf, leap through the cabin door, and run headlong into the swamp—in a futile effort to outrun his destiny.

Instead, he sat for several moments, dragging air into his lungs, getting a grip on his emotions.

Jesus, everything had been going along just fine. And now, suddenly, he felt like he was losing control of his life.

Too restless to sit, he pushed back his chair and stood, then had to reach for the chair back to keep it from tipping over.

He wasn't going to ask Sara anything. He was going to stay away from her.

He wasn't going to talk about this bag of herbs—to her or anybody else. Yet.

Maybe he'd show it to Delacorte later, if it turned out the lawman was playing straight with him. For all he knew, the sheriff was protecting the murderers cavorting in the swamp. An unsettling notion, but one Adam couldn't dismiss out of hand. For the moment, he was on his own. And his first step was to do some checking in town. Ask some questions and hopefully get some of the answers that he had been seeking since this morning.

But not now. Because he wasn't the kind of manager who just took off when the spirit moved him. So he stuffed the contents back into the bag and put the whole thing into a plastic grocery bag, then into the bottom right-hand drawer of his desk.

After that, he checked in at the office, then went on a small inspection tour of the park, asking staff members who had been on water tours if they'd seen anything unusual. Nobody had, which might simply mean that they didn't have his eye for detail. Or they were lying.

He ended up back at the park office and stayed around until closing time, taking care of the usual jobs, then trying to occupy his mind by going back through some park records.

His tour guide spiel on the boat trip into the swamp had gotten him thinking about the history of the park. One thing he hadn't known was exactly when Austen Barnette had acquired Nature's Refuge. Now he saw that the swampland had been purchased twenty-five years ago. So the park wasn't all that old.

Barnette had done pretty well by the natural environment, Adam mused. But opening the park to Granville Pharmaceuticals didn't quite fit the pattern. Why was he inviting big business into Nature's Refuge?

Pulling out the correspondence file, he found the letter Barnette had written him about Sara Weston. When he'd seen it the first time, he hadn't been paying much attention to the details. Now he read it with a lot more interest. She was here for six months. And she was staying right on the east edge of the park, in a cabin that Barnette was renting to the pharmaceutical company.

Not far away. Certainly close enough for a wolf to visit.

So would you like a visit from a wolf? he silently asked Sara.

In his imagination, she smiled. *Yes I would.*

You wouldn't be frightened of me?

She shook her head.

"Yeah, sure," he muttered aloud, banishing another one of his imaginary encounters with Sara from his mind before getting up and stomping back to the filing cabinet.

CHAPTER
EIGHT

ADAM CLEARED UP after dinner, feeling a kind of leaden fatigue weigh him down. He had thought he'd go into town this evening, but he silently acknowledged that he was in no shape for anything but rest.

The tainted smoke from the night before was getting to him. Not that he was having a flashback or anything. But he knew his body better than most people did.

He needed a good night's sleep. And he needed to think through his next move.

So he stripped off his clothes and crawled into the double bed that had come with the cabin. He lay on the hard mattress for long hours, glancing now and then at the green number of the digital clock. Eleven P.M. Twelve A.M. One A.M.

Against his will, his thoughts went back to the nights of his sixteenth year, when his body was changing from boy to man, and he knew that soon Dad would take him out to the woods for the first time—where he would change into a wolf or die.

He had wanted to talk to Ross about it. Ross had made the change and survived. He had already left home, but Mom knew where to find him. Only he couldn't ask her, because he didn't want her to see his fear.

He thought of Ross now. Some deep, buried impulse made him want to reach out and connect with his brother. But he knew that it would come out badly.

Still . . . back when they'd been friends; they'd made trips to the library together. He'd read about the natural environment.

Ross had read about witches and vampires and werewolves.

Would Ross be able to tell him anything about the bag of herbs? Maybe he'd read something that would be useful.

Longing tightened his chest. He rarely admitted it even to himself, but he missed his family with a very deep and fundamental longing. He missed his brother. And he missed his mother. And in some strange, twisted way, he even missed his dad—the Big Bad Wolf, as Ross had called him.

He wanted to see them. Yet he knew that the old phrase, "You can't go home again," applied to him in spades.

Ross had moved out while he was still in college, after a knockdown fistfight in the kitchen with Dad. Mom had thrown a pan of water on them to break it up, and Adam had watched wide-eyed from the doorway.

He hadn't understood then why Dad was so harsh and why; as soon as his sons grew up, they couldn't get along with him at all.

Then he'd read about wolves in the wild and even watched them. There was always one dominant male, the alpha male, and the others were subservient to him. They had a definite pecking order, with each wolf understanding his place in the pack. Apparently, it wasn't the same with werewolves. Each guy needed to be the alpha male. Nobody was willing to give any ground. So they fought for the top spot. Maybe they didn't even understand what they were doing, but they did it.

So how old was Dad now? In his sixties. Adam could probably go back to Baltimore and wup his hide.

But then what? He'd feel satisfied for a few minutes. Then he'd look into Mom's eyes and feel ashamed.

Mom loved the old bastard. She had no choice; she was the werewolf's mate.

As he lay there in the darkness, he thought about the wild and crazy relationship between his mother and father. They needed each other in a way that had amazed and frightened him ever since he'd been old enough to understand it. The werewolf and his mate. There was a bond between them stronger than the bond between an ordinary man and his wife. He'd heard them making love at night with a passion that had embarrassed him. He supposed no kid liked to imagine his parents making love.

But during the day, it had been so different. His father had dominated his mother. Probably he frightened her. Certainly he hadn't hesitated to raise his hand to her when he'd been angry—which had been frequently.

She could have left him. But she stayed, and she came to him at night like none of the bad stuff had ever happened.

He didn't understand it and he hadn't wanted anything so sick in his own life. Or so intense.

He'd told himself he'd known how to avoid it. He'd had lots of women. It had been easy to attract them ever since his teens, after he'd made that transition from man to wolf and back again.

Girls had flocked to him. He gave a short laugh. Apparently that was an advantage of his animal nature.

And he'd enjoyed playing the field, never getting serious about anyone. That had gotten him in trouble more than once. In fact, he'd been glad to leave Big Bend for Wayland because he'd started to sleep with a woman who, it turned out, was in a serious relationship with someone else.

Of course, he wouldn't have approached her if he'd known she had all but promised to marry another guy. Unfortunately, it had already been too late to make amends when he'd found out. He'd almost gotten himself killed, actually. And he'd vowed to be a lot more careful about his sexual partners in the future.

Wayland had been a new beginning for him. He'd been cautious about getting tangled up with anyone until he knew the town. But there were some women he'd had his eye on. And they'd had their eyes on him. Now the only woman he could think about was Sara Weston.

His right hand clenched and unclenched around a wad of rumpled sheet. He'd met her yesterday morning in the swamp.

Yesterday morning! It seemed like a lifetime.

Yet when he stopped to consider the actual number of hours, he could barely believe the time had been so short. It was easy to imagine her lying in the bed beside him. Easy to imagine her there every night of his existence— so that he could turn to her and make wild, passionate love to her anytime he wanted. He had never thought of another woman permanently in his life. He had only thought of short-term pleasure. And now, suddenly everything felt different.

He reached back and arranged his pillow more comfortably under his head. He had to get some sleep. He had to get Sara Weston out of his mind, he told himself as he closed his eyes.

When he opened them again, the room felt different. There was a vibration in the air. A feeling of expectancy. And the rich, female scent of the woman he had met in the park the day before.

He knew he must be dreaming. But this felt more real than any dream he had experienced before—or could ever have imagined. He had been envisioning Sara in his bed. Longing for her. And his dream had put her there. Slowly, as though he were afraid he was mistaken, he turned his head to look at her.

His breath caught when he saw she was lying next to him. In the park her blond hair had been tied back. Now it was loose and spread across the pillow like a delicate fan. She wore a short cotton gown that covered her hips. His gaze traveled down her body and then back up, pausing to admire her breasts and then rising to her face. She was looking at him as though she couldn't believe she was here.

And she was making the same intimate visual tour. His chest was bare. The lower part of his body was hidden by the wrinkled sheet, and he was thankful for that. He hoped it hid his erection. He didn't move. He was almost afraid to breathe.

He was afraid that if he twitched a muscle, she would disappear. And he was desperate to keep that from happening. He might know he was dreaming, but he didn't want the dream to end.

"What are you doing in my bed?" he asked, hearing the rough, uncertain quality of his own voice.

"You wanted me here," she answered, and he found it reassuring that she looked and sounded as bemused as he felt.

"Yes," he admitted to her dream image.

"What do you want?"

He laughed softly. "What men want with a woman who attracts them. To make love with you."

He saw her swallow. "I don't know you well enough to make love. We just met."

"We can get to know each other real fast."

"You weren't exactly charming yesterday morning. I was pretty sure you didn't like me."

In the waking world, the remark would have made him feel defensive. But this was a dream. He didn't have to be defensive. He could say anything he wanted. "I'm sorry. I was upset. Not with you."

"With those people."

"Yes." He didn't want to talk about those people. Not when he had Sara in his bed. So he said quickly, "I should have said I couldn't believe that a Ph.D. botanist could be so young and beautiful."

One of her beguiling blushes spread across her cheeks. "Thanks. I think."

"You're very beautiful," he murmured. Daring to move his arm the barest little bit, he slid his hand across the surface of the sheet. When his fingers touched hers, she made a small sound, and he went instantly still. But she didn't draw back. Thank God.

They lay there, barely touching. The contact was tentative and also electric. Different from anything he had ever experienced.

His relationships with women had always been hot and sexual. He was hot now. But he felt a kind of sweetness that he had never expected to feel.

Her fingers curled against his, and now he was the one who drew in a quick, sharp breath.

"I want to know about you," she murmured.

He felt tension pulse through him. He wanted her to know him, but he was sure she would run screaming in the other direction if she found out the truth. Yet he knew he couldn't simply remain silent and hope to keep her here.

Scrambling for something to give her, he said, "I love the outdoors."

"The swamp?"

"I've worked all over the country. Like I told you, I

was in Texas last. It was dry and hot. But it was majestic. My first post was in Colorado. It was so different from where I lived as a kid. I was at a park high in the Rockies, and it took a couple of months before I could get used to the oxygen level."

"Where did you grow up?"

"Maryland."

"Up north."

"Yeah," he answered, but he didn't want to talk about himself. He was hungry for information about her. "What about you?"

"Wilmington, North Carolina."

"What did you like best?"

"We were really close to the beach. I used to love going down there with my parents. We'd bring back shells and driftwood and other stuff we found."

Eagerly he demanded, "Tell me some more. What else did you love?"

"Barbecue. Playing with my dolls. Building a fort in the woods."

"Did you like school?"

"Yes."

"What subjects?"

She told him about her school days, and he drifted on the sound of her voice, pressing and stroking his fingers against hers, growing more sensual in his touch when she didn't pull away.

It was the bare minimum of contact. Yet that small link of man to woman was the most electric he had ever experienced in his life. Two inches of his flesh and bone against hers, and he knew he was feeling more than he had in any sexual encounter he had ever experienced.

He wanted it to last forever. Yet at the same time, it wasn't sufficient. He wanted more from this woman. Much more.

Slowly, very slowly, he increased the contact, stroking

his fingers against hers, all of his being focused on the sliding sensation of his fingers against her. But it wasn't enough. And when he couldn't suppress his physical need for her, he rolled toward her and reached to pull her against his heated body.

"No!"

"Sara . . . please."

In the next moment, she was gone, and he was left on the bed feeling hot and hard and desolate.

Awake now, he lay there breathing raggedly. The dream had seemed so real. Like she'd actually been there with him, exchanging personal information. He couldn't stop himself from reaching to touch the pillow next to him, almost expecting to feel the indentation of her head or the heat of her body The pillow was smooth and flat and cool.

Of course it was! It was just a dream.

Yet the memory of her rich scent seemed to linger in the room like a tantalizing illusion.

He looked over at the clock again. It was after four A.M., and he knew he wasn't exactly in great shape. But perhaps a walk through the Olakompa would help settle him.

He got up and stripped off his briefs. Naked, he padded to the door of the cabin. An owl hooted. Small animals scurried into the underbrush as he walked to a grove of trees and disappeared into the shadows. He stood in the darkness, marshaling his resolve.

He had been sick from the smoke the night before. And that would make the change more difficult. But he longed for the freedom of the wolf.

"Taranis, Epona, Cerridwen," he muttered, almost under his breath, then repeated the same phrase and went on to the next.

"Ga. Feart. Cleas. Duais. Aithriocht. Go gcumhdai is dtreorai na deithe thu."

Earlier, he had been thinking of the first time he had done this.

Tonight the pain was almost as great, but he knew how to deal with it as he felt his jaw elongate, his teeth sharpen, his body contort. Muscles and limbs transformed themselves into wolf shape while gray hair bloomed on his body. Dropping to all fours, he dragged warm, moist air into his lungs and could detect no trace of the tainted smoke of the night before. After a moment's hesitation, he trotted off toward the east edge of the park, feeling a sense of excitement that he fought to suppress.

He told himself he was simply checking to make sure that Barnette's letter had given him the correct information about where Sara was staying. But he knew deep in his heart that the excuse was only that.

All his senses were on overdrive as he moved like a gray shadow through the park, aware of the incredibly lush environment around him. A wonderful playground for a wolf, he thought, as he skirted the deeper waters of the swamp and the open prairies.

His route led him close to the highway, then through a thick grove of trees to the cabin where Sara was supposed to be living.

He waited in the shadows, listening, sniffing the air with the appreciation of a hunter. Only last night he had been the hunted—and that had counseled caution.

Finally, he made his move, gliding toward the dark shape of the cabin. He couldn't see through the walls, of course. But now he had his full faculties, and he knew she was there. Inside. His nostrils flared as he caught the same incredibly rich scent that had filled his dream. A shiver traveled over his skin, ruffling the hair along his spine.

He had done this before, made the change from man to wolf and visited the homes of women who interested him. A therapist might have called it stalking. He had thought of it as a kind of delicious foreplay that had led to incredibly good sex because it drew out the anticipation.

He appreciated women. He was a good lover. But he always made it clear before he took them to bed that he wasn't looking for a permanent relationship. Maybe they didn't want to believe him, but they couldn't say that he hadn't warned them first.

For a time it didn't matter, because when he finally climbed into bed with his lover of the moment, he devoted himself to her service, turning her on, bringing her to the peak of pleasure again and again.

And then when he left her, he did it gently, regretfully, telling her that it wasn't her fault, that it was some deficiency in himself.

Of course that was true. Only his sexual partners simply didn't understand the magnitude of the problem.

He was a werewolf. And no matter how well he fitted himself into human society, it was just a sham.

Tonight he had made his way to Sara's cabin because a compulsion was on him.

The man would have fought the irresistible impulse. The wolf accepted it.

He moved closer to the house, drawn by her scent and by tantalizing mental images. In his dream he had been ready to make love.

He was ready for that now. He pictured himself changing back to his persona of Adam Marshall, then opening the door, stepping inside, and going to her. In the dream she had said she didn't know him well enough for intimacy. In his supercharged state, he was sure he could change her mind.

They would kiss and touch and cleave together, and it would be incredible. The images swam in his head, blocked out almost all other thought.

But his wolf's awareness finally penetrated the sensual fog. Something wasn't right.

Lifting his head, he sniffed again, and caught another scent. Not an animal who belonged in the still Georgia night, although there were plenty of them around.

He wasn't the only watcher here, he realized. Another man was in the shadows, his gaze tuned toward the house.

CHAPTER
NINE

A SURGE OF anger and possessiveness welled up from the depths of his soul.

The need to protect the woman in the cabin filled his mind, driving out everything else. With no thoughts of guns or bullets, he sprang forward in a rush of fur and fury, his teeth bared, his only goal to bring down the watcher who was out in the darkness where no one should be.

But with his focus entirely on the intruder, the wolf took a misstep in the darkness under the trees. Coming down onto a patch of soggy ground, he stumbled and struggled for several steps to right himself.

The mishap gave the stalker precious seconds. He heard a muffled cry of alarm, then running feet. Moments later a car door slammed, then an engine started.

The car's wheels spun, as the vehicle lurched from its hiding place and then down the road, picking up speed as it went.

The wolf leaped forward, unwilling to abandon the

chase. Murderous rage seized him. It was the rage of the werewolf, an anger he couldn't control when it came upon him.

Four strong legs pumped as he tried to keep up with the rapidly departing vehicle. But muscle and bone were no match for the internal combustion engine.

After a quarter of a mile, he was left gasping in a cloud of exhaust fumes that choked his lungs. The man within him snarled a silent curse as he gave up the useless chase, stopping in the middle of the road.

His body was still weakened from the smoke and the mad desperate dash of the night before. And now it was all he could do to stay on his feet.

The boiling anger was still there as he looked down the narrow track where the car was rapidly disappearing. The driver hadn't turned on the exterior lights. Which meant the license plate hadn't been visible, even to a creature with excellent night vision.

The wolf wanted to slake his anger by finding some animal in the park and tearing it to pieces. But the man managed to stay focused on his mission.

He couldn't see who had been watching Sara. But that didn't leave him without resources. The night before, the drugged smoke had confused his senses, made it impossible for him to identify the naked people who had invaded his turf.

Tonight the air had been warm and clean, and he had picked up the intruder's distinctive scent. The man was no one he'd met, but he could search for him in town, follow his trail to his lair. And when they met, he would recognize him.

What had the bastard been doing here? Did he mean Sara harm? Had he simply come to watch her? Or was he here to protect her?

The last thought was as disturbing as the first. Protect her from what?

Turning, the wolf trotted back to the house. Sara must have heard something outside. She had turned on a light, and he could see her standing at the window, peering out into the darkness.

He stayed under the trees where she couldn't see him. He wanted to go to her and find out if she was all right. But he hung back, because he had only two options. He could approach her as a wolf. Or as a naked man.

As soon as he pictured that second tantalizing alternative, it filled his head, driving out all other thoughts. Yes, he could come to her, naked and aroused. And he would mate with her. Complete the promise of the dream.

The vivid picture of the two of them together burned inside his brain. He took a step forward and a twig snapped under his front paw.

Instantly he stopped, shocked at the intensity of his need.

He forced himself to back away. Then he was running, because if he didn't escape from her now, he never would.

He ran headlong into the swamp, the way he had run the night before. But not in fear for his life.

He wasn't sure what drove him. He only knew that he had to get away. Distance from the cabin helped. By the time he had returned home and changed back into human form, rational thought became possible again.

And the fear was under control. He had the perfect excuse for going over to Sara's place in the morning. He had seen a man hanging around her house. He needed to tell her.

But what would he say? If he warned her that someone had been watching her, she would want to know how he knew. What answer could he give her besides that he had been prowling around her cabin himself?

But he couldn't simply ignore the situation. He had scared the intruder off with his wild rush of lupine fur and fury. Maybe that was enough of a warning. Or maybe the wolf would have to come back tomorrow and the next night and the next to make sure that all was well in the little cabin.

THE UPS truck had delivered more lab equipment around nine A.M. Sara had been up and ready to receive it because something had awakened her early in the morning. A car engine starting? Tires grinding on gravel? She wasn't sure if she had imagined that, or if it had been real because separating reality from fantasy was becoming more difficult every moment she remained in Wayland.

To keep herself occupied, she'd started unpacking glassware. She stopped and swiped an arm across her forehead, pretending that she was inspecting a retort when she was really looking out the window. It was the third time in a half hour that she'd checked the outside view. As she had before, she saw no one, but she couldn't shake the feeling that eyes were watching her.

Did they belong to the old man who had come poking around earlier? Or to Adam Marshall?

She could easily imagine Adam coming to her after the vivid dream of the night before. She'd been in his bed, wanting him. But she'd kept the two of them talking because that was the only way she could control the situation.

She made a snorting sound. She'd been desperate for control, yet it had only been a dream. Hadn't it?

Of course it was a dream, although it had seemed very real. She'd awakened hot and needy and feeling like she really had been lying next to Adam, his fingers knit with hers.

No! That was simply the work of her subconscious. Nothing real had happened. Yet it was like the other dreams she'd had since coming here. Too real. Too vivid.

Her lips pressed into a firm line, she reached for another

box, then another. They contained more carefully wrapped lab equipment. Beakers. Measuring cylinders. Retorts. Petri dishes. Each had to be handled carefully. And each had to be washed.

There was no running water in her lab. The kitchen sink would have to do. Carefully she carried the glass items to the washboard, put some liquid detergent into a dishpan and added hot water.

Then, a few at a time, she began immersing the beakers and other items. The chore was soothing and familiar. She could do it without even thinking.

Again she stared out the window into the dark, forbidding landscape. Then, she felt her vision blur. The scene outside seemed to fade and re-form before her eyes. She should have felt a shock of alarm. Instead she felt peaceful. Her mind drifted in a kind of warm haze, and when she focused again, she realized she wasn't staring into the dimness under the spreading branches, but into a scene where more light filtered onto the grass in front of the little house. Because the trees were smaller, she realized.

With a sense of anticipation, she turned and left the sink, crossed the kitchen and the living room, and opened the front door. Smiling, she stepped out into the sunshine.

The scene was different yet so familiar that she felt her heart leap with a kind of unbounded joy.

The air was softer, cooler, and she drew in a deep breath and let it out before walking around the house to the herb garden that she loved so much. It was planted for beauty as well as practicality, with paths wandering among the patches of rosemary and dill, feverfew, tansy, and lavender. She'd lined some of the beds with lamb's ears, and she smiled as she bent down to stroke her fingers over the furry leaves.

Reaching farther into the foliage, she pulled some weeds. There weren't many because she worked in the garden every day. With a feeling of satisfaction, she took the invaders to the compost pile several yards away. Then she came back to gather herbs for a healing tea she had planned to make.

She knew the formula by heart, and she moved among her plants, selecting what she needed until she saw something on the ground nestled in the foliage. A piece of yellow cloth, tied into a bag.

She went absolutely still, her heart pounding. The bag didn't belong here. Not at all. When she bent to reach for the nasty thing, a voice shouted a warning.

"Don't!"

She didn't know whether she heard it with her ears or only in her mind. But she snatched her hand back, then turned to look out across the sunlit field. She expected to see a man watching her. Instead, a wolf was standing in the open area, his gaze fixed on her.

Had he spoken to her?

Impossible. A wolf couldn't speak.

A ripple of fear went through her as he took a step closer and then another. Yet she saw he moved slowly, step by step, perhaps so as not to alarm her.

He was large, about the size of a big German shepherd. The top half of his face was dark gray. The lower half was lighter, except for his black muzzle.

She should run, she knew. He could hurt her. But his beauty rooted her to the spot. Her eyes feasted on him, taking in details. Like his face, the upper part of his body was darker than the bottom. And his pointed ears were an enticing mixture of light and dark fur, framed by a line of black.

Her fingers itched to stroke his shaggy coat and find the softer spot just behind his ears. A strange impulse, she knew, since she had never been particularly attracted to wild animals.

Her gaze was drawn back to his eyes. They were yellow and infused with an unnerving intelligence.

"What do you want?" she asked.

He didn't speak. Could a wolf speak? But he raised his head and the answer echoed in her mind. "You."

"For dinner? Like Red Riding Hood and the wolf?" she asked.

He shook his head, dug with one beautifully formed front paw against the ground.

"Please. Tell me what you want."

His pink tongue flicked out, stroked along his lips, and she watched the movement, feeling it almost as though he had licked her hot skin and not his own flesh.

She raised her arm toward him like an invitation. And he took another step forward, just as the scene around her began to fade.

"No . . . wait," she cried, because she had to know what happened next. But it was no good. There was no way to cling to the strange reality. She didn't possess that power.

The scene snapped to a halt, like a strip of broken movie film. One moment she had been outside in the sunshine. Now she was inside standing in front of the kitchen sink, her hands clamped around a wet measuring cylinder.

She dropped it back into the dishpan, the water cushioning its fall.

Her whole body began to tremble. Lord, what had just happened to her?

She'd been standing here washing lab glassware. In fact, as she looked toward the drainboard, she saw that she'd washed quite a bit of her equipment. Apparently, her hands had kept working. But her mind had drifted off somewhere else.

She'd been standing in the kitchen of this newly rented house. Then she'd gone outside. Craning her neck, she peered out the window. The view was different from what she had just seen in her . . . daydream.

She snatched at the word like a lifeline. That's what had happened! Her vivid imagination had taken over again. Somehow living in this place was bringing out all the fantasy elements of her personality that she'd worked all her life to suppress. It had happened last night, too. She'd put herself in Adam Marshall's bed where they'd had a long, heart-to-heart chat. And just now she'd been having another imaginary conversation. Only this time she'd talked to a wolf.

Her hands were unsteady as she wiped them on the hips of her jeans, then hurried through the kitchen and the living room to the front door. Outside, she charged around the house to the spot where the herb garden had been. She could still see it vividly in her mind. But there was only scrubby grass and weeds where the neatly tended beds had been.

Even when she walked over the area, she could find no sign that a garden had ever been there.

Then her eyes lifted to the shadows under the trees. She was looking for the wolf, but he wasn't there.

Of course he wasn't there!

She didn't want him to be there.

Suddenly wobbly on her feet, she reached out a hand and steadied herself against the side of the house.

She could feel her heart pounding in her chest, feel her breath coming in little jerky puffs.

She wanted to tell herself that nothing like this had ever happened to her before. But she knew it would be a lie. Her mind had drifted off like this before—and into . . . what?

This time she made herself supply an answer—into another person's life. When she'd been little, she'd tried to talk to her parents about it. And they'd let her know it was a bad thing. So, she'd worked hard to make it go away.

She'd gotten good at driving those intrusions out of her mind, because they had frightened her. And because she'd wanted to be a good little girl. But this time she had totally lost control, and she hadn't even known it was happening.

In the past, the episodes had always been brief. Now she didn't even know how many minutes she had lost.

Heart pounding, she looked at her watch. But she hadn't checked it when she'd started washing the lab equipment. So she didn't know.

She didn't know!

And she couldn't even say for sure that she'd been in another person's reality. Some of the thoughts in her head had come from outside herself. But some of them were her own. Or at least that's what it had seemed like.

Closing her eyes, she lowered her head into her hands, trying to sort out what was real and what was fantasy. It seemed like she'd lived in this house years ago when the trees outside had been much smaller.

But what about the wolf?

She felt her stomach clench and knew the reason. She knew the wolf had come to her. Not the woman who had lived here before. *Her*.

And the knowledge was more frightening than the rest of the dream.

Last night when she'd looked out the window, she'd sensed someone out there.

Well, not someone. Something that she didn't understand. Now she was pretty sure that it had been the wolf.

She raised her head and glanced around the kitchen, seeing it as if for the first time. She should pick up and leave this place. The rational part of her that had always stepped back from the strange and the unknown urged her to run away from this place. This house. This town. The vast wilderness that stretched away from her doorstep.

But the other part was silently whispering something entirely different in her ear.

"Stay. Stay and find out."

The scared little girl inside her still wanted to run. But

she no longer thought that was possible or even that it would do her any good. Because it seemed that down here in Wayland, Georgia, at the edge of the great Olakompa Swamp, another part of her—the long denied part—had taken control.

ADAM thought about eating dinner in town, at one of the restaurants that were doing reasonably well along Main Street. But then he'd have to explain his eating habits. Mostly he preferred meat and other protein. With only small amounts of fruit or salad or vegetables.

Since the low-carbohydrate craze had come in, he had a pretty good rationale for his requirements. He told people he was on the Atkins diet. But tonight he decided it was simply easier to grab something at home.

He opened the freezer and took out one of the steaks he'd bought on sale at the local Winn-Dixie, "the meat people."

He thawed it in the microwave, then cut it into chunks and ate them, grinning as he thought about Amy's reaction to feeding Big Jim. She might hate handling the alligator's rations. He'd had evil thoughts about snitching some grub for himself. Of course, that might lead to the beast's scarfing up another toy poodle, so he'd restrained himself.

After dinner, he made sure he didn't have any blood on his chin, then strode to his SUV.

Exiting the park, he turned left toward town, slowing as he reached the Reduce Speed sign, since he knew from experience that Sheriff Delacorte or one of his deputies was likely to be hiding in the bushes waiting to hand out a speeding ticket.

Straight from the wide-open spaces of Texas where he could easily push his SUV up to a hundred on the freeway, Adam had been caught in the speed trap the first time he'd come to Wayland. Seeing as he was the new head ranger, Delacorte had let him off with a warning. Since then, he'd vowed to keep from being hauled in.

His destination was an old stone church a block off Main Street that now housed the Wayland Historical Society.

He was always cautious when entering a new situation. So he climbed out of his SUV, closed the door softly and stood looking at the neatly tended graveyard that stretched away to his left, then at the gray stone building with its peaked roof and spire.

From the outside, it still looked just like a house of worship, complete with a rounded stained-glass window over the doorway through which the interior light shone out.

It was pretty, in a stylized sort of way. If you liked that sort of thing.

After climbing the front steps, he paused inside the door and looked around at the interior. The Gothic roofline of the church was accented by high rafters and the old stained-glass windows depicting what he assumed were the usual Christian themes. With no light shining in from outside, it was difficult to make them out.

The Marshall family hadn't gone to church. Sometimes his mother had attended. But his father had seen no use for worshiping in an institution that undoubtedly considered him and his sons an abomination.

Adam had followed his logic. He had been in few churches in his life, although a time or two, a colleague had gotten married and invited him to the ceremony, and he'd gone out of politeness.

He didn't like weddings any more than he liked houses of worship.

Ironic that the historical society was housed in one.

He could see clearly, though, that the pews and podium had been removed, replaced by wooden tables and bookshelves that lined the walls and divided up sections of the large room.

Looking around, he saw only a few people in the building, chiefly a couple of wizened men with their noses buried in books. Not surprisingly historical research appeared to be a pastime of the older generation in Wayland.

He had been standing just inside the door, taking it in, when a woman's voice asked politely, "Can I help you?"

He looked to his right and saw a narrow desk where a white-haired, round-faced woman sat reading a large leather-bound volume. She was probably in her late fifties, he judged. Her name tag identified her as Mrs. Waverly. No first name.

He approached the desk and almost choked on the wave of perfume coming off the librarian. Still, he managed to give her a disarming smile before saying, "I'm the new head ranger at Nature's Refuge."

She raised her head, looking him up and down. "Then you're Adam Marshall. I've heard a lot about you."

He didn't bother to inquire how she'd come by his name. This was a small town, and he'd learned that the new guy in a closed community was always of interest. Particularly if he appeared to be an eligible bachelor.

"I hope what you heard was good, Mrs. Waverly," he answered easily.

A flush came to her cheeks. "Oh yes, certainly." She shuffled the papers on her desk. "What can we do for you?"

"Well, when I start a job in a new area, I like to find out about the local history. I was wondering what reading you'd recommend."

"We have an excellent local history, written by a former member of the society. It was published in nineteen fifty-seven, but it will catch you up on everything up until then."

Nineteen fifty-seven. He stifled an inward groan. Probably some folks thought things here never changed. Still, he responded with another smile.

"Actually, I'd like some more recent history as well."

"We have newspapers and other materials, but they can only be used in the building because often they're one-of-a-kind items."

"Yes, I understand. Can you show me where to find the newspapers?"

"Certainly." She got up from behind the desk and bustled over to an area at the back of the room. He had expected to see a bank of microfilm readers. There was one reader and high shelves stacked with large, black-bound books.

"We have local newspapers dating back to before the War of Northern Aggression," she said.

War of Northern Aggression? Oh, yeah, the Civil War, he mentally translated.

"I don't need to go quite that far back," he allowed.

Mrs. Waverly went into what must be a long-practiced spiel, her voice taking on a sing-song quality. "We started microfilming in nineteen ninety-seven," she said, obviously proud of their modern equipment. "Before that, you'll have to consult bound volumes." She pointed to her right. "You can take them to this table over here."

"Thank you, ma'am," he answered politely.

"Don't put them back because you may file them incorrectly," she added sternly. "The staff will reshelve them after you're finished."

"I understand."

"And we close at nine-thirty sharp."

"Yes, ma'am."

He wasn't sure where to start. But he figured the volumes from twenty-five years ago, the year Austen Barnette had bought Nature's Refuge, might be interesting.

He found January of that year on a low shelf, stooped to gather it up, and brought it to the table that Mrs. Wav-

erly had indicated. It was a hefty volume, and he wondered who carted the heavy stuff around.

Up until the early eighties, the *Wayland Messenger* had
come out once a week, so it wasn't difficult to thumb
through the entire year. At first he didn't encounter anything beyond births and deaths, routine police reports of
robberies and traffic accidents, and feature articles on various people like the owner of the largest peanut farm in
the area who had commissioned a batch of peanut recipes
and the botany teacher at the local community college
who was starting a new course on herbal remedies.

Herbal remedies. That stopped him, and he read the
article carefully.

It was interesting, but it told him nothing besides the
fact that a local guy was interested in old-time herbs.

He kept looking for additional information. It was in
one of the April issues that he found an article cut out of
the paper.

What?

He guessed he'd find out because it looked like someone had put it back by folding it up and tucking it into
the binding of the volume.

CHAPTER
TEN

THE FOLDED RECTANGLE of paper was brittle, and he opened it carefully. When he had spread it out, he saw that the headline on the article read, "Woman Burned to Death in Cabin."

The story began: "Jenna Foster, a young woman living in a rural area on the old Wayland-Lanconia road, was found burned to death in her ruined cabin early this morning. Although the woman was unmarried, she was reported to have a daughter, Victoria. The girl was not found."

According to the article, Miss Foster was using a space heater that exploded, setting the cabin on fire. Sheriff Harold Delacorte claimed the heater had a faulty cord.

There was more, but no other useful facts. Adam compared the hole in the paper to the folded article. They did, indeed, match. Then he thumbed through the rest of the bound volume but found no other mention of Jenna Foster.

He started to put the large book back, then remembered

that visitors weren't trusted to return research material to the shelves. Instead he got up and fetched the next.

As far as he could see, the fire and her death had been reported, but then nothing else. He found that startling. The daughter was missing, but there was no report that she had been found or that she hadn't. He thought about the media furor that sprang up these days whenever a youngster went missing. Today, the child's picture would be all over the national news channels.

And the attention would be even more intense in the local media. There would be teams of people combing the swamp for her. But apparently that hadn't happened twenty-five years ago in Wayland, Georgia.

A woman had died, and her little girl hadn't even registered as a blip on the local radar screens.

Why? Hadn't they cared? Or had some relative come and claimed her? He could easily picture that happening.

But even if that were true, he would expect the fact that she was safe and cared for to be reported in the local paper. But there was nothing.

It was as though someone had decided to erase Jenna Foster and her daughter from the local records, including cutting out the one story about her. Then somebody else had rectified the situation.

He looked over toward Mrs. Waverly and found that she was watching him. When she realized he'd caught her staring, she glanced quickly down at the papers in front of her.

Getting up, he carried the bound volume and the article to the desk.

"I was hoping you could help me," he said as he set the large book down.

"Of course."

"I found an article cut out of the paper, then stuffed into the binding."

Her voice turned sharp as she stared down at the vol-

ume he'd set before her. "Cut out? How is that possible?"
She sounded like she was accusing him of being the one
to destroy historical records. Then she focused on the article he'd unfolded.

"Where did you get that?" she demanded.

"Like I said, it was tucked into the binding of the
book."

"That's trash," she said, as she snatched it away and
put it into her desk drawer. "Why were you looking at
this particular volume anyway?"

Her reaction was so out of proportion to what he expected that he considered his answer carefully, then said,
"I came to Wayland to work at Nature's Refuge, and I
was curious about what was happening in town the year
the park was acquired."

"Oh yes. Of course," she agreed, her tone more con-
trolled.

"Naturally I was wondering about the woman and the
child."

When Mrs. Waverly simply sat there staring at him, he
asked another question, "Did some relatives come and
claim the little girl?"

"I don't know anything about that," the librarian said,
her tone of voice making it clear that the subject was
closed.

Adam took in the shuttered expression on her face. She
was looking decidedly less friendly than she had an hour
ago.

"Thank you for your help," he murmured.

She had the grace to flush.

After waiting a beat, he turned and exited the building,
then stood on the steps staring out at clouds turned pink
and lavender by the setting sun.

The natural beauty was a stark contrast to the article
he'd been reading. Something ugly had taken place in
Wayland, and he wondered what it was, exactly.

Paul Delacorte had told him that a woman had been murdered in her cabin at the edge of the swamp twenty-five years ago.

The newspaper story said that a woman named Jenna Foster had been burned to death in her cabin, the fire started by a faulty space heater. But what if that account wasn't exactly accurate? What if the cause of the fire hadn't been an accident at all?

He thought back, recalling the details that Delacorte had given him. He'd said only that the woman had been killed. He hadn't said how. But he'd been reluctant to talk about the incident, just like Mrs. Waverly had been reluctant to talk about the woman in the newspaper article.

On the face of it, they didn't sound like they had much in common, except the way both Waverly and Delacorte had clammed up. And then there was the startling fact that somebody had cut the article out of the paper—and somebody else had put it back.

Well, he needed to find another source of information about the Jenna Foster death. But now that he knew he was stepping into a pool of swamp mud, he was going to be discreet about asking questions.

STARFLOWER walked into the Road House bar. She didn't have to look around to locate the group. She knew where they were. Not just because they always occupied the back left corner of the room. She could feel their presence because they were part of her, and she was part of them.

And she loved the connection.

In the regular world, she was nobody. A clerk at Great Greetings on Main Street.

But with the clan, she was different. Strong and proud.

She swept back her blond hair and stood in the doorway for a moment. Billy Edwards, one of the guys from town, was watching her. He'd had a yen for her since she'd moved to Wayland. He had a nice new pickup truck and a good job out at the farmer's coop. She might have settled for a guy like him. But that was before Falcon had found her living in Macon and explained why she should come back to the community her parents had fled.

At first she'd been skeptical and afraid, if you wanted to know the truth. She knew that her parents had been run out of Wayland when she was just a baby.

But Falcon had told her it would be different this time. He'd taken her to meet Willow and Grizzly. And he'd brought a couple of gallon jugs of water from the Olakompa Swamp. He'd poured them into a washtub and made everybody join hands and breathe in the rich, rotting scent coming off the water. The water and the connection with the group had made her feel wild and potent.

She'd craved that feeling ever since. Craved being with these people. Craved the power she felt growing within herself.

Falcon looked up, saw her and waved. He wasn't a handsome man. His nose was too big. His eyes were too close together. And teenage acne had pitted his skin. But none of that mattered.

He was a natural leader, and she would follow him where he wanted to take her.

He flashed her his killer smile, and a little frisson went through her as she suddenly remembered the thrill of feeling his even white teeth worry her nipple.

His smile turned knowing, and she wondered if he was sharing the same memory.

"Hey!" he called across the restaurant.

"Hey." She wove her way through the tables and chairs to where the group was sitting.

The entire ten members of the clan only met on prearranged occasions. But six of them were present this evening.

Willow moved over to make room for her on the banquette. Razorback's gaze swept over her, settling for a moment on her breasts, tightening them.

What a sexy bastard. She always made love with him when the group got together for one of their special sessions. And they'd had some fun on their own, a time or two.

Too bad he was always pushing Falcon, making her wonder if the two of them were going to end up fighting it out for the leadership of the clan. That would be exciting. But she hoped they could work out their differences, because she'd hate to see one of them kill the other.

She switched her attention to Falcon. "How's the old homestead comin'?" He was a talented carpenter. When he'd come back to town, he'd found a job that used those skills. And he'd also started rehabbing the house out in the country that his parents had left standing vacant. First he'd made sure the structure was sound and weather tight. Then he'd begun adding rooms. When it was finished it was going to be a palace, where a lot of them could live.

"Great. We've got two of the new bedrooms framed. And we got the spa tub into the new bathroom."

"Wow!"

"Copperhead's a big help."

Copperhead was shy and subdued, good at taking orders. Now he smiled with pleasure at being complimented.

She smiled at him. She was looking forward to moving into the house. The other women might not know it yet, but she was going to be the queen of the place.

"So when are you gonna tell us why you invited us for a drink after work?" Willow asked.

Falcon touched his finger to his brow. "Right now, honey." He paused for dramatic effect. He was good at that. "I spotted a woman in town. Someone who would be an asset to the clan."

Starflower could feel the sudden energy flowing around

the table. Being an asset to the clan meant something very particular. It meant that the woman was descended from the same stock as the rest of them, the early English settlers who had developed special powers living in the swamp or at its margin. She didn't know what to call those powers. Falcon had said they were paranormal. He'd given her some books to read, but she wasn't much on book learning. She preferred to think of herself as a modern day witch. And most of the rest of them did, too—when they talked about it among themselves.

They were all here because Falcon had gone to a great deal of trouble, talking to his parents and some of the others who had moved away from Wayland. He'd come up with a list of people who had been shot, hanged, and burned up over the years. From that, he'd gotten a bunch of last names.

"She's from one of the families?" Greenbrier asked, her voice taking on a lilting sound.

"No."

"Then how can she be one of us?"

Before Falcon could answer, the waitress bustled up to ask if Starflower wanted anything to drink and if the others wanted a refill.

The guys ordered more beer. Starflower ordered one, too.

Falcon watched the server leave, then leaned forward and lowered his voice. "She doesn't have to be on my list. We all know there's intermixin' in this town, between their kind and ours."

There were nods of agreement. The famous Jenna Foster was a case in point. As far as anyone knew, she hadn't been married, but she'd had a child. Nobody knew for sure who the father was, but they did know he'd been ashamed to let the town know that he'd been consorting with one of those people. Of course, there was something else about Jenna Foster. She'd been known in the old-

time witch community as the woman who had gone over
to the other side. She'd shunned her own people. Which
had made her a misguided fool.

"The woman you spotted—what's her name?"

"Sara Weston."

Razorback looked Falcon up and down. "I never heard
that name around here."

Their leader nodded. "Me neither. But I know the kind
of vibrations that are coming off her."

Razorback leaned forward. "Oh yeah? Who is she? Has
she been here the whole time? Or did she move back, like
us? How old is she?"

Falcon gave an easy laugh. "That's a lot of questions.
I can answer some of them. She's in her twenties, I'd
guess." He nodded toward Starflower. "She looks a little
like you, honey. Maybe she's your long lost sister."

"I don't have a long lost sister."

"You know for sure your daddy didn't sew any wild
oats?"

She shifted in her seat and shrugged. Actually, she did
know her father had been a ladies' man in his youth.

Falcon was speaking again. "I did a little asking around.
She's in Wayland doing a plant research study for one of
the big pharmaceutical companies. And get this." He
paused, obviously enjoying their eyes on him. "She's living out at the Foster place."

A hush fell over the group. They all knew about the
Foster place. It was part of their mythology, a house at
the edge of the Olakompa that had taken on the status of
a kind of shrine among them, because it was where the
very public murder of Jenna Foster had taken place. It
didn't matter whose side she had been on. She had been
burned to death like an old-time witch. Everybody in town
knew about the murder and the cover-up. But nobody
talked about it. Least of all that damn sheriff, Paul Del-

acorte. It was his daddy who had swept the whole thing under the rug, like yesterday's garbage.

"I thought that house burned down," Starflower whispered. "I mean Jenna Foster died in a fire."

"Only part of the house was damaged. A thunderstorm put the fire out. Austen Barnette owned the place then. He still does."

"Do tell," Willow murmured.

"Your boss?" Starflower asked.

"Yeah. The old dude has his fingers in all kinds of pies in town."

"Cow pies?" Razorback smirked.

Everybody laughed.

Falcon waited for them to settle, then continued. "I don't just work out at the estate. I come down here to fix things at a bunch of different shops for him. He's got residential property, too. Like the cabin. He had it built back up so he could rent it out."

Razorback laughed again. "Yeah, to unsuspecting goobers."

"So if that woman is living there, maybe she's . . . she's absorbing some kind of aura from the place. Maybe the house has Jenna Foster's powers."

"Maybe. But there are ways to find out if it's the house or her."

Again the conversation halted while the girl served the drinks.

Razorback took a swig of beer. "Like how?" he demanded.

"I saw her come to town a little while ago. She was doing some shopping on Main Street. We can test my theory tonight."

Starflower felt her nerve endings tingle as a buzz of excitement went around the table.

Falcon lowered his voice and began to describe his

plan. It was clever, damn clever. Starflower liked it. Willow seemed excited by the idea.

But Razorback had an objection. "We've never tried anything in town before. It could be dangerous."

Falcon fixed him with a direct look. "Who's going to know?"

AUSTEN Barnette wouldn't have liked knowing that he was the subject of conversation among the witches. In this case, ignorance was bliss. At least for the next few moments.

He was sitting in his study smoking one of his specially imported Cuban cigars when the phone rang. It didn't ring in the office because he always turned it off by eight o'clock.

In this day and age, he could have let an answering machine screen his calls. But he hated many of the devices of the modern world. So, instead, he used James.

The old butler picked up the phone in the kitchen. Then he decided whether it was worth bothering the master of the house.

Austen waited for the verdict. When he heard a knock on the door, he looked up. "Come in."

James shuffled into the doorway. "Mrs. Della Waverly would like to speak to you. Are you available?"

He considered his answer. He had given a very generous donation to the historical society because he believed in keeping the town records in good order. The history of a place was as important as its present and its future. But he was interested in more than historical records. When he'd given the donation, he'd made it clear that the ladies who ran the society would come to him with certain information.

In a way, he'd been waiting for this call. So instead of answering James, he simply picked up the receiver.

"Della," he said in what passed as a jovial voice for him. "What can I do for you?" He and the woman went way back. Not just the two of them, but their families, too. Over the years the Barnettes and the Waverlys had stuck together when the going had been rough. Della's husband had been one of his best friends. Greg had been struck with a heart attack ten years ago when they'd been out on a deer hunt. A good way to pass, he'd always thought. Out with your buddies having fun.

He brought his attention back to Della.

"There was a man in here a few minutes ago going through old newspaper editions," she said, her voice filled with importance.

Austen sat up straighter. "What man?"

"That Adam Marshall."

"My head ranger. Yes."

"He said he was looking for material from the year the park opened."

"And?"

Della heaved a sigh. "You know that article on Jenna Foster? The one we cut out of the paper?"

"Of course!" he snapped.

"Well, somebody put it back."

"How the . . . heck could they do that?" he asked, modifying his intended curse.

"Well, I don't mean it was taped into the paper. But somebody stuffed it into the bound volume."

"I appreciate your telling me," he said.

"I took it away from Marshall. And I didn't tell him anything else."

He kept his voice calm and even. "You did fine, Della. I appreciate your informing me," he said again. "But Marshall won't be any problem."

"I just wanted to be sure."

"Thank you, Della."

She cleared her throat. "I put the article in my desk drawer. Should I burn it?"

"Yes," he answered, making the decision for her. Then he let the old bat prattle on for a few more minutes before extricating himself from the phone call.

He dragged in more cigar smoke, then blew it out in a heavy stream.

A long time ago he'd taken care of that article in the historical society records. He'd also made sure there wasn't any other mention of Jenna Foster or her daughter in the newspaper. And he'd made sure Sheriff Harold Delacorte did the right thing.

He'd thought that the whole incident had gone away, at least in public. Now he knew somebody had disagreed with that decision.

Who the hell had gone against him?

Well, he had a lot of enemies in town. A lot of people could have done it.

Of course, the article didn't say anything damaging. But years ago there had been other materials that could be more of a problem. He'd had those destroyed, too.

At least he'd assumed so. Now he was thinking it was better to be safe than sorry. But he couldn't exactly send James down to the historical society. He'd have to go himself. In a couple of days, when his joints didn't ache so much.

He leaned back in his desk chair, puffing on his cigar, thinking about the good citizens of Wayland, wondering who had dared to put that article back into the paper.

CHAPTER
ELEVEN

ADAM WALKED SLOWLY up the block, pretending interest in the shop windows. But really, he was watching the people going by on the newly bricked sidewalk. It was after nine, and he thought that this was the time when the kind of men and women who had been cavorting around the campfire might be out and about.

Of course, he had no hard evidence of that. It was just a hunch.

He eyed a lanky guy holding hands with his girlfriend, a young woman with medium-brown hair. From where he stood now, either one of them could be part of the group from the other night. But he had no way of knowing, and that set his stomach churning.

He'd relied on his wolf senses for all of his adult life. But they were no help to him in this situation. The smoke had clogged his nostrils, and the paint on the dancers' faces had obscured their features.

Of course, there were bits and pieces he'd focused on. Maybe if the little brunette would take off her tank top, he'd recognize her breasts, he thought with an inward laugh. Or maybe not. Probably he'd been too far gone to recognize anything. And lucky for him he'd been in the shadows, so they wouldn't know who he was either. At least he hoped to hell that was true.

He wandered along toward the Winn-Dixie, thinking that he could pick up a six-pack of bottled water.

After that, he might as well head home, because it was starting to get dark. And he wasn't going to see much without his werewolf's vision. He was halfway to the grocery store when he felt a tingling sensation at the back of his neck.

Stopping in his tracks, he lifted his head. The atmosphere around him had the charged, heavy feel of the air before a storm, yet there was no gathering of dark clouds above the town.

His breath stilled in his lungs. Something was about to happen, but he had no idea what.

As if to give him a better view of the downtown area, the street lights flicked on. Twenty feet down the sidewalk a woman stepped out of the drugstore, the yellow glow shining down on her blond hair.

One of the women at the campfire had been blond. A real blonde.

Was that her? Her height was about right. And her body type. At least he thought so. But he couldn't be sure of anything. Dammit.

She looked like she was waiting to cross the street. When she turned her head to check out the traffic, he knew who she was.

Sara. The woman who had been in his thoughts almost constantly over the past two days. He had only spoken to her once, in real life. But he had dreamed of her, stalked her house, held countless conversations with her in his head.

* * *

SARA looked toward the parking lot across Main Street. She'd felt closed in and cut off from the world in her little cabin, so she'd come to town and checked out some of the antique and clothing shops. Her last stop had been the drugstore to pick up a few things she needed, like paper towels and toothpaste.

Pausing on the curb, she opened the zipper of her shoulder bag and fumbled inside to locate her keys.

A woman alone was supposed to have her keys in her hand when she stepped outside a store, especially after dark. She'd started doing it after there had been a rape on the college campus. Probably the advice wasn't so important in a small town like Wayland, but she figured that the habit wasn't a bad one to keep.

With the hard metal keys clutched in her fingers, she stepped between two parked cars and looked both ways up and down Main Street. There were no vehicles coming, so she started across the street. Halfway into the traffic lane, a sudden pain knifed through her head.

It felt like a blast from a ray gun cutting through flesh and bone, slicing into the soft tissue of her brain.

The needle-sharp sensation made her gasp, made her vision blur. For a moment all logical thought completely fled her mind. She didn't know where she was or who she was or even what she was doing. Her whole body had gone rigid, unable to move. Unable to function on any rational level.

She didn't know how long the spell lasted. Just when she thought the unendurable was going to send her to her knees, the intensity lessened. Below the surface of the pain, like bubbles bobbing up through layers of swamp water, she sensed words forming in her mind.

Not her words. Words beamed in from some other consciousness.

Watch out, Sara. You're in danger. Danger. Danger. There's a truck coming. Get out of the street. Watch out Sara. You're in danger, danger, danger. The truck, the truck, the truck.

She raised her hand, pressing her fingers to her forehead as the warning echoed in her mind like vibrations coming off the surface of a drum, sending the words bouncing around the inside of her skull.

It wasn't one voice but a babble of people, men and women, all saying the same things like a Greek chorus.

Watch out, Sara. You're in danger. Danger. Danger.

Her skin had gone clammy. Her heart was pounding wildly in her chest. Somehow through the cotton filling her brain, she knew that she had to bring her thoughts into focus. Danger. She was in danger. But the pain in her head had made it hard to think, impossible to move.

Her fingers clamped around the cold metal of the keys that were still in her purse, deliberately pressing the teeth into her flesh, as she struggled to anchor herself to reality.

Looking to her left, she saw that a black pickup truck had rounded the corner and was coming toward her, as she'd been warned. And she had to get out of the street before it mowed her down.

But she couldn't move. Feeling like an insect caught in amber, she simply stood there, watching the truck bear down on her.

ADAM sprinted down the sidewalk, the scene burned into the tissue of his brain like a flaming brand: Sara in the middle of the street, and a black pickup heading right for her.

He couldn't get there in time. It was all happening much too fast, yet some part of him felt as if he were viewing the scene in slow motion. With no thought for his own safety, he leaped between parked cars, crossing the few feet still separating him from Sara as though his running shoes had sprouted jet propulsion devices.

He grabbed for her, his fingers tangled in her knit top, clutching the fabric as he pulled her away from two tons of metal speeding down the blacktop.

She screamed as his hands dug through her shirt and into her flesh, screamed again as the vehicle whizzed by.

Raising his head, he tried to get a look at the driver. He thought he could make out a large head covered with a cap and shoulders hunched over the wheel. But he only caught a fleeting glimpse through the back window, and he couldn't even be sure if it was a man or a woman.

He lost sight of the driver in the wash from the tailwind. It buffeted them so strongly that he was almost knocked off his feet. Swaying, he braced his hips against the side of a parked car, pulling Sara against himself to prevent the two of them from tumbling to the pavement.

She was safe. And in his arms. His breath wedged in his throat as he folded her close, cradling her slender body protectively against his. She was trembling. Her fingers must have let go of the plastic shopping bag she was holding, because he heard it drop to the ground.

"It's okay. You're safe with me."

"They warned me," she rasped, her fingers closing and unclosing on his arm.

He didn't understand what she was saying. All he knew was that at this moment in time, he needed to shut out the world and simply hold her. Closing his eyes, he wrapped her tightly in his embrace. An inarticulate sound welled in his throat as he lowered his face to the top of her head, unconsciously moving his lips against her golden hair.

In response, she lifted her arms, clinging to him as though they had been separated for a long, long time. And now they were finally together again.

The strength of his emotions made no sense. But as he

gathered her against himself, he was filled with an incredible feeling of connection to her, as though the two of them had known each other for a thousand lifetimes. He had never believed in destiny. Yet at this moment, he understood that she was the woman the fates had ordained for him.

And she seemed to understand that, too.

As they stood at the edge of Main Street, clinging to each other, he forgot where they were, forgot why he had folded her into his arms. The feel of her body pressed to his was too overwhelming to leave room in his mind for anything else. He would put her in his car. Take her back to Nature's Refuge, where he could keep her safe. Where he could keep her for himself. She belonged to him as no other woman had ever belonged to him. And he belonged to her in the same way.

A voice snapped him back to reality. "Hey, buddy, you all right?"

He remembered, then, why he was holding Sara and why she was clinging to him.

"You all right?" the voice asked again. It came from somewhere outside the invisible bubble that enclosed himself and the woman in his arms.

He wanted to ignore the intrusion, but he knew that if he didn't answer, the questioner would persist.

"Yeah," he replied, without shifting his attention away from Sara.

"Who was that jerk?" asked the man standing a few feet away.

"I'd like to know," Adam growled, the low, strained quality of his voice coming as much from annoyance with the guy who wouldn't leave him and Sara be as his reaction to the aborted hit-and-run.

But it wasn't just one guy, he suddenly realized. A whole crowd of evening shoppers had gathered on the sidewalk, destroying the private moment.

Lifting his head, he stared at the people who had materialized around them.

"We're fine," he said again, addressing the group at large.

He heard Sara swallow hard. "Yes, fine," she echoed automatically, even though her skin was pale as moonlight, and she was staring up at him with wide, shocked eyes.

Somebody thrust a plastic shopping bag at him, and he took it, then used his shoulders to part the sea of humanity so that he could draw Sara away from the center of attention and into a little courtyard between two buildings.

She was still shaking, and he draped the hand with the shopping bag awkwardly around her shoulder, stroking his other hand up and down her arm. He was waiting for her to pull away from him, but she stayed where she was.

Did she feel what he did? The intensity? The sudden need to caress her mouth with his.

The anticipation of the kiss burned through him like a fire devouring him from the inside out. He knew how it would be. Passionate. Consuming. Branding.

The reality of her overwhelmed him. He was swamped by sensory input: the sweet smell of her hair, the feminine shape of her body, the fine tremor that went through her.

Every instinct urged him to claim her mouth, to claim her for his own. Yet at the same time, he felt as though he had broken through solid ground and was sinking into the black waters of the swamp. In some part of his mind he knew that if he lowered his mouth to hers, there would be no going back. Not ever.

She stared up at him, looking shocked, and he thought maybe she felt the same thing he did. Maybe she knew that they stood on the brink of some discovery that neither one of them was prepared to make.

While emotions roared through him, Sara took the decision out of his hands and pulled away from him.

"Don't," he managed, feeling as though his own flesh were being torn from his body.

Her eyes were wide and round. When she spoke, her voice was barely a whisper. "I have to go."

"Sara." His fingers closed over her arm.

"What do you want?" she asked, her voice a little stronger.

Seconds passed as they both waited for the answer. He couldn't give it because he was afraid to frame the words, even in his mind. All he could say was, "I want you to be careful."

"I will," she told him, then pulled away and fled into the darkness.

FALCON joined the clan where they had gathered in the lot in back of the ice-cream parlor.

Razorback's head swung toward him. "Where did you park, man?"

"A block over."

"What if someone made your license plate?"

"I smeared it with dirt. There was no way to see it."

"Clever!" Copperhead approved.

Razorback kicked his foot against the blacktop.

"So what did you think about the woman?" Starflower asked the group.

"Did you see her go stock still like she'd been drilled with a laser? She got the message we sent her, all right. She knew the truck was coming," Razorback said, his voice emphatic.

"She didn't get out of the way," Grizzly pointed out. "She just stood there in the middle of the street."

"She was spooked. Didn't you see the way she went pale, the way her hand went to her head." Starflower jumped back into the conversation. "We did it too strong.

We didn't know it was gonna paralyze her."

"Yeah," Grizzly conceded.

"The way she stood there. That's not proof," Willow argued.

"What do you think?" Starflower asked Falcon.

He spread his hands. "By the time I got there, she looked like a deer caught in the headlights. It's hard to be sure."

Grizzly craned his neck back toward the shopping area. "The street was full of people minding their own business. But it's that one guy who spooked me. The guy who pulled her out of the way. Did you see him zero in on her before he even saw the truck?"

There were exclamations of agreement around the group.

"Who is he?" Grizzly asked sharply.

"He's got . . . power," Starflower murmured, her voice low.

"How do you know?" Grizzly pressed.

"I can feel it. Maybe it's a man-woman thing. Falcon recognized the woman as one of us. And I got something from the guy."

"Yeah," Falcon growled, his eyes narrowing as he stared at the place where the couple had disappeared. It was the guy he had seen the other day at Barnette's house.

He looked at Starflower. "That's the new head ranger of Nature's Refuge."

"Oh, yeah?" Razorback muttered.

"He could be the snoop who was spyin' on us the other night."

That got everybody's attention.

"So we take care of him, like we took care of Ken White?" Grizzly muttered.

"Not necessarily," Starflower said quickly. "Let me find out if he's with us or against us."

"You want to test him? Like Falcon tested her?" Willow asked.

Starflower grinned. "Actually, I have something else in mind."

CHAPTER
TWELVE

A RACCOON APPEARED at the side of the road, and Sara slowed. The animal hesitated for a moment, then turned and disappeared into the open field at the side of the blacktop.

Sara continued along the darkened highway. She was six miles from downtown Wayland, and the farther she got from Main Street, the more calm she felt.

Strange. She had fled her cabin this evening to get away from the old ghosts who crowded into the small rooms with her.

Now the old ghosts were preferable to the new voices echoing in her mind. The thought brought a trace of her earlier headache, and she gritted her teeth. "No," she said aloud. She wanted it to disappear, along with the memory of what had happened when she'd stepped off the curb. But she couldn't wish the incident away.

Tonight people had called out to her. And she'd felt their words echoing in her brain like the reverberations from a steel drum that had stopped her in her tracks.

They had sounded their alarm moments before the truck had come at her in the street. At the same time, she'd thought she heard them yammering in her head. Now she was able to come up with another explanation that she liked better.

Somebody in town was playing an evil practical joke on the lady from Granville Pharmaceuticals. They knew her name. They'd called out to her, and then one of them had aimed his truck at her.

The scenario wasn't exactly reassuring, but it had the power to make her feel better. Because it put a creepy experience into more normal terms. She clutched it to her breast, even though it didn't fit all the facts.

What about the pain in her head, she asked herself, then came up with another good answer. She had been working hard for the past few days. Too hard. She'd been under a lot of stress. In a new environment. And it was perfectly reasonable to believe that the whole combination of factors had given her a headache.

She breathed out a small sigh, feeling some of her tension evaporate as she drove on into the night.

The voices hadn't been in her mind at all. They had come from people hiding just out of sight. People having some fun with her.

She didn't like it much. And she didn't know why they had picked on her. Or whether they would try something else. But she had given herself an explanation for the truck incident. Which left her free to think about the next part.

Specifically, Adam Marshall.

He had risked his own life to snatch her out of the street when she'd lost the power to move. Afterwards, he had gathered her in his arms as though he were a lover coming back to her after a long absence. And she had clung to him with the same fervor.

The intensity of the encounter had overwhelmed her,

replacing the earlier fear. In the real world, she barely
knew the man, yet she'd cleaved to him as though . . . as
though he were her only salvation.

The idea was absurd.

And scary. Which was why she'd wrenched herself
away and run back to the safety of familiar old Miss Hester.

She'd never felt half that much for any other man. Not
even the two with whom she'd made love.

And she'd waited months before taking that step with
either of them. Adam Marshall was a stranger. So why
was she responding to him as though they were two
halves of one whole? Why had she met him in a dream
that seemed more real than any of her previous bedroom
encounters?

She pulled into the parking space in front of her cabin
and sat with her eyes squeezed tightly closed, trying to
shut out the feelings that had swamped her when he'd
pulled her into that courtyard and the two of them had
been alone. Banishing the memory was impossible. With
a sigh she opened the door and stepped out of the old
Toyota, taking a deep breath of the damp air, conscious
of how dark it was out here in the middle of nowhere.

When she'd left the little house at the edge of the
swamp, it had still been daylight. But she should have
thought to turn on the porch light. In the future, she
wouldn't forget that.

As she reached for her keys, headlights cut through the
inky blackness along the road.

Goose bumps peppered her skin. Whirling, she turned
to face the intruder, her arm rising to shade her eyes. But
it was impossible to see the vehicle behind the headlights.
The only thing she could think was that the guy with the
pickup was back.

Earlier, she had frozen in the middle of the street. Determined not to make the same mistake twice, she re-

versed direction and sprinted for the house, fumbling again for keys in her purse. Her gun was inside the cabin. If the driver or his friends meant her harm, she would defend herself. And call the sheriff.

Should she already have reported the incident? She'd been so muddled up on the way out of town that she hadn't even thought of it.

She heard gravel crunch as she shoved the key into the lock.

"Sara! Wait. It's Adam."

She went dead still. "Adam?" Turning, she saw a tall figure moving toward her across the yard and felt something inside her chest clench. A complex mixture of emotions welled inside her. Joy. Fear. Need.

She had been thinking about him. Puzzling over her feelings for him. And now, here he was, as though she'd called to him, and he'd come to her.

Her lips moved, and she heard her voice quaver as she asked, "What are you doing here?"

WORDS of apology tumbled from his mouth, "I'm sorry. I didn't mean to frighten you. I followed you home to make sure nobody else did. I wanted to be certain you were all right. And I have your shopping bag," he added lamely.

He didn't explain that the need to protect her had sent him bolting for his SUV the moment she'd left him. Or that the feeling of being separated from her after holding her in his arms was intolerable.

"I'm fine," she assured him, the answer sounding like an automatic response.

He reached her as she turned the key in the lock, pushed the door open, and switched on the porch light. Both of them stood blinking in the sudden brightness.

He set down the shopping bag on the worn floorboards,

thinking that he shouldn't have gotten out of his car. He should have made sure nobody else was coming along behind her, then driven on past and given her the drugstore purchases another time. But he was here, and the need to reach for her had him pressing his palms against the sides of his jeans.

The pulse pounding in his ears made it difficult to hear what she had said.

"Did you ask me in?"

"Yes."

"I should go."

"I should thank you for snatching me out of the street."

He found himself following her inside. She took several steps into the room. He closed the door, then watched her moving about, turning on a lamp in the corner and one on an end table.

He loved the way the warm light glinted off her blond hair. He loved the grace of her movements. Loved her slender, long-fingered hands.

Pulling his gaze away from her, he focused on the cabin. It was sparsely furnished, yet she'd made it her own in the short time she'd been there. She had set an old metal milk can in one corner and filled it with tall grasses. Indian throws brightened the old sofa and overstuffed chair. And a piece of old lace covered what was probably the scarred top of the oak chest against one wall.

Set out on the lace was a collection of small boxes, some china, some metallic, some wooden.

"The place looks nice," he said, thinking that the words sounded inane.

"I brought some stuff from home."

"Wilmington."

Her head jerked up. "How did you know that?"

His breath caught. How *did* he know it? "I can guess, from your accent," he answered, because it was the only answer he could come up with.

"Are you an expert on accents?"

He shrugged.

Her gaze pinned him. "Or did you know because I told you in the dream?"

He swallowed hard. "What dream?" he managed to say.

She kept her gaze steady on him. "Did you dream about me last night?"

He clenched and unclenched his hand. "Yes."

"Wouldn't it be . . . strange if we had the same dream."

"How could we?" he asked.

"Was I in your bed?" she challenged.

"Yes. But it's not difficult to figure out why. I've been thinking about you ever since we met in the swamp." He stopped abruptly, realizing he'd given too much away. It was one thing to admit as much in a dream. And quite another to say it in real life. *Change direction.* He added lamely, "And if you were thinking about me . . . it might seem like we met."

She gave a tight nod. "You can explain it that way if you want."

"How do *you* explain it?"

"I can't. And I don't want to. All I know is that strange things have been happening to me since I moved here. Dreams that seem real. Daydreams where I feel like I'm in someone else's head. Then that incident with the truck."

"How do you mean?"

"It's hard to talk about it. Maybe a cup of tea would settle us both down."

He gave her credit for a quick change of subject. "I don't drink tea. Well, not unless it's herbal tea," he said, feeling like he were babbling.

"I have mint. Is that okay?"

"Yes."

She moved to the kitchen and switched on another light. The room was small, and as she turned to snatch the kettle off a burner and fill it, she clanked it against the faucet.

"Sorry," she said as she whirled back to the stove and set the kettle down again.

He was consumed by the urge to go to her, make her face him, and fold her close, but he managed to stay where he was.

"Tell me about the truck," he said.

For long moments, her gaze turned inward, and he thought she wasn't going to speak. Then she sighed. "I've decided the driver didn't really mean to hit me," she said in a rush of words.

"What makes you think so?"

"Someone—a group of people—warned me I was *in danger*."

He stared at her, struggling to make sense of that. "Warned you? Why? How?"

"They shouted a warning."

"I didn't hear anything or see anybody."

"Maybe they were right near me, where you couldn't see them, but I could hear them. Maybe it just sounded like a shout," she said, acting like she wasn't quite sure. Acting like she was trying out the theory on him.

"Maybe. Why would they do it?"

She shrugged again. "Because they're into mean practical jokes? Because they hate Granville Pharmaceuticals? Because they like to test the nerves of newcomers? Has anyone tried to test your nerves?"

He hesitated. "Well, somebody tried to kill me two nights ago."

She sucked in a strangled breath, raising her head so she could meet his eyes. "The people having the drug party? They tried to kill you?"

"Yes."

"You didn't mention that!"

"I didn't think you needed to know."

"Oh Lord, Adam. What did they do?"

"Chased me like a pack of . . . hyenas. Took a couple of shots at me."

Her hands gripped his arms. "Stay out of the swamp."

"I could say the same to you."

"It's my job."

"Mine, too."

"Did you tell anyone else . . . about what happened?"

"Sheriff Delacorte."

"And he said?"

"That there's been trouble in Wayland. Over the years. Incidents he was reluctant to talk about."

"What kind of trouble?" Sara asked.

"I don't know for sure. But I'm going to find out."

She studied his face, trying to read his expression. He had pulled her out of the truck's path. He had followed her home to make sure she was safe. And now he was telling her things that he could have kept to himself.

Maybe she was testing him—or testing herself—when she said, "I can believe . . . strange things have happened here."

"Why?"

"Because I get feelings about places and people. And my impressions usually turn out to be true. There's evil here. And something else."

When he didn't laugh at her, she went on. "Ever since I came to Wayland, to this cabin, I've felt . . . off balance. Things keep happening. Things I can't explain in any normal terms."

"Such as?"

"What I told you. Dreams. Daydreams. And something that happened just before that truck came flying by."

She watched him carefully to see what he thought about the way she'd put it. When he kept his gaze steady on her, she continued.

"I told you somebody shouted a warning. That's what

I'll say if anybody asks about it. But I'm not sure that's what really happened. First I felt like somebody was aiming a ray gun at my skull. Then I heard the voices. But not out loud." She swallowed. "Inside my head. So maybe I'm going crazy."

"No."

"How do you know?"

"I just know. You're not crazy!"

The conviction in his voice warmed her.

"Why not?" she said, the words barely above a whisper.

"Because, like you, I have good instincts about people."

He took a step toward her.

"Adam . . ."

The kettle started to whistle. They both grabbed for it; both drew their hands back. She felt his gaze burning into her as she moved the kettle off the heat, then got out two mugs and two tea bags. She felt her heart racing as she poured the hot water into the mugs.

The sweet pungent aroma of mint filled the kitchen as he reached for her. Maybe he was offering comfort. Or reassurance. Whatever it was, she wanted it.

When he folded her into his arms, she melted against him, letting her head drop to his shoulder.

"What's happening to me? To us?"

"What do you mean . . . to us?" Adam asked.

"Are you going to lie and tell me that nothing . . . important . . . happened . . . after you snatched me out of the path of that truck?"

He had felt the intensity of it all right. But he couldn't talk about it. "We hardly know each other."

"That's usually the woman's line."

"Yeah."

"I'd say what we're feeling has nothing to do with the length of our acquaintance. It's like time has been compressed, like we're living in a speeded-up universe."

As she spoke, she stroked her fingers along his arm. It

was only a light touch, but he felt it scorching his skin through the fabric of his shirt.

He'd thought the dream was intense. It was nothing compared to the here and now.

He knew he should step back before it was too late.

Too late for what?

He didn't want to answer the silent question, couldn't answer because his brain had stopped working. But he didn't need words to know what he wanted, what he had wanted since the first time he had seen her.

Instead of backing away, he hauled her closer, allowing a kaleidoscope of sensations to swamp him again. The feel of her slender body that fitted his arms so well. The brush of her soft hair against his cheek as he lowered his head. The rich woman scent that was making him dizzy.

She stood with her head bent to his shoulder. He crooked his hand under her chin, lifting her face to his, his gaze focusing on her beautifully shaped lips.

He ached to kiss her. But he held himself still, because some part of him wanted to hear her tell him "no."

He wanted her to say this was a mistake. He wanted her to be the one to make the decision, so it would be taken out of his hands.

He held his breath, waiting, willing her to pull away as she had on the street. This time she stayed where she was, her lips slightly parted.

But she didn't understand that she was playing with fire. He hardly understood it himself.

And he was helpless to do anything besides lower his head to hers. The first mouth-to-mouth contact was like a lightning strike, deep in the forest, creating a hot, instant blaze that swamped his mind, his body.

He had never tasted anything so rich, so heady as this woman's mouth. And he drank from the sweetness she offered like a man deprived of all sustenance and finally bidden to partake of a feast.

She made a small, needy sound that sent sparks to every nerve ending in his body. He angled his head, first one way and then the other, changing the angle, changing the pressure, changing the very terms of his existence.

With no conscious thought on his part, one of his hands slid down to her hips, pulling her lower body in against his erection, desperate to satisfy his craving for intimate contact with her.

The other hand clasped the top of her, pressing her breasts against his chest.

The drive to mate with her was suddenly an all-consuming purpose. His only purpose. He needed to be on top of her, needed to be deep, deep inside her.

She kissed him as though she felt what he did. And he gloried in her response to him.

Breaking the kiss, he lifted his head, his gaze barely focused as he stared down at her.

He had wished her into his bed the night before. But this was reality. And suddenly he couldn't cope with how much he felt.

"I'm sorry," he managed, knowing that it wasn't an apology for anything he had done.

The desperation of his own need was like a dash of cold water.

Earlier she had fled from him.

Now he was the one who lacked the courage to find out where the heated kiss would lead. He took a step back, then turned and stumbled away, stumbled out of the house. He wasn't even aware that he had climbed into his SUV and started the engine until he realized he was backing away from the house.

*   *   *

ON unsteady legs, Sara crossed the living room and closed the front door, then threw the bolt. She wanted safety where none existed. And in some part of her consciousness, she knew there never would be safety again.

One kiss, and she had wanted Adam Marshall with a force that robbed the breath from her lungs. In her mind, a picture had formed of the two of them, on the kitchen floor, naked, in a fevered embrace.

He had left her shaking. In danger of losing her balance. Physically, emotionally. Mentally. Barely able to stand, she crossed the few steps to the easy chair and sank down.

She had thought they were getting close. Not just sexually close. Something deeper, more profound. Then he had pulled away, and she could have sworn he was afraid to take it to the next step.

Adam Marshall afraid?

Another image came to her. She saw herself throwing clothing into a suitcase and fleeing the cabin. Fleeing Adam. Fleeing Wayland. Because she was afraid that if she didn't get out of Wayland, she would be sucked under the black waters of the Olakompa—never to be seen again. If not literally, then figuratively.

As that panicked thought surfaced, she knew something even more fundamental. Earlier in the day, she had thought about leaving. She was still here. And now she knew that bailing out would be the worst thing she could do. Fate had brought her here to this place at this time. And turning away from what waited for her was worse than staying. She had to face her worst fear and conquer it or she was surely doomed. She hugged her arms around her shoulders, rubbing her hands up and down her arms, trying to ward off the sudden chill that made her teeth begin to chatter.

*   *   *

ADAM drove into the night, feeling pursued by devils that had always lurked in the darkness. And now they had burst forth.

The raw force of what had happened between himself and Sara astonished him. He knew it had started building on the street in Wayland. Well, before that, really, when he'd first seen her in the park. Alone with her in the kitchen, the need to join with her had gripped him with a savage strength that had shaken him to the core.

He had fled those feelings, and now he didn't know what the hell he was going to do.

Run. He wanted to run. Yet he knew deep in his soul that would do him no good.

If he ran from Sara now, it would be like half his mind and heart had been hacked out of his body. On some deep instinctive level, he understood that. Yet he wasn't able to come to terms with the new reality: He must have this woman or die. Till death do them part.

Although that sounded simple, it wasn't simple at all.

Like, for instance, was she involved with the people who had tried to kill him in the swamp? He didn't want to think so, but he still couldn't be sure. Part of him prayed that she wasn't. And part of him welcomed the theory. Because that would give him an excuse to tear ass out of the state.

Right now his fear was as strong as his need. She had kissed Adam Marshall, the man. What about Adam Marshall, werewolf? Would the wolf send her screaming in terror? He had never worried about that with any of his other women because he hadn't been around long enough for them to find out. He had made love with them. Enjoyed their bodies. Given them pleasure. But none of that added up to a teacup full of real intimacy, the kind of intimacy he wanted, needed with Sara.

His jaw clenched as he imagined her terror.

Jesus. What had his father done about that?

Had Ross faced it?

He dragged in a breath and let it out in a rush. It felt like he had come to some sort of fundamental crossroads in his life. And he couldn't cope with what was happening to him.

When he realized he had almost plowed into the barrier that closed off the main park entrance after hours, he slammed on his brakes.

Unlocking the bar, he drove through into Nature's Refuge, an island of peace in the middle of the great Olakompa Swamp. But not for him. There was no refuge for him. Never again. Not in this world.

CHAPTER

THIRTEEN

ADAM SPENT A restless night, turning the covers into a twisted mass of rope. He told himself he didn't have to make any decisions. He knew he was lying.

He got up early and dressed, prowling the park's public grounds looking for hard manual labor that needed to be done.

There was a place where a path was crumbling into the swamp. The plan was to shore it up with a fieldstone retaining wall. The rocks had been delivered, but the work hadn't started yet because it was going to be a messy job. This morning, Adam put on his grubbiest clothes, then got out a wheelbarrow and started moving loads of stone.

By the time other rangers began arriving, he was covered with sweat, and his arm muscles were protesting. But he had transferred most of the building material from the pile in back of a storage shed to the work area. The staff tried to hide their surprise that the boss was doing the grunt work. Dwayne and Eugene offered to help. He hesitated for a moment. They might take his mind off his problems, but he knew he wasn't fit for human interaction at the moment. So he said he was just getting to the messy part, and he might as well continue by himself.

Eugene looked like he wanted to say something else. But he kept quiet. Adam asked him to check the day's schedule and do any rearranging necessary, as he planned to be here for a few more hours.

Alone again, he marked off the construction area with yellow tape, then figured he'd better get a pair of rubber boots if he didn't want to ruin his shoes. After pulling the boots on, he waded into the water along the path and began evening out the edge in preparation for putting down two layers of stone.

He'd never shied away from hard work. In that way he was like Ross, who had gotten him a couple of construction jobs before he'd left home.

Again, as he had in the past few days, he let himself think about his brother, wonder if he was still alive, even. Werewolves were a violent sort. There were all kinds of things that could have happened to his only remaining sibling.

He bent down, laying the first level of stone in the muck and evening it out, then standing back to judge the length of the wall. The stone was just peeking above the surface of the muddy water, and he figured he'd get his level full of mud if he tried to use the instrument.

He continued, selecting stones that would fit together well, working by feel as much as by eye.

Thinking about Ross kept his mind off Sara. He had been on his own for a long time. What would it hurt to call home and find out where to contact his brother? Or maybe he could even get him through one of those Internet search engines.

He had just set the last rock in the second row when a voice broke through the sounds of chirping birds.

"Seems like you have the makings of a second career, son."

He was glad he'd put down the stone, otherwise he might have dropped it on his foot.

Looking up, he met Paul Delacorte's dark chocolate eyes. "Howdy, sheriff," he managed.

"You the new field hand at Nature's Refuge?" the black man drawled.

"If I want to be. Rank has its privileges."

"You're right on that one."

"Are you making an inspection tour of the lowlands?" Adam asked.

"I hear you had a little bit of trouble in town last night."

"News travels fast."

"Sure does, in a place like Wayland."

"You're referring to the near miss with the pickup truck?"

"Was there something else?"

"Mrs. Waverly damn near kicked me out of the historical society library."

"Oh . . . well." Paul looked him up and down. "I'd say you could use a break."

"Yeah."

"Why don't we set a spell."

"Sure. Let's go up to my cabin and get a couple of bottles of chilled water out of the refrigerator."

As he climbed up to the path, Adam caught sight of Amy Ralston watching them. Probably she was curious about what Delacorte was doing here, if she didn't already know.

Since the sheriff had heard about the near hit-and-run incident, everybody else probably had, too. On the way to the cabin, he stopped at an outdoor faucet and washed his hands and face—and boots.

He contemplated sticking his whole head under the stream of water but decided that looking like a drowned rat wasn't an advantage when talking to the law.

Delacorte brought only one bottle of water and set it on the table beside Adam's chair. He picked it up and downed half of it in one gulp.

"Hard work, laying stone," the sheriff observed.

"Yeah."

"Ken White would have left it to the staff." The sheriff shifted his weight from one foot to the other. "He went by the philosophy that on a mule team, the scenery is the same for all the mules except the leader."

Adam laughed. "Yeah, well, I like to trade places with the mules in the back. That way I know what's involved in all the jobs."

"A good policy."

"Is that why you lie in wait for speeders?"

"Partly. But I enjoy taking tourists down a peg."

Adam lowered himself into a wire mesh chair and drank more of his water, waiting for the sheriff to make the next move.

The man joined him in the empty chair, crossed his legs comfortably at the ankles, and asked, "Did you recognize the pickup truck or the driver?"

"The driver was hunched over. The truck looked like a hundred others in town. I didn't have time to glance at the license plate."

"It was smeared with mud."

"You saw it?"

"I got a couple of eyewitness accounts."

"So why do you figure someone tried to mow down Sara Weston?"

"You think that's what happened?"

"It looked that way to me. The question is why? You have many incidents like that in Wayland?"

"Not many. It could have been a drunk teenager showing off. Or some guy who had a run-in with her."

"Who would that be?" Adam asked sharply.

"She doesn't know."

"You talked to her?"

"This morning."

Adam leaned forward in his seat. "How was she?"

"A little shook up."

Yeah, he thought. So was he. And not just from the accident.

"She says she's kept pretty much to herself. And she doesn't think she's had time to make any enemies in town," Delacorte continued. "She did advance the theory that somebody might not like Granville Pharmaceuticals."

"Has Granville stuck its nose into town before?"

"No. But they make drugs. If somebody thinks they were harmed by one of the company's products, they could have taken it out on the lady."

Adam ran his finger and thumb up the sweating side of the cold bottle. "That doesn't make a hell of a lot of sense."

"Sometimes crime is like that."

"Yeah."

Adam shifted in his seat. "Since you're here, I'd like to follow up on some research I was doing at the historical society."

"I'm no historian."

"You've been in Wayland all your life. And I'm sure your daddy passed plenty of stories down to you."

The sheriff nodded.

"I was reading an article about a woman whose cabin burned up and her along with it."

Delacorte's shoulders had tensed. *Interesting.* "How did you happen upon that?"

"Funny you should ask. Mrs. Waverly had the same question. What I told her was that I went back to the year that Austen Barnette bought Nature's Refuge. I wanted more information about the park."

"Makes sense."

"So why do you think somebody cut the article about the woman in the burned cabin out of the paper? And somebody else put it back?"

The sheriff shrugged.

Adam watched the man carefully as he continued, "Well, I got to thinking about our earlier talk. You told me about a woman who was murdered around the same time. And I was wondering how many women could die violently around here in a cabin at the edge of the swamp."

Delacorte recrossed his legs again but didn't speak.

"Are they the same case?" Adam asked.

"Yeah. They are."

"So the newspaper article was really about the murder?"

"That's right."

"The story attributed her death to a faulty heater."

"That was the official explanation."

"But?" Adam asked, never taking his attention off the sheriff's face.

"A mob went after her."

"Why?"

"People came to her for herbal remedies. She was said to have special powers with healing. Then a little boy she treated died."

"Oh yeah?"

"Probably he would have died anyway. My guess is he had a heart defect. But the mob blamed this woman."

"Jenna Foster. Her name was in the article. That was about all—besides the faulty heater story—to cover up a murder . . ." Adam qualified, ". . . when your daddy was sheriff."

"That's right." Delacorte's eyes blazed with anger. "He was in the pocket of the white folks that run this town. That was how he made his decisions. I'm not proud of that. And I haven't continued the tradition."

"Probably there are white folks here who expect you to," Adam said, keeping his own voice mild.

"I've already showed them it's not gonna happen. I've made arrests my daddy never would have made. And the legal system has gotten convictions." Delacorte's expression was fierce. "You want the details?"

"I'll take your word for it."

"Appreciate it."

They were both silent for several moments.

It was Adam who spoke first. "Well, you told me right off it was a murder."

"Yeah. And if I knew who killed her, I'd go after him."

"It's a pretty cold case."

Delacorte nodded tightly.

While the lawman was in a talkative mood, Adam pushed for more information. "Did her cabin really burn?"

"Yes. But the owner built it back up again."

"The owner is?"

"Austen Barnette."

The answer sent a tingle of sensation along Adam's arm. "That's interesting."

"He rents the place out." Delacorte paused for emphasis. "Right now Granville Pharmaceuticals has the lease."

As Adam absorbed that, along with the tight lines of the other man's face, his mind made connections. "The cabin where Sara lives?" he asked, his voice low and gritty.

"Yeah. So there could be a couple of other reasons for someone going after her. It could have to do with the location. Or it could have to do with Barnette."

"I thought everybody in town loved Barnette. Didn't he make Nature's Refuge into a major attraction, which brings in wads of tourist dollars?"

"That's true, of course. A lot of folks are grateful to him. But you can't be the big fish in a little pond without gathering some algae. He's had problems over the years.

He's done things for the community like build the library and the recreation center. But he insisted on having a say in the staffing of both of them. Some folks don't appreciate that."

"He picked me to run Nature's Refuge," Adam pointed out.

"The difference is, he owns this place."

The silence between the two men stretched again. Adam was thinking that it might not make a difference who owned the park. Some people were probably pissed off that the job of head ranger hadn't gone to a local guy. Like Ken White, for example. Who'd been born and raised in Wayland and knew the Olakompa from childhood.

He pulled his mind away from his own problems and back to the long ago murder. "There was mention of a little girl. What happened to her?"

"She disappeared."

"You think she died in the fire? In the swamp?"

"Her body was never found. My daddy said that someone might have gotten her out of harm's way. Maybe arranged an adoption out of state when the smoke had cleared, so to speak."

"Who would have done that?"

"Jenna Foster wasn't married. But she had a daughter. The child's father could have rescued her."

"And that would be?"

"Whoever he was, he kept it a secret."

Adam absorbed that new detail, his own speculations taking wild leaps. "You think he's still alive?"

"Why do you ask?"

"I told you, I like to walk around the area at night. I was over by Sara's place, and I saw a guy hanging around there."

"A guy. Young? Old?"

"The best I can say is that he was agile. He got away from me."

"I guess I should put some patrols on the house."

"I'd appreciate it."

"Personally?"

"Yeah," Adam answered, his voice tight. He didn't want to talk about his relationship with Sara. If he had a relationship with her. He couldn't be sure of that. He was the one who had walked out the door last night.

Delacorte stood up, and Adam thought the interview might be over. But after walking to a tupelo tree several yards away, he turned and came back to the seating area. He stood rocking on his heals, and Adam felt his heart start to pound. Delacorte had more to say. Something important. But it was obvious he was pretty uncomfortable about spitting it out.

CHAPTER
FOURTEEN

ADAM WATCHED THE sheriff's throat work. "You look about as comfortable as a long-tailed cat in a room full of rocking chairs," he observed.

Delacorte laughed. "Where did you pick up that country expression, boy?"

"Texas."

"Right. They've got some fine southern traditions in Texas. So do we. Like persecution of people. But I'm not just talkin' about the Ku Klux Klan lynching uppity blacks."

"What are you talking about?"

Delacorte hesitated a beat before answering. "Going after people who have . . . talents that are out of the ordinary."

"I think you're going to have to be a little more direct here," Adam muttered.

"Okay. I'm talking about the line in the bible that says, 'Thou shalt not suffer a witch to live.' "

The way Delacorte said the word made goose bumps

rise on Adam's arms. "Witches? Like Wiccans?"

Delacorte stuck out his jaw. "No. Like evil old hags who go off by themselves in the swamp under a witching moon and cast spells that hurt people."

"You don't believe in that stuff, do you?"

"Some people around here do. That's why they burned up the herb lady."

"She was an old hag?"

"No. But she had . . . powers."

Adam made an exasperated sound. "An herb lady. That doesn't sound so unusual."

Delacorte ran a hand over the tight curls that covered his head. "Boy, you're not listening. Right, that doesn't sound so strange. But I heard tell she could lay her hands on you and figure out what was wrong."

"You said they killed her because she made a mistake."

"Look, I'm just telling you the town legends. I never saw any of this stuff myself. One story I heard was about an old man. Old Man Levering. He was supposed to have the evil eye. He could put a hex on you if he didn't like you."

Adam managed a nervous laugh. "You believe that crap?"

"It doesn't matter if I believe it. People in town believed it. And I'm not just talking about the black folks being into powerful superstitions. Everybody talked about Old Man Levering and a woman named Mrs. Gambrills, who had spells, and when she woke up she could tell you stuff that was going to happen. Like if you were going to get yourself eaten by a gator. Her daughter Emily could . . . could make things move without touching them."

Adam stared at the man. It was obvious that he'd heard stories of these people—and other "witches"—since childhood. And he believed them. And at the same time, he was embarrassed to be telling this to a stranger, someone who had lived in Wayland for only a few months.

Jesus, suppose he found out that the stranger liked to go off into the swamp and turned himself into a wolf?

He struggled to hold his voice steady as he asked, "You say there used to be people in town who could do this stuff. What happened to them?"

"What usually happens to witches! Like in the middle ages. Or Salem, Massachusetts. Over the years the regular folks would gang up on them and kill them. The last one was the lady who was burned up in her house. The rest of them cleared out."

Adam stared at him, trying to take it in, trying to read between the lines.

"So you're saying that the problems in town now are somehow related to what happened in the past?"

"That's what I'm thinking."

"But the . . . um . . . the witches cleared out."

"I think some of them are back," Delacorte said, his voice going thick with an emotion that sounded pretty close to fear. "And they're angry about what happened to their daddies and mommas."

"And what do you base that on?" Adam demanded.

"To start with . . . Ken White's death."

"He was shot to death."

"That's what people think," the sheriff said.

"And you're saying it's not true?" Adam felt the hairs on the back of his neck stir. "What do you think happened to him?"

"The autopsy report said he died of a heart attack. He was shot after he died."

Adam struggled to take that in. "What are you trying to tell me?"

"That he was scared to death. Or that somebody hexed him to death. I don't know how else to say it."

"Then why shoot him?"

"Hell, I don't know. To make it look like a conventional murder, so they wouldn't be found out? Or maybe the witches thought they weren't strong enough to kill him with mind power, so they brought along a gun."

"Or it was the other way around. He was trying to hex someone to death. And they shot him."

Delacorte looked doubtful.

"You don't think so?"

"I knew Ken White all my life. He was a pretty stick-in-the-mud kind of guy. I don't see him as the witch type."

"He might have been hiding it. According to you, being a witch around here is dangerous."

The sheriff nodded.

Adam was ready with another question. "Why didn't you tell me any of this choice information when I first got to town? Or when we had our little chat the other day?"

Delacorte gave him a direct look. "At first I was thinkin' there was no point in bad-mouthing Wayland unless you were going to stay."

"That comes from loyalty to the town?"

Delacorte scuffed his shoe against the ground. "I was born here. I grew up here. I have a responsibility to these people."

"Including lying to outsiders?"

"I wasn't lying to you."

"Not in so many words, but by omission."

"Well, now I'm telling you what I know. And I expect you to do the same."

"I have. I told you about the sex and drug party in the swamp."

"Uh . . . you mentioned drugs. You didn't say anything about sex."

Now it was Adam's turn to be embarrassed. "Yeah, well that was part of it."

"A witches' sabbath."

"Oh, come on!"

"On the night of the full moon."

"The witches around here did that kind of stuff?"

"Maybe."

"Would they hold a grudge against Sara because she's living in that cabin?"

"Maybe."

"Okay, so the witches could be nosing around her place, because that's where one of them died. Or maybe it's the other way around. Somebody from town is going after people connected with the witches. And since she's in the cabin, she makes a convenient target." He fixed the sheriff with a piercing look. "So, are you going to give me a scorecard?"

"What do you mean?"

"Like who are the families who went after the witches? And who are the witches?"

The sheriff's gaze turned inward. "I'm checking out potential witches. As for the others . . ." He shrugged. "My father didn't keep records on stuff like that."

"Too bad," Adam muttered, wondering if it were true. Delacorte claimed he was coming clean on the "witch problem." But apparently he was only prepared to go so far.

"Are you willing to talk about Barnette?"

"Sure."

"Why do you think he bought Nature's Refuge?"

"I think he wanted to show his faith in the town. I think he wanted to provide a source of income for people around here."

"Or atone for what happened at the cabin, since he owned it?"

"That could be part of it." The sheriff took a step back.

Adam stood up. "I've got one more question before you leave."

Delacorte quirked an eyebrow.

"Something I found in the swamp. Why don't we go

inside and have a look at it." He kicked off his muddy
boots, then stepped inside. Aware that the sheriff was
staying several paces behind him, he went to the dresser
where he'd put away the square of fabric with the herbs
and chicken feathers and black gunk. The whole thing was
inside a plastic bag. He brought it out and set it on the
table, then extracted the cloth and the herbs.

When he looked up, he saw Delacorte staring intently
at the contents of the bag.

"So, did the witches leave this as a calling card?" he
asked. "Does it have something to do with the herb lady
who was burned up?"

The sheriff reached out and touched a sage leaf, which
crumbled along the edge where his finger brushed it.
"That's a charm people used to ward off evil. I remember
my granny making something like this," he said, his voice
thick.

"Like a voodoo gris-gris?"

Delacorte gave him a considering look. "You know
about that stuff?"

"I've read about it."

"I guess this could go back to African traditions."

"But I take it you didn't leave it out in the park?"

Delacorte snorted. "Not likely. I don't protect myself
with charms and spells. I don't believe in stuff like that."

But he did believe in the witches. Interesting.

As Delacorte ambled off, Adam propped his shoulder
against a pine tree thinking about the campfire in the
swamp. The drugging smoke. The naked figures who had
come after him with murder in their eyes.

He'd thought they'd shot at him. Had that only been
an illusion? What if it hadn't really been a shot fired from
a gun. What if it had been some kind of mental energy
bolt? And his mind had put it into conventional terms?

He pondered that question for long minutes. It was a
strange line of thought. Maybe he could go back to the

firepit and look for bullets embedded in trees. Yeah, sure, when he had the time.

He shook his head. Instead of worrying about witches hurling thunderbolts, he'd better go check up on his staff. But first, he'd better get cleaned up before he scared away the tourists.

BY brute force, Sara managed to work most of the morning. Although she spent minutes at a time staring off into space, she was able to make several more plant extracts and start checking their antibacterial properties.

But she'd awakened with a trace of the headache that had stabbed into her brain the evening before. And as the day wore on, it grew steadily worse.

She took an over-the-counter remedy, but it didn't help. Finally, after picking at the salmon salad she'd fixed for lunch, she stuck her bowl in the refrigerator and put the spoons and fork she'd used into a pan of soapy water.

The throbbing in her head had made it impossible to eat. Now it was coming in waves that seemed to beat with the pulse in her temple.

Her fingers clamped onto the edge of the drain board in a death grip. She stood there, unmoving, willing the agony out of her head, picturing it leaving her body and flowing away from her, as if the force of her will could really accomplish that goal.

To her surprise, the technique seemed to work. Thinking she might as well wash the dishes, she lowered her gaze to the pan of water in the bottom of the sink.

What she saw made her gasp. Small waves were rippling across the surface of the water, pulsing like the waves of pain that had been in her head.

She froze in place, staring at the liquid in motion.

Her first thought was that the wind was blowing it. But when she looked at the trees outside the window, they were perfectly still, the Spanish moss hanging limp and gray.

It took a tremendous amount of effort, but she lifted her hand, then thrust it into the water. The waves didn't stop, they beat gently against her skin, each little ripple hitting like a small electric shock as it brushed against her flesh.

The strange feeling raised the fine hair on her arm, the sensation traveling upward to the back of her neck.

She had struggled to force away her headache. It looked, felt like she had thrust it from her body and into the pan of water. Lord, was that possible?

She made a small sound in her throat. She wanted to tell herself that nothing like that had happened to her before. But that would be a lie. She could remember times when she'd done it. Well, she hadn't seen anything like this rippling water. But she remembered willing hurt away. Like the time when she was ten and she'd been riding her bike and hit a patch of gravel. The bike had tipped over, sending her sprawling, her leg badly abraded by the rough surface. She'd known she had to get home. And she'd thought the burning in her leg was so bad that she couldn't walk the three blocks. But she'd gritted her teeth and forced the pain away. Somehow it had worked, at least until she'd staggered into the kitchen and into Mom's arms.

There had been another time, too. When Dad had been driving them home from a movie, and a station wagon had plowed into the rear of the car. She'd been sitting in the back without a seat belt, and she'd been slammed forward so hard that she'd dislocated her shoulder.

The agony had been almost more than she could bear. Even moving a quarter of an inch had made her feel like she was going to faint. But somehow she'd forced the terrible sensation away long enough for the emergency room staff to give her IV painkillers, so they could put the shoulder back into place. She had never really thought much about what she'd done on those occasions.

But now the previous experiences came back to her with a kind of sharp clarity that gave them elevated meaning.

She had done it again—today. But now there was a visual component, too.

The water. The ache had moved from her head into the liquid medium in front of her.

On the face of it, that idea was nonsense. Yet on some deep level of self-awareness, she knew it was true. And the realization was frightening. Her heart was pounding as she reached with both hands, seized the edge of the wash pan and flung it over, sloshing the water onto the wall and into the sink, pouring away the evidence, as it were.

A film of perspiration coated her clammy flesh. She had never fainted in her life, but she had a good idea what the sensation must be like. Taking shallow breaths, she leaned over the sink and squeezed her eyes shut, telling herself a pan of water wasn't evidence of anything—when she knew she was lying to herself.

Finally, she raised her gaze to the window and stared outside, her eyes unfocused. She wasn't sure how long she stood there, trying to make sense of something that she couldn't fathom. Or didn't want to fathom, she silently corrected herself.

Then a stirring in the bushes caught her attention. The movement resolved itself into the figure of a man.

Adam! It flashed into her mind that she'd been unconsciously waiting for him to come back.

When she saw it wasn't him, disappointment and relief surged through her.

Then her mind took another leap to the night before, to

the pickup truck and the people who had warned her moments before the truck came bearing down on her.

Were they stalking her here? At the cabin where she lived?

CHAPTER
FIFTEEN

SARA BLINKED AS details resolved themselves into a recognizable figure. She was staring at the person she now thought of as the blackberry man, poking around in the bushes. He had his basket with him, but he kept glancing toward the cabin, like he was hoping she would come out. Or that she wouldn't! She couldn't tell which.

Maybe this was his regular berry picking area. He hadn't spoken to her since their first encounter, but she'd seen him lurking in the underbrush several times. What was he doing here? Watching out for her? Or looking for trouble?

She wiped her hands on the thighs of her jeans, glad to have something besides the rippling water or Adam Marshall to occupy her mind. Purposefully, she crossed the small living room, then stepped outside and strode toward the man.

He went still for a moment as he saw her, then pulled himself up straighter. The basket in his hand bobbled. He steadied it, before holding it out toward her. "I brought you a present," he said.

She goggled at him, then shifted her gaze to the plants. She saw hairy, divided leaves, long stems, and knobby rhizomes.

"Cranebill or wild geranium," he said. "The leaves are used as a mild astringent, but it's the rhizomes that have the most potency."

"I know," she murmured, wondering how he had come by the knowledge.

"I thought you might want to use it in your project. And you'd have to go wading through the swamp to get to where it grows."

"I appreciate your bringing it to me," she said, thinking that the words weren't exactly true. This guy made her nervous.

He gave her a small nod. "I can bring you other stuff. Like mock pennyroyal."

She called up her mental files on that member of the mint family. "I thought that only grew in dry soil."

"That's right. So you might not be looking for it around here. But it grows on higher patches, where the water can't reach it."

She nodded, thinking that the stuff was supposed to be good for digestion and headache, although she'd never actually used it.

He thrust the basket toward her, and she took it to prevent an awkward moment.

"How did you get interested in medicinal herbs?" he asked.

She cast her thoughts back, carefully considered the question. Actually, she couldn't remember when plants hadn't been part of her life. Mom had loved gardening, and she'd asked if they could have some herbs. They'd planted them together. Mom had used them for cooking.

And she'd treated her dolls with the medicinal ones. Somehow she'd always known that foxglove was for heart problems, and witch hazel was good for insect bites.

Now she shrugged. "I guess I've been interested in them since I was a little girl. Then when I was old enough, I got books out of the library."

He nodded.

"What about you?"

"What do you mean, what about me?"

"You seem to know something about the subject."

"I studied up on them."

He looked like he might say something else. But she heard the sound of a car engine.

Again she thought of the night before. The guy in the pickup had missed her last time, and now he was back. She whirled to see a large black limousine coming majestically up the road.

A limo. Along the edge of the swamp? Some rich guy out slumming? Or picking blackberries?

The windows were dark, and she had no idea who was inside looking out at her.

She expected the vehicle to go on by her modest cabin. But it glided smoothly to a halt.

"Who could that be?" she asked the man she'd been talking to. When he didn't answer, she swivelled to look at him. But he'd slipped silently away.

She scanned the underbrush and thought she caught a flash of his yellow shirt. But it disappeared almost as soon as she saw it.

Behind her, the limo door opened, and she whirled toward the sound.

The driver had gotten out. He was a black man, dressed in a white shirt and a dark suit.

"Dr. Weston?" he asked politely.

"I'm Sara Weston."

"My name is James. I work for Mr. Barnette."

The owner of Nature's Refuge. "What does he want?" she asked.

"He wishes to speak to you," the driver said. He looked pressed and polished, while she was dressed in dirt-streaked jeans and a limp T-shirt.

"When?"

"Now."

Her hands fluttered at her sides. "I can't go like this."

"Mr. Barnette said for me to fetch you."

She glanced back toward the house. "Well, he should have given me some warning."

James shrugged. "Mr. Barnette is used to getting what he wants, when he wants it."

"All right. Give me twenty minutes." She didn't wait for permission. Instead she dashed into the house and skidded to a stop in the bedroom. After grimacing at her reflection, she settled for the fastest shower on record, then gave her naturally wavy hair a quick blow dry before pulling on one of the few dresses she'd brought to Wayland. It was a simple, black, sleeveless cotton knit, which she topped with a black-and-white camp shirt. She hesitated over panty hose, then shrugged and shoved her feet into a decent pair of sandals. A little lipstick and blusher completed her preparations. In twenty minutes she hadn't exactly turned herself into someone who looked like a Ph.D. botanist. But it was the best she could do.

James was waiting in one of the rustic porch chairs that had come with the house. He climbed quickly to his feet when she came back out. She had her briefcase with her and some of the notes she'd been taking, so at least she could talk about some of the plants she'd started testing.

She'd never ridden in the back seat of a limousine. But she tried to relax as James turned the car around and re-traced his path up the narrow road.

Now she was wondering if she should she have paid her respects to Barnette when she first arrived in Wayland.

But she hadn't thought he'd necessarily want to be involved with her.

They swung in between brick gateposts and rode up a curving drive through manicured green lawns toward an enormous red brick mansion with a two-story portico.

It was strange to think that one person lived in a house this big. From the driveway, it looked like her parents' entire house could fit inside the detached four-car garage with room to spare.

The interior was dimly lit and opulent. She didn't know much about fine furniture and fabric, but she suspected that everything here had been purchased with no regard to cost.

James led her down a hall to the back of the house, into a conservatory that would have done the Czar of Russia proud. The floor was flagstones. And the roof was high enough to accommodate several thirty-foot palm and ficus trees.

They crossed a small stream bordered by more tropical foliage and flowering plants to a round patio nestled among pots of blooming azaleas. She'd never seen anything like it except in the Botanical Gardens in Washington, D.C.

If Barnette was trying to impress her with his wealth, he'd done it.

The man himself sat in an old-fashioned wicker rocking chair. She would have guessed his age at somewhere between sixty-five and seventy. He had salt-and-pepper hair, wrinkled skin, and piercing blue eyes. He wore a rust-colored sports coat, a beige button down shirt, khaki slacks, and old-fashioned brown-and-white saddle shoes.

"Forgive me for not getting up," he said, as she stepped onto the patio. "My doctor told me I need a couple of knee replacements, but I figure I can get along with the knees God gave me, if I use them judiciously." He looked her up and down. "Thank you for seeing me at such short notice. I'm Austen Barnette."

"Sara Weston," she replied automatically, although he obviously knew who she was. "I'm sorry I didn't stop by when I got to town," she murmured.

"No need. I wanted to wait a few days before we chatted." He gestured toward the chair that sat across a round table from his own. "Make yourself comfortable. James can bring us some iced tea."

She took the seat opposite the old man, trying not to look overwhelmed.

"How are you settling in?" Barnette asked.

"Very well, thanks," she answered automatically, waiting for a question about her work and wondering what she was going to say.

There must have been a serving area near the conservatory. Before the small talk could continue, James was back carrying a silver tray with a pitcher of tea, glasses, and a plate of cookies.

"Molasses cookies," Barnette said. "My weakness."

"I love them, too. My mother used to make them."

He raised his eyes slowly and looked at her. "Which mother?"

She went very still. "I beg your pardon?"

"You were adopted. Are you referring to your birth mother or the mother who raised you?"

Her heart had suddenly started to pound. "How do you know I'm adopted?" she demanded. "And how could that possibly be relevant to . . . to . . . anything?"

Barnette answered calmly. "Everything is relevant in the grand scheme of things. You joined your family when you were four, I believe."

"What about it?"

"Do you remember anything about your life before coming to live with the Westons?"

"No." She took a quick swallow of tea. She'd thought

the cookies looked good. Now the smell of them made her stomach turn because she realized that Barnette had brought her here to ask nosy questions.

"I can see you bonded with your new parents. Your loyalty to them is commendable. But I wouldn't have approved you to work in Nature's Refuge unless I knew your background. I wanted to make sure you were a responsible person who wouldn't go around destroying my property."

She struggled to keep her voice level, but she could hear it rising. "You don't think my educational record was indicative? The references from my professors? The reports from my internships?"

He took a swallow of tea and leaned back in his chair. "I took all of those into consideration, of course. But I've nurtured Nature's Refuge for twenty-five years. I wasn't going to let Granville Pharmaceuticals bring in somebody whose background I didn't know."

Lord, had he sent an investigator to poke into her personal life? She was thinking that he'd given her the perfect excuse to pack up and leave—with the way he'd invaded her privacy. She opened her mouth to say something scathing, then thought better of acting rashly.

"I thought you were perfect for the job," he was saying.

Wondering if she could believe him now, she managed a small nod.

He made a quick change of subject. "I was distressed to hear that you had a bit of trouble in town last night."

"You're referring to the pickup truck that almost plowed into me on Main Street?"

"Yes. And it seems that my head ranger saved the day."

She nodded. Right. All he knew was what people had seen. He didn't know about the voices in her head, and she certainly wasn't going to blab about those.

Or had Adam told him? Was that the reason for this interview—to evaluate her sanity. She fought off a sudden sick feeling in her throat. She had talked to Adam about the incident in confidence. He wouldn't have said anything, she assured herself. He wouldn't go spilling her secrets. Would he? Suddenly, the need to talk to him about her frightened confession last night was like a terrible pressure building up in her chest.

She wanted to stand up and leave. She wanted to go to Adam. But she couldn't simply walk out of here. And she couldn't come across as unstable or impulsive. She reminded herself that Austen Barnette wielded a tremendous amount of power in Wayland. She needed to understand what he wanted from her and deal with it.

"You think somebody wants me out of town?" she asked, keeping her gaze level.

"I hope not," he answered. "Because I'm looking forward to the completion of your research. How is that getting along?

"Very well," she told him, "I was so pleased to find *Impatiens capensis* in the park." With the introduction of the subject, she launched into a long, boring discussion of how an extract from the plant might be the next great cure for poison ivy.

She was pleased to see her companion's eyes glazing over. She loved plants. And she loved nature. But she'd learned in graduate school how to write papers that would satisfy her most pedantic professors. She thought the old man was on the way to falling asleep when he sat up straighter. "I'm glad we had this little chat," he said.

"Oh, so am I," she answered, the words almost sticking in her throat.

"You probably want to get back to work."

"Of course." Recognizing the tone of dismissal, she rose and picked up her briefcase "Thank you for inviting me to tea."

She crossed the conservatory, then walked rapidly into

the hall, intending to go straight to Nature's Refuge. To Adam.

Then she remembered that she had come here in a large black limo. No, she'd better go home first and get her own car.

THE day's attendance had been good, Adam thought as he looked at the pile of entrance receipts. There had been over three hundred admission tickets sold. And thirty boat rides into the swamp.

Maybe that wasn't spectacular by Walt Disney standards. But it was quite good for a small natural preserve in rural Georgia.

The crowds had cleared out, because the park closed early on Wednesday. The staff had left, and Adam was filing some forms when he looked up and saw a woman standing in the doorway.

She was blond and nicely shaped, and as she stood backlighted by the afternoon sunlight, he felt his heart leap.

Sara.

Then she stepped into the room, and he realized she was someone else, wearing shorts that hardly reached her crotch and a skinny little knit top with pencil thin straps and a bottom edge that left three inches of skin exposed around her middle. She wasn't wearing a bra, and her nipples were standing up behind the orange knit fabric.

She was dressed to attract male attention, and he responded the way his hormones had programed him to respond. He felt his body tighten as he looked from her long legs to her erect nipples to her carefully painted lips.

"Can I help you?" he asked in a gritty voice.

She slid her own gaze up and down his body with a proprietary air, and he knew she was well aware of the effect she was having on him.

He closed the file drawer and forced himself not to shift his weight from one foot to the other like a sophomore in high school being eyed by one of the "fast" senior girls.

"I'm looking for Adam Marshall."

"The park is closed. Didn't you see the sign?"

"The gate was open."

Oh yeah? Someone on the staff was going to explain that to him tomorrow morning. "I'm Ranger Marshall," he answered, using his title like a sort of shield.

"Well, that's wonderful. I'm so glad I found you. I'm interested in a boat tour."

"I'm sorry. The park is closed," he repeated, keeping his tone even.

She tipped her head to one side and thrust her chest toward him. "Can't you make an exception for me?"

"I'm afraid not. We have our rules," he managed to say.

She wore no perfume, but her scent was strong. It was as though she hadn't washed her crotch that morning. And the heat from her body was wafting the evidence of her arousal toward him. He tried to take shallow breaths, but it wasn't doing much good. Even a normal man would have to react to that raw female scent. And he was no normal man. He was a werewolf, and even in human form he was caught in the sensual web of that tantalizing aroma.

He saw her lips moving, and her words came to him over the buzzing in his brain.

"Oh. That's too bad." She took a step into the room, looking like she wasn't all that upset.

"So this is the Nature's Refuge office. It's a bit primitive, isn't it?" she asked, eyeing the scarred wooden desk and the battered metal filing cabinets.

"We're not going for the designer look," Adam answered as he took in the predatory gleam in her eye. The frank sexual interest.

Most women were more subtle. But he had the feeling she was planning to crowd him into a corner. Crowd him—and more.

And from his vantage point this encounter had the feeling of a trap closing around him.

He didn't know why the trap image sprang to his mind. He only knew it was strong and vivid.

To get out of the confined space, he came around the desk, stepping closer to her so that she'd have to back up. She held her ground.

"I've heard how sexy you are. I thought I'd find out about that for myself."

"I thought you came for a boat ride."

"Well, since that attraction's closed, maybe we can move on to another one."

SARA stopped at the entrance to the park and read the sign that announced the hours. It was ten after five. And the listing said that closing time on Wednesday was five.

The gate was open. But normally, she'd just turn around and go back. Today she needed to talk to Adam, so she drove through and headed toward a cluster of buildings she could see in the distance.

She'd collected some of her plants from the wild, unkempt expanse of the swamp, but she'd never been in the areas that were maintained for the public. When she'd come in the back way, she'd driven over a narrow gravel track. The road leading from the front entrance was two lanes and paved with macadam. To keep it from flooding, it was built up above the level of the swamp.

The drive ended in a rectangular paved area divided into sections by garden ties.

Natural looking, weed-free garden beds bloomed with an assortment of cultivated annuals and perennials interspersed with plants native to the Olakompa. Most of the indigenous plants were labeled with small signs giving their common and Latin names. A nice touch, she thought. The buildings clustered on the other side of the almost empty parking area were either log cabins or simple wood structures painted dark brown.

It was all tidy and well-kept, with a notable absence of trash on the ground. The state of the park spoke well for Adam Marshall. Apparently he ran a tight ship. And he knew how to make a natural area attractive for visitors.

A sign pointed to the office. Getting out of her car, she walked up a short path toward the building—then froze as she saw Adam and a woman standing just inside the door.

THE woman stroked her forefinger along Adam's upper arm, dipping under the edge of his green uniform shirt. The touch of that one finger sent a ripple of reaction through him.

She was well aware of her female power because she smiled and gave him a smoldering look from beneath lowered lashes as she took a step back into the reception area. He followed, pulled toward this uninhibited woman. A buzzing had started in his brain. Probably the result of lack of blood in the upper part of his body.

Last night with Sara, he'd been aroused and achingly ready for sex before he'd wrenched himself away. He'd run from her cabin before he could rip off her clothing and throw her to the floor. Now here was another woman frankly offering herself to him.

"Sugar, we're going to be very, very good together," she purred. "You and me, we're the same kind."

He didn't answer. He didn't understand what she meant. Was she trying to tell him she was a werewolf? His fuzzy brain struggled to wrap itself around that idea. As far as he knew, there were only male werewolves. But maybe she was something new to his experience.

She touched him again. This time her hand stroked across his chest and slipped open one of the uniform buttons so that she could caress the heated flesh beneath.

Plenty of women had come on to him before. But never quite so explicitly, so shamelessly.

She was like a bitch in heat, and the wolf part of his nature was responding with an animal force.

He drew in a sharp, painful breath, and she answered him silently by sliding her tongue across her lower lip.

He watched that erotic pink tongue, mesmerized by the slow, enticing motion. And when she opened her mouth and repeated the provocative action along the edges of her even white teeth, he made a low, helpless sound in his throat.

She reached for his hand, lifting it to her breast, stroking his fingers back and forth across the crest of one taut nipple through the knit fabric of her top. "Harder, do that harder," she whispered.

Somehow the sound of her voice released him from the spell. Or perhaps some dark, primitive god had taken mercy on him. His hand dropped away, and he stood there staring at her. He'd been hard and hot.

Suddenly, he was limp and cold and wondering how he could have thought he wanted to fuck this woman.

There was only one woman he wanted, and it was Sara Weston. "I'm sorry," he muttered.

"You want the same thing I do."

"No."

She took a step back, looking him up and down, taking in his rigid stance and the obvious fact that the erection she'd seen straining behind the fly of his jeans was no longer in evidence.

Perhaps she hadn't believed his verbal denial. But she believed that his body had stopped responding to her.

Anger flared in her eyes as she reached out to stab a

stiffened finger into his chest. "You'll be real sorry you turned me down."

"Don't count on it," he shot back.

"Smart ass." Her eyes narrowed, her face contorted, and he felt a sudden pain in the pit of his stomach. It was as if her anger had a physical force that had him grabbing the doorjamb to stay on his feet.

CHAPTER
SIXTEEN

ADAM FELT MISS Sexpot brush past him, then watched her surge out of the office and march toward the parking lot.

His eyes widened as he saw Sara coming toward her from the parking lot.

The seductress stopped in her tracks, raising her chin defiantly.

"Oh perfect. You! What was I doing, getting him ready to fuck you?" The sharp words rang out in the afternoon silence like a war cry. The fury he'd felt directed at him suddenly had another focus.

"Sara," Adam shouted. "Watch out."

He didn't know what he was warning her about. He only knew that under that flaming hot exterior, the blonde in Sara's path was dangerous.

There was a charged moment when the two women stood in silence facing each other.

The seductress balled her hands into fists and jammed

them against her hips, looking like a street fighter daring a rival to take another step.

Sara went very still, her arms loosely at her sides and her eyes questioning, as though she had no idea what to make of the challenge.

There were several seconds of dead calm. Of utter silence. Even the birds that normally sang in the trees went silent.

Then five doves flapped away, their wings beating the air in a frantic bid to escape. From what?

They had barely cleared the tall pine at the edge of the parking lot when the sky darkened as though a storm were rapidly overtaking them.

Moments ago, Adam had seen no clouds. Now they hung low and ominous over Nature's Refuge. As the sky darkened, the wind suddenly rose, shaking the branches of the trees around the parking area, sending up an eerie clatter as twigs and branches rubbed against each other. Leaves and bits of Spanish moss tore loose, flying through the air.

It felt like something supernatural was happening. And from deep inside Adam's mind came the knowledge that he had to protect Sara, but he couldn't make his arms or legs work.

What happened next was hardly supernatural. He watched in a kind of shocked disbelief as the woman on the path marched up to Sara, drew back her fist, and socked her in the stomach.

As she gasped in pain and surprise, the woman dodged around her and dashed to the parking lot.

Seeing Sara doubled over and swaying on her feet released Adam from his trance. Quickly he crossed the few yards that separated them.

She fell into his arms, and they collapsed together onto the mulch beside the path. He cradled her in his embrace, pulled her onto his lap, folding his body around hers as though he could protect her—when he'd already failed to do any such thing.

Dimly he was aware of an engine roaring to life and a car blasting out of the parking area. But his focus was on Sara.

She was shaking. So was he.

"What happened?" he finally asked.

"I don't know," Sara whispered. "I felt so strange. I can't explain it . . . I thought . . ."

"What?"

"I don't know. I felt like the two of us were going to fight. But not physically. A fight where nobody else could see what was going on. Like with those voices last night." She gave a helpless shrug, lowering her head to his shoulder, pressing her face into the fabric of his uniform shirt.

"Who is she?"

"Hell if I know."

"You two looked pretty friendly."

He made a helpless gesture. "She walked in here and came after me. Maybe somebody dared her to get it on with the new park ranger," he clipped out, hoping Sara would drop the subject. He didn't want to think about the woman who had come here with seduction on her mind. He only wanted to focus on the woman in his arms.

He stroked his hand tenderly over her hair, her shoulders, feeling some of the tension go out of her. Still, when she lifted her head again, the troubled look on her face tore at him. "Okay, forget her. You're sure I'm not going crazy?"

"No!"

"Why not?"

He knew his answer wasn't based on logic, but he gave it anyway. "Because I care about you," he whispered. It was so hard for him to say. Even that much. He'd never told a woman anything that came close to what he'd just said. He'd taken his pleasure with them, and he'd given pleasure in return. But he'd never been compelled to make an emotional connection. Now he felt that compulsion. But he couldn't tell that to Sara. The concept was still too new, too threatening.

She was staring into his eyes, and he was the one who felt stripped naked. If she had secrets, so did he. He couldn't tell her about them, so he rocked her in his arms, his hands soothing up and down her back and across her shoulders.

"You're going to move out here," he heard himself say.

She blinked. "What?"

"I want you where you'll be safe—in the vacant cabin where one of the rangers used to bunk. We keep it ready for visitors, so it's all nice and clean." She opened her mouth, but he rushed on. "I talked to Delacorte about that damn place where you're living now. A woman was murdered there. She was an herbal healer. A boy she treated died, and a mob went after her."

He heard Sara suck in a sharp breath and let it out before saying, "I think I daydreamed about her."

"About the fire?"

"No. About her living there." She kept her gaze steady on him. "All my life I've felt like I was different. I would . . . see things that weren't really there. And I knew they were true."

"Like what?"

She took another gulping breath. "Sometimes they were things happening in other people's lives. And sometimes I didn't know *what* they were. I didn't want to see them, so I pretended they didn't exist. And finally, they really were hardly there. Or maybe it was that I had trained myself to ignore them. Then . . ." She stopped again and shuddered. "Then I came to Wayland. And right after I moved into that cabin, I went back and stepped into that

woman's shoes for a little while. She had a garden. With
herbs."

His hands gripped her shoulders. "Yeah, well I don't
know why Barnette put you in that damn haunted house,
but I want you somewhere else. I feel like you're a teth-
ered goat out there drawing . . . a predator. And I want
you where I can keep you safe."

Sara made a small, distressed sound. But he kept talking.

"I'd say there's still a lot of interest in that damn place."
He evaluated his options and decided to tell her more of
what he knew. Not all of it, but enough. "Delacorte says
that the woman who lived there wasn't the only person
the town went after. Apparently there were a bunch of
people who lived around here, people with strange . . .
powers. They were persecuted as witches."

She gasped, "Witches!"

He went on quickly, "Delacorte says most them left
town. Or maybe some of them went underground. I don't
know. But he thinks their children have come back to get
even with the community. They could be focused on the
place."

"Witches," she said again. "Are you sure?"

Adam ran a shaky hand through his hair. "I don't know
if it's true. But whether it is or not, there are probably
townspeople who think that living in that cabin makes you
a bad person."

"What are you trying to say?"

"That I saw someone lurking around your house a couple of nights ago."

"Why didn't you tell me about it?"

"I started to last night. Then we got sidetracked. I'm
telling you now. I chased the guy, but he got in his car
and drove away. I don't know who he was. But I'll know
him if I find him in town."

"How?"

"I . . . picked up his scent."

"His scent," she repeated slowly.

"It's a talent I have." He laughed. "You see ghosts, and I smell out trouble."

"Really?"

"Yeah. Maybe that's why the smoke from that fire in the swamp sent me into a tailspin."

She was watching him, taking it in. There was a lot more he could say, but the idea of telling her the rest made his chest constrict. Not yet. Not when he needed to keep her safe.

"I want you to move out here," he said again.

He saw her wedge her lower lip between her teeth. "The last time we were together . . . we . . . about burned up the floorboards under our feet."

He swallowed around the constriction in his throat. "Yeah."

"If I'm out here . . ."

"I'll behave myself."

"How do I know?"

"Because I want you to trust me. That's important to me."

He leaned toward her and brushed his lips against hers. The touch was light, but it sent heat leaping through him. Yesterday he would have acted on the need to shift her in his arms and press her body to his. Yesterday he might have rolled her to her back and come down on top of her. Today he held himself in check, because he needed to prove something to her—and to himself.

Some inner strength he hadn't known he possessed helped him keep the kiss light. It was a unique experience for him, simply savoring her taste and the contrast between what he felt now and what he had felt when Miss Sexpot had come on to him. He didn't have much experience with restraint, but he could see it had its advantages.

Sara made a small sound, and he pressed his lips more firmly to hers, just for a moment before he lifted his head.

"Sara, I promise you that it's going to be fantastic between us . . . when we're both ready."

She looked dazed. He found that very satisfying.

He helped her up, then turned her to him and held her gently, savoring her, savoring feelings he'd never expected to experience.

"Come see the cabin," he said.

"We have to move all my lab stuff."

"We can use the park truck. And there's another vacant building where you can work."

"Are you sure that will be all right with Barnette?"

"It'd better be!"

He led her along a path in back of the public area. "This is where I live," he said, then showed her the other residence which was about fifty yards farther. He'd had his pick of the two places, and he'd chosen his because it was more to his taste.

The door wasn't locked. Neither was the one to his cabin, and he wondered if that ought to change. Pushing open the door, he stepped aside and let her go in first.

In the living room was a sofa, a rocking chair and a rag rug. White curtains hung at the window. A pine table with two chairs sat in front of a kitchen area along one wall. Someone had draped a quilt across the back of the sofa, a small homey touch.

The cabin's other room had a double bed, a chest of drawers, and an armoire instead of a closet. Besides the toilet and sink, the bathroom was big enough for a stall shower.

Not a very impressive refuge to offer Sara.

"It's smaller than where you're living now," he said, keeping his arms pressed to his sides to stop himself from reaching for her. "But it's comfortable."

She turned back to him, and the breath froze in his

lungs as he waited for her to say it wasn't going to work.

What she said was, "You're sure it's okay for me to be here?"

"Perfectly sure. Barnette lets me make the decisions at the park."

"Are you trying to rush me into moving in, before I change my mind?"

"You catch on fast. Come on; let's get your stuff."

He drove the truck to her cabin. She took her own car. On the two-mile drive, he had time to consider what he'd been thinking. The need to protect her had been his primary motivation. But the consequences for him were massive. He wondered how he was going to live near her and keep his hands off her. And he wondered what he was going to do at night, when he needed to roam the park as a wolf. Well, he'd told her he walked around at night. He'd just have to make sure he was deep in the swamp before he changed.

Yeah, but what if she comes into your cabin and finds you eating a hunk of raw meat? How are going to explain that? he asked himself.

STARFLOWER hooked a right onto the dirt road and headed for the meeting place. It was a spot near the swamp where locals sometimes hung out. This evening she could hear rock music blaring from a boom box.

Tonight the music irritated her. But everything had irritated her since the scene at Nature's Refuge.

Adam Marshall had turned her down, despite the power she'd exerted over him—and she'd instantly hated him for that. She could have any man she wanted. But not him. What did he think—that he was too good for her? Then the woman, Sara Weston, had come along and hatred had turned to fear.

Yesterday, when they'd shouted a mental warning at

her, Weston had been confused. She'd seemed weak.

But she hadn't been weak today.

The woman had power. Great power. And it looked like she was learning to use it. She'd called up storm clouds and a wind out of nowhere. Apparently she didn't know what to do with them—yet. If she ever found out—God help anyone who was in the way.

When Falcon had brought Starflower into the group, she'd been excited by the contact. Excited at being with others of her kind. But she'd discovered that wasn't enough.

Falcon was the leader. The strongest man. And so far she was the strongest woman. She liked that position, at the top of the heap. And she didn't want anyone around who could challenge her. Like Sara Weston. Which meant pretty little Dr. Weston had to be eliminated. Her and her boyfriend, Adam Marshall.

He was dangerous, too. And totally expendable, as far as she was concerned. He'd rejected a good thing a few hours ago. And he was going to find out the consequences of that.

Starflower climbed out of her car and eyed the portable CD player. She wanted to tell Falcon to turn off the damn music, but that would give away her mood.

So she kept her simmering hostility to herself.

Her gaze zeroed in on the six-packs of beer sitting in a tub of ice. Tonight she needed a couple.

She'd spent the past several hours thinking of how to put the best possible face on what had happened at Nature's Refuge. She'd worked out a good story, and she was sticking to it. And really, most of it was true. There were just a few little details that she'd changed.

Usually she liked being the center of attention. Not this evening.

"How did it go?" Willow asked, taking in the scanty shorts and top she was wearing.

"Not exactly the way we planned," Starflower tossed off as she walked toward the beer, snatched a can out of the ice and flipped it open. She took several swallows before she turned to face the group.

"He didn't want to get it on with you?" Grizzly asked.

"Of course he did. Then that Sara Weston came along and interrupted us."

"Interrupted how?"

"I had him ready, willing, and able. Then she showed up, and he was embarrassed about getting caught with me."

Of course, that wasn't exactly how it had happened. But she was pretty sure none of the other participants was going to get a chance to revise the story.

In the light from the camp flashlight, she could see Falcon watching her closely. She kept her gaze trained on him.

"So are you saying the park ranger is fixated on her?" he asked.

"Yes. And she's fixated on him, too. She lashed out with her mind and called up a storm when she caught me fooling with him. She was going to fight me for him. Only she didn't quite know how to do it, because she doesn't have anybody to teach her how to use her powers."

"We could teach her," Willow said.

"No!" Starflower caught Falcon's piercing gaze and lowered her voice. "I mean. She's strong. And dangerous. I felt it. Together they make a dangerous pair."

"So how do we deal with them?" Falcon asked.

"I don't think either one of them would work out in the group."

Razorback had been silent until now. "Because she's a rival?" he asked with a knowing smirk.

The question hit too close to home. "Because neither one of them is going to go along with our plans. Because both of them are too locked into the . . . the world of the regular folks in Wayland. They fit into the system. They don't have anything to gain by joining us," she answered. She wasn't going to admit that she'd developed an intense hatred for Sara Weston and Adam Marshall. She wasn't going to explain that her personal plans included making sure they both ended up dead. At least not yet.

Falcon gave her a considering look. "Let's not do anything hasty. I think we ought to wait and see how things develop."

"Just don't wait too long," she said, making the warning low key because she could see that pursuing the subject was only going to reveal too much of her own feelings.

"Let's get back to the fun stuff. I've been waiting to tell you what I have in mind for later this evening. A little raiding party in town that I think you're going to like. But we need to wait until after midnight."

Starflower was only half listening to the plotting session. She couldn't stop thinking about Sara Weston and Adam Marshall. Falcon might want to put off making a decision about them, but the matter was of more urgency to her. The sooner they were eliminated from the face of the earth, the better she was going to feel.

CHAPTER
SEVENTEEN

ADAM SPENT A long restless night, unable to sleep. He knew that a satisfying run into the wild, untamed acres of the park would settle him down. He needed to turn off his human thoughts and submerge his personality into a simpler, more primitive being. He wanted to be a wolf—his only object to stalk prey and satisfy his craving for warm flesh and blood.

But he kept picturing Sara waking up early in the morning and going outside. Sara coming upon a wolf tearing apart a deer, and the image made his blood run cold.

So he tossed in his double bed, and got up early, thinking that running as a man would work off some of his excess energy. It wasn't the same, he conceded as he sped down the access road to the park entrance; then he did another couple of miles along the highway before heading home.

Back in his cabin, he pulled a beef roast out of the refrigerator and hacked off several slices, which he ate raw.

He was in the office early, waiting for the others to arrive, looking at each of his fresh-faced rangers with new eyes. When all the full-time staff had reported in, he called a meeting. The office was too small, so he used the room where they did nature programs for school kids. Moving aside an alligator jaw, he leaned back against the table at the front of the room.

"I want to talk about security," he began, looking at each of the men and women sitting on wooden chairs ranged around him.

"Because there's been some trouble in town?" Rosie Morgan asked.

"You're referring to the truck incident?" Adam responded.

"And the break-in at the historical society," Dwayne Parker added.

"When? What break-in?" Eugene Brody and Lisa Hardin asked, speaking at the same time.

"Last night," Dwayne answered. It was obvious he'd enjoyed dropping that bombshell. "I found out about it because my mom is tight with Mrs. Waverly," he said importantly.

Adam saw Amy Ralston shift in her seat. "Why would anyone break into the historical society?" she asked.

"Who knows? They don't keep any money there."

"Just old books and papers," Rosie said. There were nods of agreement around the room.

"Okay. I didn't know about that," Adam said, thinking he was damn well going to find out what he could—later. "But I am concerned with a breech of security at this facility. Last night, someone came through the gate after hours claiming it was unlocked." He looked toward Eugene, who had the duty of closing up the night before.

He saw the boy blanch. "I locked it," he said.

"Are you sure?"

"Yes."

Adam gave a tight nod. He was inclined to believe the kid. Eugene was a good worker. He was smart and conscientious. And he wanted to get ahead. Adam had been thinking that when he eventually moved on, Eugene would be a good choice to run the park.

"So then we have to assume that someone unlocked the gate after you left." He looked at each of his staffers in turn, thinking that they all had keys to the padlock. Amy was the one who looked the most uncomfortable. What did she have to gain by letting Miss Sexpot onto the grounds?

"If anyone has something to tell me, we can speak in private," he said. "Meanwhile, I have something else to discuss with you."

The staffers waited for what he was going to say.

"I'm sure you're aware that Nature's Refuge is the site of a project being conducted by Dr. Sara Weston for Granville Pharmaceuticals."

There were nods of agreement.

"She's been living and working at a cabin near the back entrance to the grounds."

"The witch house," Rosie murmured.

"What do you know about it?" Adam asked sharply.

She looked down at her hands. "Most people know about it. I mean that's what people call it."

"You know it burned down," he asked, putting the question in pretty bland terms, considering what had happened there.

"Yes."

"So should I assume that everybody in greater Wayland knows about that except Dr. Weston and me?"

"Pretty much everybody," Dwayne answered. "It's hard to rent the place, you know."

"Yeah, well, considering its history, I've determined that living there might not be good for Dr. Weston's health. So I asked her if she wanted to move into the vacant cabin here on the grounds. She accepted the offer. And she's using the old workshop next to the cabin for her plant experiments. So you'll probably see her around. She's got the run of the facility."

"Sure. Okay," Dwayne answered for the group.

Adam went on to discuss work schedules, then went back to his office, closed the door, and made a phone call.

The sheriff picked up on the second ring. "Delacorte here."

"I hear you've had some more trouble in town. At the historical society."

"News travels fast."

"What was taken?"

"I've got Mrs. Waverly working on that. So far, she hasn't told me about anything that sounds valuable."

"Interesting. So what do you think it means?"

"I'd like to know."

They talked for a few more minutes before hanging up. Adam rocked back in his chair, thinking that a wolf he knew was going to pay the society a visit after it got dark.

He thought about going over to Sara's cabin to tell her what had happened downstairs. Then he stopped himself. He wasn't going to charge over there this morning. He was going to give her time to settle in.

SARA knew that Adam was deliberately staying away from her. Did he regret his impulsive invitation to move her to the main grounds of Nature's Refuge? Or was he simply giving her space? she wondered as she arranged her petri dishes on the long tables in the workroom.

She'd spent the morning giving the place a good scrubbing. It was dusty from disuse, but really it was a better place to work than the old cabin.

There was even a utility sink with running water.

As she arranged her equipment, she saw various staffers

going about their duties. But they—and Adam—kept their distance.

In a way she was grateful. At the same time, she was disappointed.

But she held the disappointment in check while she considered her reasons for coming here. Fear had been one of her motivators. She'd never been comfortable at the cabin.

The dark foreboding atmosphere had played a part in that. And now she knew that people were watching the place. She'd felt it, hovering in the background of her consciousness. Adam had confirmed her subliminal impression.

Of course, it could be that the man he'd seen lurking around had only been the blackberry man. But she couldn't count on that. She couldn't even assume that the blackberry man wasn't going to turn from mild to aggressive. If it was him, what was he doing down there at night?

The danger had been a good reason for letting herself be persuaded to move onto the grounds of Nature's Refuge.

But she knew that wasn't her only motivation. The admission brought her back to Adam. She'd wanted to be near him. She'd welcomed the excuse. Even if she wasn't going to tell him.

THE phone rang in the Nature's Refuge office at two in the afternoon.

"This is Austen Barnette," the testy voice on the other end of the line announced.

"Yes, sir." Adam's hand tightened on the phone receiver. He'd been expecting the call, and now he had to deal with it.

"I didn't authorize you to move Sara Weston into a cabin on the park grounds."

"Do you disagree with the decision?" Adam asked, keeping his own tone mild.

"That's not the point. What did she do, come running to you right after she left my house yesterday?"

"I wasn't aware that she was at your home."

"She's in Wayland because Granville approached me about using the park as a research site. I invited her over to find out how she was settling in. She seemed upset about the incident with the pickup truck."

"Almost getting run over could do that to you," Adam answered blandly.

"Why is she at your place?"

"She's not at my place. She's in the vacant cabin on the grounds."

"That's what I meant," the old man snapped.

"She was concerned about the history of the cabin where she was living," Adam said. "And I was concerned, too."

"What do you know about that?" the sharp voice on the other end of the line demanded.

"I know a mob killed a woman there."

"That was years ago!" Barnette said, emphasizing each word.

"Uh huh. But I discovered someone lurking around the place this week."

After several seconds of utter silence, the old man spoke, putting his retroactive stamp of approval on the action Adam had already taken. "You have my permission to do what you think best."

"Thank you, sir," he answered. "Can I do anything else for you?"

"Keep me informed of what's going on at the park."

"Yes, sir. In my monthly report." Adam hung up, wondering how long he was going to hold his present position.

* * *

"DR. Weston?"

Sara looked up from her worktable to see a young, dark-haired woman wearing khaki pants and a ranger shirt standing in the doorway of the shed.

"Yes?"

"I'm Rosie Morgan. Mr. Marshall sent me over to see how you were doing."

"I'm fine. Thanks."

"Do you need anything?"

"No. But I appreciate your asking. This is an excellent work space."

The young woman lingered.

"I love the way the park looks," Sara offered. "The grounds are so well kept. And those plant identification signs are a nice touch."

"Yes. We've had them for a few years. But a lot of them were missing. Mr. Marshall had a bunch of new ones made."

Sara nodded.

"Did you hear about the robbery at the historical society?"

Sara set down the beaker she was holding with a clunk. "No. I didn't know about it."

"Somebody smashed a basement window and got in. But they don't know what was taken."

"Oh. Thanks for telling me," she answered.

"We talked about it at the meeting this morning. And the break-in here, too."

"The break-in?" she echoed, feeling her chest tighten.

"Well, Mr. Marshall said somebody came in after hours."

Sara nodded, pretty sure she knew who that was.

The young woman glanced over her shoulder, then back at Sara. "There's a lot of bad stuff going on in town. Mr.

Marshall said that probably everybody in town knew about it, everyone but you and him."

"Like what?"

Rosie lowered her voice. "Like, some people think the witches are back! There are old-time stories about them. But now people are talking like they're real."

Sara felt the air freeze in her lungs, but she managed to say, "I'd like to hear more about them."

Rosie examined her fingernails. "I shouldn't talk about it. I just thought you ought to know."

"Know what exactly?"

The woman shrugged. "It's good that you're out here now. It's safer here than at that cabin."

Before Sara could ask another question, the woman turned and hurried away. Leaving Sara standing with her heart pounding and wondering why the park staffer had said so much.

IT was after one in the morning, which was perfect for Adam's purposes as he drove through downtown Wayland.

Leaving the business district, he headed for a house he knew was vacant. After pulling around the back of the garage, he cut the engine, then climbed out and sniffed the wind, sniffed for danger.

He was taking a chance. But he wanted to know who had been at the historical society. Slowly he took off his clothing and stood naked in the starlight. After stepping into the darker shadows cast by the house, he began the ancient chant that had been such a familiar part of his life since his teenage years.

The change from man to wolf was painful as always. It would be nice if there were some way to make it easy, he thought as muscles and bones contorted and transformed.

Still, he felt the old familiar exhilaration as he came down on all fours and looked around, sniffing the wind again. He had been born for this. It was his destiny.

He was a creature of the night. At home in his familiar surroundings, he breathed more deeply, suddenly excited by the prospects of the environment. The scents were richer now, more distinct. There was a squirrel in a tree several yards away. Fresh meat.

A very small meal. Hardly worth the effort. And food wasn't his primary concern tonight. He was hunting men. Not to eat them, but to sort them out.

Down the block, a dog suddenly howled. Apparently it had caught the scent of wolf. He trotted off in the opposite direction, keeping to the shadows and heading for the historical society.

SARA looked through the darkness toward Adam's cabin. Earlier there had been a light on inside. Now the place was dark. She'd thought about inviting him to dinner, then decided that was being too forward.

After that, she'd waited for him to come over and see how she was doing. He'd stayed away.

Now he'd probably gone to bed.

The sudden image of herself walking over there in only her nightgown flashed into her mind.

She pressed her shoulders against the back of the chair where she was sitting. Where had that come from? She wasn't the kind of woman to throw herself at a man.

But then, it wouldn't exactly be throwing herself. Adam wanted her. That was pretty clear. Yet he'd backed off. And now maybe he was waiting for her to be the one to make the big move.

Well, she had a good reason for going to his cabin. She wanted to talk to him about the conversation she'd had with Rosie. The woman had brought up the subject of the witches, then run away like she was sorry she'd mentioned it.

That was something she and Adam should discuss. But at one in the morning? she asked herself, unable to hold back a shaky laugh. The laugh turned to a groan. Talking wasn't the real reason she wanted to see him.

The image of herself and Adam alone in the cabin came back to her, sending a hot tremor of chills over her skin. There was no point in lying to herself. She wanted him, the way she'd wanted no other man she could remember. He'd said it would be good between them. She knew it would be. But still, she knew on some instinctual level that she'd be playing with fire. He'd brought her here to keep her out of danger. Danger outside the park. But he was the danger close at hand.

ADAM waited a long time before emerging from behind a monument in the cemetery next to the old church that now housed the historical society. Most of his wolf expeditions had been in open country. Being surrounded by the trappings of civilization made him nervous.

Probably he was responding to some primitive animal instinct, he thought as he moved from gravestone to gravestone, then slowly approached the building. He'd heard that the break-in had been through a basement window. He stopped when he got to the boarded up rectangle and drank in a long draft of air.

There were many human scents mingled together. He could distinguish men and women. The men smelled more raw. The women had a dainty aura that always called to him. Some were people he had met in town. Others he didn't recognize.

He got a near-choking draft of Mrs. Waverly's perfume. What had the woman done—crawled through the window on an inspection mission? Or was she the one who had broken into her own precious building, to make it look like something had been stolen?

SARA had just changed into her nightgown when a sense of overwhelming danger closed in on her, choking off her breath. She staggered back, hitting her shoulder against the bedroom armoire, then sprang away, gasping, trying to fill her lungs with air.

Something bad was outside in the night. But it wasn't coming for her. Somehow she knew Adam was in danger.

Not here at the park, but in Wayland. Downtown. Outside an old stone building that shimmered in the vision of her mind. A church that looked dark and forbidding. And ominous.

She reached out and grabbed the bathroom door frame, her fingers digging into the vertical surface. Somehow she was able to ground herself, to ease the tight, sick feeling in her chest. Just a little. Just enough to keep herself from fainting.

A flicker of movement at the edge of his vision startled the wolf, and he whirled. But there was nothing there.

Well, not exactly nothing. He caught the ghost of a shadow image just below the level of his vision. A shadow he could see and yet couldn't see at all. It was something completely beyond the realm of his experience. A phantom image with no scent. No substance. Yet it raised the wolf hairs along his spine.

Not *it*.

Them. Watching him.

He went very still, trying to bring them into focus. But he simply couldn't do it. And then he didn't know if he had made the whole thing up because he already felt like he was treading on broken glass.

He shook his head. This was no illusion. He felt something at the edge of his consciousness where he couldn't reach it.

He didn't like the sensation. And the wolf in him wanted to turn and run away before it was too late. But the man inside the wolf forced him to stay where he was and gather what information he could. He went back to what he was able to detect with his sense of smell.

Paul Delacorte had been here. Of course, the sheriff had been investigating the break-in. And a whole crowd had apparently come by to goggle at the broken window.

Another individual leaped out at him. Miss Sexpot, the woman who had appeared yesterday at the park office and tried to get into his pants. He'd been halfway toward fucking her when thoughts of Sara had stopped him.

Her scent was mixed with a bunch of others, male and female. Because he had been so intimately involved with her, she stood out to him, although her presence here proved nothing. She could be one of the curious or one of the people who had broken in. But he had no way of knowing.

SARA blinked. The image of the church stayed lodged in her mind. But she saw something else as well. Big booted feet stealthily crossing a patch of gravel. She didn't know who the man was or why he was there.

She tried to get a better look at him. Her view expanded enough for her to see a gun in his hand. A dark-skinned hand.

She still didn't know who he was. All she knew was that the gun was pointed at Adam.

Panic seized her.

"Adam!" she screamed. "Adam, watch out."

She couldn't see him. She didn't know where he was

in the midnight picture wavering in her mind. And that was as terrifying as anything else.

ADAM was pawing at the edge of the window frame when a voice rang out in his head.

Sara's voice.

"Adam!" she screamed. "Adam, watch out."

He whirled around, smelling the strong scent of man. A very familiar scent. Not from earlier in the day.

Now. He strained his eyes into the night and caught a man-shaped shadow standing out against the darkness around him.

He had been so intent on his mission that he hadn't heard the crunch of shoes on gravel.

But Sara's voice had cut through the focus of his concentration.

He leaped back as the beam of a flashlight hit the spot where he had been standing.

"Holy Moses!" a voice rang out in the blackness behind the light. A glint of metal flashed in the man's hand. He knew that voice. Knew the scent. It was Paul Delacorte, probably prowling around for the same reason that Adam was here himself. He was hoping to find out who had broken in.

Only the sheriff was armed with a gun, and the wolf had only his teeth and claws.

Would the lawman risk a shot here?

Adam didn't wait around to find out. He turned and fled into the night, dodging through the cemetery, expecting the hot pain of a bullet slamming into his flesh.

CHAPTER
EIGHTEEN

SARA'S HAND CLAMPED into a fist. She pressed the fist against her lips, trying to hold back a scream—or a sob.

Adam was in danger. Terrible danger. Being stalked by a man with a gun.

She had seen that much, along with the bulk of a large stone church. And something else. Something that raised goose bumps on her bare arms. In the background were flickering shadows. People-shaped shadows. Not solid. She could see through them, like ghosts.

She made a little moaning sound. Could they be the witches? Adam had told her about them. So had Rosie. And she'd started wondering if they were the people who had shouted at her. Now she was seeing them. Well, not exactly. They had been at that place. But they weren't there now. Somehow she was picking up their afterimages. And those images rocked her to her soul. Just like their voices echoing in her mind.

Their forms were blurred, indistinct.

And she hadn't seen Adam. Just a blur of motion like an animal running from danger. And she didn't understand why that fitted into the warning reverberating in her head.

The whole ghostly vision began to dissolve. She tried to clutch onto it, but it was suddenly gone, and she saw only the bedroom of her little house. She had been standing by the bathroom door. Now she found herself sitting on the edge of the bed.

Seconds ticked by. Then endless minutes. She waited for something else to happen. The past few minutes had left her cold and shaking. She should get dressed, she thought vaguely. But she didn't have the energy for that.

All her strength was focused on trying to bring back the mental picture she'd just seen. But it wouldn't come!

For a lifetime she had ruthlessly shoved such visions out of her consciousness. In Wayland that had been impossible because she didn't seem to have any control over the images that came into her mind. Or the images that faded away, either, leaving her weak and shaking. Now she wanted desperately to find out what had happened with the man and the gun, but she couldn't make the dark scene come into her mind again.

Chills rippled over her skin. Wandering into the living room, she snatched up the quilt from the sofa, opened it up, and wrapped it around her shoulders like a large shawl as she moved to the window and stared out into the darkness.

She didn't know how long she stood there before the headlights of a vehicle cut their twin beams through the night.

It was Adam. Or it was Delacorte. Or someone else official coming to give her bad news.

Clutching the quilt around her shoulders, she opened the door and dashed into the night, her bare feet pounding the mulched path to the parking lot.

A vehicle's door slammed. She headed for the sound and saw a man standing beside an SUV parked at the edge of the lot. One of the overhead lights shone down on him, and she could see his face.

"Adam! Thank God. Adam." She ran toward him as he started toward her. They met on a soft bed of pine needles under a cluster of trees.

The quilt fell from her shoulders as she lifted her arms and reached for him.

ADAM reached for her at the same time. He had been longing to come back to her, yet all the way home he had been dreading the reunion. He had heard her voice shout a warning to the wolf. But she hadn't been there. Not physically.

He heard her breath come out in a gasp as he pulled her toward him, then stopped with his hands on her shoulders.

"You called out to me!" he said, hearing his voice rasp like sandpaper on rough tree bark.

"You were in danger."

His hands tightened on her shoulders. "How did you know? How did you warn me?"

"I . . . I don't know." She stopped, closed her eyes for a moment, then started again. "I had . . . had . . . one of those visions that I hate. But this time, I knew you were in trouble."

He dragged in a painful breath and let it out in a rush. He had to struggle to keep his fingers from digging into her shoulders. "You saw me?"

She stared up into the harsh lines of his face, looking confused. "No. That was the strangest part."

"What did you see?" he demanded.

"Not you. I saw another man's feet. I saw his boots. And I saw he had a gun."

"Delacorte."

"Oh!"

"But you didn't see me?" he pressed.

"No."

He felt like a condemned prisoner given a stay of execution. On a sigh, he pulled her to him, his arms closing around her.

"Do you believe me?" she whispered.

"Oh yes." If she had seen him, she wouldn't be in his arms now. Would she?

She lifted her face to his, her eyes troubled. "I told you I've been having strange experiences . . . strange perceptions since I came here. That dream we had. When I was in your bed. We both had it. It was real. Somehow, it was real. And what happened tonight. That was real, too." Her fingers dug into his shoulders. "Adam, what's happening to me?"

"I don't know. We'll figure it out," he promised, because he didn't know what else to say.

"Having . . . visions is wrong."

"What do you mean—wrong? Was it wrong to keep me from getting shot?"

She went on as though she hadn't heard him. "My parents thought it was a bad thing. They didn't like it . . . so I made it stop."

"Jesus! What did they do, beat you?"

"Of course not. They would never have beaten me. They adopted me because they loved me."

"You're adopted?"

"Yes. But that doesn't make a difference." She looked like she was on the edge of tears. "They just made me understand that it made them uncomfortable."

He swore again. "Don't tell me anything you do is wrong," he clipped out. "And certainly not tonight. You saved my life!"

"I wanted to help you," she murmured. "But I didn't

even know where you were. Were you outside a church?"

"A church building. The historical society took it over. I was trying to figure out who broke in there last night."

"And Delacorte thought you were one of the witches come back to the scene of the crime."

A bolt of tension went through him. "The witches? How do you know it was the witches?" he asked, hearing the strain in his voice.

"I saw them," she whispered. "I mean . . ." She stopped and started again. "I don't know what else it could be. I saw that they had been there. Last night I guess, when they broke in. They were like ghosts, flickering in the darkness."

"Yeah."

"You saw them, too?"

"Not exactly. I could *almost* see them. And I felt . . . something strange. I didn't know what it was. I think you just told me."

She wrapped her arms around his waist, pulling herself tightly against him. "Adam, I was so scared for you. And scared for myself, too. I don't like this."

She was trembling in his arms, and at the same time running her hands over his back, his shoulders, her touch telling him how relieved she was to have him safely home.

The need to soothe away the remnants of her fear was like a deep, primal longing that seemed to envelop him and at the same time wrap the two of them in a curtain of silk that sealed them away from the world and sealed him to her.

After the heat of their first kiss, he had vowed to take things slowly with her. But her touch and the warm look in her eyes was making that impossible.

He was aroused. And while he'd been holding her, arousal had passed beyond pleasure to pain. It felt as if he had been turned on for days. Turned on since he had first come across her in the swamp and known that she was his destiny. He had raged against that destiny. Some part of him was still trying to outrun it. But how could he fight his own need when she was in his embrace, silently telling him that she wanted the same thing he did?

A thick fog of sensuality was rapidly obliterating his ability to think. Her face was turned upward toward him, and he drank in the honey and sunshine scent of her mouth, feeling each exhalation of her breath drawing him toward her. He didn't make a conscious decision to lower his mouth to hers. It simply happened.

And that first touch of their lips was like a jolt of molten intensity that sizzled its way to every one of his nerve endings.

He drank from her like a man who had crawled out of the desert and found a cool, clear pond waiting in a shaded oasis.

She made a needy sound, her mouth opening to give him better access, and he knew that this time if he didn't make love with her, he would lose his sanity.

He should have warned her to run for her life, but he was beyond warnings. His hand slid down to her hips, reveling in the feel of her silken skin beneath the thin fabric of her gown.

Under the protective canopy of the tree branches, he stepped back long enough to drag the gown up and over her head.

Now there was nothing between the wonderful curves of her body and his hands and lips.

He stroked his fingers over her back, down her flanks, pulling her against his aching erection.

When she made a whimpering sound and rubbed against him, he felt as if his body was going to ignite and set the grove of trees on fire.

He reached up to take her breasts in his hands, his

thumbs stroking over the hardened tips, bringing another whimper to her lips.

He needed to get rid of his clothing. She made a sound of protest as he stepped back.

But when he pulled his T-shirt over his head, her hands went to the waistband of the sweatpants he had worn so he could get in and out of his clothing quickly.

He kicked off his shoes, then helped her scrape the pants down his hips.

Naked, he pulled her in against himself, desperate for intimate contact. His cock nestled against her belly; his hands stroked over the rounded curve of her bottom.

He needed to be on top of her. Inside her. Here. Now. He looked down at the pine needles under his bare feet and blinked when he saw a quilt lying on the ground.

Sara followed the direction of his gaze.

She laughed. "It must have fallen off my shoulders. How convenient for us."

They both knelt, spreading out the quilt. Then he pulled her back into his arms, tumbling her to the makeshift bed on its soft mattress of pine needles.

Their bodies crushed the needles, flooding the air with the pungent aroma of pine mingled with the dark, rich scents of the night.

It seemed right that he was making love with her for the first time out here, the wind a light caress on their naked bodies.

He clasped her to him, hot and hard and needy. He had never wanted a woman more. Yet his own satisfaction was only a small part of what he craved. He ached to give her pleasure, ached to bring her to the same peak of satisfaction that waited for him.

"Sara," he murmured through trembling lips.

Lowering his head, he caressed her breasts with his face, then turned his head so that he could take one pebble-hard nipple into his mouth, sucking on her, teasing her with his tongue and teeth while he used his thumb and finger on the other nipple.

She arched into the caress, her fingers winnowing through his dark hair. He shifted so he could trail one hand down her body, finding the hot, slick core of her.

When he dipped his finger between the silken folds, she made a low, needy sound and pressed her hips upward, telling him silently that she craved more.

She was ready for him. Thank God, because he knew that he was too close to the edge to wait.

Positioning himself between her legs, he entered her in one swift stroke.

She cried out at the joining of their flesh, circled his shoulders with her arms as he began to move within her in a fast, hard rhythm.

She matched him stroke for stroke, her nails digging into his back, the intensity quickly building to flash point. He felt her inner muscles tighten around him, the contractions like small electric shocks jolting his nervous system. And while orgasm still gripped her body, his own release grabbed him and spun him into a whirlwind of sensation that left him gasping.

He had never felt anything as profound, not with any other woman. Shaken to the depths of his soul, he collapsed against her, his head drifting to her shoulder, and she reached to soothe her fingers through his hair, turning her head so that she could stroke her lips along the line where his hair met his cheek.

They lay there for long moments. On the verge of sleep, he finally roused himself with visions of the staff arriving in the morning to find them lying naked on a quilt under the pine trees.

"We can't stay here," he murmured.

"A bed might be warmer," she conceded.

Which bed, he wondered, as he thought about protecting her reputation. He didn't want people in town gossiping that he'd asked her to stay at Nature's Refuge and invited her into his bed the next night.

"Your place," he said in a gruff voice. "So I can get back to my own cabin before anybody else shows up."

She nodded against his shoulder, then roused herself. Together they collected clothing from the ground around them. She picked up the quilt and put it back where it had been, over her shoulders. He put an arm around her waist, holding her close as they made their way back to her cabin.

In her bedroom, he lifted and pushed aside the covers for her, then stretched out beside her and took her in his arms.

He'd dreamed of this. But the reality was better than any dream. Sara, warm and pliant in his arms.

He was still shaken by what he was feeling. Still unable to put it into words. But as he gathered her close, fear was one of the elements circling painfully in his brain.

He had asked her what she'd seen. She had seen Delacorte. But not the wolf. Earlier, he'd been relieved.

Now—

Now he felt his chest constrict so painfully that it was difficult to draw a full breath. She had made love with a man named Adam Marshall. Would she run screaming from the werewolf? And what would he do if she turned away from him after giving herself to him?

His arms tightened around her, and she snuggled into his warmth. But she didn't speak.

What was she thinking now? He was afraid to ask.

But he needed to talk to someone who had faced this crisis. Had his brother, Ross, dealt with this? And what had he done about it?

The questions tore at him. In the warmth of Sara's bed, he made an effort to unclench his jaw.

He closed his eyes, thinking he would just lie here holding her. But the night's activities had worn him out.

Sometime before dawn, he drifted into sleep.

And sometime after the sun had come up, he woke with a start. The bed was cold. He was alone. Sitting up, he fought a wave of dizzying fear as he staggered through the cabin looking for her.

She wasn't there. And when he got to the dining area, he found a folded note waiting for him on the table. With a shaking hand, he reached out to pick it up.

CHAPTER
NINETEEN

WAS SHE A coward? Sara asked herself as she headed north in Miss Hester, her rattletrap Toyota.

She'd snuck around the cabin, throwing a few things into an overnight bag because she hadn't been able to face Adam in the morning. Not because of anything he'd done.

A warm flush heated her whole body. Making love with him had been more wonderful than anything she could have imagined. She'd given herself to him with a joy she'd never known before.

Last night she had been swept along on a tide of passion, and then in the morning, reality had set in. Her world had turned upside down since she'd arrived in Wayland. Not just by Adam Marshall. Something was happening within herself, and she needed to understand what it was.

It had borne fruit in Wayland. But she knew that the roots went much further back. To the time before she'd come to live with Barbara and Raymond Weston.

Last night she'd talked a little to Adam about her parents. They'd loved her. But they'd let her know that they wanted her to be a "normal" little girl. She'd done her best. And for a while, it looked as if it had worked. But now she felt like the fabric of her life was unraveling. There were things she needed to understand. Things that only Mom could tell her.

She knew the Westons hadn't been able to have children of their own. And they'd been in their late forties when she'd come to them. Probably it hadn't been an adoption through an agency. Probably they'd worked through a lawyer or something like that. They'd never talked about how they'd gotten her.

She'd loved her parents. And they'd loved her. They'd given her a good foundation for going out into the world. When Dad had died of a heart attack five years ago, she'd mourned his loss.

But she'd come to understand that they were people with rather rigid and traditional values, people who didn't know how to cope with a child who saw things that weren't there.

Had they done her a favor? Certainly they'd helped her fit in to the conventional world. But their upbringing hadn't prepared her for what had happened after she'd come to Wayland.

Come back to Wayland, she thought now. Because the minute she'd driven into town, the place had seemed familiar. She hadn't wanted to admit that then. Today she had to.

As she pulled into the driveway, she stood looking at the house. Dad had taken care of the home maintenance. But since his death, there hadn't been anyone to do the work. And Mom couldn't afford to hire out.

That was one of the things Sara hoped to remedy. When she got a steady job, she was going to take out a loan and get the house back into shape.

Even Mom's beautiful garden was a little less polished than in previous years. There were fewer annuals among the perennials. And she saw weeds poking up in the un-mulched beds.

Mom was in the kitchen when Sara knocked at the back door. Her mother dropped the colander she was holding into the sink and rushed to the door.

"Sara! What are you doing here? Is something wrong?"

With a shake of her head, she hurried to reassure her mother. "No. Nothing's wrong. I just got a little home-sick," she answered, thinking that was just a bit far from the truth. But she wasn't going to come bursting through the door complaining about her problems—or making de-mands.

"But you drove all this way!"

"It's not so far." She crossed to her mother, and they gave each other a tight hug. Once again she was back in the warm, sheltered environment of her childhood.

"You should have warned me, and I would have fixed extra for lunch. I've only got my spaghetti."

"I love your spaghetti."

"We can stretch it out with a salad."

"Wonderful. And I want some of your iced tea."

"There's a pitcher already in the refrigerator."

She and her mother fell into the familiar rhythm of putting together a meal. Twenty minutes later, they sat down at the dining room table with the place mats and flowered china she remembered so well.

Mom watched her from across the table.

She forked up some spaghetti and sauce, chewed, and swallowed. "This is so good. I missed your cooking."

"If I'd known you were coming, I would have made chocolate chip cookies."

"We can make them together after lunch," she an-swered, thinking that if they were both busy it might be easier to talk. She still wasn't sure what she was going to say. The only thing she was sure of was that she wasn't going to chicken out.

* * *

ADAM sat at his desk pretending to go over a list of books he was considering for the gift shop. But his mind was on Sara. She had gone to her mother's. She said in the note that their lovemaking had been wonderful. But she had some issues to resolve about her own background.

He made a snorting noise. She might think *she* had issues. But how was she going to react to the tooth and claw monster watching over their shoulders?

He wanted to know if she would run screaming from the wolf. He *had* to know. He wasn't going to be able to think about anything else until she came back.

A knock at the office door made him jump.

He looked up to see Delacorte standing in the doorway carrying a large cardboard box. "You got a package from UPS," the sheriff said.

Adam's hand froze on the paper he was holding, and he had to force his fingers to unclamp.

Without asking permission, the large black man came into the office and closed the door, setting down the box beside the desk.

Adam gestured toward one of the wooden chairs across from him. "Have a seat."

Delacorte accepted the invitation.

"What can I do for you?"

"Since you asked about the break-in at the historical society, I thought I'd keep you posted on . . . developments. I've been keeping an eye on the place."

Adam managed a steady gaze and an even voice. "After the break-in? Isn't that like locking the barn door after the horse has escaped?"

"You can put it that way if you want. I think of it as seeing whether the witches come back to the scene of the crime."

"The witches! You think it was them?"

"I did some pondering on it. Who else would steal a devil's lot of old history records?

"An interesting way to put it. Was it a whole bunch of stuff?"

"I was speaking figuratively. Mrs. Waverly claims she doesn't know exactly what was taken. But I think she's lying. I think the witches were looking for evidence of who did what to whom in Wayland in the past."

"You think they got what they wanted?"

"I reckon we'll find out."

Adam shifted in his seat, hoping the sheriff couldn't detect the wild pounding of his pulse.

"When I was a little pitcher, I had pretty big ears. I listened to all the old tales about the witches. Some of them had more holes than a screen door at an orphanage."

"Yeah. I'll bet."

"But they all followed a kind of pattern. And I think I encountered a new wrinkle last night. I was down at the historical society after midnight, and I saw what looked like a wolf."

Adam raised an eyebrow. "A wolf? Are there wolves in this area?"

"Not that I know of." The sheriff shifted in his seat, tension crackling through him. "I came over here to try out a theory on you."

Adam's mouth was so dry that he could hardly speak. But he managed to say, "Okay. Shoot."

"Keep an open mind. I don't want you to get the notion that I'm crazy."

Adam nodded, thinking that the sheriff and Sara appeared to be having similar doubts. Delacorte seemed to relax a notch. "Like I said, I've heard the old spine-tinglers since I was a kid. About stuff the witches could do. But I never heard tell of a werewolf."

The word Adam had been dreading was out in the open. He sat very still, half expecting the sheriff to draw his gun. But he only ran a hand over his short-cropped hair.

"What if the witches have developed a new talent?"

"Are you talking about shape-shifting?"

"It's not impossible."

"It sounds like a stretch to me," Adam managed to say. "Why would they add something new?"

"Because they're growing and evolving. They're getting stronger."

"You sure are into this paranormal stuff."

"When I was a kid, I didn't really believe it. It was just stories the bigger boys and old men told to scare you. But now that I'm in the middle of it, it looks kind of different."

"Yeah," Adam muttered. "But that doesn't mean you saw a werewolf. You said it was last night, right? Why wasn't it just an ordinary wolf?"

"You would have had to be there," the sheriff answered. "He wasn't just trotting around town. He was sniffing around the exact place where they broke into the historical society. He was pawing at the plywood tacked over the broken window. He was acting intelligent. Like he had a purpose."

"What did you do?"

Delacorte laughed. "I panicked. I pulled my gun. And he ran like hell."

Adam wished he could share the humor. In a tight voice he asked, "Would you have shot him?"

"I would have last night. Now I think that would have been a mistake."

Adam sighed. Well, that was something anyway. He pretended to be carefully considering what Delacorte had said, pretended that his heart wasn't threatening to beat its way through the wall of his chest.

"You think I've gone off the deep end," the lawman finally said.

"No. I'm thinking about what you said. Let's agree for

the sake of argument. Suppose you saw a werewolf. If he was part of the witch group, why would he have gone back there? What would have been his purpose? I mean, you're assuming he has human intelligence. What would he have to gain by sniffing around the place where his friends broke in?"

Delacorte rocked back in his chair. "I don't know."

"Well, since we're getting into the twilight zone, let me try a theory on you. You think that a . . . uh . . . coven of witches has come back to town to get revenge. Suppose there's another faction. Suppose somebody with . . . um . . . psychic powers is fighting the witches. And the werewolf is part of that other faction. So he was down there . . . investigating."

The sheriff's brows knit together. "That's an interesting hypothesis. I suppose it's a possibility. But who would it be?"

"Folks who were never friends with the witches?" Adam suggested. "Folks who have figured out what they're doing and want to stop them."

"Yeah. But folks with . . . powers."

"Superman!" Adam said, cutting through the tension.

"More like wolfman."

Adam leaned back in his chair and dredged up a laugh that he hoped didn't sound like he had a throat full of ground glass. "So the wolf got away. How are you coming on tracking down the witches?"

"I'm compiling a list of new people in town. Including Sara Weston."

Adam had told himself he was starting to relax. "Not Sara," he said.

"She arrived just when you tangled with that group dancing around a drugged campfire."

"Not Sara," he said again, flashing on what had happened last night. Not the lovemaking. Before. When she'd told him she'd had a vision of him in trouble.

Delacorte was watching him carefully, and he wondered what showed on his face.

"You're telling me you've gotten to know her pretty well," the sheriff said.

"Yes," he answered, speaking around the lump that clogged his throat.

"You're sure you know what kind of person she is?"

"Yes," Adam answered, hoping that he was telling the truth. Shifting in his seat, he said, "If you're looking at new people in Wayland, what about me?"

"I thought about you," Delacorte said. "And I checked into your background. You're from Baltimore. You've got no connection to this town."

"Sara's from Wilmington, North Carolina."

"Sara's adopted," the sheriff said.

Adam sat forward. "How do you know that?"

"Barnette did a background check on her. She's about the same age as that little girl whose momma burned up in that cabin. If she's that little girl, that would sure give her reason to hate the fine upstanding people of Wayland."

THEY were washing the dishes, when Sara screwed up her courage. "I'm not sure I ever told you how lucky I feel to have found a home with you and Dad."

"Why thank you, dear."

Sara finished soaping a plate and set it in the tub of rinse water. "We never talked about my real background. From before I came to live here."

A glass slipped out of her mother's hand and bobbed back into the tub of water.

"Can you tell me where I came from originally?"

"I don't really know. Why are you asking? I mean, why now?"

Sara listened to the quaver in her mother's voice. It

sounded like she was either lying or worried about telling Sara the answer to the question.

She cleared her throat. "I met a man. I think we might be right for each other. But . . . that got me thinking about my . . . genetic heritage, you know," she stumbled through the plausible explanation she'd thought of on the way up from Wayland. "I mean, what if I were in danger of passing something . . . bad to my children? Or what if . . . um . . . it turned out that I could develop some genetic disease? Like Huntington's chorea."

"Oh no, Sara. I'm sure there's nothing like that in your background."

"Why not? What about that stuff that used to happen to me? When I'd hear and see things that weren't there."

Her mother sucked in a sharp breath. "I don't want to talk about that."

"But just because you don't want to talk about it doesn't mean that it will go away."

"It did go away! Long ago."

"Yes, Mom. You and Dad made sure of that," she said, hearing the strident note in her own voice.

Her mother's face had tightened. "You were little and scared. We did what we thought was best for you."

Sara made an effort to soften her tone. "I know that, Mom. I know you had my best interests at heart. But I'm grown up now. And I need to know about my background. I'm hoping you'll help me.

FALCON watched Starflower working on the drywall joints of the new addition to the house. He liked seeing her rounded bottom when she leaned over to get more mud out of the plastic tub. Even though she wasn't much of a worker, she had other attributes. Basically, she was a sex magnet. But she needed to learn a little discipline.

She was going to be the mother of his children when

they got this house finished and set up their commune. As far as anybody in town would know, they'd be a bunch of retro hippies living in the country and getting back to nature with their brood of kids running naked in the bushes.

The image pleased him. A nice freewheeling commune was the perfect camouflage for the clan. There was a lot of land here. They'd build other houses when they got this one finished. Then they'd get money out of some of the low lifes in town who had tormented their parents. Before they killed the sorry bastards.

He came up to Starflower and ran his hand down her back from her shoulder to the nice rounded curve of her butt.

"You might as well take a break from the finishing work. You're not getting much done."

She gave him a saucy grin. "I was hoping you'd notice."

"You and Willow and Water Lily can start dinner."

Her face fell. "I'm not the chief cook and bottle washer."

"But we all pull our weight here. And you're a good cook." That wasn't exactly true. But she was getting better.

She gave him a little nod. "Can we have some fun later and use that cool smoke?"

"You like that, do you?"

She swayed against him. "You know I like it a lot. You know I'd love to get high and have a nice hard cock inside me. Yours especially."

The suggestion made him instantly hard. "You know, we can't use the smoke too much. The more you use it, the less effect you feel."

"But it's still a lot of fun."

"Yeah." He stroked his hand over her right breast, feeling her pebbled nipple. With his thumb and forefinger, he gave her a nice hard squeeze, and she sucked in a sharp breath. Another woman might have yelped in pain. But she liked that. Liked it rough. And he was more than willing to accommodate her. He liked fucking her fast and sharp. And he liked being the leader of the clan. He liked making the decisions about when they had group sex.

They could break off into couples if they wanted. But the group gropes and fucks were important—and not just for fun. Arousal increased their powers. So it wasn't just having a hot time. They needed to be together in a group. They needed to practice with the power they generated.

He glanced over his shoulder. The others were outside clearing away construction debris. It had piled up for a couple of weeks, and he was afraid somebody was going to end up stepping on a nail.

"We'll have a party tonight," he said.

"Good." She shifted her weight from one foot to the other. "Something you should know."

"About tonight? You're having your period?"

"No. About Sara Weston. My spy at Nature's Refuge told me she went out of town."

"Oh yeah."

"But she's coming back. She left all her stuff. And everybody in town knows she's working for Granville Pharmaceuticals. She's got a fancy-ass research grant, and she left her science experiments, so she can't be away long."

"And? What's your point?"

"We can set a trap for her. Like we did before. Only this time, she's toast."

Falcon gave Starflower a long look. "You hate her, don't you?"

She took her lower lip between her teeth. "I'm only trying to protect us. She's dangerous. She's got powers. And if she learns how to use them, she can hurt us."

He gave a tight nod. "What kind of trap did you have in mind?"

She smiled and he saw some of the tension go out of her. "I've been thinking about what kind of death would work for the scum who hunted down our parents. We want to kill them, but we don't want anyone to know we had a hand in it. What do you think about a one-car auto accident?"

"Tell me more."

She started outlining a very well-developed plan, and he realized she'd probably been thinking about it since the afternoon Adam Marshall had rejected her. And Sara Weston had scared the shit out of her.

The rejection was minor in the grand scheme of things. But Sara Weston was another matter. At first it had looked like she might be an asset to the group.

But he trusted Starflower's judgment. Dr. Weston was dangerous. She had the power to challenge their plans and disrupt the clan.

So she had to be eliminated. And Marshall, too. Because he had gone to the trouble of protecting her, by moving her into Nature's Refuge. He cared about her. Which meant that if he found out the clan had offed her, he'd come after them.

CHAPTER
TWENTY

AFTER THE SHERIFF'S visit, Adam couldn't even pretend he was focused on paperwork.

Thinking about Sara being in danger from Delacorte made his insides ache. He couldn't deal with that. Yet he couldn't put Sara out of his mind. She crept into every empty space in his thoughts like fresh air seeping into the hard crevices of a dark cave. His mind zinged back to the morning—when he'd awakened in bed alone. He had made a frantic search of her room. Most of her clothing was there. And the lab was still set up in the shed.

She was coming back.

She had to be coming back, because he couldn't deal with the alternative.

Closing his eyes, he let his thoughts drift back to that first morning in the swamp, feeling again the primal burst of attraction between them. He had wanted her then. Wanted her every moment since. Last night he had made love with her. Binding her to him for all time, the werewolf and his mate. The way his father had told him it would be.

And instead of waking up next to her, he found she had fled.

From him? Or was she telling the truth about going home to talk to her mother about her background.

She'd told him she was adopted. And Delacorte had wondered if she was Jenna Foster's daughter. The woman would be about the same age as Sara. What if they were the same person? That was hard to believe. A real coincidence. But what if it wasn't a coincidence at all? What if somebody had brought her back to town? Back to that cabin where her mother had died.

With a tight feeling in his throat, Adam got up and wandered back to the cabin where Sara was living now. For a long time, he simply sat in the front room, breathing in her scent. If he closed his eyes, he could picture her walking through the door. Picture himself reaching for her. Picture her melting into his embrace. But she wasn't there. And he could torture himself only so long.

Heaving himself out of the chair, he walked stiffly down to the supply shed, where he got out a bag of feed for the deer that frequented the park.

He measured out the day's portion, then headed out to the area where the animals had been coming for their handout.

After spreading the pellets around, he stood staring for a long time at a pair of sandhill cranes poking through a marshy area. He knew from his reading about the swamp that old-timers in the area had mistaken them for whooping cranes. But they'd gotten the species wrong.

He managed to occupy his mind with bird lore for another five minutes, then sighed and headed back to the shed with the empty plastic container. Sensing that someone was watching him, he looked up. A tall, fit-looking man was leaning against the corner of the wooden building watching Adam's progress up the path.

He froze in his tracks, feeling like he'd been punched in the pit of the stomach.

The man was standing with his arms casually at his sides. Maybe he was trying to look calm. But the tension radiating off of him was like heat radiating off molten lava.

After finding Sara gone and then his meeting with Delacorte, Adam's own stress level had already shot through the roof. He had little control left, and the first words that came out of his mouth were, "What the hell are *you* doing here?"

The man gave a bark of a laugh. "That's quite a warm greeting for your long lost brother."

Adam swallowed. "Sorry, Ross. You have to admit it's a bit of a surprise seeing you here. How did you find me?"

"I'm a private detective. I'm good at locating people. I've been following your moves around the country."

"And now you're in Wayland, Georgia. Why now, after all these years?"

"I know you're investigating Ken White's death."

"Oh yeah, well I don't need your help."

Ross Marshall sighed. "I figured you wouldn't."

Adam shoved his hands into his pockets, trying to rein in the emotions warring inside him. Some deep buried part of him wanted to stride across the space between them and embrace his brother.

But Ross had taken him by surprise. And there was a more urgent need than that of physical contact. He wanted to protect his turf. This patch of Georgia was his. And another werewolf was invading his territory.

He knew that was a knee-jerk reaction, the animal inside him acting on instinct, and he struggled to curb it. It appeared as if Ross had come in friendship. But was friendship between two adult werewolves really possible?

Ross was watching him with keen, dark eyes. "I figured you were probably struggling with some personal stuff now."

Adam's breath was shallow in his chest, but he gave a small shrug.

"Can we go somewhere and talk?"

"What's wrong with right here?"

"Okay. This is your dominion. You call the shots." Ross shifted his weight from one foot to the other again. "You're the right age to be looking for a mate."

When Adam didn't speak, his brother went on. "I guess the most important thing I came down here to tell you is that I'm happily married. I met a wonderful woman. Her name is Megan. And the miracle isn't just that she can put up with a husband with my . . ." He stopped and looked around, mindful that they were standing outside where anyone could come upon them. "With my wild nature."

"Congratulations," Adam said.

"The best part is that she's a medical doctor. A geneticist. She's done some research into our . . . problem. We have an extra chromosome that causes our genetic aberration. It's a sex-linked trait. I can give you more details if you want. The bottom line is that she's working on how to keep boys from dying when they . . . reach puberty. She's got a few years to do that. Our son, Jonah, is two and a half. And she's pregnant with our daughter."

"A girl!"

"It's okay," Ross said quickly. "She's fixed it so she doesn't have the fatal genetic problem our sisters had."

Adam nodded tightly, fighting against the lump that had formed in his chest. He remembered all those babies who had died at birth. And all the brothers who hadn't survived into adulthood because being a werewolf's child carried a heavy chance of mortality.

So he understood the importance of what Ross was telling him. He hadn't been thinking about his terrible heritage when he'd been pursuing Sara. He should have been, he realized. But he'd only been focused on his own selfish needs. His own overwhelming drive to mate with her.

"I came down here to tell you that if you find the woman you can't run away from, Megan can help you avoid the tragedy of our parents' life."

Ross paused and studied Adam, who could imagine what he looked like. Ragged around the edges. Strung out. Sick.

"You've already found her, haven't you?"

"I'm not discussing that with you!"

"Right. You're too uptight to get personal with me. And I understand that. We haven't seen each other in eight years. Maybe I should have sent you an e-mail. But once I decided to get in touch with you, I wanted to do it in person. I wanted to let you know it's possible for us to get along with each other."

"You really think so?" Adam asked, unable to keep the note of scorn out of his voice.

Ross sighed. "If you want it as much as I do, we can work it out. Violence was a big part of my adult life. I guess you've had some of the same problems. I'm going to raise my sons a lot differently from the way the Big Bad Wolf raised us."

"The Big Bad Wolf! I haven't heard that in years. That's right. That's what you used to call him." He found himself asking, "Is the old bastard still alive?"

"Yes. And Mom, too. She'd love to see you, if you ever get up to Baltimore."

"But not him."

"He'd probably like to see you, too. For about five minutes. He might not want to be in the same room with you for long, but he'd be proud of how well you've done."

Adam gave a harsh laugh. "Proud or jealous."

They stood facing one another, each caught in his own thoughts. Each remembering the dysfunctional home life at the Marshall house. His mother had tried her best. But the Big Bad Wolf had dominated the family. And his idea of dinner table ambience had been a cuff on the ear for any little boy who annoyed him.

Ross spoke first, in a firm, level voice. "I know what you went through as a kid because I went through it, too. I'm going to make sure I get along with my sons when they grow up. If I can do it with them, I can do it with you."

"How are you planning to accomplish that?"

"I see a shrink once a week. He's helping me cope with my aggressions."

Adam could literally feel his jaw drop open. When he'd closed it, he said, "You're kidding. Right?"

"I've never been more serious. It doesn't hurt as much as you think."

"I'll take your word for it."

Ross took a step back. "I came down here to make contact with you. I wanted to make sure you were all right. You can call it curiosity if you want. I call it caring about my brother. But I'm not going to push you into anything you can't handle. I just wanted to let you know that I'd like to keep in touch. And I'm here to help you any way I can."

"Okay. Thanks," Adam answered because he couldn't think of anything better to say.

"I know seeing me is a shock. So I'll back off. I'm in Maryland. Howard County. I've got a nice patch of woods where I can roam at night. And a family I care about. You're welcome to visit us anytime you want."

"Okay."

Ross turned away. Then he was gone. Adam wanted to run after him. But he stayed where he was. He had enough problems right now without trying to figure out how he felt about his long lost brother.

SWALLOWING her frustration, Sara wandered out into the garden, looking toward the spot where her swing set had stood. Dad had taken it down when she'd been in her teens and replaced the old play area with a slate patio with some wrought iron furniture. Along the border were beds of tall annual phlox in white pink and lavender. They were at their peak and lovely. But the furniture was covered with dried leaves and other debris. In the utility room she found an old T-shirt, which she used to wipe off the chaise longue. The long cushion was in the garage. She brought it out and laid it on the metal frame. After sweeping off the patio, she lay down in the late afternoon sun.

It had been a long time since she'd relaxed out here. Memories came back to her. Some good. Some bad. She had played hard in this sheltered garden by herself and with the neighborhood kids. She had helped her mother pull weeds and plant flowers.

But there was a strong memory that dominated all the others. Out here was where she'd had her first strange experience when she was five years old.

She'd been playing on the swing. And suddenly her head had started to pound. Like the headaches she'd had since coming to Wayland.

The scene around her had disappeared. And she was someone else. Timmy. She was inside her childhood friend Timmy's head.

She didn't know where he was. All she knew was that he was in a box where the lights were flickering. Then they went off, and it was dark and scary and closed in, and she felt like she couldn't breathe.

She heard Timmy crying. Or was it herself crying? She didn't know, and she didn't want to be there. Terrified, she yanked her mind back to herself. In the process, her hands lost their grip on the metal chains that held the swing, and she fell onto the ground, knocking the breath out of her lungs.

The sensation left her shaking. When she could get up, she ran to the house, weeping.

"Daddy! Daddy! I was scared. I couldn't get out."

Daddy caught her in his arms.

"What is it? What happened, sweetheart? Did you skin your knee?"

"I was there! In the dark. I . . . I was inside Timmy's head!"

She had felt her father go very still. Over his shoulder, she saw Mommy looking down at her with a strange expression on her face.

Daddy was saying. "You're here with us. Right here. Everything's okay." His gaze burned down into hers, and he gave her a little shake. "You're right here with us. Right here. Nowhere else."

He frightened her then with his eyes drilling into hers and his voice as hard as bricks. She wanted to please him. She was afraid that she might be sent away.

So she clamped her lips shut and fought away the image behind her closed eyelids. And later, when she saw Timmy in the park, and he told her how scared he'd been when he'd gotten stuck in an elevator downtown at his doctor's office, she listened like she didn't already know about it.

The next time something like that started to happen, she clenched her fists and squeezed her eyes shut, and somehow she fought it off. Because she would do anything to please her new parents. Anything including suppressing a part of herself that had always struggled to break out. She'd understood that part of her was bad. That it wasn't normal. And she'd understood that her parents wanted a normal little girl.

So here she was, in the spot where she'd had that first frightening psychic experience. Because she was all grown up, she knew what to call it. And she finally understood that repressing part of herself over the years had taken its toll. It had made her closed-up. Made her play it safe.

Now, whatever the cost, she had to embrace her own uniqueness. And since this was where she'd first shut away part of her personality, this was where she'd come to bring it into focus.

The trouble was, she wasn't really sure how to invite it back.

She made a frustrated sound. Then she thought of the pain that had drilled into her head when she'd stepped into the street before the truck came rushing toward her.

She remembered the intensity of the headache. And she didn't want to feel it again. But maybe she had to. Leaning back, she closed her eyes and focused on the sensation of a blast from a ray gun drilling into her head.

As she tried to open herself to whatever would come next, a terrible sense of guilt clutched at her. She had been taught that this was wrong. And she had tried her best to do whatever would gain Mommy and Daddy's approval. It was hard not to feel like she was betraying them.

"No!" she said aloud. She wasn't betraying them. She was an adult, and she was reaching for her true heritage.

She'd pleased her parents with her denial. She had tried to be normal. For a while it seemed to have worked. She'd been successful in school. She'd made a life for herself. But she'd never really gotten close to anyone.

Then she had come to Wayland, Georgia, and everything had changed. And she realized she had never felt normal. Not deep down.

She squeezed her eyes more tightly shut, trying to open herself to what she had always known was forbidden. It had happened in Wayland without her permission. It could happen here just as well. It had to happen here.

Need was greater than fear. She wasn't sure what she was doing, except that she was reaching out with some kind of mental hook and pulling something dangerous toward her.

And suddenly, her consciousness was no longer in the garden. She was somewhere else. In a child's narrow bed. In the dark. In a nightmare.

She didn't want to be there! Not there. And she tried with desperation born of fear to escape from the terrifying place where she found herself.

CHAPTER
TWENTY-ONE

BUT IT WAS too late for Sara to flee. She was trapped in a nightmare. In the cabin at the edge of the swamp. The same cabin, but different.

In the front room, she could hear Daddy and Momma talking. Not the Daddy and Momma who lived in the house in Wilmington, North Carolina. The other Momma and Daddy.

She wasn't Sara. She was Victoria, and she started to swing her small legs over the side of the bed. Then she heard something scary in the sound of Daddy's voice—and his words.

"Come on, we have to leave. We don't have much time."

As one of Daddy's arms tightened around her, he reached for Momma with the other. "Come on. Let me get you away from here, before it's too late."

Outside, above the babble of voices, she heard a man shout, "Come out and show yourself—you damn witch."

"Yeah, you can't hide from us," another man joined in. "You and the rest of your damn tribe."

"No. I'm not one of them," Momma screamed from the front room.

"Don't lie to us," the man who had spoken first shouted.

Others joined the chorus. "Come out before we burn you out."

Victoria buried her face against her father's shoulder, her free hand clutching Mr. Rabbit.

Daddy started to go after Momma in the front room, but before he reached her, the window beside the door shattered, sending glass spraying across the wood floor.

Momma screamed. Then a strong, dangerous smell filled the air. All at once, Victoria could hear a strange roaring noise.

"Save her! Save her!" Momma screamed.

Her father cursed, trying to get to the front of the house. But the heat beat him back. Turning with Victoria in his arms, he sprinted across the bedroom, then bent to push up the window sash.

"Daddy! I'm scared, Daddy," she whimpered, trying to breathe through the cloud of smoke choking her nose and throat.

"It's okay. Everything will be okay," he said between coughs. "I'll get you out of here."

After lowering her out the window, he quickly followed. With his body bent over hers, he ran into the darkness of the swamp, carrying her past the old crooked tree where she'd liked to play.

Behind her Victoria heard a sound like thunder. Raising her head, she saw the whole house explode into flames.

"Momma! Where's Momma?"

*   *   *

SARA'S eyes blinked open. Her breath was coming in
painful gasps. Her heart was threatening to explode.

She folded her arms across her chest, trying to ward
off the sudden chill that gripped her body.

She had been there. Been right in the middle of it. And
now she knew what had happened.

She had lived in the cabin at the edge of the swamp
long ago. With Momma. And a mob of townspeople had
killed her mother. Townspeople from Wayland. There was
no shred of doubt in her mind about what had happened.
In the waking nightmare, she'd seen the old bent tree. The
same tree that was still there.

The woman who had been killed in the little cabin,
Jenna Foster, had been her mother. The witch had been
her mother!

And what did that make her?

She squeezed her eyes closed, trying to drive away the
answer. But it had lodged in her brain like shards of glass.

The scared little girl part of her wanted to escape—into
madness, if that was her only option. But the woman she
had made herself into—the scientist—stood back and approached the subject with cool logic.

She might have died in that cabin. But she had survived. And now, twenty-five years later, someone had
brought her back to Wayland. To the scene of the crime.

But she was in Wilmington now. At her adopted
mother's house. And she had to find out what Barbara
Weston knew about it. Because there were details the little
girl would never be able to learn unless someone could
fill in more of the puzzle pieces.

On shaky legs she went back to the house to confront
the woman she had called mother for most of her life.

Mom was sitting on the living room sofa, a magazine
spread on her lap, but she wasn't reading. She was pleat-
ing the edge of a page in her fingers.

As soon as Sara entered the room, her mother's gray

head came up. Her gaze was questioning and troubled.

Sara stood in the doorway, unsure of what to say. She'd come charging into the house, bent on confrontation. But now she saw how small and old her mother looked. Her face was pale, and her lips trembled as she stared at her daughter.

Sara crossed the room and sat down on the couch. "It's okay, Mom," she murmured.

To her horror, tears welled in the older woman's eyes.

The hard shell Sara had tried to erect around her heart instantly melted. "Mom . . . don't . . ." Sara whispered. "What's wrong?"

Her mother brushed the back of her hand under her eyes. "I knew . . . when you came home . . . when . . . when I saw the look on your face."

"What look?"

"Determined." She sighed. "That determination you taught yourself."

"Did I?"

"Yes. Then when you started asking about your background, I got scared."

"It's been on my mind a lot lately."

Her mother's head bobbed. "I told Raymond this would happen!"

"What?"

"That it would all come back to haunt us eventually." Her mother swallowed hard. "When you first came to us, I wanted you to . . . to be yourself. He thought that you'd be happier if you forgot about your past. If you were like all the other little children."

"Oh!" She'd never realized that her parents hadn't agreed on how to bring her up.

"I promised him I'd keep the secret."

Sara felt shivers slither over her skin. "What secret?"

"About your mother."

"I know who she was. She was a woman named Jenna

Foster, wasn't she? And I was her little girl, Victoria."

Mrs. Weston moaned softly. "Was that her name? We never knew."

Sara nodded, trying to put herself in her parents' situation all those years ago. She covered her mother's wrinkled hand with her own. "I had a good childhood. But . . . I can't function as an adult like this. I have to know what you can tell me. Did you know I came from Wayland?"

"Wayland? Where you have that research job?"

"Yes."

Her mother made a small, distressed sound. "We never knew the town where you lived. We only knew it was somewhere south of here."

"How did you know that?"

"Because the money always came from down south."

Sara's eyes widened. "What money?"

"He would send us money orders. From different banks and from different towns."

"Who?"

"Your real father."

"You knew my father? How did you adopt me?"

Her mother stared across the room, her gaze unfocused. "We were too old to get a child through an agency. So we put an advertisement in several newspapers saying that we wanted to provide a loving home for a baby or a toddler. For months we didn't get any response, and we were thinking it wouldn't work. Then we got a phone call asking if we wanted a little girl. Of course we did. A man arranged to meet us down at the Big Boy restaurant. He had you with him. We had lunch and talked. Then the next day he came to our house. You were so quiet. You stayed right by his side all the time. It seemed like you were in shock."

Sara nodded, picturing the little girl who had just lived through a terrible experience. At the same time, she tried to imagine the situation. Raymond and Barbara Weston had taken in a child they didn't know. A child who was obviously traumatized.

"You were taking a chance on adopting me, weren't you?"

"We didn't think about it that way. You were so sweet. So fragile. And we just gave our hearts to you."

Sara squeezed her mother's hand. "And I gave my heart to you."

"When you went off to the bathroom, he told us there had been some trouble, that your mother had died. The man said he was your father, and he couldn't take care of you. And he wanted to find a good home for you with people who would love you. He made it a condition of the adoption that we not know his name. The legal details were handled by a lawyer."

Sara tried to process everything she'd heard. "If you didn't know where I came from and you didn't know the identity of my father—how did you know about the murder?"

"You had nightmares. You told us about the night your mother was killed."

Sara gasped. "It came from me?"

"Yes. And we would comfort you and tell you the best thing was to forget all about it. And we thought the bad stuff had gone away. But I was always afraid that it would somehow come back."

Sara looked down at her and her mother's joined hands. "I understand," she murmured.

"Do you forgive me?"

"Yes," she said, then reached to hug the woman who had raised her with love, a simple woman who, understandably, hadn't wanted to deal with a child with psychic powers.

They sat together on the sofa for a long time. Then Sara stirred herself. She had to get back to Wayland. But first she had to make sure that Mom was okay.

"So, are we going to make those chocolate chip cookies?" she asked.

"Oh yes!" her mother answered, relief flooding her voice.

BY four in the afternoon, Sara was too keyed up to stay any longer. So she hugged her mother good-bye and started back to Wayland to face her past and to face Adam. Making love to him had been like nothing she had ever expected to experience in her life. It had been like something out of a romance novel. Like a man and a woman finding their soul mates.

Yet how could a man be soul mate with a witch?

Her hands clamped around the steering wheel. Part of her wished that she had never come back to Wayland, because coming home had awakened that deep, buried component of her psyche. The part she had always feared. Yet if she hadn't come back to the town where she was born, she never would have met Adam.

But she was the wrong woman for him. Her mother had been a witch. She was a witch. And being with a witch could be dangerous for so many reasons.

She wanted to turn the car in the other direction and flee. But she couldn't make herself do it.

Her mind was a disordered jumble as she drove through the late afternoon and into the night. So many pieces of her personal puzzle had fallen into place. She had been having psychic experiences ever since she'd arrived at that damn cabin. But they didn't just come from the cabin. They came from within her. And some of them had to do with Adam.

"Oh Lord, Adam. I'm sorry," she said into the darkness of the car.

Adam had told her about the witches. He'd told her that their children had come back to town to get even.

Witches with an evil purpose.

Her mind made another jump. They had attacked her. She knew that now. They had sent pain shooting into her head, then warned her that a truck was speeding toward her. So what had they been doing, testing her because they knew she was like them?

A cold chill traveled from her hairline down her spine.

Why had they hurt her? Was she some kind of threat to them? And what about her own psychic power? The power she could feel developing within herself. She didn't think she would use it to hurt Adam or anyone else. But how could she know for sure?

There was so much to think about. Herself. Adam. And her natural father.

He had saved her from the fire. But he had given her up. Then he had sent money to the Westons.

"So who are you, Daddy dearest?" she asked into the closed compartment of the car. "Are you still in Wayland? Are you even still alive? Did you somehow arrange for me to come back to the little cabin beside the swamp?"

That certainly seemed like a radical step. And if he'd done it, what did he hope to gain?

As she drove on through the darkness, her mind spun back to her interview with Austen Barnette. He owned the cabin. He'd had it rebuilt. He was connected to her past. Did that mean he was connected to her? Was *he* her father?

She kept thinking about him as she drove south. But as she drew closer to Nature's Refuge, her thoughts went back to Adam.

She longed to see him, yet she was afraid, too. Thinking about him made her heart pound and her mouth go dry. Then all at once, she realized that wasn't the only reason she felt like her nerves were rising to the surface of her skin.

She tried to analyze the sensation.

Maybe it came from her witch's instinct.

She shuddered. Something was going to happen. Something vibrating in the background of her mind. Something bad.

Pain shot through her head. The same kind of pain she'd felt just before Adam had snatched her out of the way of the pickup truck.

CHAPTER
TWENTY-TWO

SARA'S HEART LEAPED into her throat as a car shot straight toward her out of the darkness, its lights off, and she knew it wasn't some driver losing control. Last time the witches had been playing game with her. But this was no game. This was for real. They were trying to kill her. Fear might have paralyzed her. But anger and determination were stronger. She was damned if she was going to let herself get run off the road along a deserted stretch of highway. She wasn't going to have a fatal accident here. She was going to see Adam again. She had to see Adam again!

Without conscious thought, her mind called out to him, even as she yanked the wheel to the right.

Luckily she had already slowed her speed. Still she whizzed along the shoulder, bumping over potholes, grazing tree trunks, hearing metal tear off of poor old Miss Hester as she pressed on the brake. She threw up her arm to shield her face as the car bashed into a tree branch, then lurched to a halt against the trunk of another tree.

The impact sent her flying forward. Then the seat belt caught and pulled her back again.

She sat behind the wheel, dazed, struggling to drag in a full breath, thankful that nothing worse had happened. Looking over her shoulder, she tried to find the car that had come out of the darkness and crossed the double yellow line, barreling toward her. But it was gone.

With a shaking hand, she unbuckled the seat belt and leaned back against the headrest, trying to bring her emotions under control. Miss Hester's engine had stopped, and she doubted it would start again. And even if it would, driving would probably not be such a great idea.

The danger was over. It should be over. But it didn't feel that way. Through the windshield, she peered into the darkness. Too bad she didn't have a cell phone, because she was alone on this deserted stretch of rural highway, and there was no one to help her.

But she was pretty sure she was only a quarter of a mile from Nature's Refuge. That would be an easy walk.

Her fingers closed around the door handle, but some deeply felt instinct kept her from getting out of the car.

Out in the darkness, she felt eyes were watching her. And she knew who they were.

The bad witches. The ones who wanted to hurt her, and she didn't even know why.

Her chest tightened with apprehension, and she reached to snap the door locks shut. But how much protection would that be?

Oh God, Adam. Adam, help me, her mind screamed—although she didn't know where he was or what he could do.

But he had pulled her out of the street the first time the witches had attacked her. And she clung to that memory, clung even harder as another terrible pain arrowed into her head.

They were doing it. She felt them, even though she

could see nothing as she stared into the darkness. Mist rose from the surface of the road now. It spread beyond the blacktop, obliterating underbrush and tree trunks, turning the landscape into a strange, forbidding place. A place of terror and black magic where anything could happen.

Through the car windows, she strained to see into the darkness and caught a flicker of movement, forms gliding through the trees. People. Like apparitions in a horror movie.

They were coming toward her slowly, slowly, ghosts moving through a graveyard, the horror movie effect magnified by their black-hooded cloaks. But it wasn't their physical bodies that threatened her.

Ahead of them, they were sending a wave of pain that filled her brain, swamped her senses.

Her hands clenched. The pressure inside her skull was too much. She was going to die. Right here in the car along this fog-shrouded stretch of road. And everybody would think that the auto accident had killed her.

That thought brought a wave of anger pounding through her. Those bastards! They had made her crash. But they weren't going to kill her.

She roused herself. Leaning forward, she sent back her own wave of energy, instinctively fighting the pack of witches with their own paranormal weapon. She saw them pause, saw their hooded heads turn toward one another. One woman raised a hand toward her face.

Sara had momentarily stopped them. But her feeble weapon wasn't enough. The coven started moving forward again, and Sara felt an invisible noose was closing around her neck, choking off her breath.

She struggled to send another energy burst. And she managed some kind of power surge. But it was like trying to put out a forest fire with a garden hose.

She was still choking, still gasping. Still on the verge

of passing out, when suddenly the pressure lifted. She struggled for breath, sitting forward and peering out of the windshield, trying to figure out what had happened.

Through the fog she saw a gray shape charging at the black-hooded figures. An animal. She saw it leap on one and then another, knocking them down, sending high-pitched screams through the group as they flailed at the marauder with their arms and kicked at it with their legs.

The animal looked like a large dog. Or a wolf.

And in that moment of recognition, she knew she had seen that wolf before. In a daydream. A daydream that had overtaken her after she had arrived in Wayland. She'd been standing at the kitchen sink. And her mind had gone back in time. She'd stepped into her mother's life. She knew that now.

But it hadn't just been her mother. The wolf had been there, too. Warning her of danger.

She was pulled back to the present by the screams of the witches echoing through the night as they scattered into the swamp. She watched the wolf chase one of the men, nipping at his legs, almost knocking him to the ground.

The coven was in full flight. Probably the wolf could have killed at least one of them.

Instead he turned and raced back toward the car. He reached her door, standing with the mist swirling around him, staring up at her through the window. And she would have sworn that he was begging her to tell him she was all right.

She should have been terrified. He had savagely attacked the people who had come to hurt her. But she felt a kind of awesome calm settle over her. In her heightened state of awareness—her witch's state of awareness—she knew who he was.

It made no sense. But she knew the wolf was Adam, and that he had come in response to her call for help, come to her with no regard to what might befall him.

Last night, the reverse had happened. She had known he was in danger. And she had been terrified. Then she had seen the sheriff's boots and called out a warning. But she hadn't seen Adam. Now she knew why. He had been a gray wolf in the darkness, and her mind had rejected that vision.

Tonight it was impossible to turn away from the knowledge of the wolf. Man and animal were the same. She was staring down at him through the glass when flashing lights in the rearview mirror suddenly captured her attention.

A police car. The wolf saw it, too.

He waited for a few more seconds, then turned and dashed away, disappearing into the fog. And she was left sitting in the car, breathing hard, trying to deal with the unthinkable.

Paul Delacorte stepped out of the police car and came toward her car, shining his light through her window.

She raised her hand to shield her face, and he directed the beam away from her.

"Dr. Weston? Are you all right?"

She opened the door. "Yes. I . . . I had an accident."

"Are you all right?" he repeated.

"I'm all right," she assured him, trying to keep her voice steady.

"Please get out of the car."

She did, wanting him to know that she hadn't been driving under the influence. As he shined the light on her, she started shivering.

He moved the beam away from her and inspected the damage. "What happened? Did you fall asleep?"

"No."

He played the beam around the bottom of the car, then at the trees along the side of the road, then onto the black-top.

"Did you swerve to avoid an animal?"

"No."

He made a more thorough inspection of the area, then came back to her.

"I always call for an ambulance. But it looks like you don't need one."

"No, I don't."

She waited while he spoke into the microphone clipped to his collar, canceling the emergency vehicle.

She was debating what else to say to him, when more headlights cut through the night.

A surge of fear shot through her. She was sure Delacorte caught her contorted features. Then he turned toward the newcomer pulling up in back of the police car.

It couldn't be the witches coming back, she told herself. Not now. Not when the sheriff was here. But logic had nothing to do with the sudden chattering of her teeth.

She cringed against the car, then breathed out a small sigh as she saw who it was—Adam, looking disheveled, as though he'd just thrown on his clothing.

A feeling of unreality seized her as she stared at him. He had been here only a few minutes earlier. He had come to her rescue. But the last time she had seen him, he had been a wolf.

She fought off a jolt of hysterical laughter. If she thought he had been a wolf, she had another reason to doubt her own sanity. Yet she knew it was true.

He ran across the road, his eyes fixed on her, yet he stopped a few yards away, and she knew that he was hesitant to approach her, now that she'd seen the wolf in action. Then another thought struck her. She hadn't said anything to him. He didn't even know for sure if she had recognized him.

Yet she felt unspoken messages passing between them. A sane person would be afraid to get near him now.

But she wasn't frightened of him. Really, she was more afraid of herself.

"Adam." She raised her hand toward him, and he closed the distance between them, taking her in his arms.

"Are you all right?" he asked, and she felt the question rumbling deep in his chest.

"Yes."

"Thank God." He pulled her tightly to him, and she leaned into his warmth. He was here. He had come to her again. Even when he didn't know if she was going to run screaming from him.

His hands stroked up and down her back, and she knew he must feel the fine tremors of her body.

Behind her Delacorte was speaking. "I was trying to find out what happened."

She turned to face the sheriff, letting Adam hold her against his body. "I . . . I . . ." She stopped and started again. "A car was coming toward me. I swerved off the road to avoid it."

The lawman looked around. "I don't see another car."

"It managed to keep from hitting me. I guess . . ." She stopped, wondering what to say.

Adam filled in the gap. "What I think is that the witches were lying in wait for her. They forced her off the road. Then they came to finish her off."

Her head swung toward him. Then to Delacorte. Then back.

FALCON gripped the arms of the easy chair.

"What the fuck are you doing? Trying to burn my skin off?"

"I'm trying to disinfect this bite," Willow answered as she dabbed antiseptic on his mangled flesh. "You don't want to end up in the hospital, do you?"

Falcon gritted his teeth as she slopped more of the stuff

on the places where sharp teeth had punctured his skin. He had a bunch of deep bites on his legs.

So did the rest of the clan. They were gathered in the living room of the house where a big plastic sheet hung between them and the construction mess.

Until a few days ago, the addition had still been open. Now he was profoundly glad that the house was secure and that the wolf or dog or whatever it had been couldn't get in.

"What was that thing?" Razorback asked, echoing his thoughts.

"I don't know. But it was something strange," Starflower answered.

"It was a dog gone mad," Razorback said.

"And it came streaking out of the night and started tearing at us just when Sara Weston needed help," Starflower said. "Don't you think that's a little convenient for her?"

"What are you saying?" Falcon demanded.

"Maybe she's the kind of witch who has a familiar. In fairy tales, it's a cat. But maybe she's got a damn wolf."

"Oh yeah, right," Razorback said, trying to sound sarcastic and not quite pulling it off.

"If it's true, it's another reason we have to get rid of her. Because next time, that wolf of hers could rip us to pieces."

"WHY would the witches be after her?" Delacorte asked Adam in a slow, careful voice.

Adam watched Sara drag in a breath. He thought she was going to speak, but she evidently changed her mind and closed her mouth. He pulled her closer and filled the silence by saying, "I think they're afraid of her."

"Why?"

"She's some kind of threat to them. They didn't just

drive her off the road. They came after her with their psychic powers! The way they came after me that night in the swamp."

The sheriff was watching him closely. "How do you figure that?"

His own tension level was so high that he didn't have to fake a show of emotion. He ran a hand through his hair in a good imitation of a man who was thoroughly perplexed. "Maybe I've got a little of their . . . their powers. All I know is that I sensed that Sara was in trouble out here—from them. And I came running. Or rather driving."

Which left out the part when he *had* come running. But he wasn't going to bring that up. He was pretty sure Sara wouldn't, either—if she'd understood what had happened. He didn't even know that much.

He kept his gaze fixed on Delacorte, to see how the explanation had gone over. The sheriff nodded as if the answer didn't really surprise him. "I've got a theory about that," he muttered.

"Oh yeah?"

"It's the Olakompa. There's something in the swamp that seeps into your system. From the water. Or the rotting vegetation. And if you've got the right receptors in your brain, it acts like a drug to . . . to . . . give you psychic power."

Adam tried not to gape at him. Obviously the man had been mulling over this rationale for Wayland's supernatural troubles for quite some time. The lawman focused on Sara. "Have you found any plants that might be involved?"

"There are plants that cause hallucinations. I . . . I don't know about ones that . . . that increase psychic power," she stammered.

Adam tipped his head to one side, torn between this fascinating discussion and his need to be alone with Sara.

"That's a pretty enlightened point of view from a small-town sheriff."

"I've lived in Wayland all my life. I grew up with the witch tales. I've had a lot of time to think about what's happened here over the years."

Adam nodded.

"If you've got a better hypothesis, I'd like to hear it," Delacorte said.

"I don't. And I'm not going to stand on the side of the road speculating about it," he added, finally unable to control his own emotions a moment longer. He could feel Sara leaning more heavily on him, and he suddenly wondered how she was managing to stay on her feet at all. Probably she'd had an emotionally draining experience at her parents' house. And she'd come home to *this*. Now she must be beyond exhausted.

"I'm going to take this woman home," he said, hearing the tightness in his own voice. "We can arrange for towing tomorrow. Unless you need her for something else."

Delacorte looked at the wrecked vehicle. "I'll call a truck and have the car towed to Jerry's Garage in town, if that's agreeable with you."

"Yes, thank you," Sara murmured.

When Adam started to shepherd her toward his SUV, the sheriff shook his head. "Before you leave, I need some basic information from you."

"Like what?" Adam demanded.

"Dr. Weston sideswiped a tree. I have to fill out an accident report, and for that I need her driver's license, vehicle registration, insurance card, home address, phone number—that kind of information."

Adam nodded tightly, stepping back so Sara could comply with the request. She had to call him back, though, to ask for the phone number at the park.

He waited for Delacorte to finish, listening to Sara's

even voice, trying not to look like a pressure steam valve was about to burst in his chest.

When the sheriff had taken the basics, he put away his notepad. "Did you recognize any of the . . . witches?"

Sara shook her head. "They were all wearing black capes with hoods."

"Okay." Delacorte didn't write it down. Obviously the witch part wasn't going into the official report.

"Are we done?" Adam asked.

"Yes."

Adam silently led Sara to his vehicle, opened the passenger door for her, and then closed it after she climbed in.

He had been desperate to be alone with her. Now he walked slowly around the car, putting off the moment. But finally there was nothing left to do besides slip behind the wheel.

He looked back, seeing Delacorte watching them. The sheriff had already seen him pull Sara into his arms and hug her, so he knew something was going on between them. But it could be over in the next few moments.

So instead of dragging her close and hanging on to her, he started the engine, then headed back to the safety of Nature's Refuge.

Taking his eyes from the road, he glanced at Sara. She didn't speak.

His voice was gritty as he asked, "So, what about the wolf?"

CHAPTER
TWENTY-THREE

ADAM HAD DROPPED the question into a deafening silence. He clamped his hands on the steering wheel, thinking that he'd made a terrible mistake.

But he wasn't going to take it back. He risked a glance at Sara. She had knit her hands in her lap so tightly that her knuckles were white.

Instead of answering his question, she said, "We were talking about the witches like some science fiction movie we'd seen! But it's not a science fiction movie. I'm one of them."

"Jesus! That's not true!"

"What am I?"

"A woman with . . . with some special talents."

She twisted her hands in her lap. "I told you I was going home to find out about my background. While I was there, I had one of my old *daymares*. Only this time, it made better sense. It was the one about the little girl and her mother in the cabin. I put some of it together, and I made my adoptive mother tell me some of it. I'm Jenna

Foster's little girl. My mother was the witch they killed. My father was there that night. He got me out of the cabin, then found adoptive parents for me."

She let that settle into the darkness before demanding, "Say something."

"I was starting to wonder if you were her daughter. Delacorte was, too."

"You talked about that? About me?" she demanded.

"That's not how the conversation started. He dropped by while you were away to talk about the wolf he'd seen downtown at the historical society building. The wolf he almost shot."

She made a low, moaning noise.

"So, yeah, we were having a pretty . . . intense conversation. And you came into it. I told him that even if you were Jenna Foster's daughter, you hadn't come back to town to get revenge on Wayland. You weren't one of them."

"It doesn't worry you that I'm her daughter?"

"That didn't bother your natural father when he was having a relationship with your mother."

"Oh, I think you're wrong. He was ashamed of his liaison with her. He kept it hidden from everyone in town. After she died, he took me to North Carolina and found a childless couple to adopt me."

"It didn't have to have anything to do with the damn witch thing. He could have been married, for all you know."

He saw her taking that in and went on quickly. "But he loved you. He didn't let you down. He found good parents to bring you up."

"Far away from Wayland where nobody would know who I was."

He made an exasperated sound. "Maybe he sent you far away to keep you out of danger."

She shot him an astonished look. "I didn't think about

it that way. But it doesn't change anything. I'm still worried about my . . . background. When I was driving back here, I kept wondering how I was going to face you."

He started to speak, but she waved him to silence.

"Let me finish! The closer I got to Wayland tonight, the more I felt the world closing in on me. I kept thinking, What happens when he finds out the real truth about the woman he made love with? I kept thinking, The witches are after me. And they could hurt Adam. Or I could hurt him. Somehow, something bad could happen."

"No!"

She kept talking, staring straight ahead, as though he hadn't spoken. "Then . . . then they forced me off the road, and they started that stuff with me that they did the other day. Only it was worse. They had on those damn hoods. And they were using their minds to attack me. Sending mental energy bolts at me. And you know what I did? I fought back the same way!"

"Good."

"You can accept what I'm telling you . . . just like that?"

"Yes."

"Why?"

He thought about the answer for a moment, recognizing the importance of what he told her—to both of them. "I guess because my whole life has been lived knowing there were things in the world that would scare the . . . the spit out of ordinary people. If there are men who change themselves into wolves and roam the woods at night, who knows what the hell else is lurking in the genetic heritage of humankind."

As they'd been talking, he had been driving, going on automatic pilot, going home. When he looked up, he saw that he was in the parking lot of Nature's Refuge. He'd left the gate open when he'd come tearing down the road in his car.

He'd driven inside the park grounds without even thinking about what he was doing.

Sara sat staring straight ahead. "The witches would have finished me off except that the wolf came along and started tearing into them. He could have gotten hurt. Or killed."

"The wolf did what he had to do! The problem is that he *is* a wolf."

She had avoided looking at him. Now she turned and met his eyes. "I saw the wolf before tonight. Not in real life. In a daydream about the past. When it started off, I was my mother, living in that cabin. Then I looked up and saw the wolf. I didn't know his identity. But I knew he had come . . . for me."

"Were you afraid of that?"

"Yes."

"And now?" he asked, hardly daring to breathe.

Instead of answering the question, Sara asked one of her own. "Why aren't you running screaming from a woman you know is a witch?"

"Because I love her!" he fairly shouted, then realized what he'd said.

AFTER Adam and Sara drove away, Paul Delacorte focused on routine tasks, like drawing a quick sketch of the scene. Then he took some measurements, triangulating the vehicle to a big tupelo tree, so three or four years later, he could place the car in the exact position where it had come to rest—in case there was going to be a trial for some reason. Next he took some flash pictures of the Toyota and the road surface and a couple of comprehensive shots covering the scene from different angles.

Finally, he looked around for any evidence he might have missed: drugs, alcohol, anything that might have been thrown out of the car. But he found nothing. So he drove to a nice quiet spot on a side road and began writing up the accident report. When he'd first come upon Sara Weston's battered Toyota at the side of the road, he'd wondered if he'd come upon a case of falling asleep at the wheel or DWHUA, driving with head up ass. Swerving to avoid a porcupine or a raccoon fell into that category, and she looked like the tender-hearted type who wouldn't want to hurt a small animal. Instead, she'd come up with the story about another vehicle that had vanished into the night.

She'd been shaken. And she'd been trying to figure out what to say. Unfortunately, Adam Marshall had driven up and started speaking for her.

Marshall blamed the accident on the witches. But there was more to it than that. Stuff that neither he nor Weston was saying. Paul had been a cop for too long not to recognize evasive answers when he heard them. They were leaving something out, and he was going to find out what it was.

Was Sara Weston involved with the people he'd come to think of as the bad witches?

Adam had said it wasn't true. Paul was still waiting for the rest of the chickens to come home to roost. And he had a lot of questions. Like, for example, he wanted to know how Adam Marshall had gotten there so fast. Did he really have some psychic power that had drawn him to the accident site?

He sighed. That was the least of his problems. At the moment, he had to figure out how to write up his report. Because he sure as hell wasn't going to mention anything paranormal. Not hardly.

ADAM heard Sara's indrawn breath. "Is love enough?" she asked.

"What the hell do you mean—is love enough?"

"It's a fair question."

"The hell it is!"

"Adam, I'm scared."

"Of me?"

"Not of you. Of . . . of . . ." Her hands fluttered. "Of what's happening. Of the witches. Of myself. Didn't you hear what I said? When they hurled thunderbolts at me, I started fighting back the same way. Adam . . . I'm frightened of what I am. Of what I can do."

"But not of a man who changes into a wolf and roams the woods at night?" he asked, putting the question in the most stark terms he dared.

"Not of you!"

"In that case, we'll make it work," he growled, unhooking his seat belt, then unhooking hers so he could haul her across the console and into his arms.

He cupped the back of her head with one hand, bringing her mouth to his in a kiss that started as a desperate attempt to show her what she meant to him. What they meant to each other.

The other hand dragged her closer so he could feel her beautifully rounded breasts pressed more firmly to his chest.

The contact delivered a jolt of sexual need that drove everything from his mind except the feel of her, the wonderful taste that he had discovered so recently.

She might have resisted, but her fingers kneaded his shoulders, moved to his upper arms, and back again, her touch questing and erotic.

He had driven home as though he were traveling through a dream landscape. He was still in a fog. He had forgotten where they were. Forgotten everything but the enticing woman in his arms.

With a jerky motion, he released the lever and pushed back the seat to its maximum extension. Lifting her up, he pulled her skirt out of the way and settled her in his lap, positioning her so that she was facing him, her legs straddling his.

He accomplished all that without lifting his mouth from hers. When he had her where he wanted her, he pushed up her knit top, then reached around to unhook her bra so that he could take her breasts in his hands.

She moaned into his mouth, moaned again as he played with her nipples, the feel of those hard pebbles against his fingers driving him close to insanity.

Her hips moved restlessly against his, and her lips were soft, warm, and open, silently begging him for more. He obliged, deepening the kiss, using his tongue and his teeth and his lips in all the ways he'd learned to please a woman.

It wasn't enough, and he realized that he had moved her onto his lap too quickly. The layers of clothing separating them were driving him beyond the point of madness. And when she made a frustrated, whimpering sound of agreement, the blood in his veins turned to molten lava.

Somehow he kept himself from screaming in protest when she pushed away from him—until he saw that she was trying to struggle out of her panties. He ripped the fabric and tore them free of her body, so that he could dip his fingers into her throbbing center. She was hot and wet, and the stroking touch of his fingers seemed to make her whole body pulse and tremble.

Her fingers scrabbled at the snap of his jeans, then the zipper. And when she took him in her hand, he thought he would self-destruct.

"Sara," he gasped. "Don't. I want to come inside you."

"God, yes!" As she spoke, she lowered her body, bringing him into her with a sure, swift motion that robbed them both of breath.

He brought his mouth back to hers, caressing her breasts as she moved frantically above and around him, her moans of pleasure mingling with his.

They climaxed in an explosion of passion that felt to him like a rocket blasting off into outer space.

She wilted against him, her face damp, her breath ragged.

He kissed her cheeks, her lips, his hands stroking possessively over the silky skin of her back.

For long moments, neither one of them moved.

He was the one who spoke first. "Don't give this up because you're afraid of the future."

"There's more to working out our relationship than great sex."

"Was it?"

She reached up and gave a tug at his hair. "You know damn well it was!"

He laughed, a low rumble in his chest. "Yeah." Laughing felt good. She felt good, her body covering his, clasping him. He kissed her again, slowly, tenderly, then with more urgency as he felt himself getting hard a second time, still inside her.

She raised her head, looking down at him, smiling. The smile turned to a small gasp as he found her breasts again.

"Good, that's so good," he whispered.

"Yes."

They kissed and touched, arousing each other more slowly now that the urgency was sated. This time they enjoyed the delight of being together. Of giving and receiving pleasure, of working their way from peak to peak until climax overwhelmed them once more.

When they could finally move again, he helped her up, and she flopped into the passenger seat.

He stepped out of the car, pulled on his jeans, then circled around to her door. Helping her out, he stuffed the ruined panties into his pocket, then swung her up into his arms and carried her along the path to his cabin, determined to keep her safe no matter what the cost.

CHAPTER
TWENTY-FOUR

IT WAS TOO early in the morning for a business meeting. But Paul Delacorte was responding to a summons from the most powerful man in Wayland. The message had been on his voice mail when he'd arrived at the office. He'd figured that he might as well get the interview over with.

James Lucas had apparently been waiting for him. The two men met outside the front door of the mansion next to one of the variegated ivy topiaries that flanked the wide entrance.

They eyed each other gravely. They weren't really friends. But they weren't enemies, either. Their skin color made them allies. Although they were of two different generations, they were both African American men who had done very well for themselves in the small town of Wayland, Georgia. Each was conscious of his position in the community.

They were both wearing uniforms that proclaimed their status. James, who was in his late fifties, was dressed in the neatly pressed black suit and crisp white shirt that his employer required him to wear. There were folks in the black section of town who thought that suit was a badge of oppression. He ignored them and had survived bigotry from both the black and white communities with grace and determination and an ability to keep his mouth shut when faced with stupidity from either race.

Paul, who was in his early thirties, wore the crisp navy blue police uniform and plain black trooper boots provided by the Wayland taxpayers. He and James had grown up in a different world. James had come from a generation where Negroes were considered to be inferior to whites for a variety of racist reasons, ranging from skull thickness to body odor. Paul had been born into a world where equality was supposed to be within reach, if you trod carefully among the tar pits and quicksand traps of life in a small southern town.

Ironically, each thought the other had gone too far in bowing to the subtle and not so subtle pressures that the white folks imposed on them. But neither of them would ever have voiced that opinion. They were allies in a struggle that remained on the collective radar screens of the African American community.

Paul might be the sheriff, but as the younger of the two men, he allowed James to take control of the conversation.

"I got a summons to the big house this morning. What's up?" he asked.

James lowered his voice but spoke in tones dripping with sarcasm. "The massa's scared," he said, mocking a term of respect once used in slavery days.

"The field hands are rebelling?" Paul asked.

"Naw. I hear tell the witches have a grudge against him."

"You got any idea why?"

"He don't confide in me."

"Yeah, well, maybe I can get the straight story out of him."

"Good luck."

Paul had been summoned to the mansion a few times in the past. The last occasion had been when Barnette had wanted a police background check on the farm manager he was considering hiring. Paul had seen no harm in earning some brownie points by doing the town benefactor a favor. It had turned out the guy had a slew of DWI convictions, and Barnette had hired someone else.

"Where is he holding this audience, in the study or the conservatory?"

"Neither. You're in the front parlor."

"Well, well. The black folks is comin' up in the world," Paul muttered as he followed James inside.

The butler squared his shoulders and stood up straighter when he led the way down the hall to the house's main sitting room.

"Sheriff Delacorte, sir," he intoned, as though he were announcing an important courtier to an eighteenth century English monarch.

Paul strode through the doorway, then stopped and studied the man sitting in a carved wooden chair that might have been a throne. It had been almost a year since their last face time. The patriarch of Wayland, Georgia, looked older and on edge, despite his studied casual air.

"I appreciate your coming," Barnette said.

"Yes, sir," Paul answered, hating the way he'd added that *sir*. But it seemed to come automatically out of his mouth when he was in this house.

"Have a seat," Barnette invited.

Paul looked around at the uncomfortable furniture and selected a Chippendale chair about five feet from the master's throne, waiting for the man to say what was on his mind.

"I understand we have a situation in town," he began.

"A situation?"

"Newcomers moving into the area and making trouble."

"What trouble?"

"I expect you know what I'm talking about!"

"I'd like your perception, sir."

Barnette permitted long seconds to stretch before allowing, "You know that over the years, we've had some unfortunate . . . incidents."

He paused, but Paul remained silent and remained sitting quietly in his chair, although his pulse rate had picked up. He knew very well what the last unfortunate incident had been. It was decidedly different from what was happening now. Did Barnette recognize the difference?

The old man spoke again. "Things have been quiet for a while. But we both know there have been people in town who . . ." He stopped and cleared his throat. "Whose behavior doesn't conform to the community norm. Or any other norm. I expect that you're alert to that?"

"Yes, sir," he answered, sorry that they were still tiptoeing around the subject.

"Down through the years, there's been a history of incidents involving those people and the rest of us."

Paul nodded, thinking that what Barnette meant was that homicide had been committed here. Out of fear and hatred.

Barnette rocked in his seat. "What happened was . . . documented."

Paul blinked. "You mean murder? You mean somebody was stupid enough to write it down?"

Barnette's face contorted. "We're talking about papers that were supposed to be destroyed. Apparently, they ended up in a locked safe at the historical society."

"Is that what the break-ins were all about?"

"Yes. And I wouldn't call it murder."

"What would you call it?"

"Self-preservation."

"We have a different interpretation of the term."

"I believe your daddy and I saw things the same way," the old man snapped.

"I'm not my father," Paul said in a low but firm voice. "I don't sweep homicide under the rug because that's what the white folks want me to do."

A flush spread across Barnette's wrinkled face. "That's not what I'm asking."

"What *are* you asking?" he inquired, keeping his voice low and even.

"First, that you recover the stolen property."

"I'm doing my best. But we have no leads."

"You know as well as I do who took those records."

"Do I?"

"Troublemakers who have moved into the area. New people who ... who are connected with families that might have lived here at some earlier time. I want them brought to justice."

"I don't have much to go on," Paul repeated.

"You have employment applications. Real estate transactions. Phone records. Credit receipts. All kinds of information."

"I've made a start on that. But I don't have the resources to go through months of random civil records with little hope of finding anything useful."

Barnette snorted. "I can provide the resources."

Paul raised an eyebrow.

"A special grant to the sheriff's department. More money for additional personnel. You run the department with eight deputies. That's not much manpower."

So the old man was paying attention to things like staff numbers. What else was he into? "The offer of additional money is very generous of you, sir. But we can't hire personnel off the streets. Officers must have special training for their jobs. According to our charter, we can only take candidates who have graduated from the state police academy or who have been working in law enforcement."

"I thought you'd give me some excuse like that!"

"I'm willing to hire suitable candidates after a thorough background check."

"Which means it will take months."

"I'm afraid that's so. When sheriff's departments skip that step, they can wind up with felons on the payroll. That happened in Dade County, Florida, not too long ago."

Barnette's eyes narrowed. "Well, I don't intend to make myself a sitting duck. I'm hiring a private security company. I'm starting with two men right here."

"At your estate?"

"Yes."

"Do you have some reason to worry about your personal safety?"

"No more than any other normal citizen of Wayland." He made a throat clearing noise. "I'd appreciate your keeping me informed on what you find out about any troublemakers in town."

"I'm afraid I'm not authorized to do that, sir."

"Yes, well, perhaps we should elect a sheriff who's more cooperative. When are you up for reelection?"

"Next year."

Barnette stroked his chin thoughtfully. "That soon."

Paul ignored the implied threat and stood. "If there's nothing else, I need to get back to work."

"Of course." Barnette gave a dismissive wave of his hand, as if he was sending away one of the house slaves.

Paul pressed his palm against the side of his uniform pants, thinking that it was a good thing he was getting out of here before he lost his cool and said or did something that would make his daddy roll over in his grave.

As he left, James appeared in the hallway. They walked silently toward the front door, then exited onto the porch.

"Well?"

Paul looked around, wondering if the portico was bugged. He made a quick negative gesture with his head, then walked slowly down the steps. James followed.

"You're right. He's actin' like a cat on a hot tin roof. He wants me to find out who broke into the historical society."

"I guess that old lady, Mrs. Waverly, has her skirt in a twist."

"It's more than that. What I got out of the conversation is that somebody kept some notes on who did what to whom over the years."

"You're kidding."

"No. Barnette thought they'd been destroyed. Apparently, he was wrong!"

USUALLY Adam was up early. But exhaustion kept him asleep until long after the sun had risen.

He woke with a feeling of disorientation, followed immediately by a terrible tightness in his chest. The tightness eased when he found that Sara was still in bed with him. She was sleeping on her back. The covers had slipped part way down her chest, revealing the tops of her creamy breasts. He wanted to reach out and slide the sheet the rest of the way down so he could see more of her. But he held himself still, thinking he should be content with what the morning had given him.

Really, he thanked God for the morning's gift because he had been secretly afraid that Sara was going to disappear again.

They had cleared that hurdle. Now all he had to do was make sure he woke up next to her every morning for the rest of his life.

His right arm was in an uncomfortable position. But he was afraid to move, afraid to wake her. So he feasted on what he could see. The mass of blond hair spread across her pillow entranced him. So did the curl of her ear and the curve of her eyebrow.

Long moments later, he saw her lashes flutter, and his breath stilled. Her eyes opened, and he caught her momentary sense of confusion. Then she turned her head and looked at him.

"Good morning," he whispered, shifting to ease the cramp in his arm and hearing the gritty quality of his own voice.

She gave a small nod.

"Thank you for being here."

"I'm not going to run away again."

The sense of relief was profound, followed by the need to pull her into his arms then, and make love to her all over again. But her next words stopped him.

"That isn't a promise that I'll stay forever."

"What is it?" he managed to ask as he sat up and plumped his pillow behind him, giving himself something to do so he wouldn't have to meet her eyes.

She looked at him, then slid up carefully, pulling the sheet with her to cover her breasts. Then she took several moments to arrange her own pillow.

"A promise that I'm going to try and act like an adult, not a scared little girl."

"Good." He wasn't sure what else to say. What else to do. But he couldn't stop himself from reaching for her hand and holding on. He had gone to sleep wondering what he could say to influence her thinking. And he'd known it would have to be the truth. But the speech that had sounded so plausible as he'd silently rehearsed it last night now rang hollow in his mind. Still, he had to try and make her understand.

"I was always a very happy bachelor. I loved playing the field. I loved having a good time with a lot of different women. Those kinds of times are over, because now the only woman I can think about making love to is you."

"Making love with you is wonderful," she breathed.

He shifted his hand and knit his fingers with hers, then couldn't stop himself from leaning over and brushing his lips against the tender place where her cheek met her hair. He ached to hear her tell him she loved him. But there was no way to force her response or her feelings. She had made discoveries at her parents' house that he knew had jolted her. Then she'd come home to an attack from the witches. And to the wolf. He knew she was still grappling with the aftershocks. All he could do was hold on to her and hope that she'd come to feel about him the way he felt about her.

"I'm not very experienced with men," she murmured.

"Is that supposed to be a negative?"

"Isn't it?"

"No. But at least this morning you're worrying about man-woman stuff. Not witch stuff."

"I'm still worried about witch stuff."

"Okay. But let's demolish the man-woman problem first. At least from my point of view. I knew the moment I saw you that you were the right woman for me. But that scared me. I tried to run away from it. I tried to tell myself it wasn't true. None of that did me any good. I kept thinking about how much I wanted you . . . needed you. Don't tell me you didn't feel something . . . significant that morning in the swamp!"

"Are you trying to get me to say I felt an instant attraction to you?"

"Did you?"

She heaved a little sigh. "Yes."

"So it wasn't all one-sided. That's a relief."

"You know it wasn't all one-sided."

"Yeah. But I like hearing you say it."

"And do you like hearing me say that I pick up information from your brain?"

He kept himself steady, knowing that she was trying to get a reaction out of him. "Like what?"

"Like your watching the witches that night in the swamp. I saw it in your mind."

"You tapped into my consciousness because some-thing . . . bad had happened to me. Then you did it again, when you thought Delacorte was going to shoot me."

"You can call it what you like. I say we're right back to the witch stuff."

He wanted to physically shake the negative thinking out of her. Instead he turned and reached for her, pulling her close against him. "All my adult life I've run from real intimacy. But you are the woman who completes me. Maybe all my life I was waiting for a witch."

She laughed, then quickly sobered again. "Living with me isn't going to be easy."

"Then I guess we're even." He swallowed hard. There were still things he didn't want to tell her. He wanted some time to show her how good they could be together before he had to get into the really bad stuff. But Ross had given him hope that life with a werewolf wasn't going to be the total disaster of his parents' marriage.

He was desperate to make her understand how he felt, yet at the same time, something else teased at the back of his mind. Something important. Perhaps she felt his sud-den tension, because she drew back and asked, "What?"

"Something . . ." He closed his eyes, trying to bring a scent into focus. And when he did, his body jerked.

"What? What's wrong?"

"Her smell!"

"Whose smell? Who are you talking about?"

He tried to make his muddled thoughts clear. "I was thinking that when the woman came to my office and tried to seduce me, I didn't respond, because the only woman I wanted was you. Then I started thinking about the way that other woman smelled."

"Good? Bad?"

"That's not the point. The point is that her distinctive scent wasn't masked then. Later, I picked it up down at the historical society building. Her and a lot of other people. Too many people for me to sort them all out. Then last night in the mist, there were only five witches. I couldn't see their faces. But I could distinguish their scents. Including that woman. She was there. Lord, maybe I should have figured out before that she's one of them."

Sara shuddered, her gaze turning inward. "Maybe I should have. That woman hates me," she whispered. "I saw it in her eyes the afternoon when she came on to you. She's so sure of her womanly power. But you turned her down. In front of me. Then last night, she tried to kill me. It was her. She was the one driving it. I know that know."

Adam felt a wave of cold sweep his skin. "She'd kill you because I want *you* instead of *her*?"

"Well, not just that. I think she's afraid of me. And I think she hates both of us, because we didn't give her what she wanted. And she always gets what she wants."

"Jesus." He turned and grasped her by the shoulders. "Maybe you're right. Maybe she's the motivating force. But whatever it is, I want you to promise me to stay in the Refuge where you're safe. Promise to stay here!"

She gave a tight nod.

"And I want you to do something else. Practice."

She looked puzzled. "Practice what—my plant experiments?"

"No, your witchcraft."

"What . . . ?" she gasped.

"You said that they hit you with mental thunderbolts. And you hit them back. But they were stronger than you. So practice doing it."

Her voice rose in panic. "I don't know how! I don't know what I did. I don't even know where to start."

"Figure it out, because they tried to kill you once, and they're going to come back looking for you."

His words had been harsh. The look of terror on her face tore at him. He reached for her, held her tightly, rocking her gently in his arms. "I'm sorry," he murmured as he skimmed his lips against the side of her face and her silky hair on the top of her head. "I hate to scare you."

"I know why . . . why you did it. I have to face facts."

He nodded against the top of her head. "Yes. We both do. Tonight I'm going to go out looking for the bastards. I don't need to see their faces, like I told you . . ." He still couldn't say the word *werewolf*, so he put it in third person terms. "The thing about the wolf is that he has a fantastic sense of smell. And tonight, he's got something to work with."

"Adam, for God's sake, be careful. Last night, you hurt them. I could feel their fear and their anger. It's not just her now. The whole coven is out to get you."

"Yeah, but I'll bet they don't know that the wolf is me."

"Don't count on it."

"Okay, and I'll be careful," he growled, because it was the answer she wanted—needed—to hear. And he would do anything to keep her happy while he tracked down the Satan's spawn who had tried to kill her.

CHAPTER
TWENTY-FIVE

AMY RALSTON WAS in the office down at the boat dock when her cell phone rang. The number on the screen brought a kind of sick feeling to the pit of her stomach. Furtively, she looked around. No one was in the immediate vicinity, so she pressed the Receive button.

"Hello?" she said in a lowered voice.

"What's up?"

"Nothing."

"Where's Marshall?"

"At the office."

"And where's Weston?" The voice took on an ugly ring as the speaker said the woman's name.

"She's in that shed, working with her laboratory stuff."

"Tell me if either one of them leaves the park."

"I'm only here till dark. It will look funny if I stay after hours."

"I know that! Just do your best. Try to get some extra evening hours. And one more thing, if you take any tourists out into the backcountry, see if you can spot any more of those cloth bags."

"I hate those things."

"Somebody put them out in the swamp to warn us away. I want to know if there are any more."

"Okay," Amy whispered.

The line clicked, and she was left listening to dead air. She wanted to turn off her phone, but she left it on because she didn't want to get into trouble.

Brenda had hurt her once, given her a terrible pain in the head. And her cousin could do it again if she wanted.

But that wasn't the only reason why she'd agreed to be Brenda's spy at Nature's Refuge. She had been surprised when her cousin had come to town and looked her up. She had heard stories about some of the people in her family. Her great-great grandfather had been killed by a mob. And her uncle and aunt had gotten out of town after another woman had been killed.

Brenda had come back with a group of friends. Friends like herself, she said.

Amy wasn't exactly sure what that meant. Her own family had never had any of the problems of Brenda's parents. And she knew she was pretty ordinary.

But Brenda was special. At first, Amy had been excited about that. Now she was afraid of Brenda and her friends. Especially that spooky guy who was fixing up his parents' old house outside of town. She didn't like him or the others. She wished Brenda wouldn't hang around with them. But Amy knew she wasn't going to stop her. And she knew that if she didn't do what Brenda said, she could get hurt—real bad. So she'd tell her when Adam Marshall or Sara Weston left the park. And she'd look for some more of those yucky bags in the swamp.

*   *   *

ADAM knew Sara had spent the day in her laboratory. He suspected she hadn't gotten much done. But he wasn't going to press her for details, because he was trying to show her that he could give her space. If that was an issue.

Still, he could only stay away from her for so long. When he went off duty, he invited her to his cabin for dinner. Steaks on the grill and salad. A nice normal meal. Only his steak was almost raw and he went easy on the salad.

She didn't comment on his dietary habits. And he did his best to steer the conversation to her work and his stewardship of the park, because those were safe topics.

But she had a way of turning everything back to the subject that was uppermost in her mind. He watched her playing with the wax that had dripped down one of the candles he'd set on the dining room table for atmosphere. He knew how to set the stage for physical intimacy. He had a lot less experience with sharing his thoughts.

"I was thinking about why I went into botany," she said.

"Why?"

"Probably I have some of the same interests as my mother."

He nodded, admiring what the candlelight did to her pale skin.

"But science is so . . . logical. There are reasons for everything . . . even if you don't know what they are. That appealed to me. I think I was looking for control and structure."

"Would you have liked some other field better?"

"I don't know. Maybe I'll give up plants and become an artist."

"What kind of artist?"

"I loved working with oil and acrylic paint. I think I'd be good at painting the swamp. The birds and animals.

The vegetation. Landscapes." Her voice had taken on an excited glow.

He covered her hand and lightly stroked it. "You should do what makes you happy."

"And does your job make you happy?"

"You probably know I picked it so I could be outside. Close to nature."

"Yes."

"But I was never exactly happy. Until you walked into my life."

"Adam . . ."

"Sorry. I'm not trying to force you into anything," he lied.

Finally he reached for his plate, intent on carrying it to the sink.

"Let me do the cleaning up," she said.

"You don't have to."

"You cooked. I'll clean."

"Okay," he answered, thinking that being with her, sharing chores with her felt natural. Simple. But nothing in their lives was really simple, was it?

He cleared his throat. "I'm going out. Will you wait here for me?"

"Yes."

He wanted to add, *in my bed*. But he didn't press his luck.

"Are you driving into town?"

He had debated about that. He could travel faster in his car. But he wasn't taking any chances on the witches watching the park entrance. He wanted them to think he was here guarding Sara. "I'm going the back way."

He let that statement settle in the candlelit room. The back way. Through the swamp.

She nodded, then reached toward him. That was all the invitation he needed to pull her into a tight embrace.

"Be careful," she murmured.

"I will. And you lock the door as soon as I'm gone."
He bent and kissed her. Just one undemanding kiss that
made him instantly hard as one of the candle shafts. Before he lost his resolve, he turned and walked through the
front door, feeling her gaze follow him as he strode into
the wilderness.

SARA stood quietly by the window watching Adam disappear down one of the nature trails. Then she locked the
door, feeling reassured by the rasp of metal against metal.
But as she seated herself on the couch, she knew that a
locked door only provided a false security. Anyone who
wanted to get in here could break a window. Unless she
stopped them. The gun she'd brought to Wayland was in
her purse which was resting on the floor near her feet.

She had boldly pulled out the weapon that first time in
the swamp with Adam when she hadn't known who he
was. And before that, she'd had several sessions at a practice range to make sure she knew how to use the gun and
how to take care of it. But she still wasn't certain if she
could actually shoot anyone.

There was something so awful about pulling the trigger
when you were facing a person, not a paper target.

And even if she could do it, what if a whole group of
people attacked the house, the way they'd done with Jenna
Foster.

The thought brought a clogged feeling to her throat.
She had brought the gun for security, but it might not do
her much good. Adam was right. She needed another form
of protection. The power that she'd inherited from her
birth mother.

Strangely, she didn't feel the same reluctance as when
she thought about a gun. A gun was a mechanical device.
The skills Adam had told her to cultivate came from
within her.

But how did she call them up? She'd flailed out in response to the witches' attack. But what guarantee did she have that she could do it again?

Had her mother tried to save herself on that terrible night? Sara didn't think so. Her mother had been a gentle woman. A woman oriented toward healing. That had been her special talent, and maybe she hadn't even known there was a way to defend herself.

Sara sighed, feeling weighed down with a deep sorrow. Jenna Foster had died so young. Lord, she probably hadn't been as old as Sara was herself. And not only that, she'd borne a child by a man who couldn't even admit their relationship to the world.

Adam was different. He had told her he loved her, blurted it out when he'd been trying to make her understand why he wasn't afraid of her.

She was sure he wanted her for his wife, although he was being careful not to press her. Was she the right wife for him? She still wasn't sure. But the idea of living without the man she loved made a cold knot form in her stomach.

The man she loved. She knew it was true, even if she'd been afraid to say it to him.

Her hands clenched and unclenched. Fear seemed to rule her life. And she hated that.

When she felt her nails digging into her palms, she deliberately tried to relax. Tried to open herself. Tried to bring back the feeling of power that had seized her when the witches had come hunting for her.

WHEN Adam was deep in the swamp, he took off his clothing and changed, then headed toward Wayland, sticking to the paths through the wilderness, moving quickly, intent on staying out of human sight.

The thought of going into town made his steps falter.

A wolf was made for the natural environment, with trees or open sky overhead and soft dirt under his feet, not hard pavement lined with buildings.

More than that, the town was dangerous, now that Delacorte was on the lookout for a werewolf. Every minute he spent on the streets was a minute too long. But he had no alternative. It wouldn't do him any good to simply pick up the trail of a witch. He needed to trace it back to the man or woman's house.

His thoughts flashed to his brother. Ross had offered to help him. And if he couldn't find the damn witches in a reasonable amount of time, he might have to ask for help. Two noses would certainly be more efficient than one.

He had reached the residential area and began moving more cautiously. At the edge of the downtown, he stopped dead and sniffed the air, hoping he wasn't going to pick up the strong scent of Paul Delacorte.

He didn't. But that proved nothing. The sheriff could be in his cruiser, metal and glass between himself and the outside air.

The wolf moved cautiously from building to building, a gray shadow gliding down back alleys when he could, cataloging the odors he encountered.

Garbage. Marijuana. Roses. And in one of the houses he passed, fresh baked bread and a pot of beef and vegetable soup slowly cooking.

Once or twice he stopped. The witch woman's scent was strong outside a Main Street shop that sold greeting cards. He stopped and dragged in a deep breath. She had been here. He was certain of that. But the trail ended in the parking area. Did she work in the store? He could come back during the day and find out.

No. He could only come back at night until the witches were put out of action. The minute they knew he was off the park property, they might go after Sara. And he couldn't take that chance. They knew where to find her, and he was the only thing that would keep them away.

IN the warm glow of the table lamps, Sara looked around the small room where she waited for her man to return. It was rustic and simple, but she liked it. Maybe because it was where Adam lived. She felt his presence here, even when there wasn't much to see of his personality in the room. He hadn't set out any family photos. Or mementos of his assignments. Probably he'd lived in a lot of parks around the country. But you couldn't tell it from looking at his house. He was a man who had lived a solitary life. And now he was reaching out to her. More than that, he had totally changed her perception of herself. He accepted her for who she was. What she was. And she hadn't really thanked him for that, she realized.

"Adam." She murmured his name, partly because it filled the silence of the room. She supposed she could put on the television set or the radio. But she wanted neither distraction.

Leaning back, she closed her eyes, opening herself to something that came from within. Inviting psychic energy to bubble up in her mind. It was a strange task, because she had no idea what she was doing. She didn't have one shred of control over her special abilities. Long ago, she had worked hard to shut a door in her mind. She had taken her father's word that the visions from her past or her flashes of insight into the present were strange or abnormal, bad elements to be rooted out of her life. And now Adam was telling her they weren't bad. He was telling her they might even be the key to her survival.

She tried to imagine where he might be. He had walked away from the cabin on two legs. He hadn't exactly said so, but she was pretty sure it was the wolf who had gone into Wayland.

A little frisson went through her. Going into town as a wolf was dangerous. But he had done it for her.

She tried to imagine him now, a gray shadow moving through the darkened streets. A clear image formed in her mind. But she was still unsure of herself. The image was just as likely her imagination as anything real.

ADAM waited at the entrance to an alley, his gaze darting up and down Main Street, probing the darkness between the overhead lights, his ears tuned to danger.

No one moved on the street, and he trotted forward again, then stopped short as he caught another familiar smell.

It was the hidden watcher he had spotted outside Sara's house. One of the witches! It had to be.

The man's distinctive essence filled his head. It started outside one of the shops. The dry cleaners.

That night at the cabin, the guy had escaped in his car. But now Adam had picked up his trail in town. Did he work at that shop? Or had he just been dropping off or picking up his cleaning?

Riveted to the man's odor, intent on the hunt, Adam followed the trail down the sidewalk, praying that the guy lived nearby, praying that he hadn't gotten into a car and driven away, leaving another dead end. He trotted along one block, then another, his breath burning in his lungs from the tension of not knowing. Three blocks from the dry cleaners he came to a small house, a bungalow walled off by a low boxwood hedge.

He went past, and the scent was less sharp. Turning back he stepped onto the front walk, breathing deeply.

The guy lived here. Or he had spent a lot of time here.

It wasn't what Adam would have pictured for a witch's lair. It was an ordinary house. But very well kept, he decided as he looked up at the porch which sat three steps above the walk. His gaze skimmed the white wicker furniture and the pots of impatiens. The wide porch roof was supported by massive stone pillars. The siding was yellow clapboard and looked newly painted. Stepping back, he took in the grounds. Even in the darkness, he saw that every inch of the front yard was planted with neatly mulched beds of flowers and vegetables set among paths of natural wood rounds.

He made out beds of daylilies. Some yellow flowers he'd seen before but couldn't name, tomato plants. Green bean vines. Hydrangeas. The front of the house was dark. He stepped around the side. Through a lighted window, he saw a man sitting in a leather recliner.

He was totally focused on his quest, so intent on his purpose that the rest of the world had ceased to exist. A dangerous situation for a wolf on the streets of Wayland.

CHAPTER
TWENTY-SIX

SARA FELT A shudder go through her. Once before when Adam had prowled the dark streets of Wayland, she had warned him to run.

Now it seemed like she was there with him again. Only the scene was more vivid. More real. This time it felt like she was standing right next to the wolf.

He was in the side yard of a small house, looking up toward a lighted room.

Someone was inside. And a shock of recognition went through her as she took in the man's face.

At any other time, he would have commanded her total attention. But she knew there was something else more important in the scene.

She had caught a glimpse of the street in front of the house where a police car was gliding slowly and silently forward.

It must be Delacorte. Or one of his deputies. And he must have seen the wolf.

"Adam—Watch out!"

She was sitting alone in the living room of the cabin. But her vision was focused on the garden of a house miles away. In that scene, she saw the wolf's body go rigid, saw him raise his head and look around.

"Run," she shouted again into the empty living room. "Use the alley and not the street. Delacorte's out there."

Her body was back at the cabin, but her mind was somewhere else. With Adam. With the wolf. At least part of her mind.

A split second later, he faded back into shadows, then trotted off into the backyard and hurried through the alley.

She saw the sheriff stop the car and get out, shining his light into the bushes and up and down the street. But the gray shape had made his escape. And all Sara could do was sit there on the couch, her arms wrapped around her shoulders, waiting for Adam to return.

AS Adam turned the knob on the front door, he saw Sara through the glass. She was huddled on the sofa, her shoulders hunched and her eyes closed. When he'd left, he'd pictured her in his bed. Now he was glad that she was still up and dressed.

The slight noise had her gaze shooting in his direction, and she was off the sofa and throwing the door open before he could get out his key.

She flung herself into his arms, pressing herself to him, her hands locking over his shoulders. "Are you all right?"

"Yes." He waited a beat. "Because you warned me again."

He stepped through the open door and closed it behind himself, leaning back against the solid surface as he hugged her to him.

"I was trying to do what you told me, trying to . . . to hook into . . . my powers. And then I saw you. Only I didn't know if it was real. But . . . it . . . it felt real. And when I saw the police car, I knew you had to get out of there." The words were high and shaky, and he realized she was near to hysteria. "Then I couldn't tell if it had worked, if you'd gotten away."

"It's all right. It's all right," he whispered, his fingers kneading the tense muscles of her neck and shoulders.

He had come rushing back here to tell her something important. But now that she was in his arms, all he could do was hold on to her. She was the one who eased away so that she could meet his eyes. "Before Delacorte came, you saw the Blackberry Man," she gulped out. "Inside the house."

He tipped his head to one side, trying to make sense of her words. "Who?"

"Well, that's the name I gave him. I saw him in the woods a few times near my cabin."

"I think he's one of the witches."

"He's not!"

"How do you know?"

"I . . ." She stopped, made a helpless gesture. "I don't know. I just think you're wrong. He was always friendly."

"Yeah, he'd have to act friendly, wouldn't he, if he didn't want to seem like a threat? But we're going to find out."

She goggled at him. "How?"

"We're going back to his house. I'd like to confront him on my own, but I'm not going to leave you in the park without protection."

She glanced from him to the darkness out the window, then back again. "You mean we're going now?"

"Yeah, now."

She gave him a panicked look, and he knew she was frightened. He could have told her that he'd rip the guy's throat out if he tried to hurt her. But he kept that insight to himself.

"Wouldn't . . . wouldn't it be better to wait until the morning?" she stammered.

He shook his head. "This is the perfect time. It's so late that the witches may not be watching the park entrance. I think the guy's alone in the house. I want to confront him while he's not with his buddies."

"But what . . . what if you're right about him? What if he attacks us?" she gasped out.

"I'm hoping he keeps up the pretense that he's friendly. And if he doesn't, we can handle him together," he said, projecting confidence because that was the only way to deal with the situation.

He hurried her into the car before she could marshal another protest. Then, as a precaution, he took the alternate route out of the park, using the road where she'd come in that first day. It was only a quarter mile from the main entrance, but it might fool the witches.

He drove with his headlights off down the narrow gravel lane and didn't switch them on until he was a mile down the highway. As far as he could see, there was nobody following them. But, of course, the coven, or whatever they called themselves, could be using the same tactics that he was employing, driving in the dark with their lights off.

Sara sat rigidly in her seat, and he wished to hell he didn't have to drag her to this confrontation. But leaving her alone was not an option. A few minutes later, he pulled up in front of the small house, then went around to open the passenger door.

She stepped out, and they both stood on the sidewalk, staring at the residence.

"It looks so normal," she whispered.

"Yeah."

When a flash of movement caught his attention, he turned his head and saw a police cruiser rolling to a stop beside them.

Shit! He should have driven around the block, looking for the cops. He should have realized that if Delacorte had been here earlier, he might have staked the place out, checking to see if the wolf came back. Unfortunately, his mind had been focused on the guy Sara called the Blackberry Man.

Now they were going to have some explaining to do.

The lawman got out, walking stiffly toward them.

Adam cursed again under his breath.

"What's up?" Delacorte asked.

He stuck with a version of the truth. "The guy who lives here was the man I saw lurking around Sara's house. I want to talk to him, but I don't think it's safe to leave Sara by herself. So I brought her along."

"How do you know it's the guy?"

It was then that Adam knew he'd made another bad mistake. What reason could he give now, a reason that wouldn't tie him to the werewolf?

He was a good talker. But he'd jumped in with an explanation before his brain was fully engaged.

He realized Sara was speaking. "I asked him to bring me here," she said.

Delacorte's attention focused on her with the intensity of a laser beam. "And why is that?" he asked.

He saw her swallow, wondered what in the hell she was going to say. "The other night you asked why the witches might be after me. I didn't want to tell you then because . . . because it was too personal." She dragged in a breath and let it out in a rush. "What I didn't want to tell you then was that I'm Jenna Foster's daughter."

The sheriff gave a tight nod. "I was wondering if that might be true."

"Why?"

"Because you're the right age. Because it looked like somebody wanted you back in that house."

Adam moved to Sara's side and put his arm around

her. "You don't have to tell him any more," he muttered.

She turned to him briefly. "I think I do." Addressing the sheriff again, she said, "When I moved into the cabin, I started having memory flashbacks. I didn't know what was happening to me, so I went back to my adopted parents' house and made my mother tell me some things she's kept hidden all these years. That was last night. I was on my way back to the park to talk to Adam about it when the witches forced me off the road."

"And when she told me about the guy hanging around her house, I figured he was one of them," Adam jumped back into the conversation.

Delacorte looked doubtful. "The man who lives here?"

"Yes," Adam answered, hoping the sheriff wasn't going to question the logic gap in their explanation.

"I'll be surprised if he's one of them," Delacorte said.

THE clan gathered in the shadows under the trees. Falcon and his band of followers. Willow. Water Lily. Grizzly. Razorback. Copperhead. Raven's Claw. Greenbriar. Water Buffalo. And Starflower. He was glad the rest of them were here. He needed to feel their presence. They had become part of him in a way that he couldn't explain. All of them. But the one he needed the most was Starflower.

She was the strongest of the women. Almost his equal. And she would play a key role tonight.

They were all naked—except for loincloths. And they would shed those later.

All of them except Starflower were wearing bright designs of paint in streaks and circles all over their bodies, the way they'd been on the nights of the ceremony. Because tonight was another special occasion. This was a crucial test of their power. And a time for celebration, because they were finally turning the tables on one of their enemies. More than one if everything worked out the way it should.

They came through the swamp, drifting like brightly painted birds through the fog that rose from the cooling ground.

A large bulk loomed in the background. The house. But Falcon knew his way around. Which was why he headed for one of the guest houses. Through the window, he saw a man sitting in an easy chair.

"Go get him," he said to Starflower.

She smiled, thrusting out her magnificent naked breasts before she stepped up to the door and knocked.

ADAM shifted his weight from one foot to the other. "If you don't think the man who lives here is one of the witches, then who is he?"

"Dr. Montgomery didn't just move to town. I remember him when I was a little kid."

Sara looked stunned. "He told me his name. He didn't say he was Dr. Montgomery."

"Well, he was the botany teacher at the community college until he retired a few years ago."

Adam felt a shiver travel down his spine as he remembered an item from the newspaper he'd seen. "The botany teacher . . ." he repeated. "Back in the year Barnette bought the land for Nature's Refuge, Dr. Montgomery was starting a course on herbal remedies at the community college."

THE night air was cool, but Sara felt beads of sweat break out on her skin. She backed away from the two men and darted quickly up the walk. Before she could give herself time to think, she rang the bell. She was aware of Adam and the sheriff climbing the stairs behind her, but all her attention was focused on the slim man with salt-and-pepper hair who had turned on the porch light and was peering through the front window.

When he saw her, his wrinkled face went pale.

But she wasn't seeing him exactly as he was. She was seeing his face without lines. Seeing him with dark hair. Seeing him come striding toward the cabin with a jaunty step, like he was escaping from his everyday existence into a world of magic.

The lock clicked and he opened the door, his eyes fixed on her.

Something she couldn't name passed between them, and in that moment she was sure.

"You figured it out," he said in a raspy voice.

"Yes. You're my father."

He stepped back, and she followed him inside. Adam and Delacorte were behind her, but she didn't take her gaze from the old man.

"How do you know?" he asked.

"I guess I was a little slow. But I finally got it."

He nodded, studying her face. "You look just like your mother, you know. I saw you at the cabin that first time, and for a few moments, I thought it was her, come back from the dead. I've missed her every day since that night. I've missed you."

She fought a choking sensation. It was hard to keep standing in front of this man who had betrayed her and had chosen to keep lying to her. "You abandoned me."

"What choice did I have?"

"You could have taken me to live with you!" Somehow she managed not to shout the words.

"I found you a good home. I sent you money."

"Money. Yes, money," she whispered, her eyes blazing. "Did that help salve your conscience? Did that make up for your being ashamed of me and my mother?"

"I wasn't ashamed of you!"

"You only came to our house when you could sneak away from town."

"You don't understand how it was."

"Why don't you tell me?" she shot back, unable to keep the sarcasm out of her voice.

He looked at her pleadingly. "I used to go off into the swamp gathering plants, just like I do now. That's where I met your mother. She was a ray of sunshine in my life. I couldn't believe that someone so sweet and beautiful could be interested in me."

"So you seduced her. Why didn't you marry her?"

"I would have, if I could. But I was already married!"

Sara struggled to assimilate the information. She'd made certain assumptions, assumptions that weren't quite right.

"Dora, my wife, was sickly. She couldn't give me children. She couldn't give me much of anything. My life was a wasteland. Then I met Jenna and fell in love with her. But I couldn't give up my responsibility. I couldn't leave a sick woman on her own."

She could only stare at him, trying to take it in, her mind forced to reject old assumptions. If he was telling the truth.

From behind her, Delacorte cleared his throat, and she turned briefly to look at him. She'd forgotten that anyone else was in the room with her and her father. "You're the one who got the child out of the cabin," he said.

"Yes."

"You saved her life."

Sara's head was swimming as she listened to the conversation.

Adam stepped toward the man who he'd thought was one of the witches. That was the biggest irony of all, Sara thought. He was no witch. He was her father.

"Do you have something to do with Sara's coming back to town?" Adam demanded.

Montgomery gave a tight nod.

"What?"

He dragged in a breath and let it out. Addressing himself to Sara, he said, "I funded the grant to Granville Pharmaceuticals. I made sure they contacted you. I convinced Austen Barnette it would be good for the town to let you work in the park. And, of course, he liked the idea of making some money by renting Granville that cabin nobody in town wanted." When he finished he looked relieved, like he'd finally gotten a burden off his chest.

"You?" Sara breathed.

"I wanted the association kept secret."

"Why did you bring me back here—to that house?"

He lifted his hand toward her, then let it fall back to his side. "So you could realize your full potential. I knew you had your mother's heritage. I kept pretty close tabs on you. As close as I could. The Westons were good for you. But I was afraid they had failed you in one important way. I was pretty sure they had made you turn away from . . . from your special abilities. So I arranged a job that would bring you to Wayland—to the cabin—because there's something in the swamp—something that brings out the paranormal powers in people who have them."

Delacorte made a sound of agreement.

Adam jumped back into the conversation. "So you wanted her back here. But you picked the wrong time. Others, with a similar heritage, have come back, too. To get revenge on the town. And she's caught in the middle of it."

The old man blanched. "No!"

Delacorte faced the old man. "If you know who they are, I want you to tell us."

Her father—she was still having trouble thinking of him in those terms—looked helpless. "I don't know anything about that."

"The only one of . . . the people with power you knew was Jenna?" Delacorte asked.

"Yes," he answered in a shaky voice. "She kept to herself. She didn't like them. Then, when she was killed, there was only that one little article in the paper. And some bastard cut it out of the volume down at the historical society. But I put it back. I wasn't going to let them wipe her out of existence."

Suddenly, it was all too much for Sara to take in. She felt no affection for this old man. He had never acknowledged her. He had given her up for adoption years ago. Then he had brought her back to town and spied on her, without telling her who he was.

"I need to get out of here," she whispered, turning and stumbling out the door.

ADAM followed her, hurrying to catch up, drawing her close, as she paused at the end of the front walk.

Shivering, she leaned into his warmth.

He wondered exactly what to say. "It must have been a shock, meeting him."

"He brought me back here, but he still couldn't be straight with me."

"He was trying to do what he thought was best."

"Are you defending him?"

"I feel sorry for him."

"Why?"

Adam's voice was raspy now. "He lost the woman he loved. And he gave up his child. He thought that was for the best."

"For his best," Sara answered, pulling away because she needed to be alone now. "Take me back to the park."

"Yes."

Delacorte came out.

"Did you get any more out of him?" Adam asked.

"No."

"Keep us posted if he comes up with any more information."

"You do the same if you find out anything more about . . . the situation."

They both nodded, and Adam helped Sara into the car.

The sky was lightening as they drove back to Nature's Refuge. Adam was thinking that tomorrow was going to be a hell of a day. Maybe he could snatch a nap sometime in the afternoon. Otherwise, he was going to be wasted by closing time.

In the gray light, he shot Sara a glance. She sat rigidly in the front seat, her hands clasped in her lap, unable to rid herself of the tension that was coursing through her.

A few miles out of town, both of them sat forward in their seats as they spotted a figure stumbling along the shoulder of the road.

It was a man running toward them, waving at them to stop.

CHAPTER
TWENTY-SEVEN

ADAM SLOWED, STARING at the wild man. He was black, dressed in a dark suit and shiny dress shoes, totally inappropriate for an early morning jog, and it took only moments to realize who he was.

"It's James," he said, pressing on the brakes, his mind scrambling for explanations. What the hell was Austen Barnette's butler doing looking like a wild man out here?

"Yes. I remember him from the other day, from that command performance with Barnette."

Adam screeched to a stop on the shoulder, and Austen Barnette's butler came staggering toward them. He stopped beside the SUV, his eyes wild, his breath coming in gasps. His mouth working for several moments before he was able to speak.

"Praise the Lord it's you! They got Mr. Barnette." James sounded frantic. "They drug him off into the swamp."

"Did you call the police?" Adam asked, climbing out of the SUV and going to the man's side.

James shook his head violently. "No. They said they'd kill him if I did." He went on breathlessly. "They cut the phone lines. They did something to my car," he puffed. "I had to come down here to the road. Cars went by, but nobody would stop. Black and white, both. Damn them."

The man looked like he was on the verge of having a heart attack. Adam opened the back door of the SUV and helped him in. The butler flopped onto the seat, leaning his head back for several moments before sitting up straighter.

Adam squatted beside the open door. Sara knelt in the front seat and turned around so that she was facing James.

"Okay, take your time. Tell me what happened," Adam said.

"I was in my little room off the kitchen, where I relax in the evenings waiting for when Mr. Barnette calls. I didn't know anything was happenin'." He stopped and swallowed. "I looked up, and outside the window I saw . . ." He glanced at Sara.

"Tell me what you saw," she encouraged.

In the illumination from the dome light, his dark skin turned ruddy. "A . . . a naked woman. With war paint all over her body."

Sara kept her gaze steady.

Adam felt a jolt of recognition. Naked people with war paint. That sounded a lot like the witches in the swamp. "A white woman?" he asked.

"I only got a flash . . . you know." He stopped and cleared his throat. "But, yes, she was white under all that paint. Then somebody came in and hit me over the head." He reached up to gingerly touch the back of his head. "I guess I was out cold for a while. I came to all hog-tied—lyin' on the floor."

"What about the security guards?" Adam asked.

"Dead."

"Oh, God," Sara breathed.

"How long ago did this happen?" Adam asked.

"An hour ago, I reckon. It took me a while to get free of the ropes. Then I ran around the estate looking for the guards." He stopped and swung his gaze from Adam to Sara and back again. "What am I going to do?"

"Call the sheriff."

James jolted upright. "No! I told you. They'll kill him if we call the law."

"They told you that?"

"They left a note on the table in the front hall." His gaze focused on Adam, and he blinked. "Inside it was addressed to you, but I had to read it!"

Adam touched his shoulder. "Of course you did."

"They said that if you called the police, they would kill Mr. Barnette. They said they wanted half a million dollars. They said you should handle it."

"Let me see it!"

James pulled a folded piece of paper out of his pocket, and Adam snatched it away. "Why me?" he asked.

"Maybe 'cause you run the park for him."

He still didn't know why he'd been singled out, but he scanned the message quickly. "Money?" he muttered, wondering what the hell was going on. Were these people planning to collect a ransom and leave town? It didn't fit in with the image he had of them. He had been assuming they'd come to Wayland to make the old-time residents miserable. But he supposed he could have gotten it all wrong. They could have been planning to disappear and live high on the hog off Austen Barnette's money.

"I picked up the note, and then I didn't know what to do," James was saying. "I jumped in the car, but it wouldn't start. So I ran down the drive."

"We can't keep this a secret. We have to call the cops."

He could see James's teeth chattering. "They'll kill him."

"They may kill him anyway!"

"How can we take the chance?" the butler demanded.

Adam didn't know. He saw Sara reach back and put her hand on James's arm. Softly she said, "They took Mr. Barnette off somewhere. They won't know we called the sheriff. They were just saying that to give themselves a free hand to do what they want."

"You think so?"

"Yes."

Adam looked at James. "I'm going to make the call. Okay?"

"Don't put it off on me," James muttered. "The note was addressed to you. You take the responsibility."

Adam felt his throat tighten. But he knew that they couldn't handle this by themselves. And he was pretty sure Mrs. Waverly down at the historical society wasn't going to be much help. Pulling out his cell phone, he dialed the number that Delacorte had given him. The sheriff answered on the second ring.

"Delacorte here."

"This is Adam Marshall. I just picked up James Lucas along the road. He says that Barnette has been kidnapped. Taken into the swamp."

"The swamp. Jumping Moses! Where are you?"

"About a quarter mile from the estate. And I took the responsibility of calling you. The kidnappers left a note addressed to me, saying they'd kill Barnette if the police got involved. They said they want money, but I don't know if it's true. So maybe you'd better come in some kind of unmarked car. And we'd better meet you up at the house, so we can get James off the road."

"I'll be there as quick as I can."

"Good." Adam turned to James. "He's coming in an unmarked car."

Starting the SUV, Adam headed up the road, then turned into the private drive that led to the house. There were dead men up there, and he didn't want Sara to see them. But he needed to know what had happened, and he couldn't leave her down on the road.

They pulled up in front of the house. "Anything inside that Sara shouldn't see?" Adam asked.

James caught his meaning immediately. "The house is okay."

They all went in. James showed them where he'd been sitting. The remnants of his rope bonds lay on the floor. It looked like the kidnappers had done a half-assed job of tying him up. Apparently, they'd just wanted it to last long enough to give themselves a head start.

Down the hall in the master's den, there were signs of a struggle. Small items from the desk were scattered across the floor, and the desk chair was overturned.

Adam heard a car engine outside and tensed. "Stay here," he ordered.

When he saw a pickup truck pull up in front of the house, he looked around for a weapon. But the man who climbed out was the sheriff, wearing jeans and a flannel shirt. A baseball cap was pulled down over his eyes. Adam glanced toward the tree line. If somebody was spying on them, it wouldn't look like the law had arrived.

Delacorte jumped out and trotted toward Adam. "Lucky your coming along and finding James Lucas," he said.

Adam wondered if there was some kind of hidden meaning in the comment. He chose to answer with a tight nod.

"What do you think happened here?" Delacorte asked.

"Barnette's gone." Adam hesitated for a moment, then gave his theory. "I think the witches kidnapped him."

"The witches? Why the witches?"

"James saw one of them through the window. He described a naked white woman with war paint. That's a pretty good description of the group I saw in the swamp the night they came after me."

Delacorte nodded. "It could be somebody imitating them."

"Could be. But who would do that? Who would know enough to do it?"

Delacorte shrugged. "If it's the witches, what do they want with him?"

"Well, they asked for a ransom. But that doesn't fit what we've discussed about them."

Delacorte nodded again. "Anything else you want to tell me before I talk to James?"

"He says the security guards are dead. He says one's out on the grounds. The other is in the guest house where they were living."

"Hard to get the jump on guys like that."

Adam nodded.

"Okay. I'll get some deputies up here to secure the area." He spoke into the microphone attached to his collar as he followed Adam into the house, then down the hall to the sitting room, a location that the witches didn't seem to have invaded.

Stepping back, he listened to the sheriff question the butler. James recounted the same story that he'd given them. Under Delacorte's careful questioning, a few more details emerged.

Barnette had been nervous that evening. He hadn't been out of the house for several days. He had called his lawyer for some kind of consultation. James had gotten the impression he was making a change in his will.

"For what?" Delacorte demanded.

"I have no idea, sir," James answered with dignity.

"It sounds like he was afraid something was going to happen to him," Adam muttered.

As they spoke, two deputies arrived, also dressed like the sheriff. They fanned out to search the area.

"Does Barnette have any relatives nearby?" Delacorte asked.

James shook his head. "No. But he's got a sister in Atlanta."

"Are they close?"

"No, sir."

Delacorte scowled. "Then there's probably no point in getting her all riled. But we need to set up recording equipment, so we can monitor the phone if they call with a location for dropping the ransom. And it looks like it will have to be here. I'll leave two deputies with you. That's all I can spare."

"They won't know the phone is tapped?" James asked.

"No." Delacorte answered, then gave him some instructions for what to say if he received a call. "Try to keep them on the line as long as possible. Try to get them to let you talk to Barnette. Tell them you want to make sure he's okay."

Adam listened, growing increasingly restless as the conversation progressed, because he didn't really think the ransom was the point.

He was pacing back and forth across the room when he finally reached the end of his patience.

"The longer we wait, the less chance there is that we find Barnette alive. I'd say we can risk two guys in the swamp if they look like they were out there for a nature walk or something." He nodded toward Delacorte. "You and me. Your clothing is good. But a green shirt would work better. Or a camouflage outfit. I'll wear something similar."

The sheriff considered the plan, then bobbed his head. "Okay, we'll use cell phones. If one of us finds Barnette or one of the . . ." He stopped short and started again. "If one of us finds the kidnappers, he calls the line I'll have set up for information. But it's a lot of territory for two guys to cover."

"Not that far. They're limited to the distance Barnette can walk. Or they can carry him."

"What about by boat? They could go to one of the islands."

"Let's assume they aren't into boats. They didn't use them the other night. I think they're not comfortable deep in the swamp, that they'll stick to the fringes."

Adam turned and focused on James. "I work for Mr. Barnette. I want to help find him. But I can't go looking for him unless I know Sara is safe. I think the people who took Barnette have been threatening her, as well. Are there some relatives of yours in town where you can take her? That's the last place where the kidnappers would look for her."

James blinked. "You went to take Dr. Weston down to the east end of town?" he said, referring to the black community.

"I'd be honored to go there," Sara said.

Delacorte looked thoughtful. "Yeah, it's a good idea."

FALCON stepped back and looked at the old man whose hands were tied around the back of a tree. Austen Barnette pressed his shoulders against the trunk and stared wide-eyed at the group of naked, painted figures around him, then brought his gaze back to Falcon. He was trying to keep his voice steady as he said, "Your name is John Ringell. You work for me. How dare you do this." The words were imperious, but the tone was faltering.

Falcon laughed, conscious of the clan members in back of him. "You're not the lord of the manor out here. Yeah. I go by that name sometimes. But not today. Today you can call me Falcon."

The captive stared at him, trying to take in what was happening. "Why are you doing this?"

Falcon lifted one shoulder. "You killed Jenna Foster."

The wrinkled face contorted with fear. "No!"

Falcon kept his voice mild. "Of course you did. It's all

written down in those secret records from the historical
society. The ones you thought were locked up. But I know
how to open a safe. Pretty stupid of you to keep that stuff
around. What, do you have a death wish or something?"

"I thought . . ."

"What?"

"Those records were supposed to be . . . gone."

Falcon snorted, "Well, it's too bad for you they were
in that safe—big as life and twice as plain. Maybe you
weren't the one who tossed that firebomb into her cabin.
But you were the one who stirred people up against her."

"No!"

It was time to make this man face the consequences of
his actions. Falcon stepped forward and gave him a good
slap across the face.

"Don't lie to me! You were the leader of the God-
fearing people in town. You rented her that cabin so you
could keep an eye on her. And when you decided she had
done evil, you whipped up the town against her."

Barnette goggled at him.

"You killed her, and you and your good buddies drove
the others like her out of town. That's how you got the
land for your damn park. I always wondered why my
uncle sold that property. But I've put two and two together—and they add up to over three hundred acres he
let you practically steal, so he'd have money to move his
family. That's true, isn't it?"

The old man moaned.

"Say it!"

"Yes. It's true. I wanted that land to benefit the good
people in town. I opened the park to bring money to the
area."

"How much other stuff like that did you pull?"

"Nothing."

"Sure."

Barnette's eyes filled with tears. "Let me go," he pleaded. "I can pay you."

"How much?"

"A million dollars."

"That's very generous of you, but money's not the point. We don't want your damn money."

"But I heard you say you were leaving a ransom note."

"That was the story we wanted James to believe. But we knew Adam Marshall wouldn't fall for it. We knew he'd come out here looking for you. And when he does, we'll be ready for him."

He turned to Razorback. "Light the fire."

The old man cringed. "Are you going to burn me?"

Falcon laughed. "You burned her up. Maybe that would be poetic justice; but actually, we have other plans for you."

CHAPTER
TWENTY-EIGHT

WHEN THE FIRE was blazing, Falcon nodded toward Starflower. She brought a long stick with a wad of cloth at the end, cloth that had been soaked in a drugged solution.

Everyone in the clan watched eagerly as she thrust it into the fire, watching it smolder.

The first hints of aromatic smoke drifted toward him, and he took a breath, smiling as he looked over at Barnette. The smoke didn't work quite so well for them now as it had the first few times. The effect was less, and they were going to have to find a way to boost the pleasure. But it was still potent, and he knew that it would hit the old man hard because this was his first time.

"You'll like this," he murmured.

"What is it?" the captive quavered.

Falcon laughed. "Something to put you in the right frame of mind for the festivities."

"No. Please."

"Don't waste your breath," Falcon growled, then turned away.

Starflower brought the brand toward her face, inhaling deeply. Her eyes took on a dreamy look as she held out the offering to the rest of them.

Each in turn, they leaned over to drink in the smoke.

Falcon was last. After he had taken his first portion, he turned and walked toward Barnette, thrusting the brand into his face, forcing him to breathe the smoke.

Starflower had come up behind Falcon, caressing the bare skin of his back, trailing her hand down to his hips and then his buttocks. He felt himself getting hard and looked back toward her.

"Later. We'll have fun later. But business before pleasure."

She made a pouting face but took her hand off his body.

Falcon turned his attention back to the old man who coughed and swivelled his head away. But there was no escape from the inevitable. All Falcon had to do was move the stick so it was in his face again. He watched with satisfaction as the old man's eyes glazed over.

With a smile, he picked up the knife that he'd left on the ground near the tree. "I think you're overdressed for this party, don't you?" he asked, inserting his knife into the fabric of Barnette's shirt and ripping it open.

SARA listened to the men talking about their rescue plans. She was confident she'd be safe with James's sister, but she wasn't so sure about Adam. He'd done enough already. She wanted to beg him to stay out of the swamp today. But she imagined he wouldn't listen to her.

She turned to face him. "I want to talk to you about this."

"About what?" he demanded.

"Can we have some privacy?"

"I'd like the sheriff to be in on the discussion," he answered, his tone brusque.

She swung her gaze to Delacorte. There were reasons why she wanted to keep the conversation with Adam private. Like, was he going into the swamp as a wolf or a man? But how could he go as a wolf, if he was supposed to be staying in communication by cell phone.

It struck her then how much her thinking had changed over the past few days. She had accepted the wolf because the wolf was part of Adam.

She studied him now, convinced that he was deliberately making sure she couldn't talk him out of looking for Barnette. She sighed. "Okay. Did you talk to the sheriff about what happened the last time you encountered those people in the swamp?"

"Yes."

"So he knows that they were having some kind of ceremony using drugged smoke. He knows that the smoke made you high. He knows that they chased you through the underbrush and almost killed you."

From the corner of her eye, she saw James's eyes bug out, as he took in the exchange.

Adam's gaze had narrowed. "I told him what happened. The smoke was a problem, but I don't think it will be a problem now."

"Why not?"

She saw him hesitate for a second before going on, and she wanted to challenge that hesitation. But he was already answering the question.

"Because they have a kidnap victim. It's not like the last time when they were having a party."

His reasoning made sense, but she wanted to tell him she was still worried. She wanted to beg him to keep out of it. But she knew that he wasn't just going after the people who had abducted Barnette. He was also going after the people who had tried to harm her. Probably the sheriff knew that, too.

She gave a tight nod, feeling like she had no choice but to agree. And once she said the word, the plans proceeded with lightning speed.

James called his sister, and after a few minutes conversation, she offered to take Sara in.

As James put down the phone, Sara looked at Adam, wanting more than ever to be alone with him. "Can you drive me down there?" she asked.

Delacorte shook his head. "It would be better if I did it. That way you'll be introduced to Tyreen by a neighbor."

"Who happens to be the sheriff," Adam pointed out.

Sara nodded, understanding the wisdom of that approach. Still she didn't like the look of relief on Adam's face. He didn't want her to beg him to stay out of danger.

"We'd better go," Delacorte said.

"I wish I could change my clothes," Sara murmured. "I've been dressed in this outfit since . . ." She stopped short, unwilling to give away that she had been waiting up for Adam to come home from his spying trip into town.

Lord, it seemed like a thousand years ago since he'd tracked her father to his house.

She glanced at Delacorte. He was waiting for her. Letting him wait for another few moments, she crossed to Adam and reached for him. He went still for several heartbeats, then he raised his arms and hugged her to him.

She wiped their audience from her mind, focusing only on Adam as she tipped her head up and pressed her mouth to his. He looked shocked, then settled into the kiss. And she felt the familiar consuming passion that she always felt when they came together.

But he only allowed himself a few seconds of the intimate contact before he raised his head.

"Be careful," she ordered.

"I will," he said, the answer sounding automatic.

"Adam. I mean it. I don't know what I'll do if anything happens to you."

His face took on a look of sudden intensity. She felt him clench his hands on her arms before asking, "Does that mean you'll marry me when I come back?"

Totally unprepared for the question, she gasped. "That's not playing fair!"

"I want it settled before I go. I want to be thinking about how much I'll appreciate coming back to you."

She knew what he was doing—manipulating her. Yet she was willing to be manipulated because the crisis had done wonders to clarify her thinking. "Yes," she breathed.

He hugged her tighter with a kind of savage triumph, almost crushing the breath out of her. When he released her, she felt momentarily dizzy. Then the world snapped back into focus. A few feet away, she heard two men shuffling their feet and clearing their throats.

She looked around and blinked, seeing the bemused expression on Delacorte's face.

"Good going, son," he said with a note of awe in his voice.

Her own face flamed. "Let's go," she muttered, marching toward the door.

"You go on out," he said, "I want to have a word with the sheriff."

She glared at him. "You don't want to be alone with me. But you want to talk to him in private?"

"Yes."

SARA had left the house angry, angry with Adam for keeping secrets, even if he thought it was for her own good.

She sat tensely in the front seat of the sheriff's pickup

truck. But as they rode toward town, fatigue won out over tension. She'd been up all night, and now she slumped against the passenger door. One moment she had closed her eyes. In the next, she felt the truck come to a stop.

Looking up, she saw she was in a driveway between a beat-up station wagon and a large, fenced backyard where two dogs barked and jumped at the chain links. One was a shepherd. The other some kind of standard poodle mix. To her right, Sara saw a small woman with skin the color of coffee with a nice dollop of cream. She looked to be in her mid-thirties. Dressed in jeans and a baggy red sweater, she was standing inside the fence on the back porch of the two-story clapboard house.

That must be Tyreen Vincent, James's sister, she thought.

Delacorte looked around, then turned to Sara. "Best you get into the house quickly. I don't want the neighbors wondering what you're doing here."

What a white lady is doing here, she silently edited his statement. But she kept the observation to herself.

Tyreen was looking down at them, an uncertain expression on her face. The sheriff had told Sara that she lived there with her husband, Noah, and her children, Trinity and Isaac.

More than a bit uncomfortable, Sara took a tentative step forward. She was imposing on these people. And she didn't even know how long she would have to stay. Would someone be able to get her a change of clothing from Nature's Refuge? She hoped so.

The yard had been turned into a dirt patch by the dogs. They were still barking and jumping, and Sara eyed them uncertainly.

"Amos and Andy won't hurt you," Tyreen said as she hurried down the back walk.

"Amos and Andy!" Despite the circumstances, Sara grinned, glad that she'd landed with someone who had a sense of humor. She reached to open the gate, then stepped inside, staggering back as one of the big dogs leaped up, put its paws on her shoulders and licked her face.

"Amos! Mind you manners," Tyreen called out as she pulled at the dog's collar.

"It's okay. I love dogs," Sara told her as Amos detached himself from her shoulders. "And I love your names, boys." She continued talking to the dogs, partly because she did like animals, and partly because she knew that they were helping to break the ice with their owner.

"Let's get inside," Delacorte said.

"Yes. Right."

Leaving the canines outside, they stepped into a country kitchen with pine cabinets, a vinyl tile floor, and a long trestle table over at one side.

"I'm sorry for imposing on you," Sara said.

"No. This is fine. I know James wouldn't ask if it weren't important."

Delacorte nodded. "I told you over the phone that this visit has to be kept confidential for the time being. We're in the middle of a kidnapping case. And Dr. Weston—"

"Sara. Please call me Sara," she interjected quickly. "You must be Tyreen. I appreciate your letting me stay here. I don't want to be any trouble to you." She held out her hand, and the other woman shook it.

"The kids are going to be home from school at three-thirty. They're going to tell their friends that a white lady is staying at our house."

"We don't want the kidnappers to know that the police are involved," Delacorte broke in. "Maybe she can hide out in one of the bedrooms for a while. She's been up for hours, and she fell asleep on the ride over."

"If that wouldn't be too much trouble," Sara said quickly.

"It's a good solution. I can take you up to the guest

bedroom, and tell the kids we've got some unexpected company. After you come down, I'll keep them inside."

"Yes. Thanks."

Delacorte shifted his weight from one foot to the other. "I'd best be going."

As he turned to leave, Sara reached out and put a hand on his arm. "Call me the minute you know something."

"I will."

Her hand dropped away, and he opened the door, leaving her alone with this woman she had just met. A woman who was taking in a stranger out of kindness and probably a sense of duty.

"So, can you tell me what's going on?" she asked.

There was curiosity, too, Sara amended her assessment. She swallowed. "I wish I could. But the bottom line for me is that the man I love is going off with Sheriff Delacorte to look for the kidnappers. And I could put him in more danger than he's already in by talking about the situation."

The black woman's face contorted. "Oh, you poor thing."

"I'd like to be alone for a while. Then, later I can help you get dinner ready."

"There's no need for that."

"I don't want to be any extra work."

Tyreen led the way upstairs to a small room that was dominated by a double bed. "It's not very plush," she said.

"It's perfect. Just let me borrow your bathroom, and I'll flop into bed and get some sleep."

ADAM stood at the edge of a patch of brackish ground and shifted the knapsack on his shoulder. Sara was safe. He couldn't have come here without being sure of that. The knowledge that she was out of danger gave him the freedom to concentrate on what he had to do now.

He and Delacorte had left as soon as the sheriff had
gotten back from stashing Sara. Before moving out, they
discussed where to look. Delacorte had chosen the area
where the campfire had been that first time. Probably he
thought that was the most likely place to find the witches.
Adam didn't agree. He was pretty sure they would be
somewhere else, somewhere less obvious.

He had a cell phone with him, and he had promised to
use it. But getting help would depend on his being able
to describe his location, which might be a problem deep
in the swamp.

He would have liked to go on this hunting expedition
as a wolf. But that was out of the question.

He sniffed the wind and caught a scent he had smelled
before. The smoke that had turned his head muzzy. In
front of Sara, he had told the others that he didn't expect
it was going to be a problem.

Actually, he'd been thinking that the witches might
well use the stuff. And if they did, it would lead him to
them. But at the same time, he'd have to be damn careful.
The fumes had overpowered him last time. This time it
wasn't going to happen, because he'd come prepared. He
hoped.

First he took a quick breath to tell him the direction the
poisoned fumes were coming from. It was still far away,
its tendrils reaching toward him, pulling at him.

The effect was dangerous. Not just because it muddled
his mind. It was addictive, and he was more susceptible
than most, because of his physiology.

Too damn bad.

Before the probing tendrils could choke off his rational
thoughts, he took a gas mask out of his knapsack and
pulled it over his head, adjusting the nosepiece and the
straps so it was comfortable.

Just before they'd left the mansion, he'd told the sheriff
it might be a good idea to bring along a mask. He hadn't

wanted to talk about that in front of Sara because he hadn't wanted to alarm her.

He'd thought he was being clever by thinking of the protective gear. He'd read a lot about gas masks on the Internet before he'd bought one. In fact, it had been in the package Delacorte had brought into his office a couple of days ago.

It was a good model. At least the reviews said it was good.

But he'd never used one before. A surge of claustrophobia made him grit his teeth like when he tried the thing on. But it hadn't been quite so bad.

Stop it, he ordered himself. *This isn't any worse than a snorkeling mask. You've snorkeled on a couple of vacations.*

Yeah, he'd snorkeled plenty of times. And this wasn't anything like same sensation.

A snorkeling mask only fits over the front of the face. This thing enclosed a lot more of his head.

He took a breath, fighting a choking sensation.

"Stop it," he ordered again, this time speaking the words aloud because he needed to hear them, as he plunged into the swamp.

CHAPTER

TWENTY-NINE

SARA HESITATED FOR a few moments. She needed to lie down, but she wanted to be ready to leave the moment she found out Adam was safe.

So she kicked off her shoes, then folded back the spread on the double bed and lay down. As she closed her eyes, she told herself she had to relax, despite the pain pounding in her head.

Adam had come back to her safe and sound when he'd gone into town to look for the witches. But now he had marched off into danger again and she'd wanted to beg him to stay out of the line of fire. Especially when he was risking his life for a man who might not be worth it.

Unable to lie still, she sat up and fluffed the pillows behind her head. Her eyes stared unfocused at the striped wallpaper on the wall.

She hadn't liked Austen Barnette when she'd met him. Despite how she felt about him, she knew he was in a horrible situation. Unfortunately, that situation had put Adam in danger.

Pressing her fist to her mouth, she struggled not to scream out her fear and frustration.

She had to stop thinking about Adam, had to stop worrying about him.

So she focused again on her father. She still hadn't gotten over the shock of finding out his identity. And she still didn't know how she felt about him. He'd abandoned her all those years ago.

Well, not abandoned, exactly. But it had felt like that to the little girl he'd left to the kindness of strangers.

She'd grown to love those strangers. They had given her a warm, supportive home. A good foundation in life. But she'd always known a piece of her heritage was missing.

She'd met her father tonight, and she'd walked away from him because she'd been in shock. Could she forgive him? She didn't know. But he had brought her back to Wayland. He had made contact with her, although he hadn't said who he was.

Maybe he'd been afraid she'd reject him, which was what it looked like she *had* done. But when she thought about it more objectively, she could see it would be a terrible shame if she never got to know him as an adult.

Her mind made another leap back to the Olakompa. Adam and the sheriff were out there somewhere. She kept picturing the vast wilderness area. The trees blocking out the light. An alligator sliding into dark water.

Then she was seeing a group of naked men and women, their bodies painted with bright slashes and circles, dancing wildly. This time the campfire wasn't the only focus. This time, as they gyrated, they also circled around a tree. And tied to the trunk was a naked man, his face a mask of terror.

She gasped when she saw it was Barnette.

There was no way to know if the image was real or if

she had made it up. But it stayed firmly in her brain like a piece of festering shrapnel.

THE dancing stopped, and a hush fell over the group. Falcon stepped up to the old man who was sagging against the bonds that held him.

He struggled to stand up straighter as the leader of the clan approached him. Falcon counted that as a mark of respect—for all the good it would do the old bastard.

"Listen up," he said.

Barnette tried to focus on him. The smoke had whacked him out some, but not completely.

"You didn't give Jenna Foster a chance," Falcon said. "But we're going to give you one. We're going to let you loose. We'll give you a head start. And if you can keep us from finding you until it gets dark, we'll let you go."

Barnette struggled to keep his eyes in focus.

With the delicacy of a surgeon, Falcon cut the old man's bonds and pulled the rope away.

"Go on. Git!" he ordered.

Barnette wavered on his feet as he looked around at the circle of faces.

Then he made a moaning sound and staggered off into the underbrush.

"How long do we give him?" Copperhead asked.

"It won't be any fun if we go after him right away."

"We could lose him," Razorback muttered.

"You think so? I think he's going to leave a trail an elephant would envy."

The rest of the clan snickered. Razorback flushed and clamped his teeth together.

PAUL Delacorte kicked at the cold ashes of the campfire. He had been sure the witches would be here again. But he had been wrong. And now he had no idea where to look for them.

He removed the phone from the holder on his belt and dialed the private line that would connect him to Adam.

After several rings, the park ranger answered. "I can't stay on long," he said.

"What's up?"

"I had to take my gas mask off to talk to you. And I have to put it back on pretty soon."

"You're using it?"

"Yeah. There's drugged smoke here."

"Where?"

"Near that cabin where Sara was living. You'll know by the fumes. Gotta go."

The line went dead.

Paul sucked in a deep breath. He smelled something strange. Something evil. He remembered Adam's description of the stuff. It was nasty.

Unpacking his gas mask, he pulled it over his head.

ADAM wavered on his feet and shot out a hand to steady himself against a tree trunk. He'd had the mask partially off for less than a minute, and his head was swimming.

Shit. He shouldn't have answered the phone. But he'd had to do it in case Delacorte had some important information.

Now his brain felt like cottage cheese. He sat down heavily, staring off into the distance, trying to remember where he was and why he was here. And the damn Halloween mask over his face was choking off his breath. What he needed was air.

He reached up to free his nose and mouth. Then he stayed his hand.

The thing that felt like it was cutting off his oxygen was a gas mask. He'd put it on because of the drugged

smoke. And he'd gotten a couple breaths of the stuff just
then. Only a few breaths, and his brain had gone mushy.
Because it was worse for him than for other people. It
took only a little bit to turn him into a space cadet.

He closed his eyes and leaned his head back against
the tree trunk, thinking of Sara. Thinking about how much
he wanted to be with her. To be holding her in his arms.

She should be here with him. She'd like the smoke. It
made him feel really good. She would feel good, too. The
witches had used it for sex. That sounded like fun.

He blinked. Not good. Bad. This stuff was bad, and he
wasn't responding normally.

He hadn't gotten too much of it. Just a little. He was
going to be okay if he just sat here for a few minutes.

SARA'S body jerked, then went rigid. Another picture
leaped into her mind. Once again she saw the wild, natural
landscape of the Olakompa. But the dancers were gone.

The scene was calm. Still.

She recognized the location because it was right near
her cabin. Well, not the cabin where she was living now.
The cabin that belonged to Austen Barnette.

In the center of the mental picture was a figure sitting
with his back propped against a tree trunk. A man, wearing a camouflage shirt and pants. But his face . . . his face
was so strange: elongated like an animal's muzzle, but
with the features obscured.

She made a small, strangled noise. Her head pounded
as if someone were using it for a drum set. Her vision
blurred, but she struggled to understand what she was seeing.

Was it Adam—his face turning to that of a wolf? No.
That was no wolf. As she tried to take in more details,
she focused on the man's hair. Black hair. Cut just a little
too long.

It *was* Adam. Or someone who looked just like him from the forehead up.

And there was something over his face. Something she'd seen before in a movie or on television.

She wasn't sure what it was. Some kind of protection? Then the answer leaped into her mind. It was a gas mask, attached by straps that went over the top and sides of his head.

She watched another figure appear in the scene. A naked man staggering out of the swamp, staggering toward Adam, screaming something she couldn't hear.

Mud coated his feet and legs. Long scratches ran down his thighs and across his chest. His gray hair was matted to his head. His features were contorted with terror and pain. But she knew who it was: Austen Barnette.

She had seen him with the witches. Now he was fleeing through the swamp. Naked as the day he was born. Had he somehow gotten away?

He ran up to Adam, clutching at him, clawing at the mask that obscured his face.

Adam raised his hands, but they seemed to move in slow motion. She watched as the mask came off his face so that she could see his reddened skin and the wide, vacant look in his eyes.

She was out of bed and pulling on her shoes before she knew what she was going to do.

RAZORBACK poured water on the fire.

"What the hell are you doing?" Falcon demanded.

"Getting rid of the damn smoke."

"Why?" the leader of the clan demanded.

"'Cause I was thinkin' we need to be on top of the situation here. People could be looking for Barnette. What if they find us, and we're all wasted?"

"There's no *they*. There's only Marshall."

"He could have figured out we don't give a shit about the money. He could have gotten help."

Some of the clan murmured their agreement. Falcon's eyes narrowed. Razorback was challenging his authority. And that was bad. Bad for him. Bad for the group. But maybe the guy was right. Maybe they'd had enough of the smoke.

"Come on, we've given Barnette enough time. Let's go find out if a gator's got him. Or if we need to finish him off ourselves."

There were shouts of agreement from the clan. Falcon had them back in hand. But over Starflower's head, his gaze met Razorback's eyes, and he knew this wasn't the end of the rebellion.

SARA came pounding down the stairs and into the kitchen, her eyes wide. Tyreen must have been keeping a lookout for her, or maybe she'd simply heard the heavy footsteps, because she came running toward the back of the house.

"Honey, what's wrong?" she asked.

Sara dragged in a shuddering breath. "Adam is in trouble!"

"I didn't hear the phone ring. Did you get a call on your cell phone?"

Sara swallowed, thinking about what she could possibly say that wasn't going to sound completely crazy. "I . . . I had a dream . . ." she said.

"You dreamed something bad?"

"Yes. But I know it's true! Adam is in trouble. I have to go to him."

When the woman only stared at her, Sara blurted, "My . . . my dreams can be about things that are really happening."

Tyreen spoke gently. "Honey, you need to calm yourself. You're under a lot of pressure right now. And your imagination is working overtime."

Sara clenched her hands at her sides. She *knew* that Adam was in terrible danger. She also knew with absolute certainty that there wasn't going to be any way to convince Tyreen of that.

Sara's gaze flicked to the black purse sitting on the kitchen counter—and the key ring next to it—before she brought her attention back to Tyreen. "I . . . I'm really worried . . ." she murmured. "Could you call Sheriff Delacorte and find out what's happening?"

"We don't want to bother him when he's out on a kidnapping investigation."

"Please. Call him!"

Sara waited with her heart pounding, waited to see if the other woman would do what she asked.

CHAPTER
THIRTY

TYREEN GAVE A small nod. "All right. I know you have to be jumpin' out of your skin. If it will make you feel better, I'll call the sheriff. But I left his card in the den."

Sara spoke around the knot in her throat. "Okay."

Waiting until Tyreen had disappeared from sight, Sara grabbed the keys and exited the kitchen, closing the door quietly behind her. She'd never stolen anything in her life. And she wouldn't be starting now. But she needed the woman's car. Because she had to get to Adam before it was too late.

As soon as she was out of the house, the dogs ran toward her, and she stopped to speak to them in a soothing voice. Then she ran to the car. Climbing in, she locked the door behind her and inspected the keys. When she found a standard ignition key, she jammed it into the slot and turned. The car shuddered, but finally the engine caught, sending a puff of black smoke shooting from the exhaust pipe.

Sara was backing out of the driveway when she heard

Tyreen shouting at her. "Wait! Come back. What do you think you're doing?"

Sara stepped on the brake, needs and emotions warring inside her. Then she rolled down the window and stuck her head out. "I'm sorry. I need the car. Tell Sheriff Delacorte that I've gone to my old house. That's where they are. In the swamp near my old house."

She thrust her head back. Then, teeth clenched, she pulled onto the road, hearing the tires squeal as she reversed direction and sped away. She hated what she was doing. But she saw no other option. Adam was in trouble and she had to go to him.

But now it was hard to drive, hard to see what she was doing, because of the phantom scenes flashing before her eyes, scenes of what was happening in the swamp.

THERE was no problem following the old man's trail. As Falcon had predicted, he had crashed through the underbrush with the grace of a wounded ox.

They splashed through shallow water, then came out onto a wide, dry stretch of ground. Across the clearing, the old man's skinny white body was crouched beside a tree trunk.

It took several moments for Falcon to figure out what he was seeing. Another man dressed in fatigue pants and a shirt sat propped against the tree.

He must have caught a flicker of movement from their direction because he looked up.

Falcon and the clan stared at him.

"It's Adam Marshall," Starflower crowed. "I told you he'd come looking for the old bastard. Kill him."

"Wait." Falcon pointed toward the seated figure. "Look at him. He's not moving. I think he's in no shape to fight us."

"You're taking a chance," Razorback muttered.

"I want to do the old man first. Give him what he deserves for leading that gang of townspeople against Jenna Foster because he branded her a witch, then running my uncle out of town and grabbing his land for that damn park. When we're through with him, we can take care of Marshall." He glanced at the figure slumped against the tree. "He's not going anywhere."

Barnette must have heard them because he turned and screamed, then staggered away. Falcon captured Starflower's hand. The others saw what he was doing and reached for the hand of someone next to them.

He waited until they were centered, until the clan was working together in harmony. Then he stretched out his free arm toward Barnette. The group's power flowed through him, through his mind as he hurled an invisible thunderbolt at the pitiful, naked figure.

He felt like the god Thor, raining destruction down from heaven. Barnette cried out and fell to his side, then lay still.

"Make sure he's dead," Falcon said to Water Buffalo. The other man loped over to the huddled body while Falcon strode toward Marshall.

The ranger raised his head and blinked, staring at them with dull eyes.

PAUL was in the pickup speeding toward the back entrance to the park when his cell phone rang.

"Delacorte here," he answered as he pressed the Receive button.

"This is Tyreen. That crazy woman you left here stole my car."

Paul's hands clenched on the wheel. "Why? What happened?"

"She came tear-assing downstairs, saying that she knew her man was in trouble. I asked her how she knew, and she said she'd dreamed it. Sure! Then she tricked me into going and calling you. While I was looking for your number, I heard my car start." Tyreen stopped and made a huffing sound. "She yelled a message out the window before she took off."

"What message?"

"She said to tell Sheriff Delacorte, 'I've gone to my old house. That's where they are. In the swamp near my old house.' "

"Okay. Thanks!"

"Paul what the hell is going on?"

"Tell you later." He hung up and tried to get Adam on the line.

FALCON walked toward Adam Marshall. "Good of you to join the party," he said to the ranger in a conversational tone. Before he could say anything else, a ringing noise made him start. A cell phone. Marshall tipped his head to one side, listening. Then, slowly he reached into his pocket and brought it out.

Falcon snatched it away from him and threw it into a pool of water where the ringing cut off as it sank from view.

"Any other toys on you that we ought to know about?" he asked.

Marshall's lips moved, but no sound came out.

"Like the smoke, do you?" Falcon asked.

Razorback stooped and picked up something black and rubbery on the ground. "He was wearing a gas mask. Lucky for us he took it off."

Falcon lifted the mask from the other man's hand and tossed it away before turning his attention back to Marshall. "He's overdressed for the party. Strip him."

"I want him dead," another voice rose from behind him.

The speaker was Starflower. "Once he's dead, we can get Weston, too."

"Not yet. I want to know what he knows." He turned to Razorback. "Go back and get the rope. I want him secured."

Marshall said something, but it sounded like gibberish.

"Send one of the women!" Razorback challenged.

"I told you to do it."

There was a moment of silence while the two men stared at each other. Then Razorback shrugged and started back to the campfire.

Falcon bent over the ranger. "I'm the leader of this clan. You can call me Falcon," he said. "If you can talk. You can beg me for mercy."

SARA sped past the cabin and continued down the road, then turned off onto a side trail. Her teeth were clamped together to keep herself from screaming.

She pulled to a halt just before the trail disappeared into a flat stretch of black water and started running into the swamp.

Jumbled images were still coming to her.

Austen Barnette lay crumpled on the ground. Unmoving. Probably dead.

Adam still sat propped against the tree trunk, the group of painted witches standing over him.

She watched them kneel down, watched them tearing at his clothing.

God, what were they going to do to him?

She ran toward the clearing where the scene was happening. The last time she'd confronted these people, they'd been wearing hoods over their heads. Now they were wearing nothing. Just as she reached the campfire, a figure loomed in front of her. One of the naked, painted men. One of the people who had hurt her.

Only now he was alone.

He stopped short, staring at her with malevolent, glittering eyes. Before she could react, he attacked—not physically but with one of those thunderbolts that made the inside of her skull feel like she'd been strapped into the electric chair and someone had pulled the switch.

She struggled to stay on her feet. Struggled to find a way to protect herself from him. Because if she couldn't do it, he would kill her.

ADAM lay on the ground, forcing himself not to react to Falcon's goading words, or to the feel of hands moving roughly over him, stripping the clothing from his body, tearing fabric and popping buttons.

They had killed Barnette, and there had been nothing he could do about it. They planned to kill him, too. They had used Barnette to lure him out here. And he had walked right into the trap.

He recognized two of them. One was the workman he'd seen that afternoon at Barnette's house, the one who called himself Falcon. The other was the sexpot who had come to the park and tried to get into his pants. Falcon had addressed her as Starflower.

She was tearing at his pants now. But her motives were a bit different. She wanted him naked and vulnerable.

He concentrated on keeping his body limp. For a while there, his mind had been filled with the smoke. Thoughts had floated in a cloud of cotton wool. But the drug had drifted away, and now he was only a little impaired. At least he hoped so.

He kept his lids lowered and his mouth slack as they tore off his shirt and pants. Then his undershorts and shoes and socks.

By the time they had finished, he was already chanting, his voice low, barely audible.

"Taranis. Epona. Cerridwen." He tried to repeat the phrase as one of them pushed him onto his back and kicked him in the midsection.

The chant turned into a groan of pain. He lost his place and had to start all over again, wondering if he was going to manage the change under these circumstances.

Another of the bastards aimed a kick at his head, and he somehow ducked away from the blow.

Hands clenched against the pain, he focused on getting the words out.

"Ga. Feart. Cleas. Duais. Aithriocht. Go gcumhdai is dtreorai na deithe thu."

The crowd of people had sprung into savage action, flailing at him with hands and feet, making it all but impossible for him to focus.

"What the hell are you saying?" one of them shouted.

He didn't answer. He was beyond speech. The change was on him now. His vocal cords would no longer form human sounds.

One of the women screamed. Then another. All of them jumped back as his body jerked and contorted. Wolf hair sprouted on his skin, covering his body in a thick, silver-tipped pelt. The color and structure of his eyes changed as he rolled over so he could stand on all fours. He was no longer a man but an animal, far more suited to the swamp than the crowd of painted, naked people who surrounded him.

"Jesus Christ! He's the wolf who went after us. He's the damn wolf!" one of them shouted.

"Run!"

Yes he screamed in his mind. *Yes, you bastards. Run.*

Howling his rage aloud, he sprang at the man who had kicked him, tearing at a naked thigh, finding that he wasn't in quite as good shape as he'd thought. His movements were slower, more sluggish than they should be.

He could hear someone shouting, but he was too absorbed in the chase to pay attention to the words.

People were scattering, screaming. He charged a woman and brought her to the ground, slashing at her arm and leg. Then he rounded on a man, dragging him to his knees.

He was slashing the man's naked back when something hit him. A blow to the back of his head that sent him sprawling.

He thought at first that one of them had thrown a rock at him. But it wasn't something physical, he realized. It was like a mental jolt to his brain. Like what Sara had described. Like when he'd thought they were shooting at him. Only now he knew for sure that had just been an illusion his mind had manufactured to cope with what it hadn't understood.

He turned and faced the enemy. Three of them were holding hands, their eyes bright with concentration. It was the workman guy, Miss Sexpot, and another one of the women.

He felt another invisible blow slam into him and fell back, gasping with the pain.

He had watched them kill Barnette like this. They were going to do the same thing to him, because teeth and claws weren't going to cut it against their thunderbolts. His only hope was to get them before they got him. But he couldn't do it. When he tried to stagger toward them, he couldn't make his legs cooperate.

He sank to the ground, panting, trying to keep his brain from dissolving under the force of the pain. He was going to die here in this patch of swamp, because the hatred radiating from these people was going to destroy him.

He longed to disappear into unconsciousness to make the pain go away. But he knew that the moment he let go, he was giving in to death. So he focused all of his energy on keeping hold of consciousness. It was all he could do. He knew that it wasn't nearly enough.

CHAPTER
THIRTY-ONE

BY SOME MIRACLE, the agony suddenly lessened. Somehow Adam managed to raise his head in time to see the three witches jolt as though they'd been hit by rifle bullets. The woman he didn't recognize fell to her knees. The workman and the sexpot whirled around, as if to face another enemy. Had Delacorte found him?

Not the sheriff. Adam's heart stopped, then started pounding hard as he saw Sara standing beside a large tree, her eyes focused on the group.

The sky had been a clear blue moments earlier. Now storm clouds swirled over her, turning the whole scene dark and ominous. Trees swayed as the wind picked up bits of plant material and sent them flying through the air.

He wanted to howl in fear and frustration.

Sara was here! He'd made sure she was safe. He'd counted on that. But now she'd rushed into danger to help him.

She must be fighting the witches. And whatever she'd

done had broken their hold on him. The pain still pounded in his head. But he could move now.

He saw Sara sag against the tree, saw the witches move from their frozen positions. The two still on their feet, Falcon and Starflower, bent to the other woman and pulled her up, pulled her toward Sara.

Lightning flashed in the clouds above them. He heard Sara gasp and knew they had hit her with another one of their mental artillery shells.

Anger surged through him. With a savage snarl, he gathered his remaining strength and sprang, taking down the one named Falcon, clawing at his back, biting at his shoulders, mauling for no other purpose than to inflict pain on the bastard who was hurting Sara.

The man screamed. The unknown woman fell to the ground again, drew up her knees, and folded her hands protectively over her head, no longer in the fight.

The man's body went limp, and Adam instantly backed off, planning to go after Starflower.

He made a low, growling sound when he saw all of her attention was focused on Sara.

His body coiled as he prepared to spring at her. But a voice in his head rang out, "NO!"

It was Sara. Warning him off. Warning him to stay out of it. There was a charged moment when the two women faced each other, and he knew that only one of them would come out of the confrontation alive.

The clouds turned darker. The wind roared through the trees, sending leaves flying like small guided missiles.

Energy seemed to crackle in the air. Deadly energy. Sara squared her shoulders, her whole body rigid with concentration.

Then Starflower's body jerked, and he thought she would go down. But she stiffened her legs and thrust her head forward as though every cell of her mind and body were focused on her enemy: Sara.

The struggle was one he could only imagine.

Sara had warned him to stay clear. But when he heard her scream and saw her knees buckle, he went mad, leaping at the woman.

As his teeth closed around her arm, a bolt of electricity seared through his body, but he held on, bringing her to the ground, aware in some part of his mind that she was already as limp as a dead bird. That she was already defeated.

He might have ripped out the bitch's throat just for the satisfaction of it, but he head Sara shout again, "No. Don't do it!"

Lifting his head, he watched her stagger forward. Watched the clouds above her float away in the howling wind, leaving the sky as blue as it had been a few minutes earlier.

"Adam, Adam," she shouted above the roaring in his ears. "It's over."

He raised his head and stared at her, dragging himself on all fours across the ground toward her. She looked pale. Deep purple streaks marred the tender skin under her eyes, making them appear bruised. But she was moving under her own power.

They met at the edge of the clearing. She knelt beside him, and he turned his face, rubbing it against the parts of her he could reach, her leg, her hand. He was hurting and bone weary, but he scooted closer, needing the contact, needing to know she was all right.

She curved her body around his, running her fingers over his head and his silky ears, then lower to the thick hairs that ringed his neck.

He sighed with pleasure at the contact, then shifted so that he could meet her eyes.

"Are you all right?" she asked urgently.

He gave a small nod, his gaze intense on her face, because as a wolf, there was no way he could ask the questions he urgently needed answered.

But she seemed to understand what he wanted. "I'm okay," she whispered, circling him with her arms, pressing close, stroking her hand along the length of his back, her touch soothing and sensual at the same time.

Long moments passed. Long moments when all he wanted to do was nestle in her arms, feeling her magic touch. But before he had his fill of her, she made an effort to rouse herself.

"Delacorte is coming. You have to get out of here. You have to change before he sees you."

He kept his gaze on hers, asking a silent question in his mind. What good would it do to slink away now? The damage was already done.

"Don't worry about the damn witches. They won't remember the wolf. They won't remember much of anything. I figured out how to hurt them. I . . . I put up some kind of shield in my mind. It sent their nasty little guided missiles back at them. And I think it fried their damn brains."

Was she right? Well, they'd find out.

"Go on. Go! Hurry."

He gathered his last small bits of energy, then heaved himself to his feet and staggered away from the clearing and into the underbrush. He was beyond fatigue. Almost beyond remembering what Sara had said. All he wanted to do was sink into the ground and sleep.

But she had told him to change. And he had something else he must do, also. He raked the claws of his right paw down his left side, fighting off the jolt of pain. Then he turned his head and bit into his right front leg. The pain helped to concentrate his mind. With his remaining strength, he changed back to his human form, then lost consciousness.

Voices woke him.

Sara and Delacorte talking.

He pushed himself to a sitting position and dragged shaky fingers through his hair. His arm hurt. And so did his side. He looked down and saw the long scratches and the bite he'd inflicted. He also saw he was naked. But so was almost everybody else out there in the clearing. And he wasn't the one who had torn off his clothing, he reminded himself.

It took a considerable effort to make it to his feet. When he did, he staggered toward Sara.

She looked up when she saw him, then ran to him and embraced him.

"Adam! Are you all right? Where were you?"

He hugged her to him. She'd seen the wolf at his savage worst. But she wasn't running in the other direction. She was still letting him hold her. For that he was profoundly grateful. "I'm all right."

Delacorte strode toward him. "What happened here?"

He shifted Sara so that she was standing at his side, his arm still around her. "I'm not sure. The smoke did something wacky to my brain. I remember Barnette staggering out of the swamp, terrified and naked. I was already kind of out of it because I had to take off the mask to talk to you. I'd put it back on, but Barnette clawed it off again.

"Then this gang of painted savages came after Barnette. I know it doesn't make a whole lot of sense, but I think they did something with their minds that killed him." He turned and looked at the men and women sprawled around on the ground. "I mean, they used some kind of mental weapon on him. After that, I remember them tearing my clothing off." He stopped and looked around again. "I'd like to put my pants on, if you don't mind—if they aren't ripped up."

He made his way to the tree where he'd been sitting and found his clothing. The trousers were torn but wearable. One half of the hook at the waistband was torn away. But he pulled up the zipper, which more or less kept them on. Getting partially dressed gave him a chance to plan what he was going to say next.

Turning back to Delacorte, he said, "Whatever they were doing to Barnette, I think they were trying to do to me. It felt like they were sending flaming arrows into my head. It hurt like hell. It must have screwed up my memory, because that's the last thing I remember."

"Lucky it didn't kill you, too."

"I'm younger and stronger than he was."

"Some of them are clawed up and bitten," the sheriff said in a tight voice.

He could see Sara's eyes on him. He opened his mouth and said, "Maybe a bear or some other big animal came out of the swamp and attacked them. Maybe the smoke made him crazy. It looks like the thing attacked me, too." He pointed to the scratches on his side and to the bite on his leg. "But I honestly don't remember any of it."

The sheriff peered at him. "Yeah, you're kind of mauled up. You'd better get some antiseptic on those wounds."

"I will." He looked toward the witches. "Are they dead?" he asked.

"One woman is dead."

Sara held herself steady. He assumed the dead woman was Starflower. He assumed she had died in the battle with Sara. But he wasn't going to ask about that now.

"The rest of them are alive," Delacorte was saying. "But none of them is making sense. It's like their brains are cooked. I'd like to know what happened to them."

Adam gave him a steady look. "Maybe this is a case of a bunch of druggies poisoning themselves. Maybe they got too much of that smoke, and it killed too many of their brain cells. It was pretty potent stuff. Or maybe it made them so crazy that they turned their death rays on each other. It couldn't happen to a nicer group."

Delacorte took in the explanations. After a moment, he nodded.

Adam wondered if the sheriff believed any of it. Maybe and maybe not. But at least the drugged smoke and the big animal gave him something to put in his police report. It played better than the real scenario: the werewolf and his mate fighting off the evil witches.

Adam looked back at the naked men and women sprawled on the ground and added, "One of them told me his name was Falcon. He said he was the leader of the clan. I guess they had names they used among themselves. I recognized him. He was a workman at Barnette's place."

"Yeah." The sheriff looked from him to the casualties and back again. "It won't be hard to get his real name. I suppose the same ought to be true for the others. I've seen some of them around. The dead woman worked at the card shop on Main Street."

"I heard them say they were going to kill Barnette because he was the one who led the mob against Jenna Foster. Then apparently he grabbed the land of one of the witches he ran out of town."

Delacorte looked startled.

"He did?" Sara gasped.

"I don't know if it's true," Adam answered.

"Maybe the part about Jenna Foster was in those historical records that got stolen."

"Why would Barnette want them saved?"

"Hell, I don't know," Delacorte answered, his language stronger than Adam had ever heard it. "Maybe he felt guilty all those years. Maybe in some twisted way, he wanted to be punished."

"Or maybe he didn't know the dippy lady down at the historical society wasn't much for housecleaning," Adam gave another plausible explanation.

In the distance, a siren wailed. "I sent for the paramedics," Delacorte said. "And my deputies."

"That smoke and the thunderbolts about did me in," Adam said, speaking the truth. "I know you want to question me some more. But there's not much I can tell you."

Sara moved closer to him. "Adam's in pretty bad shape. Can I take him home?" she asked.

"In the car you stole?" Delacorte asked.

She flushed scarlet. "Oh Lord, I did, didn't I."

"How did you know that Adam was in trouble?" the sheriff asked.

She took her bottom lip between her teeth, then let it go before she started to speak. "A . . . a vision. I saw it in a vision. Images . . . pictures have been coming into my mind since I got to Wayland. Dreams that turned out to be real. I knew Adam was in trouble, and I jumped up in a panic and ran down to tell Tyreen. But I knew right away she didn't believe me. So I . . . I took her car. I'm sorry, but I had to do it."

The sheriff nodded.

Sara looked toward the men and women lying on the ground. "I . . . I hope you don't think I'm like them. I hope you know it's possible to have . . . psychic powers and not be . . . evil."

Delacorte gave her a long look. "The way I heard it, your momma was a good woman who was in the wrong place at the wrong time."

She swallowed. "Yes."

"You go on. I'll square the car with Tyreen. You're going back to the park?"

"Yes."

"Then I guess I'll know where to find you. I'll send someone out there to pick up the vehicle."

Sara nodded, then turned to Adam. Reaching for his hand, she led him back in the direction from which she'd come. He held tight to her, waiting until they were in the vehicle before he pulled her into his arms, crushed her against himself, and kissed her.

She kissed him with equal passion. When she lifted her head, it was to say, "Adam, don't ever put yourself in danger like that again."

"Funny, I was going to say the same thing to you. I only agreed to look for Barnette because I knew you'd be safe. Then it was like a nightmare when you showed up."

Her eyes shone into his. "But I had to come here, because I love you. Because I couldn't lose you."

He made a strangled sound and clasped her tightly again. "Sara, Sara," he murmured. "I love you so much. I need you so much."

"Yes."

"You can make a life with a man who turns into a wolf so he can tear his enemies to bits?" he found himself asking, because he needed to know it was true.

"Well, it looks like you scratched and bit yourself, too. That was a clever move."

"Yeah. I thought so!"

She dragged in a breath and let it out in a rush. "I can make a life with you, if you can make a life with a woman who hurls thunderbolts when she's pissed off."

He managed a small laugh. "More like majorly pissed off. More like your life was in danger."

"And yours."

He hugged her tightly, overwhelmed with the feel of her in his arms. Moments ago he had barely been able to stand. Now he might have made love to her right there in the station wagon if he hadn't realized that they were no longer alone. Men in uniform were hurrying past the station wagon, some of them wheeling stretchers.

"Let's get out of here," he said.

"Yes. Let's go home so I can tend to those self-inflicted

bites and scratches. And then I'll tuck you into a nice warm bed."

He grinned. "Only if you tuck yourself in with me."

"How did you know what I was thinking?"

"Maybe I'm learning to read your mind."

EPILOGUE

ADAM STOPPED THE car at the edge of the meadow and stared at the modern wood and timber house where his brother lived. It looked like Ross had done pretty well for himself.

He was glad he had come here. But he was also nervous. Two adult male werewolves were going to try to stay in the same room for more than five minutes without getting into a fight.

But he figured if Ross could keep his cool, so could he. He had to because the need for a connection with his family was greater than the need to assert his dominance over his brother.

He and Ross had been exchanging e-mails for the past month. And then phone calls. And Adam had finally convinced himself he was ready to make the trip to Maryland—with Sara beside him.

They were getting married soon. Her mother was fluttering around in Wilmington, making arrangements. And he was going to stand up in front of a minister and fifty other people and say the words. Sara said she wanted a minister. A judge would have done it for him. But he decided he didn't object to having a man of God join a witch and a werewolf in holy matrimony. If that's what it took to make sure he kept Sara for the rest of his life.

They'd talked about the wedding. And he thought Sara was probably going to invite her father, too. She had been so confused about her feelings and so angry at the man. But now it looked like she was coming around to acceptance and understanding. And Adam was glad of that, because he wanted as much joy in her life as she could gather up.

He reached for her hand.

"Nervous?" she asked.

"Yeah."

"If he attacks you, I'll hurl a thunderbolt at him."

He laughed. "I hope you're kidding."

"Well, just a little one."

He pressed on the gas pedal, and the car started again with a jerk. They crossed the meadow and pulled up in the parking area, next to an SUV that looked a lot like his.

The front door opened, and Ross came out. Followed by a pretty blond woman holding the hand of a little boy. His wife, Megan, and his son, Jonah. Megan looked like she was five or six months pregnant.

Adam climbed out of the car, then went around to Sara's door, to give himself a few more moments.

Ross had stopped several yards away. But Megan had given him the care of the little boy and came forward.

Holding out her arms, she said, "Adam! Ross has talked so much about you. I feel like I know you already." She gave him a hug, then turned to Sara and hugged her, too.

Stepping back, she said, "If Adam is anything like Ross, you're a lucky woman to have hooked up with him."

"I know."

Turning, she held out her arm to Ross, and he came slowly forward.

"I'm glad you're here," he said to both of them.

"An historic occasion," Adam answered around the lump that had formed in his throat.

"The two werewolves and the witch," Sara said.

"You must have been waiting for hours to deliver that line," Adam muttered.

She grinned. "Days, actually."

"Let's go in," Megan said. "I've made a big pot of blackberry tea. And some oatmeal cookies." Then she looked at Adam. "Your mother's recipe."

"I remember those cookies!"

"I'll get the recipe from Megan," Sara said.

It sounded so normal. So normal that it made him feel dazed. He had never dreamed of anything like this. But here he was at his brother's house. Meeting his brother's wife and son. And bringing the woman he was going to marry.

They all went inside. The boy stuck close to his parents while they got the refreshments. It was so strange seeing Ross and Megan work together, Adam thought. His dad had sat back and let his wife do the "women's work." Ross was obviously different.

They all settled down in the great room, with its huge windows that looked out over the woods and the meadow.

"So what did you decide to do?" Ross asked.

Adam turned his mug in his hand. To his shock, just before Austen Barnette had been kidnapped and killed by the witches, Barnette had changed his will and left Nature's Refuge to him—along with a trust fund to keep the place running—and an endowment to give the head ranger a very nice income. Maybe he'd had a premonition that something was going to happen to him.

There had been another change at Nature's Refuge, too. Amy Ralston had quit. He'd wondered if she'd had something to do with the witches. Like was she the one who had left the gate open? He'd found out that Brenda from the card shop, who called herself Starflower, was Amy's cousin. But he wasn't going to pursue the matter.

Now he looked at Sara. "We're talking about staying. The park is the perfect environment for me, of course. All that land where I can roam free. And Sara wants to try and find some of the other witch families. She's thinking we can have a little werewolf and witch colony down there."

"A refuge where we can live in safety," Sara clarified. "One thing I hope I can do is save children with my heritage from growing up feeling like they're different from everybody else. We know it's not all going to be smooth sailing. We know there could be problems with some of the people in town. But we think it will be worth the effort," she added.

"Sounds like a plan," Ross answered. "Just be cautious about who you invite to join you."

"I will," she answered solemnly.

Ross began to speak again. "And I want you to know there are people who don't have our . . . special genetic heritage who can still accept us. Tomorrow I want to introduce you to Jack and Kathryn Thornton. I met Jack through my P.I. work. He's a police detective, and he knows what I am. Once he even saw the wolf in action. But we're still friends."

Adam was watching him intently. "He saw what . . . ?"

Ross glanced at his son. "I'll tell you about it later."

"Yeah, right."

Sara looked at the little family seated across from her. How did you deal with a child who would grow up to be a werewolf? Well, she'd find out. She was almost sure she was pregnant, although she hadn't said anything yet.

She would tell Adam soon. But she also wanted to talk to Megan about the genetic research she was doing. Research that Adam had told her would make it a lot more likely that the children of a werewolf would survive.

Sara knit her fingers with Adam's, then looked up and saw Megan watching her. She smiled. The two of them had talked on the phone several times. She already thought of Megan as a friend. Which felt so good. She hadn't had many real friends in her life.

Ross broke the silence. "We're in this together," he said, his gaze moving from his wife to Adam and Sara.

Megan tipped her head toward her husband. "You've come a long way toward accepting yourself."

He answered with a small shrug, obviously uncomfortable with the subject. He was like Adam in that way. Quick to question the wolf part of his heritage. But Sara understood that. She'd had the same kind of worries. She still had them. And maybe if Adam had been a different person, she would have left him, at least for a time, until she was more sure of herself. But there was no question of separating herself from Adam Marshall. He was as necessary to her as the air she breathed. And she knew it went both ways.

He'd opened up with her in the weeks since the witches had kidnapped and killed Barnette. Many of the things he'd told her about his family had made her sad. His father had been a tyrant who insisted on obedience from his wife and sons. They'd lived on the edge of poverty because he'd been an uneducated man who relied too heavily on his werewolf skills. But probably he'd only been doing what he'd learned from his own father.

Adam would be different. He was her lover. Her partner. Her companion in a journey she'd never thought she'd take.

She looked up and saw Ross watching them. "I'm glad you found Adam," she told him.

"I wasn't so sure at first," Adam muttered. "Now I'm damn glad."

She knew how hard it was for him to say that. Her hand squeezed his tightly.

He was no ordinary man. But then, she was no ordinary woman. She had tried to be one, but she had failed. And then fate had brought her Adam Marshall. And her whole world had turned into an adventure. A lifelong adventure.

It wouldn't always be easy. She knew that. They were two people who didn't quite fit into twenty-first century life. But they had found a place where they could live and thrive. Near the black waters of the Olakompa swamp. Where she had learned that anything was possible.

First in her thrilling new romantic suspense series!

Shadow Game

by *New York Times* bestselling author

Christine Feehan

They are Ghostwalkers—men whose natural psychic abilities have been scientifically enhanced, enabling them to carry out the most dangerous of missions.
When something goes terribly wrong, Captain Ryland Miller and his men suddenly find themselves locked away without explanation—and, one by one, dying inexplicably.
Lily Whitney, daughter of the scientist who began the project, felt an immediate connection with the handsome captain and became determined to free him and his squad. What neither realizes is that she is at the heart of the secret people are killing to keep hidden.

0-515-13596-8

**Available wherever books are sold or
to order, please call 1-800-788-6262**